Bound
Book I

I. R. Harris

For Adriane; who somehow between sets at the gym, managed to convince me to be myself, and to my husband, who agreed

THE BOUND TRILOGY

To Ana, the Bonding ritual is a dangerous part of being human. She herself hasn't been chosen--yet. However, her dear friend Kai has, and on the surface he seems happy. However, Ana knows that Kai was lucky; his Bonder didn't make the choice to kill him. When it is her time, she might not be so fortunate. As it so happens, the choice to take Ana as a Bond was made years ago and her time is now. When Ana's peaceful life in Indonesia is suddenly intersected by a Bonder Demon named Nathanial, she is thrown into a roaring tempest of choices, of love, of ever changing loyalties, and of lies. She quickly realizes that loving someone is not the same as knowing them, and that having either of those things offers no guarantee that her heart will be protected or her life will be spared. For Ana, does being Bound mean to live in the absence of love, of autonomy, of trust or does it mean she will have to make the ultimate sacrifice in order to reclaim who she is and to save not only herself, but also the lives of those to which she is forever tied?

BOUND BOOK I

FALLEN BOOK II

AWAKENING BOOK III

Chapter One

Nathanial

I was waiting for her. Standing out in the hot, muggy heat for three hours was not something that had I anticipated, but I had waited long enough; it had to be today. Actually, none of this was in any shape or form what I had anticipated. For over three hundred years I had managed to move through the world without acquiring a Bond, three hundred years to see the relative calm co-existence between so many very different species and three hundred years to wonder if I had escaped my inevitable fate, this unfortunately was not to be the case. It was impossible to know when it would happen, the visions, the overwhelming desire, the inescapable *need* and of course the scent. Everything had developed so quickly for me, yet much later than others of my kind. Like a giant storm surge, it collided with my soul leaving me doubled over in pain, and I had no choice but to submit to what I was experiencing.

I saw her first in a dream. I knew her name, where she was living, what she looked like; I knew everything about her life. She was to be mine, my Choice, my Bond. The scent of her leaked into every memory, every sense I had ever experienced. I tasted her on my tongue and my throat ached with the very need for her. The journey to locate her had not been a difficult one as I was already in the area teaching at the local university. She was living and studying on one of the larger islands, only a short ferry ride away. Convenient, I suppose, but still it had taken me three months of watching her and studying her, calculating every word I wanted to say,

1

how I wanted to say it, before I felt that the time was right to make my presence known.

Humans understood what the Bond was, some of them even welcomed having to make the choice, but for others, it was not an easy concept to grasp. I had hoped that Ana would not be of the latter persuasion and fortunately for me, I would have to wait no longer to find out; she was coming from the University and headed for the parking lot. I heard her laughter fill the air around me and of course her unique fragrance, her essence, seeped into my skin, heating it from the inside. I watched her walk with a young man. They had their arms hooked together like you would see small children doing on a playground. I realized immediately that her companion was already Bound. I felt the heat from his metal branding dissipate into the wind serving as a signal that he had completed the "exchange". I wondered if Ana knew. I heard them laugh again; regaining my attention, I attempted to filter my way into her mind, trying to decipher what emotional state she was currently experiencing. I could do this quite easily without inducing any pain or having her know, it was one of my many "talents". I probed a bit deeper trying to decipher her emotional tenor, when I felt a sharp pain reverberate inside my head. White-hot, it shattered my concentration and I gasped for breath. What the hell just happened? I looked up, trying to catch whatever air I could and she was standing in front of me, her head cocked to the side. We stared at each other for what seemed like an endless amount of time. Her friend spoke, breaking the trance of our gazes.

2

"Ana, call me when you get home. It's going to be ok, I promise." He squeezed Ana's hand, gave me a hard stare and walked toward his car, leaving us alone.

"That's not the best way to make a good first impression," she spoke forcibly. "I haven't given you the right to know me in that way, have I?" Her tone was tinged with sarcasm. So she had been the source of the pain in my head. She had stung me with her unwillingness to let me in—apparently I was not the only one with a few "talents". My breath had returned to normal and I leaned back against her car door, reassessing this woman I had so clearly underestimated. She was standing several feet away, markedly wanting to create space between us, something that I didn't much care for. I surveyed her quickly; she was not particularly tall, maybe 5'3 with long hair that swirled in waves and curls, with a few dreadlocks that meandered down her back and over her shoulders. My original thought from private observations of her, was that her hair was brown, but now standing so close, I saw it was actually more reddish and copper in tone, with streaks of dark auburn. She appeared much young than her age, which I knew to be in her late twenties. Her eyes complemented her hair, liquid brown with flecks of gold and bronze and were almond shaped, framed by dark lashes. A light olive wash toned her skin that highlighted her Mediterranean descent. Her lips possessed a natural fullness that suited her small oval face and complimented what I was sure were a beautiful set of teeth, if she'd ever smile. She was muscular, but curvy and it suited her quite well. Her energy spoke of power and courage and a healthy dose of stubbornness—she was intriguing and she was going to be a project. I sighed, she was waiting for me to speak I guessed. "You know why I'm here," I said softly.

3

"Yeah, I know why you're here." She exhaled the breath she'd been holding. "What happens now?" she asked. I gently allowed myself to probe her mind to see her assessment of me; I sensed a bit of fear when she spoke. Another white-hot sting lashed out in my head and had me doubled over, yet again gasping for air.

"What the hell are you doing?" I tried to shout at her.

"I told you," she calmly explained. "You haven't earned the right to go digging around in my head, now please back off," she said diplomatically. I managed to take my hands off my knees and shakily stand back up.

"Jesus Christ," I panted. "I'm sorry…" She had walked around to the driver's side of her jeep and opened her door. Ana threw her books inside and leaned across to unlock the door that was barley holding me in a standing position and she glared at me across the seat.

"Are you getting in? I've been in class all day and I'm starving and I have a feeling that my evening is about to take a bit of a turn. I should at least have some food in me before we discuss my death and yours, don't you think?" Her tone dripped with annoyance. I pulled the handle on the door and slid onto the seat and I turned to look at her incredulously. "Thought this was going to be an easy get, did you?" she exclaimed as we backed out the parking space and headed toward the coast.

4

Ana

Holy shit, holy shit, holy shit!!! I was trying to keep what was sure to be a massive panic attack, at bay. This totally sucked! Why me, why now? I was driving in my jeep heading home with a frickin Bonder-Demon as my passenger—frick, frick, frick! I had been in Indonesia for four years. I had a wonderful job as an environmental mediator in the National Park. I was at the University working on my Ph.D. I had wonderful friends, a great little bungalow on the beach that I rented, two fantastic wolves that I had rescued and were now my closest family—I was happy and now there was the possibility of me dying or causing the death of another "person". Frick! I frantically tried to rack my brain in an attempt to recall what I knew about this bizarre and secretive species that was currently riding beside me. I had studied about Bonders and the ritual of Bonding, every human had, it was part of the set academic curriculum since the peace treaty had been reached decades ago, and I tried to recall the many lectures I had attended about the nature of the ritual itself. It wasn't something that I was ever invested in and I'd never paid much attention and now I was kicking myself in the ass for being so lazy and apathetic.

I did remember that Bonders were not Vampires; they were Demons. The Vampires were an almost extinct species, although a few of them still managed to roam in different parts of the world. Vampires had reputations for being extremely violent, seductive and absolutely corrupt. Unlike Demons, Vampires lived off of blood, any blood, and they were prone to attack indiscriminately. However, they shared with the Bonders the natural ability to produce venom that could both heal and incapacitate their prey. Vampires and Bonder-Demons both were equipped with uncanny, superior mental nuances; reading minds, sensing emotions and desires, the ability to plant false memories, as well as unparalleled physical strength. I always thought it would be tough to bet against either species in a fight; they were both superior and they were both predatory in nature, but in different contexts—fascinating stuff really, if you were into that sort of thing. There were a few Vampires here in Indonesia. I had always thought they were a bit lame, and since their almost complete evisceration via the Bonders, they sort of just tried to blend in and not cause any trouble...I was trying to recall a few more details from various readings... something about their blood being of great value to humans; it had healing properties...I racked my brain.

Before the latest treaty, there was mass obliteration of humans and Bonders. Humans killed Bonders for the valuable properties of their blood; Bonders killed humans for the immense powers that our blood gave them access to, and of course there were the Vampires who just killed anyone for blood. I knew that there were certain humans who possessed blood that would also supply the Vampire population with enhanced strength and abilities, but I had yet to hear of any human who had managed to secure such a relished position in that clan. The Bonder/human tie was an odd, slightly codependent relationship. Advances in science and medicine had yet to give human society enough armor to fight all of the deadly diseases and illnesses that plagued the globe. Throughout our history, we had learned that Bonders possessed antibodies for almost every known and some unknown illnesses and diseases that were sure to hit many in the human population. Their blood had the potential to heal even the most horrific of bodily traumas and of course, humans upon discovering this, had stopped at nothing to harness such a powerful substance. Therefore, the history of our relationship with these Demons was a complicated one, and it was always shifting and evolving. However, unlike our relationship with the Vampires, Bonders had maintained a relatively peaceful sentiment towards humans, at least lately and they didn't hate us.

I seemed to remember some sort of condition to the relationship with Bonders, some sort of catch. It seemed impossible for two species to coexist peacefully, with each group agreeing to a mutual exchange of "services", allowing for give and take in order to foster an entire society of humans and Bonders that depended on one another—it seemed impossible because it mostly was. I turned my face out the window to look at the ocean, trying to recall various conversations that I had with some of my Bonder friends over the last few months. I felt a sudden urgency to remember any information that I had heard, anything that might help me to navigate what was now happening to me. I snuck a glace over at my passenger. His face was turned to look out the window and I thought I heard him mumble a "good luck" in a slightly mocking tone. Hmph! I could totally figure this out; I wasn't about to come across as some helpless human who needed a Demon to facilitate her piecing things together. I heard another snicker from the passenger seat and I rolled my eyes.

Let's see, what did I know for sure? I knew that in order for a Demon to have immortality and complete their full transition into a Bonder, they must receive blood from a human. I knew the Bonder could just take it by force—which is what had been happening throughout our mutual histories, but most Bonders were willing to ask for this gift to be given voluntarily from a human, because if taken by force, well I was pretty sure that no human would ever survive that kind of attack. I also knew that if the human ultimately decided that they were *willing* to make this exchange, then there still could be consequences. If the human agrees to "donate" his or her blood to their Bonder, when the exchange is made, the Bonder receives the desired powers and completes the full transition into their form. The human could then be viewed as disposable after performing this service if the Bonder does not deem them fit to return the favor. By not allowing for the human to take the Bonder's newly immortal blood thus completing their Bond, the human would ultimately die.

I remember thinking after learning that crucial bit of information, that this whole relationship was somewhat asinine. I remembered my only friend that was Bonded, Kai, telling me that we have the right to say no, however, refusing the Bond can ultimately kill the Bonder and thus why some Bonders are compelled to take blood by force, often killing the human in the process. Once a Bonder has "branded" a human, the human's blood is the only source that can provide the Bonder with their completed form—no other. By saying "no" to the exchange, humans could be handing themselves a death sentence, so maybe the human assumption of having a "choice" in the matter, was a bit of a misconception. It was possible that the human could say no, and gamble on the fact that they might survive the forthcoming attack, but why take the chance? I was playing all of these histories out in my head, while driving along the coastal road. I was completely lost in my own thoughts and for a moment, forgot that I had a Demon as a passenger. What I was recalling historically was now apparently, my definite reality.

My friend Kai had already been Bonded. It was a fairly easy choice for him to make, he had fallen madly in love with Alec, and so he was guaranteed to stay his beautiful self for quite a long time! By Bonding with a Demon, humans could live an unnaturally long life, not immortal, but something quite close. I was sure that you could still die, even if you were part of a Bond, but I couldn't recall how and I didn't like thinking about Kai or Alec dying. Kai was my best friend, my brother in arms. He was Indonesian and I had worked with his family on stopping some industrial development that was occurring on the tribal, agricultural lands. This was one rare issue that had garnered interest from all three species, humans, Bonders and Vampires, mainly because Bonders and Vampires had always been land hungry and those who could acquire the most land had more access over the surrounding human populations. The Vampires were big miners in the area and I had spent quite a few years negotiating with certain Vampire covens over land rights for the indigenous peoples that were living in the mineral rich communities. Sometimes it ended well, sometimes it did not and I much preferred to not have to spend my time negotiating with Vampires; they were a tricky and subtle species to encounter.

That's when I first met Alec. He was working as a lawyer for Kai's family and I was serving as mediator between the covens and Kai's family. Both Kai and I had known that Alec was a Demon. They had a very distinct look even with varying ethnic backgrounds; usually very long hair that was almost always woven into dreadlocks that hung below their waists and they dressed in what I always referred to as "Boho-chic". Most Demons, like some Vampires, had strangely colored eyes; not the normal brown or blue or green, they had a mystical quality to them and a depth that was otherworldly. Alec's were bright emerald green.

We didn't know that Alec had come to work specifically because he'd chosen Kai. I remembered when it happened. Last year, Alec had shown up to Kai's 30th birthday party— uninvited I suppose. Kai, as always, amazed me with his reaction. He walked right up to him and said, *"Well, if this is what is supposed to be, then I guess we should try to at least make it fun!"* They've been inseparable ever since. That's the other weird thing about having a Bonder; they stay with you *everywhere*. A couple of my undergraduate students had Bonders that had come to them while they were still in high school. It was known that when the family accepted the relationship, nothing sexual in nature was tolerated on either end with someone so young. The Bonder would move into the house with the whole family, they would help with the chores and participate in all of the family activities—they would stay with their Bond until that person was mature enough to make the "choice" for themselves as it involved both the taking of blood and often a sexual connection. I had a feeling that my situation would be a bit more complicated than that of Kai and Alec or even my undergrads. Hell, I didn't even know my passenger's name and I doubted he'd be helping me with the pile of laundry that was waiting on my bed.

10

light against a cloth of darkness and infinite depth. Those were his eyes, the night skies staring at me. They were penetrating and a little frightening.

"I don't want you to be scared," he spoke so softly that I wasn't sure if he had actually said anything at all. "I'm a patient being and we will go as slowly as you need Ana." The way he said my name, like he had known me for years, like my name was now his, it made me tremble. Surprisingly, I wasn't as bothered by this notion as I thought, however having him in my house was a bit unsettling. I didn't know what to expect. I was glad that I had spent yesterday evening doing a bit of cleaning; at least he'd know that I wasn't messy.

"Well," I said. "I know it's probably not what you're accustom to, but it really works for me," I said, holding the door open for him as I followed behind. I loved the inside of my house. It was a great space; a rare two stories with a nice deck that I had spent an entire summer with Kai and Alec refinishing. Having a Bonder as a friend, particularly one who had various talents in architecture and design, was really pretty handy. The downstairs was the main living space; it was small but really cozy and comfortable. I had hard wood floors that were dark and a rich cherry in tone. A wood stove in the kitchen with a breakfast nook and an open living room with a small fireplace, a roll top desk that housed my computer and everything school related. Alec had built me an amazing sofa and two matching chairs that were covered in some very soft creamy, beige fabric—the sofa was one of my favorite pieces. I had a very eclectic taste in décor and I didn't like anything that was mass-produced. I enjoyed spending some of my weekend mornings scoping out the local markets for trinkets

15

that spoke to me. I got that from Noni. We would spend hours some Sundays just combing through other people's histories and bringing them home to start their next life with us. I could possibly be considered a hoarder as Kai liked to say, but I fancied myself selective enough not to be made into a reality show for people with mental illnesses, at least not yet. The unique bungalow was a loft space with the upstairs overlooking down into the living room. My bedroom and the second bathroom occupied that floor and my most favorite spot in the whole house—the tree terrace. Just off from my bedroom was an iron door that led right into the trees from the Preserve. When I moved in, there was just a drop off from the door into the canopy below, but Alec had made a wooden pathway leading into the trees and to a little balcony. I placed a small patio table and some chairs so I could sit and have coffee or tea, read or study or just listen to all of the sounds coming from the forest. And of course there were my wolves Kuckuc and Piyip. Besides Kai and Alec, they were my best friends and they were the only wolves to survive the fire at Noni's sanctuary. Fifteen wolves perished, we tried to save as many as we could, but there was too much smoke and fire. I got Noni out and went back to save Kuckuc and Piyip. Noni used to say that they were now my guardians and I was theirs. I found great honor in our dependence on each other; it was a sacred and rare relationship that I cherished. They were great with Alec and Kai, but I wondered how they would react to Nathanial. I knew they were patrolling along the beach, their favorite place to hunt for fish and taunt the chimps in the trees. I thought better of calling them, no need to create any more tension.

I turned to glance at Nathanial, hoping that he'd have some idea of what our living arrangement was going to be. I had lived with a few men before, boyfriends and one fiancé, but I was guessing this scenario might pose some different challenges. His back was to me and he was staring at the pictures that covered my refrigerator. I had made most of my favorite photographs into magnets and collaged them onto both the fridge and the freezer. My trip to South Africa, my studies in Ireland, Noni, and my friends on the Reservation, Alec and Kai, all of my most happy moments set out for me to look upon every morning—an homage to my life so far. "Umm, what do we do now?" I noticed that my voice had a slight tremor to it when I spoke.

"Why don't we get you something to eat?" He turned his attention away from the photographs and looked at me. "I believe that you mentioned you were hungry after your long day of classes, yes?" At the mention of the word 'hungry' I felt my blood sugar plummet and my stomach growled; Nathanial smiled at me. I remembered from Alec that Bonders ate human food, just not very much. I didn't want to be a bad hostess so figured I should at least ask him if he was hungry. "I'm not at the moment," he answered my unasked question. Ugh, this could get annoying very quickly. He laughed out loud. "Perhaps, it would serve you better to keep your mind uncluttered in order to be more aware of my little gift." *Gift*, more like a weapon, I thought. "As is yours Ana, your ability to keep people out, is that not also a weapon?" he said quietly. We stared at each other, unblinking.

It was odd having someone sit across from me while I ate, I felt rude having a meal when the other person was not. I sighed and pushed my plate back. I knew we needed to discuss what was happening between us. I laughed to myself, it reminded me of those talks you had just before you were either going to break up with someone or you had just realized that you wanted to be together. Both were a bit uncomfortable, not knowing how the other person was going to react, what was going to be said, how you would come away from the discussion, with a broken heart or a chance at a new life with someone who you loved and who loved you. Again, I felt the sudden depth of my situation and I looked at Nathanial as if in some desperate need for him to figure all of this out for us. "Ok, what do we do, obviously I'm new to this, and I have no idea what to expect or what to do next, I'm having a very hard time getting my head around you being here…" I trailed off. He leaned across the table and lightly brushed the tips of his fingers across my hand. Heat suddenly radiated up my arm, making me jump. He jerked his hand back and laughed nervously.

"Well," he began, composing himself by taking a breath, "you know that you now have a decision to make. You are my Bond as I have chosen you and the matter of my immortality and my completion into my life as a Bonder, falls to you," he spoke in a matter of fact tone, as if we were discussing what type of used car to buy.

"But you could choose not to save me," I interjected before he could continue. "Right? I mean I could say 'yes' to this whole immortality/power thing and then you could get what you want, decide that I'm disposable." He flinched at my use of the word. "Then I'm left to endure a slow death. I mean,

certificate to know how much he was committed to their relationship. Kai on the other hand, had always wanted to get married. He never felt that he was particularly handsome even though I thought he was one of the most beautiful men I'd ever seen. He never fancied himself smart enough to have anyone want to make that kind of commitment to him; he saw himself through a very distorted lens. To me, Kai was the very essence of true beauty. The kind that radiates from within, transforming anyone who is lucky enough to cross his path and I counted myself amongst those lucky few.

I was unsure if Nathanial was aware of the good news; he and Alec had known each other for a very long time, they had served in the armies of both Bonders and humans and fought various battles together against the Vampires. I was excited to tell Nathanial, secretly hoping that this would get him to engage me a little bit, but also because it was nice to have someone to share things with during your day, even if that person was poised to try and steel your blood. I sighed as I pulled into the driveway; his Land Rover was gone, of course. I looked at the clock in the dashboard, 6:00pm—he was in class and probably wouldn't be back until eleven, that had become his usual routine as of late. I put my jeep in reverse and backed out of the drive; I didn't feel much like being alone in the house right now. Kai had given me a list of "things to do" for the wedding planning. They had a date set for the winter solstice; it was late August which gave us about four months. I sighed again as I drove back toward town. I hit the bookstore for some coffee and a salad before stopping in at the engravers for invitations. The bookshop was buzzing and there was an unusual amount of people crowded around the tiny tables and in the booths.

"Sheesh Rhu," I called to the owner's son. "What the hell's goin on?" I elbowed my way into a barstool at the counter.

"You didn't hear Ana?" Rhu's head shot up from somewhere underneath the bar, his shaggy hair falling into his dark eyes.

"Uh, hear what, what did I miss?" I asked, resisting the urge to sweep his hair back from his face like I was his mother.

"There's been another attack at the University and this time the Bonder was killed." An icy current swept through my veins and I felt the familiar racing of my heart in my throat. In the last month there had been five attacks, all brutal but each time the Bonder had survived. God, my head was racing; not him, it wasn't him. It couldn't be him. I grasped the bar table feeling the slick sweat seep from my palms.

"Rhu, when did this happen?" my voice shook as I spoke and it sounded unusually high. I didn't know if Nathanial had come home last night, I went to bed early and he wasn't there this morning.

"Last night, the Bonder was coming out of the library and seven guys jumped him and staked his wrists right there into the ground. Then, they slashed his groin and his neck, took the blood and set him on fire, leaving him there staked into the dirt—the dude was smoked right there on the spot." I had greatly wished that Rhu had spared me the details of the attack, but he was seventeen and for some reason, unprovoked violence didn't seem to affect him.

"Who was it? I mean, who got attacked, do the police know?" My jaw was clenched and I ground my teeth together.

"Yeah, it was a grad student, some guy, I don't know his name or anything. Hey, are you alright Ana? You look a little green." Ok, ok, it wasn't him. I felt relieved and then a little guilty that I felt relieved.

"What? Oh no, I'm ok Rhu. I'm ok." I felt sick. Attacks like this were rare in the last ten or so years and especially since the latest treaties had been negotiated between humans and Demons just five short years ago. This shouldn't be happening.

"You want this to go?" He was holding my salad up in front of me.

"Umm, you know what? I'm... I'm not actually hungry..." I trailed off. I needed to get out of there. I needed to call Nathanial. I didn't care if he was in class or not, I just needed to hear his voice. I backed out of the bookstore and rummaged through my backpack to find my phone. My hands were shaking, I knew he was ok, but still the whole scenario scared the shit out of me. I was old enough to remember when the last wave of violence between humans and Bonders had happened; that's how Noni had lost the wolf sanctuary. The Bonders had scoured the Reservation, burning and attacking humans indiscriminately. It was an odd display of violence for their species, but they had reached their breaking point. I shuttered at the memory as I hit the speed dial and waited for him to pick up...it rang and rang and on the fourth ring I thought it had clicked over to voicemail, but I heard a soft voice speak.

"Ana, what's the matter? Is everything ok, are you hurt? What's wrong?" he said. Nathanial didn't sound annoyed that I was calling him during his class and that was good. I took a deep breath and started to talk.

"Nathanial, I'm sorry to bother you at work, it's just that I was at the bookshop and …" My voice shook. " I heard what happened last night and Rhu, he told me what happened and I just panicked and I haven't seen you in a few days and I just panicked…" I was babbling and coming close to hysterics. "I'm sorry I called, I think I just needed to hear your voice—I'm sorry." Silence met me on the other end of the phone. I was taking deep breaths and attempting to calm myself.

"Ana, I'm fine, we can talk about this when I get home tonight ok?" It wasn't really a question so much as it was an order or dismissal of sorts. I felt my jaw set and I clenched my teeth at his tone.

"Of course Nathanial, whatever you want." At his reaction, numbness washed over me and I spoke mechanically, blandly. I hung up the phone and went to my car, pulled out of the parking space and drove out of town toward the ferries bound for the outer islands. I felt tired, tired with Nathanial, tired with myself, and my nerves were shot. I was so frustrated. I couldn't seem to navigate any of the feelings I had for him or for our situation. I needed something, someone to help me through all of this; it was too much for one person to handle. I was angry that Nathanial hadn't been more help in our entire process of being together. Clearly he had his own "demons" to battle but seriously, ignoring me, not talking to me—it wasn't helping his case very much. I missed Noni. I missed her smile and how she always truly knew what I needed to feel better. I missed how much she believed in me, in my strength, my capacity for resilience; she was and is, a very stupid woman, I laughed bitterly to myself. I was neither strong nor resilient and especially not now.

It took me three hours to get to the ferry dock, park and buy a ticket for the last boat of the evening. I had no idea what I was doing really, and I didn't care—I just wanted to get away. I was emotionally exhausted and hearing about such brutality, it did a number on my state of mind. I boarded the ferry with a few scarce locals heading home for the evening after work. The island I was headed for was one made up predominantly of indigenous peoples. Some were from Indonesia, but quite a few were from Indigenous American groups. They had migrated from the US in search of a more communal lifestyle in a place that offered a peaceful setting far from the government imposed reservations in the States. They set up a commune of sorts and they were pretty self-sufficient. Actually, I really envied their existence. Beautiful gardens housed fresh fruits and vegetables and they built solar powered green houses for native plants and herbs. Last year Kai and I went over to help build a new elementary school for the children—I loved being there. It stirred memories of my time with Noni on the Reservation and made me feel almost happy…almost, but not quite.

Once docked, I hoisted my pack onto my shoulders and began walking into the little village. The paths were lined with bungalow type shops and homes, people rode bikes everywhere and children were outside playing. Idyllic would be a good word for the community, but this group of people fought many bloody wars to gain their cultural autonomy from the Bonders, the Vampires and of course other humans that had infiltrated every possible area of their land; this type of peace and communal harmony was long over due in my opinion.

I made my way through the narrow streets, not thinking too much about what I was doing or where I was going. My head was racing as usual and I was having trouble navigating my next plan of action. It wasn't as if I could actually "run away" from this whole situation or from Nathanial, he would be able to find me no matter how far I managed to get. So what options did I have? "None", the voice in my head answered, I had no options. I exhaled loudly and decided that I might as well find something to eat and sort out where I was going to spend the night; I had no intentions of going back home this evening. If Nathanial was going to be agitated with me for caring about him and his life, then maybe it would just be best to do this stupid Bonding thing and then go our separate ways; we didn't have to stay together, we could be Bound but apart, and for me and my life, that just seemed to make the most sense.

I found a nice outdoor café that looked busy for the late hour, but not crowded. People were pouring over newspapers and huddled together reading. Apparently, even the outer communities were not immune to the violence that had infiltrated the University. I felt sad for them for some reason. To me, it seemed that they should be shielded from all of that nonsense; they had endured so much violence of their own, and it was still so close to them, close enough for the fear to remain in their collective memory—why add more?

I sat inside because I didn't want to overhear any more details from the scene of the murder. My head hurt and I just wanted to sit and not think for the moment. I ordered a glass of wine and some brown rice and chicken. I pulled out an art magazine I'd gotten on campus today and started to thumb through it, then my phone started buzzing on the table. I glanced at the screen to see that it was Nathanial calling. What time was it? I glanced at the clock next to the incoming call and noticed that it was nine. It looked like he'd called three times before now. Hmm, I debated for a moment picking it up and telling him to come and get me. He had a boat that he took back and forth between the islands and he could easily make the trip. I turned off my phone. I wasn't ready to talk to him and it wasn't like he'd been making much of an effort as of late. Screw it, I thought, and turned my attention to my meal.

By the time I finished dinner, the café was calming down and catering to the late night coffee goers. I went to the bar and asked the guy behind the counter if he could recommend a place to stay for the evening. He told me that the commune now had small beach bungalows that you could rent. It sounded good to me and I headed off in the right direction. It was quite dark out, but small bamboo torches placed along the pathway lighted most of my walk. During the day the journey out to the coast was a beautiful one; nighttime was a bit of a different story.

As I traveled deeper down the dirt road, the torches became less abundant until there were just a few sporadically placed along the walkway. I wasn't much for darkness and I wished I had brought Kuckuc or Piyip with me. The late summer air was damp and moist, but my skin broke out into chills and I stopped to pull out my sweatshirt that I had in my pack. I noticed that my hands were shaking and my teeth were chattering. I hoped that I wasn't coming down with anything. I moved a bit more quickly along the path toward the little cluster of lights that designated the entrance to the commune. Instantly, my muscles seized and I stopped walking, well actually, my feet stopped moving, to say that I stopped walking would indicate that I actually had power over my movements—I did not. I couldn't move, not my legs, not my arms, nothing. Terror filled every bone in my body and the hair stood up on the back of my neck. It was an odd sensation, not having any control over one's body.

Suddenly, I felt a force of pressure in my head so heavy that I thought for a moment that something or someone had hit me. I doubled over in pain and fell to my knees. At least I could move now. A curl of nausea washed over me and I fell over onto the dirt, vomiting. In my head, I saw Nathanial standing over me; at least I thought it was Nathanial. He looked different, his features distorted somehow. His eyes were no longer sparkling with silver and midnight blue, but instead they were black and the black filled in his entire eye, like someone had spilled ink into the whites, shrouding their appearance. His teeth were barred and he was making a deep growling noise, not from his throat, but from his whole self—I felt it reverberate inside of me and I trembled. The vision was so frightening that I forced myself to open my eyes. I gasped and choked on the air entering my lungs. I pressed my palms into the dirt and pushed myself into a standing position. I looked to my front, nothing. I looked behind me, nothing. I tried the steadiness of my legs and found them to be shaky, but not unwilling to move—I ran.

Rage flooded through my body. Never, in my three hundred years on this earth, had I ever experienced this type of intense anger. I threw my phone down on the table and rubbed my eyes in sheer frustration. Where the hell was she? Why wasn't she answering my calls? I had called Kai and Alec, neither of whom had seen her since this morning. They were out looking for her. The only thing I could do was to unleash my anger with her by attempting to get through the chinks in her mind. I had been trying for hours to get a read on her location, but she was impenetrable, locked down like a fortress. I thought I had managed to paralyze her enough to let her see what I was experiencing, but still, she hadn't called.

I knew that she'd been upset earlier today when we'd spoken. I knew the events at the University were startling and disturbing, but I had planned to discuss her fears upon my return home this evening. Granted, since my little attack "episode", I had been having difficulty sorting through my feelings for her and for our situation. My faith in myself had been shaken and somehow the tides had shifted. My feelings about Ana had changed and I didn't know what that meant for us or for me. I was just trying to sort through everything so I could come to her and tell her what I was thinking, what I wanted. But now, now things were a mess. She was gone and the distance she had created not only physically, but also emotionally, was wreaking havoc on my ability to think clearly, to be calm and rational. Instead, I was now allowing for my most demonic nature to surface. If she would just come home and listen, I could explain to her what was happening. I could tell her just how much I now needed her and that I desired her, but that I would be patient. I could tell her not to worry. She wasn't coming home and now I was angry.

My phone rang and I jumped, grasping it as if it were a lifeline. It was Alec, he'd tracked her to the commune on the outer island; she was safe and staying in a bungalow on the beach. Alec was a natural navigator and very apt at shimmering, a demon's best mode of transportation. He could decipher almost anyone's location just by his or her mental space and scent. He asked me if he should approach her and take her home. I told him no, and that I was on my way. Thanking Alec, I ended the call and grabbed my car keys. Humans couldn't shimmer with us, unless they possessed some of our blood from the exchange, so I would need a vehicle to take us back home; I didn't want Ana driving back alone, I wanted her with me. I knew all of the short cuts to the outer islands and what usually took the average person three hours, took me about thirty minutes. I drove down the trails leading away from the Preserve and out toward the back roads. Circumnavigating the longer coastal highway route, I headed to the port where I kept my boat. From the dock, it was only fifteen minutes down the waterway to the commune. I arrived in five.

Her scent knocked the breath out of me the minute I set foot on land; she was close by. I followed the path down to the little huts scattered along the beach. Bonfires illuminated my footsteps as soft music and laughter drifted in the air. I closed my eyes and reached my mind out to feel where she was. Something strange occurred; I didn't just sense her like I usually did, but instead my mind *saw* her. A full picture of Ana entered my mental vision, clear as if she was standing in front of me. She was out on a deck with her hands grasping the railing, her face turned up toward the moon, her hair blowing in dark swirls around her face and shoulders. I gasped at this new development; what the hell was happening to me? First, I almost attacked her, and now these new, full visions. What was next? I moved slowly through the people partying on the beach and headed up the dunes to where she was standing. I saw the outline of the bungalow and her silhouette bathed in moonlight and shadow. I felt a surge of anger at her complete disregard for the trouble she'd caused, but the minute I stepped onto the deck and saw her, the anger quelled. She was truly the most beautiful and exquisite person that I had ever laid eyes on. It wasn't just her physicality that was pleasing, but the core of who she truly was that was the most beautiful site to behold and I could see it. She was radiant, even in her fear of me. She turned and our gazes locked, unwavering in their emotions.

"You're really mad aren't you?" she spoke in a matter of fact tone, and with what I sensed was just a bit of "screw you, I don't give a shit attitude". I shook my head back and forth, trying not to laugh at her tone.

"Yes, but that doesn't matter anymore, you're safe and we're together," I replied, unable to take my eyes off of her. I wanted to be near her. My body was aching with a pull so great that I was shocked by its intensity; that was new as well.

"Tell me something." She turned away from me to look out at the ocean, "are you glad that I'm safe because I'm your Bond and if something happened to me, then you would most certainly die, or are you glad that I'm safe because you care about me as a human being, as a woman, as your friend?" I paused and let silence penetrate the space between us. "Never mind," she said with a sigh of defeat. "It doesn't matter anymore—it is what it is."

"Ana," I whispered her name into the wind. I didn't know how to respond, everything that she was saying was true. I cared about my own survival of course, but I also cared deeply about her wellbeing. Maybe I had come to love her or at the very least, care deeply for her, but somehow though, I didn't see how those two feelings could ever be reconciled within myself. Nothing I could say would ever make her feel valued in this situation, not in the way she wanted. I moved quietly to her side and reached to hold her hand. I expected the touch to resurrect the violent feelings that I had had before, but this time it was different. What washed over me this time were not feelings of desperation or of survival, but of the deepest desire, of want, of need, something so forcibly primal stirred within and I felt outside of myself. I turned to her and put my hands on her waist, pulling Ana toward me. For one moment, alarm filled her eyes and I felt her body tense. "I'm not going to hurt you," I whispered into her ear. I felt her shiver as I pressed my lips softly to her neck. Her scent was absorbed into my mouth. I let my tongue sweep across her skin tasting the very essence of her. My mouth moved to hers. Sensing her reluctance at my touch, I fiercely brought her lips to mine not giving her a chance to resist. He body relaxed and I felt her trace her tongue over my bottom lip and she pressed herself harder against me. I gripped her shoulders and skimmed my lips across her collarbone and onto her chest, each movement of my mouth on her skin sent shivers up and down her body. I held her closer still as she brought my face back to hers, kissing me deeply, hungrily. I felt a soft moan escape from my throat as she slid her tongue in and out, teasing me. Heat rose inside me and I moved her against the glass doors, I kicked them open and pulled her urgently inside.

Instincts were taking over and I felt nothing but the desperation to have her, to possess her. My mouth watered as I felt her lips move slowly down my chest. I fell back against the bed and quivering, I let her unbutton my shirt and slide down my pants. I reached up to tear off her tank, jerking it over her shoulders. I grabbed her and moved her under me, pining her hands above her head. I curled her fingers around the bedposts and slid off her jeans and underwear. My breaths came in ragged intervals as my teeth grazed along her inner thigh and I felt the pulse and flow of her blood. The scent was a heady fragrance of spice and rich sweetness and I let my tongue trace slowly on her skin, trying to get as close to the source of the aroma as I could. I groaned loudly as I felt her body writhe. I let my mouth move over and inside her, tasting what I knew was to be the very reason for my existence. She moaned and pulled my face back to hers and bit lightly down on my lip, her tang lingering delicately on both of our tongues. I pushed myself as gently as my passion would allow, inside of her and shivered as I felt our bodies pulse together. She was much better at this than I was. The way she moved her body against mine, the rhythm of her hips against mine, self-control for me, was out the window. I feared that I was much rougher with her than she wanted, but her body seemed to respond in ways that sent me reeling. Pushing myself deeper into her, I felt purified and whole, the missing pieces of my existence were now filled—was this what it was

47

like? I had distant memories of engaging in sex, but nothing like what I was currently experiencing. Sweat coated her body as she moved on top of me, igniting a deep pleasure with the position and she slowed our movements to a quiet rhythm. I gasped out loud as I felt her raging toward her climax, her moans making the pulse of my hips move faster, push harder. She felt too good now and heat surged from between her legs as she came. My body tensed unwilling to wait any longer. I grabbed her waist and flipped her forcefully onto her back, holding down her arms. I thrust myself roughly against her, my body ached with pleasure and I ground deeper feeling how wet and soft she was, how her body opened for me, accepted my claim of her. Moans escaped from her perfect lips as each thrust from me brought her closer to peaking, to igniting once more. I wanted her to come again and I wanted it desperately. The sounds she made, the way her body felt as I slid inside of her; it was overwhelming. I grabbed the headboard to harness as much power as possible. I was beyond hard; I was pulsing with violence. She held me firm and tight as I pushed back and forth with as much force as I could, feeling myself begin to release inside of her, filling her with my desire. I felt myself unleash and I groaned as my body instantly came again and again, I didn't want to stop. Slowing my rhythm against her, I finally managed to bring my mind and my body under control enough to stop thrusting. God, I was going to need a bit more practice at this. I looked down at her, worrying suddenly that I had physically hurt her somehow or that things had happened too quickly. "Are you alright?" I asked breathlessly, pressing my lips to her forehead, her cheeks, her eyelids. She opened her eyes and smiled.

"Yep, I'm good!" She laughed and pushed my hair back behind my shoulders. I leaned into her neck and laughed too, it felt good to be with her, laughing; I wanted her to be mine…for eternity.

Ana

Well that was interesting, I mused as I listened to Nathanial breathing deeply beside me. I truly could not, for the life of me, understand where or when my passion for him had ignited. Had it always been there? Was it something that I had been fighting all of these months and now here we both were in this new place with each other? I smiled to myself; I wasn't going to diminish what proved to be a very sensual, yet somewhat quick experience for me, by overanalyzing. I shifted to turn on my side and glanced at the window, the sun was just beginning to stretch its rays across the horizon. Hmm, I didn't think Nathanial had actually ever *seen* me first thing in the morning. My hair was usually a tangle of curls and I was prone to have a few pillow lines and blotches etched across my face. I had a small makeup bag in my pack and thought I may be able to salvage a presentable appearance before he woke up. I shifted out of the bed as gently as I could. Nathanial was a very deep sleeper, most Bonders were and he didn't move. I rifled through my backpack until I found the little Ziplock bag that held some concealer, lip balm and a ponytail band; I could work with that.

Once in the bathroom, I pulled my hair back and splashed some water on my face. The coolness of the moisture felt good, but for some reason the back of my neck felt very warm. I tried to finger comb through some of the more invasive tangles and twisted my hair into a low braid, dabbed on some cover-up and rinsed my mouth. Like a bullet to the brain, suddenly, a surge of heat racketed up the back of my head, blazing through my spinal cord to the base of my neck. I thought something was burning into my skin. I grabbed the edges of the sink and bent my head toward the basin, trying to breathe. The heat was now producing such an acute pain at the nape of my neck, that instinctively I moved my hand to the spot and felt something wet soaking my fingers. What the hell? Another shot of heat and pain shuddered through me, and blood began streaming down the back of my skull. I slumped down onto the tiled floor, not able to scream or call out. My body was seizing from whatever was attempting to sever my spinal cord from my brain. I gasped and managed to yell as loudly as I could. In seconds Nathanial was slamming open the door. He looked at me heaving on the floor, his eyes darting to the now small puddle of blood that was oozing around me. "It's my neck," I tried to speak. "It's the back of my neck, something's wrong!" He quickly knelt to my side and lifted up the braid that was masking a now growing tear in my skin. Another contraction of fire and burning unleashed at the base of my skull. I convulsed in Nathanial's arms. Why wasn't he doing something, calling a doctor, calling someone to help?

"Ana", he spoke calmly. "It's your Bond, it's going to be alright. I know it hurts, but it will be over soon." His voice sounded distant and hollow, like he was speaking through some sort of filter. My *Bond*? What the hell was he talking about? I struggled against the pain, trying to remember…trying to understand. A memory of Kai came to me; he had a mark, something like a metallic carved tattoo at the base of his neck. Oh god, the pain! I groaned on the floor and grasped my head with my hands. My brain was being compressed, squeezed so tightly that I was sure I was going to die or hemorrhage out. The mark, Kai's mark…he said it only came once he'd made his decision. I hadn't made any decisions yet had I? He also failed to mention what he'd gone through when the "branding" finally showed up! Nathanial was speaking softly, it sounded like he was praying or chanting or something. I really didn't think that now was the time to be evoking some old Mayan god—I needed him to make this stop and make it stop now! Another jab into my brain sent me gasping and writhing, my face pressed into the bloody pool on the floor. I felt the flesh at the base of my skull rip and shred, sending a new wave of dark-red blood running down my back. Then, as suddenly as it had happened, everything ceased. The pain and heat flooded out of my body in a giant whoosh of relief. I stopped bleeding and only my head was left with a dull ache and pulse. My heart was racing and my breath was coming in rapid intervals, but I wasn't hurting anymore. Nathanial was dampening some towels in the sink and wiping off my bloodied face and neck. I was having trouble holding up my own head so he laid me down across his lap, cradling my head in his hands. The cool, moist towel helped to revive me and I could steady my breathing enough to speak. "What happened to me?" I asked weakly.

"Shhh," Nathanial whispered. "Not now, let's get you feeling a bit stronger shall we?" I closed my eyes and let him work me over with the towels and his soft caresses to my body. I sighed. It was always something with us, with me. I wondered what the world was like before Bonding. I didn't know anything else, so I had nothing to compare it to, and now with all of its pain and ritual, Bonding *was* my world.

I must have fallen asleep at some point. I woke up under the covers with the blinds pulled. It was dark in the room and my eyes were having trouble adjusting. Immediately, my hand went to the nape of my neck, the flesh was hard and the texture reminded me of armor. My fingers traced something raised and solid that seemed to follow the vertebrae down a few inches. For some reason, my mind went to cauterizing and the burning of metal to flesh, not your typical tattooing process. I suddenly realized that Nathanial was in the room, sitting so still and silent that I had thought that I had been left alone. He was perched in the chair by the window watching me.

"It suits you," he mused from the dark corner. "The pattern and colors I mean...it's you."

"What does it look like?" I asked with a hit of skepticism in my tone. I had a few tattoos, but I wasn't sure if I could quite pull off a piece of carved metal sticking out of my skin as well as others.

"Nonsense," Nathanial said, sensing my wariness and chuckling softly. "I haven't seen a single thing that you can't pull off successfully. Let's have a look, yes?" He raised himself off the chair and went to the bathroom, which I thankfully noticed had been scrubbed clean of my blood. Good man, I thought to myself. He came back holding two little mirrors, one from my makeup bag and another from the bathroom. He helped me sit up, which I was grateful for, as a sudden extreme dizziness overwhelmed me and I collapsed back against the pillows. "Easy now," he spoke softly. "Let's try again." I sat up slowly and steadied myself using my abdominals to find a solid center of balance. Nathanial held up one mirror to the back of my head and handed me the other. I raised it a bit over my shoulder so I could find the back of my reflection.

"Oh!" I gasped violently. At the nape of my neck and weaving down between my shoulder blades, was a pattern of entwined metals. One was a deep smoky silver with clusters of tiny, clear sparkling jewels that reminded me of stars, and the other was a deep midnight blue with luminous strands of silver etched inside the narrow lines. It reminded me of something that I couldn't quite place, something that I knew and loved. The entwined strands moved in an intricate pattern, the shape and lines resembling an ancient Pagan symbol or cross. The metal pair was fluid and flexible but solid in their hold on my neck and I felt them embed solidly into my flesh. There was a smoothness to their texture, and something that radiated onto the surrounding skin, almost like a spotlight, bathing my new branding in moonlight and starlight.

"It's beautiful," Nathanial whispered. I jumped. I was so enthralled with my new addition that I'd forgotten that he was right behind me.

"Hmm…" was all I could muster.

"Ana," he spoke into my ear. "You've made your decision now." There was a quiver of excitement in his voice, an undercurrent of elation that he could not hide, and he was right, I had made my choice, his life was to be spared. Nathanial was going to get what he wanted, what he was here for. As for me, my fate was now directly in his hands and there was no going back for me, no running away, no looking down from the cliffs—it was time to jump.

Nathanial

Ana and I had decided to initiate the "exchange" after Kai and Alec were married. I wasn't terribly happy about that decision, the wedding was eight weeks out and I was anxious. Of course I knew that Ana couldn't undo her choice. Once she'd been branded, she was bound to her decision, and I felt in no way that she would try to find a loophole around that, not that she could. Still, it had been months since our first meeting and I could feel the window of time for this transaction to happen, waning. Bonders had a brief opening of sorts once they had branded their Bond. The window was different for each of us, but the longer the stretch of time between a decision being made and the actual exchange, the physically weaker we became. I suppose the Human could drag out the process, but that just increased the chances of their blood being taken by force, and the possibility of that person surviving such a violent attack were slim to none, even in a Bonder's weakened state.

Ana wanted the next several weeks to be about Kai and Alec. She didn't want anything to distract attention from their happiness and the fun of planning the final touches of their wedding. For some reason, I was not in the mood to be celebratory. The pressure in my head had returned and I couldn't place the direct source of my angst. I was well distracted with a grouping of exams and term papers that were now scheduled and filtering in. I spent long nights at the office and offering extra advising appointments to my students. I knew Ana was quite aware of my current mental state, and I also knew that she was hoping I would talk to her about what I was experiencing—I wished that I could, but I had no idea where to begin, as I wasn't sure myself of what I was feeling. Our time at the beach had shifted our relationship into one that was much more intimate, something that I was unaccustomed to and I was having difficulty navigating. Ana was a very affectionate person and she oriented herself around me in such a way that allowed for her to touch me and kiss me whenever the mood struck. That was new for me. I was not, by nature, affectionate. Not because I didn't desire closeness, especially from her, but ultimately I was somewhat reserved about physical expressions of emotion or mood. Ana was tuned into my hesitations and tried to accommodate me as best she knew how. There was also the issue of my self-control around her. Apparently, our coupling at the commune had awakened some deep primal longing that was in constant need of being satisfied. I hadn't quite mastered the diplomacy of foreplay, something that Ana and a lot of women really enjoyed and sometimes needed. I hadn't been with too many women and the ones that I had shared intimacies with, there had been no connection, no passion. Whereas with Ana, all I ever felt was desire and our intimate moments were always so intense and erotic that it was hard for me to go slow with her, to be tender and calm; I wanted her all the time. Sexually, I was a work in progress, and luckily for me, she didn't seem to mind.

This was a rare evening when I was coming to pick her up from the gym. It was impressive how much she worked out, especially since she was the only female currently enrolled at the gym she attended. Of course, Ana couldn't pick one of the nicer fitness facilities that the area offered. She'd been working out at this crude, underground gym run by Bonders and some of their Vampire associates. It was my least favorite place for her to spend her time. I also was not too keen on the guy who owned the gym, he was her trainer and she'd been with him for several years. He was a Bonder who had yet to mark his Bond, which had always bothered me. Jack was dark and muscular and he was constantly thinking about Ana. I knew this because upon meeting him for the first time, his thoughts permeated my mind. I didn't even have to filter my way in as I usually did. He'd hit me with them as some sort of warning. Why? I was not sure. All I could decipher was that he fancied himself as some sort of protector for Ana. She had quite a few Bonder friends, all of whom showed an undying loyalty and concern for her wellbeing, but this was different. Jack was different and I was always on guard when he was around.

Upon entering the gym, the familiar rush of air conditioning, absurdly loud metal rock music and sweat pulsated around me. I scanned the main floor and immediately found her in the boxing ring. I didn't like what I saw. Ana trained in many areas of combat, such as Mixed Martial Arts and Budokai, and being the only female at this particular gym, well, it limited her

56

training partners to just males. Currently, I was watching as Jack straddled Ana on the ground, pinned her hands over her head and hooked his legs to hers. He pressed his knees to her hips, preventing her from moving side to side. A fierce wave of anger crashed over me. Logically I knew this was just a training exercise, and she was in no immediate danger, but I could sense that Jack was getting a different kind of high off of having her beneath him, a high that he was not trying to cover in my presence.

I heard her grunt and thrust her hips high in the air, throw her body to the left, roll him over and pin him down under her. She was quick and extremely strong for her height and weight and she'd managed to pin me rather quickly at various times during our own roughhousing. The current of anger I was experiencing only seemed to grow as I watched her laughing, sitting astride Jack.

"Ding, ding, ding—round over, it's a tap out!" I heard her yell, holding up her hands in victory. "I rule!"

"Yeah, yeah, enjoy it while you can woman! It was a lucky get. I'm off my game today." Jack turned and gave me wink. Ugh, this was too much. I was pretty sure that Ana had just kicked his ass, off his game or not. She jumped down between the ropes and trotted over to where I was standing. She put her arm around my waist and gave me a squeeze.

"Let me just get my bag and we can go." I nodded and started for the exit.

"Hey Nathanial, wait up!" Jack called. I gritted my teeth, took a deep breath and waited for him to make his way down from the ring. His mind was closed, of course, so I had no idea what he could possibly want. "I was thinking about taking Ana over to the combat training demos in California. They're at the end of the month, what do you think? I mean, I wasn't sure of the protocol with the two of you, can she leave on her own will or what man?" His tone was flooded with mockery and I had to make a super demon effort not to grab his throat and squeeze. I spoke quietly and slowly.

"You know perfectly well that Ana is able to be away from me. As far as this 'protocol' you speak of, I do not own Ana, she has the right to travel and to see the world as much as she wants, she is her own person." My eyes flashed with fire.

"Ahhh, I see," Jack said and nodded his head as if he just figured out some great mystery.

"What is it exactly that you see, Jack?" I tried to keep the tenor of my tone friendly, but my patience with him was quickly waning.

"You haven't decided to 'keep' her yet, have you?" I felt a sudden pressure deep in my mind as he tried to force his way into my thoughts. I retaliated hard, forcing him to stumble backward a few steps.

"Don't push your already limited boundaries, Jack. I've never been partial to an even playing field and I'm not known to play fair." My tone was acidic.

"What, not sure she'd be worth keeping around?" he said, turning the full force of his eyes on me. "It wouldn't even occur to me *not* to *have* Ana. To be together with her, well it would be pretty spectacular." The way he said *have* in regards to her, sent my body into attack mode. I felt a surge of power stream to all of my limbs and my lips become moist with my venom. I growled and stepped toward Jack. "Hey, hey, easy there Nate! No need to get upset." He was chuckling, but his eyes had darkened, the color filling in the whites like a shroud and his jaw was clenched. "I'm sure you'll make the right decision, but of course if you don't…" He trailed off and winked at me again. What the hell was that supposed to mean? He couldn't "choose" Ana, she was already taken, so to speak. She was mine and she couldn't belong to anyone else, could she? Something tugged at the memories filling my mind, something that I couldn't get a grasp on, something that I had heard from my father or was it from my brother…what was it? I stepped back from Jack as I heard Ana approach, talking into her phone to Kai, I was sure. She hung up and came to stand beside me.

"Ready?" She gave Jack a hug and thanked him for her session. Jack, staring at me, proceeded to run his hands up and down her back slowly and deliberately—he was taunting me.

"I'm ready, let's go." My tone was harsher than I had wanted and Ana glanced at me, rolled her eyes and led the way out the door.

"I'm gross and sweaty, but I'm going to kiss you anyway," she declared. I had been reaching to throw her bag in the car while still distracted by my confrontation with Jack and with what I was sure was something crucial that I was missing from my history, when I felt her arms encircle my waist and turn me toward her. She pressed me up against the car door and proceeded to kiss me full on the mouth. She had no idea what she was getting herself into. Had she not learned? The fact that she was sweaty seemed to make things that much more difficult for me. Her scent was vastly more potent and it penetrated every inch on my skin. Her mouth moved softly against mine, and she wound her hands behind my neck, tugging my hair gently and sending little nips of pain up and down my neck; Jesus, I loved that. I leaned into her and let my teeth graze her earlobe. She shivered and moved her hips closer to mine. That movement, her mouth, her scent—things were getting out of control fast. A soft groan escaped from somewhere deep inside of me and I weaved my fingers into the back of her neck, fastening her face tightly to mine. She laughed a little breathlessly and slowly pulled back from my embrace.

"What?" I murmured. I was just getting going. "What?" I said as I pulled her back against me and began kissing her neck.

"Hmmm…as nice as this is," she breathed into my ear, "I think the locals might find our displays a bit inappropriate." I took a deep breath and groaned in protest. "We have the rest of the evening don't we or are you going into the office tonight?" she asked, slowly disentangling herself from my grip on her waist. I did have to stop by my office, so we decided that we'd go together and then head home.

By the time we had made it over to the University, it was already dusk. My preoccupations with her lips and her neck and her bare legs on the drive over, had slowed down our travel time considerably. I had to steer us to an isolated overlook and pull Ana on top of me in the front seat. My body wouldn't wait for us to get home. I had taken her right there in my car. The taste of her still on my lips and my body quivering from what she'd done to me; I parked the Rover at the University and left Ana inside the car fiddling with my preset stations. The urgency to be alone with her, at our home, was driving my haste in gathering the papers I needed to grade. I was already desperate to have her again. There were a few messages taped to my door from students who had come by looking for extensions and extra credit. I pulled them off and tucked them into my jeans. I swung my messenger bag across my shoulder, locked the door and took off down the stairs and into the quad.

It was dark now and as I walked across the courtyard, my mind was recalling being with Ana at the beach, how she smelled, how the rhythm of her hips on mine did things to me I was sure would be considered "unholy". My pace quickened and that's when I saw them. From a distance, I could assess that there were about seven or eight of what appeared to be students. They were walking with the kind of swagger that usually comes with immature Human guys—cocky and arrogant. I passed quickly by. I wasn't exactly afraid of them, but my instincts were in overdrive and I knew that eight against one would be a very difficult battle to win. Unfortunately, I could sense that fate had decided to intervene and I was going to have to fight for my very survival. My head exploded in a crushing pressure, someone was trying to get in, to get to my inner eye. The pain proved the perfect distraction for my attackers and I whirled around, just in time to see someone come toward me with a metal pipe.

The first blow struck the side of my head, knocking me sideways. I stumbled backwards trying to get a foothold. As a species, Bonders were immensely powerful, and I was no exception, however, most of my power came from my mind and I could turn it outward if desired. Having been struck in the head served to confuse me and it was that much harder for me to transfer my physicality onto my assailants. They knew what they were doing. The second blow landed directly to my left temple, sending white-hot pain exploding in my head. I felt the blood, trickling down at first, then coming in more fluid gushes. I doubled over and fell to my knees. My back crunched under the weight of the pipe they were using to beat me. It was at that moment that I heard the clanking of metal against the concrete and I knew it was over.

"Flip him, flip him over, now, do it now!" Someone was giving orders. I felt them heave my body over so that I was facing up toward the moon. I could feel a tightening around my wrists and a pressure through my palms as the stakes crushed through the bones in my hands.

"Here's the fucking knife, hurry up asshole and just do it!" I felt a sting to my flesh as they cut through my jeans to my groin, another sting and a ragged slashing of flesh. I screamed as I felt the blood pour from my body, my veins cut and torn. A flash permeated my mind, a single vision of a woman with liquid brown eyes, flecks of copper and gold, her hair swirling in waves and curls, her lips on mine...I sighed once and then, darkness took me.

Good god, what the hell was taking him so long? From the clock on the dash, I'd been in the damn car for over forty-five minutes. This was just crazy. I turned the keys and pulled them out of the ignition, grabbed my phone and jumped down from the door. I headed off in the direction of Nathanial's office; it was on the other side of the quad, not even a ten-minute walk to where we had parked. I probably shouldn't be wandering by myself at this time of night, but seriously, waiting in the car was driving me insane. I crossed quickly into the main part of campus and started jogging toward the Anthropology building. As I pushed open the iron gate to the courtyard, a strong smell filtered into my nose and my mouth. At first, it made me smile, it was Nathanial's scent; woods and earth and musk, but I quickly realized that there was something wrong; it smelled off. This scent was tinged with a putrid decay, like when meat spoils. My stomach contracted and I gagged. Dread began to flood my body and my blood felt icy. I stepped through the gate, breathing through my mouth, which didn't help. I saw him immediately and I screamed so violently, shattering the very atoms in the air. I ran to him, I couldn't recognize his face. It was twisted, distorted. His eyes were opened but they were unseeing. His hair was matted and soaked with blood—oh Jesus! The blood, his blood was everywhere. The putrid smell of death flowed from him onto the blood soaked ground. I dropped to my knees. His hands had metal bars through the palms, tugging on them was impossible. He was barely breathing. I fell over his body and shook with terror. I screamed for Alec and for Kai, hoping beyond hope, that Alec was "tuned in" this evening. I pressed my face to his and screamed for Alec to hear me. Nathanial was gray, waxy and cold. I remembered that I had my phone. My hands shaking, I called Alec, he would know how to help. I knew that the authorities didn't care about Bonders; they'd get here too late. Holding Nathanial's face in my hands I waited for Alec to pick up.

"Ana, we're on our way, we're coming! Hold on! Hold on!" The phone cut off, they were coming, Alec had seen what had happened. I pressed my lips over Nathanial's and tried to breathe air into his lungs. He was making a strange gurgling noise. Dark clumps of blood were now oozing out of his mouth.

"Oh god, Jesus Christ, hurry Alec, please god, hurry!" Lifetimes passed. I was screaming and crying when I felt someone touch my shoulder.

"Ana, you need to let me see him." Both Alec and Kai were standing beside me, Kai was sobbing. "Ana, let go of him, I need to see what can be done—if anything," he said, speaking the last words as if things were already over, as if it was too late. I pushed myself off his body and Kai wrapped his arms around me, both of us crying. I watched as Alec moved his hands up and down Nathanial's oozing, bleeding body. He pressed his fingers to his temples, stood up and motioned for me to come over. My legs didn't want to move, my body paralyzed with the deepest terror that I had ever known. "It's not entirely too late Ana, but a decision needs to be made quickly." I blinked, what? If it wasn't too late, then what did I need to do? I'd do anything, anything to save him.

"He needs your blood now Ana, you have to make the exchange now to save him." I didn't even need to think about anything. Of course we would do it now! Of course, I was already prepared for this.

"What do I do Alec, what do I need to do?" I choked and sobbed.

"Give me your wrist, quickly now, we haven't too much time." I looked at Kai and immediately he came to my side to take my other hand. We knelt down next to Nathanial, his face distorted, his eyes dead and black. My gaze roamed over his body and I felt my bones begin to ache—a deep and sudden contraction squeezed my chest and I began to gasp for air.

"Look at me Ana, look at me ok?" Kai squeezed my hand and I buried my face into his chest. Suddenly I felt a slash against my wrist, a quick, sharp pain and then wetness. I sucked in a breath as Alec took my wrist and put it to Nathanial's lips speaking in a language I didn't know. Forcefully, and without warning, Nathanial's body jerked beside me. I felt his lips curl around the wound on my arm. I felt him begin to suck and pull the blood from my veins. I screamed out in pain and tried to pull away.

"No Ana!" Alec shouted. "Don't move!" he yelled and I screamed again and grabbed for Kai. The pain was excruciating, my body convulsed and then I felt Nathanial pull me forward into his chest. He sucked harder and I felt his teeth dig deeper into the gash. I looked into his face, his eyes—I didn't recognize him, I didn't know this man. He was strong and angry and possessed. His gaze locked onto my wrist, to the blood now flowing like a dark red ribbon, the gash wide and deep. I heard Alec gasp. "NO!" and pull me forcefully back from Nathanial's reach. Nathanial lunged for me, tearing at my arm with his hands. I was pulled onto him and we crashed to the ground. He rolled on top of me, pinning me beneath him.

"Nathanial!" I was crying. "Stop, please stop!" I was screaming desperately. He growled at me and plunged his teeth and lips once more into my now gaping wound. My body shook and the pain became something I could no longer withstand. I saw Alec leap from behind and try to pull Nathanial off of my weakening body. It didn't work. Nathanial had lost himself and not even Alec or me, could save him.

Somehow, at that moment, something in me snapped. Maybe it was all of my combat training. Maybe it was remembering I had been in this exact position with Jack in what seemed like a lifetime ago. Maybe it was my memories of being abused, of not being able to escape. Whatever it was, I felt a power within me, a heat that surged and heaved through my body, making my blood boil. I looked at Nathanial, this man that I knew I now loved, that I knew that I couldn't stand to be without, this man who was supposed to be my life; he had betrayed me. Grunting, I yelled at him, "GET OFF OF ME, GET OFF NATHANIAL!" I pushed my hips up and over while flipping and rolling my body to the right, launching Nathanial up and back off of my legs. I scrambled up, but he was too quick and he crashed into me, tackling me back to the ground, the force of his violence knocked the air out of my lungs. He slashed and tore at my skin, my neck; he was too strong and I was losing. I saw Alec yank Nathanial's hair, snapping his head and neck back. He punched Alec in the face, sending him hurdling through the air, and hitting his head on the stone walkway. Nathanial's face was so close to mine, I could feel the heat of his breath, the now rancid scent of him. There was a flash in his eyes and he suddenly stopped moving. Still holding my hands above my head, he sneered at me. His lips snarling over his barred teeth, a grimace so evil and so unfamiliar, I closed my eyes. He slackened his grip.

"Get up you foolish girl, it's over." He spat at me, my blood on his lips, spraying me in the face. I remained there stunned as Kai ran over to help me up. I was weak and bloody and the pain in my wrist was now filtering into my head, my chest and my heart. I knew what was coming as much as I knew that the sun rose in the east. I knew what he was going to do as much as I knew how I loved the moonlight and the starlight. I knew his decision, as much as I knew that I loved him… still after all of this, I loved him. Gazing at each other, I watched him laugh as he wiped his blood soaked mouth across his arm. "Thanks for your donation," he said spitting into the grass. He took a look around at Alec and Kai and then back to me. Alec had resurrected himself from the ground and positioned himself in front of both Kai and me.

"Nathanial." I took a step toward him, not knowing what compelled me, and Kai tried to hold me back. Sobbing and gasping for breath, I tried to speak. "Nathanial, it's over, just go." I tried to push one final memory into his head, one of my most happy moments with him, the moment that I knew that I wanted him to live—no matter what, even if he didn't love me. I saw a flash of midnight blue and the light from silver stars replace the cold black that was now in his eyes, just a flash

67

and then it was gone. He smirked once more at me, turned and walked away into the night.

Chapter Three

Ana

I was pretty sure that I wasn't dead. My body felt heavy and my mind wasn't working right. I was trying to remember, trying to see his face. My memories of what happened were tangled, as if a massive cobweb had encased what I knew to be real. There was a soft glow from behind my closed eyelids and a subtle smell of incense burning. It reminded me of being in a Catholic church; the harsh smell of leather from bibles, the slight acidic tinge of wine hovering in the air, scattered beams of light as they fractured through the stained glass. I hated church.

"Ana, can you open your eyes please?" A strong voice broke through my mental trance. It was unfamiliar. "Ana, open your eyes, you're ok." God, my eyelids must have been nailed shut. I *couldn't* open them. I tried to turn my head toward the sound of the voice, tried to speak. My throat was thick and dry. Swallowing, I managed to whisper.

"Nathanial."

"Ana, it's ok now, but you need to open your eyes." A second voice spoke. This voice I knew, it was soft but commanding, it was Alec. He was ok, which meant that Kai was ok too. I tried to channel every bit of muscle power I had to open my eyes.

"There you are. Hmmm, I knew you would have beautiful eyes." The unfamiliar voice softly laughed. I tried to bring the blurry face into view. It was a man, that much I could decipher as I struggled against the heavy pull of exhaustion. His hair hung down in long, very dark brown almost black dreadlocks twisted into intricate patterns and weaves. He was wearing a loose, white shirt, open at the throat revealing a turquoise and silver type amulet around his neck; the pattern reminded me of something, but I couldn't place what that something might be. I stared at his face; high cheekbones, full lips and the most shocking turquoise eyes were staring back at me and I felt a sudden rush of familiarity. I tried to concentrate on not falling asleep and held his gaze—did I know this man? I saw what looked like flames dancing in his pupils, and I felt a sudden pull inward, but toward him at the same time; that didn't seem right, I must not be seeing or feeling things correctly. I was probably more messed up than I thought.

"Ana, this is Patric, he's a Healer. He's been taking care of you." Alec's voice was tight when he spoke and I saw that his eyes were careful, not letting his gaze leave Patric's face. God, how long had I been asleep? "A week," Alec said answering my unspoken question

"A week!" I tried to sit up, but was racked with a sudden pain in my chest and back, my breath came in gasps and I sunk back onto my pillows.

"Easy. You've undergone some serious trauma, one step at a time." As Patric spoke these words out loud, there was also another voice that penetrated my mind, a mystical and light voice—like the wind was carrying the sound; *Ana, I've been waiting for you, I know you Ana and I'm going to do everything in my power to help you heal.* I gasped out loud. Who was speaking to me? I glanced over at Patric and I swore I thought I saw his eyes turn to red flames. God, I was so screwed.

I spent one more night with Patric at his clinic, sleeping mostly, but also watching Alec watching Patric as he studied me. Alec had refused Patric's request that Alec go home and leave me in his care. Patric never spoke, he just sat quietly on the edge of my bed, staring. I was cleared to go home the next day with a schedule of weekly visits back to the Clinic so he could monitor my "progress", whatever the hell that meant. I was going to die so what was the point?

Alec and Kai insisted that I stay with them, but I was already feeling guilty about causing so much trouble just a few weeks before their wedding, that I managed to convince them that staying by myself for a bit was not such a bad thing. Kai agreed, but demanded that he or Alec would be over every morning to check on me. Ugh, I hated people wanting to help me; it was a ridiculous waste of time. I was happy to see Kuckuc and Piyip and by the intensity of their howls, they felt the same. I shooed Alec and Kai out of the house and started upstairs to take a bath. My wrist had been wrapped in some mesh-like cloth that smelled like the incense from the clinic. I couldn't get it wet so a bath was my only option. Patric administered some anti-anxiety herbs and I was feeling slightly drugged and very tired. I poured all the bubble bath I had into the scalding water and sank into my tub, closed my eyes and fell immediately to sleep. My mind was dark, but I sensed a distinct rushing of energy within the blackness. Pushing open the iron-gate to my terrace, I walked tentatively out into the trees. A calm wind whirled around my face and I turned to look up into the night sky. I was dreaming. Another breeze caught my hair and played with the curls, making them dance around my shoulder and tickle my neck. A warming sensation radiated out from the metal in my skin and I went to trace my fingers along the embedded pattern. Pain hit me, like a bolt of electricity from the air and I heard laughing, dark and sinister. The scene shifted and I was on the bluffs, looking down. I saw him there, walking across the water like a god, his hair blowing dark and furious as a storm. He held out his arms and looked up at where I was standing—on the edge.

"See what you miss when you never look down? Jump Ana, I'm here, I'll catch you." The voice in which he spoke was slow and seductive, it purred into my ears. I glanced back behind me—nothing; there was nothing. "Please Ana. I want to be with you, please jump." His whisper caressed my whole body and I took another step closer to the edge.

"Nathanial," I spoke in a tremor. "Nathanial." I was falling toward him, through mist and smoke, through fire and stars, I fell, reaching for him. He laughed.

"Foolish girl, you are nothing, you are no one and you are finished," he said quietly and I screamed, choking and whaling as I felt the water submerge me in darkness. Kuckuc was yanking on my hair, trying to pull me up out of the bath. Sputtering, I hung my head over the side of the tub, trying to get her to stop pulling on my head.

"Kuckuc! Stop! I'm ok, Stop girl!" She howled and licked my face up and down. "I'm ok." I whispered and patted her head but I knew that I wasn't, I knew that things were nowhere near ok, and they never would be. I sighed and pulled myself out of the bath.

I stayed awake in bed, too terrified to sleep. This isn't what I had wanted for myself, yet here it was. The prospect of facing my own death did not scare me nearly as much as I would have thought. Death never frightened me. I had spent most of life trying to prevent my own demise or the demise of others from various abusers. The only thing that ever had the ability to scare me was fire and dying by fire. I had come close once, when I was eight. One of my older adopted brothers had tricked me into playing in a living room with him. He had distracted me with my dolls and when I wasn't paying attention, he dropped a lit match behind the sofa. He then ran out of the room and shut the door, holding it closed on the other side so I couldn't get out. The room quickly filled with smoke and flames and I remember screaming and pulling on the door as hard as I could. It was a terrible memory and one that I always carried with me. Noni was the only person who had been able to quell the nightmares that came from the abuse. Even as a teenager, she would come into my room after she'd heard me screaming in my bed and she would sit and just talk to me, about nothing in particular, but having her near seemed to ease my mind. God, how I wished she could be here now.

Noni believed that true Life begins when the soul finishes with its duties here on earth. We were never truly gone. If we had lived an honest and compassionate Life, one in which we never feared to love, or to have others love us, then when death came, it wasn't an ending, but a transition into a more spiritual sense of who we are; we became the beauty that was within us all along. With Noni, I knew her to be always with me. It had been years since I'd seen her, but everyday I heard her laughter on the wind and felt her calming touch in the

73

moonlight that danced across my skin. Tears streamed back into my hair and I sobbed. A thought occurred to me, something that I had once let into my conscience mind a very long time ago. After the abuse happened, long after I had put it away and moved on in my life, the thought returned. I spent months battling with myself, not understanding what was happening in my own mind. I was in so much pain that I didn't see any other choice and I just wanted it to stop. I fought back and decided that all that I had endured would have been in vain if I ended things that way. It was the right choice then, but now, now things were different. I had fought, and I had lost and now I was going to die at Nathanial's hand. Did I have to? Couldn't I end things on my own terms, not let him win?

"I really don't think that's a very good idea Ana." A voice broke through the darkness of my thoughts. Wait, the voice was in my room! I struggled to sit up and turn on the bedside lamp. It was dim and I was having trouble seeing. A figure moved out of the corner and into view. It was Alec.

"Christ Alec, you scared the shit out of me! What are you doing here?" I wasn't upset at him, I was tired and depressed and really wasn't in the mood to have him be concerned.

"Well, that's just too damn bad," he spoke with more fierceness than I was used to hearing from him. Crossing the room, he came to my bed and sat on the edge. I'd never really had much alone time with Alec, and quite honestly, while I adored him, he'd always scared me a bit. He had a quiet intensity and an energy that radiated power and commanded respect.

"Hmm, I had no idea that you thought so highly of me Ana," he mused, his tone softening. "Although, I would never want you to be frightened of me. I love you more than I would my own sister." He grinned down at me and tossed his dreadlocks back over his shoulder. "Now, what are we going to do about this little 'situation' you have? Clearly, I'm not inclined to let you kill yourself, and while I quite understand your desperation, that would be enormously selfish of you. Do you know how that would destroy Kai, not to mention me, if we lost you from this world!" He posed this not as a question, but a declaration.

"Kai has you now," I said softly. "You love him and you take care of him, he'll be ok." I sighed and waited for him to counter my argument.

"I would love to spend time debating the merits of your life Ana, but I need to get some crucial information from you right now." My heart began to race.

"What is it Alec, what do you need?" I couldn't possibly imagine what information I could provide to Alec, he knew *everything*.

"That's actually not true, but it's neither here nor there at the moment. I need to know what Patric said to you at the clinic." I tried to rack my brain and remember, but I couldn't place any conversation that Patric and I had had, except about the herbs I was supposed to be taking and how to redress my wound. "Not a verbal conversation." Alec cut through my recollections. "In your mind, he spoke to you, didn't he? What did he say Ana?" I looked sharply at Alec.

75

"How did you know that?"

"I was concerned when we brought you into the Clinic, that he was the Healer on call that evening." Alec's voice trembled with what sounded like anger and fear. Odd; it seemed misplaced coming from Alec.

"Why, why would you be concerned? He seemed alright." But that wasn't entirely true; I had sensed an undercurrent of darkness from him that I couldn't place.

"Hmm… I need to know what he spoke to you in your mind." Alec was leaning toward me, his eyes urgently searching my face. I tried frantically to recall that weird moment in the Clinic, that I had thought it was a side effect from my injury.

"Uh, he said that he'd been waiting for me and that he was going to do anything he could to help me." I thought that was the gist of it. Alec was shimmering in and out of his form and he looked furious. "God Alec, what's the matter?" He took a deep breath and regained his solid body.

"Ana, Patric is Nathanial's brother," he said. I guess I should have been more shocked, but I wasn't getting what the problem was here.

"Ok, so Nathanial has a brother. He may have mentioned that to me, but I thought they had lost track of each other or something. I mean, what's the big deal here Alec?" I was missing the cause for concern.

"Ana, I need to see your mark." The sound of his voice made me shiver and I swung my legs around to the side of the bed and turned my back to him. He pushed my hair aside and I felt his fingertips brush lightly along the length of the metal inscription. "What did this look like when it first appeared?"

"Um, well, it had silver and midnight blue metal things entwined together." I wasn't sure what information he was after.

"Have you looked at since it first surfaced?" Honestly, I'd stopped noticing it. The only time it occurred to me was when Nathanial would trace his fingers along my neck and back. The sudden memory of our intimacy knocked the air out me. I tried to steady myself and breathe. "I'm sorry Ana for dredging up painful memories," he spoke gently and softly, "but this is important."

"No," I murmured. "No, I haven't looked at my mark."

"Did Nathanial say anything about it to you?"

"No, never." Except that it suited me, he had said that once.

"It must have changed after…" Alec muttered to himself. "It must have been the attack that brought it out…" He trailed off.

"Alec, what the hell are you talking about?" I got up from the bed and grabbed my make-up mirror off the dresser and started for the bathroom. Positioning myself in front of the mirror over the sink, I turned around and held the vanity glass up over my shoulder so I could see the back of my head. My hand shook violently. My mark had changed; well more accurately, it had a new addition. A deep line through the entwined metals was now carved into my neck. A line of brilliant turquoise that ran directly through the main knot tying the silver and dark blue swirls together. I could make out a thin silver pattern within the line, a design that evoked something in my memory, something that I had just seen.

"It's the pattern of his amulet, the one you noticed on his chest." Alec was leaning against the frame of the door watching me.

"Patric's amulet? I don't understand, why is *his* symbol on *my* neck?" My head was now spinning. I couldn't navigate all of this at once; Nathanial's attack, my impending death, Patric as Nathanial's brother, my stupid mark—what the fuck?

"I know it's an overwhelming amount to take in right now Ana, but there's more you need to know. I need you to calm down and to clear your mind a bit, please. Come back to bed, you need to rest." I was exhausted and I had a feeling that Alec was not inclined to leave whatever discussion was coming, for the morning. "You know me well, Ana." He laughed softly and tucked the covers up around my shoulders. It was a tender action, one that reminded me of what a parent would do for their child had they been sick or scared. It made me sad and lonely at the same time. Alec touched my face and settled back against the pillows next to me. "I'm not sure where to start, it's a bit complicated if you are not of our persuasion. I'll try to get to the heart of what's happening to you." I laid my head against his shoulder; I hadn't had anyone to comfort me in a very long time and his presence made me feel safe, even if it was a fragile safety. He sighed softly and began to speak. "Bonders and Vampires have long memories Ana, they don't forget easily and they are not quick to forgive." Humph, I thought to myself, I suppose that Nathanial was the exception to that rule—he'd forgotten about me quite easily.

"I meant with regard to each other and yes, Nathanial remembers you Ana, it's just buried—he remembers." He looked down at me and took a breath. "I'm guessing you know a bit about our tiffs with the Vampires?" I nodded, again remembering the lecture I'd heard during one of my undergraduate classes. "Our war with the Vampires occurred over many centuries, with power and control shifting back and forth, mainly over territory; I suppose you could say it was more a war for cultural superiority than anything else. Both groups are susceptible to corruption, to power and wealth, but the Vampires seemed to have just enough recklessness within their species, that it made them commit vast injustices and acts of unspeakable violence to obtain all of those things. This is not to say that Bonders were not without their failings. Many of us knew what was happening to other Bonders and Humans, but if guarantees were made to us, that we too would benefit in all that the Vampires attained, well, it's just easier to look the other way, isn't it? Anyway, over time both species were viewed as cantankerous to society, but some Bonders had reached their limit of how much violence and complete disregard for life could be inflicted upon any population." He turned to look down at me, checking to see if I had fallen asleep; I hadn't because Alec was never boring. He laughed and touched the tip of his finger to my nose as he continued. "There were small uprisings here and there with Humans and Bonders, but also within the rankings of Vampires. However, the Vampires almost always beat down all of these disturbances, either by force or by their uncanny abilities to persuade and seduce. As in most wars, most conflicts between groups, there are natural leaders who emerge, those who the oppressed, as well as those in power, turn to for hope. It was about two hundred years ago when someone emerged in *our* species. Can you guess who amongst the Bonders stepped forward?" I didn't know if he was asking a rhetorical question, but I shook my head no. "Really?" he exclaimed. "Hmm, well I guess you didn't have a lot of opportunities to explore things, and he is a bit closed off isn't he?" Who the hell was he talking about, who was closed off? "Nathanial, Ana, Nathanial came forward to lead us." I sucked in a quick breath. I suddenly recalled a very brief conversation that Nathanial and I had had one late night when I was writing on my dissertation. I remembered him mentioning that his father was a great elder and leader of his people and had been the one to tell him about the Bond. "Yes, that's right," Alec spoke, recalling the memory from my mind. "Nathanial's father was a Healer and spiritual guide to the Bonders, but he was not a Bonder himself.

"I thought it was genetic," I murmured.

"It is. Nathanial received the Bonding gene from his Huron mother. She was a Bonder who fell in love with her Bond, Nathanial's father. Child bearing for a Bonder is difficult if the child is conceived from a Human and she died about five years after giving birth. One child was risky, but to conceive two at the same time and carry them to term, well that was unheard of within our species. From the start, although both brothers were destined to be Bonders, Patric possessed some unique gifts that were considered rare for our kind."

"Like what?" I asked. Of course I was wondering if one of those gifts had to do with speaking to someone in their mind.

"Yes, that would be one, but it's the most mild of the ones he possesses," Alec spoke with a hint of amusement at the mention of Patric's uncanny abilities. "He has a vast ability to coerce individuals to do what he wants, to feel what he wants, and then to have those under his power ultimately carry out those feelings in their actions towards others." I shuddered at the thought of being possessed by Patric. Alec squeezed my shoulders and pulled me closer. "Patric also managed to obtain a gift so ancient and so powerful, that hardly any in both the Vampire and Bonder species are able to harness." For some reason, I held my breath waiting for Alec to continue. "Patric is a fire wielder; he can absorb, control and manipulate fire from nothing and from everything. It's an incredible ability and one rarely seen from either species." I exhaled. I wondered what I could have done growing up had I had such power. Alec turned to look at me, his eyes full of sorrow. He sighed and continued. "For Bonders and for their war against the Vampires, well, you can see how Patric would be an asset to our cause. He could offer vast influence on the Vampires, help them to see the havoc they were causing, as well as being able to turn those Bonders who seemed to have fallen under the spell of corruption, away from the Vampires. Between Nathanial and Patric, our side became well supplied with leadership."

"But I thought back then the Vampires became nearly extinct—I mean, most of them were banned to isolated areas and reservations, so you won right? Patric helped you to win?" I asked and Alec took a breath and sighed.

"No Ana, Patric did not help us and the fact that we were able to conquer the Vampires and stop the violence was not a testament to any great plan or skill on our part; the near extinction of the Vampires, and ultimately the fact that some were spared and able to leave unharmed, well, that was more an issue of family ties than anything else."

"Wait, I don't understand, didn't Nathanial help you in the cause, he's a Bonder and what happened to Patric?"

"Remember Ana that the transformation into a Bonder for Nathanial, happened long after the Vampires had been conquered. He fought with us, essentially as a Human. Something that Patric had a difficult time accepting. Patric sees no intrinsic value in the Human race, aside from the fact that Humans are excellent vessels for corruption and greed. Patric never viewed Nathanial as one of 'us', but as disposable, someone to be used to do his will. The great flaw for Patric was that he grossly underestimated his susceptibility to being corrupted and he miscalculated the vast and subtle powers of the Vampires. Little by little, he was seduced. Offerings of money, of power, high political office, of women—he was given it all and eventually he changed sides."

"So, he became a Vampire?" I asked, incredulous. I couldn't believe that anyone would *choose* to undergo that transformation. I had always heard that it was like experiencing your own death, from the inside out.

"Hmmm," Alec murmured. "The transformation into a Vampire is not pleasant, but it's also amazing what someone will do to achieve a position of power. However, Patric is a half-Vampire; half, because his genetic destiny is to be a Bonder; he's a bit of a half-breed if you will." Alec chuckled darkly.

"Where was Nathanial during all of this, what was he doing?" I asked thinking of Patric's face and unusual eyes.

"That's an interesting question. Nathanial had developed unparalleled respect amongst Bonders. He had and still does have, an exceptional ability to understand what people need and how to go about achieving those desires. Funny enough, his gift is very similar in nature to Patric's. The difference though lies in the host of those abilities doesn't it?" I tried to stifle a yawn. "I'm sorry, I've been talking for hours, and you're exhausted," Alec said as he laughed.

"No, please. Go on, I'm good. Please keep talking."

"Well, I'm sure you can see where this is headed. We have two brothers, one who had jumped ship to revel in his newfound power as a half-Vampire, and the other being pushed to lead a group he didn't technically belong to—at least not yet. Patric rose very quickly in his new 'Life' and soon found himself running the various sectors of Vampire militias and political ventures, even advising some covens. He essentially became a leader and as his power grew, his abilities multiplied and it seemed that the combination of his genetic predisposition and his conversion into a Vampire, this combination gave him more strength than either species had ever witnessed. He seemed unstoppable. We had all but given up and were about to sign over the rights to the last of our land for the promise that the killings of Humans and Bonders would cease immediately, a treaty of sorts. We were foolish; the treaty never held and we learned, you never make deals with Vampires, never." Alec's eyes flashed as he looked at me and I thought I could see some emotion jump to life in the

83

emerald green depths. I blinked and it was gone. "Eventually, it was Nathanial who proposed a meeting between he and Patric. Sending a Human to meet with a power hungry, Human-hating Vampire seemed like a suicide mission, but Nathanial insisted on going anyway. No one ever knew what transpired between the two of them, we still don't know to this day, but upon his return, Nathanial announced that a fragile peace had been reached, and we just accepted that the Vampires were retreating—no questions asked.

"So, you don't know how Nathanial got Patric to give up and leave, I mean, no one knows what happened when they met?" That was bizarre.

'No, it was never discussed and Nathanial made sure that his mind hid whatever secret had existed between he and his brother. We do know that by agreeing to leave, Patric lost much if not all of his attained power and for some reason, in his demise, most of his newly adapted abilities became weakened, but not all, as you have personally experienced," Alec chuckled lightly as he spoke.

"So what's all this have to do with me?" I yawed.

"Ahhh yes, the glue that holds all of this together. The Human with the rare blood that everyone wants…"

"My blood's not rare, it's just blood."

"Actually Ana, your blood is rare, but beyond that, it is what your blood can offer that is of far greater value."

"What can my blood offer? I don't get it." I was awake now and my body felt rigid. Alec sighed and paused for longer than I felt comfortable. "Alec?" I urged him on.

"Nathanial and Patric are brothers, brothers from two very spiritual and powerful seeds. They are connected in ways that transcend most sibling relationships, and those connections don't just stop at their biological kinship. They are emotionally connected, and what happens to one affects the other somehow, which might explain the addition to your mark; perhaps if you are Bound to one, you are also Bound to the other." Alec's voice grew soft and I thought I felt his body tense. I didn't know Patric; it would be an odd thing to share a Bond with someone that I had no relationship with, no history. Alec studied me. "Ana, your Bond with Nathanial also affects Patric, not in the same way, but Patric needs you, he needs your blood. Your blood has powers, which I have yet to decipher. From what you were able to do to save Nathanial from his attack, it shouldn't have happened, he should be dead. I suspect that what you are, who you are, can return Patric to his former glory, something that causes me great concern. Perhaps this reality is directly tied to you saving Nathanial. Somehow your decision is connected to Patric and connected to the restoration of his powers—I just don't know how or why." Alec was clearly frustrated with so many gaps in what he knew, but there was something beyond the frustration that he resonated, something that I had never seen in Alec before; it was fear.

My discussion with Alec had left me reeling. I wasn't fully grasping any of this; moreover, I really didn't want to. Kai and Alec had decided to postpone their wedding until we could

85

come up with a plan, a plan for what, I was not sure. Alec had explained that since both Nathanial and Patric shared the same blood, that Patric essentially could be the one to save my life, replacing what Nathanial was supposed to have completed. Of course, we thought that this might mean that I would have to undergo the painful transformation of becoming a Vampire and then there was the whole idea of Patric performing this act. His reputation did not place him as one who typically allowed for a human to undergo the process into a Vampire and he would most likely just kill me. On top of that, we weren't even sure if half-Vampires *could* perform such a transition. Alec ventured to guess that Patric may be aware of my role in all of this, and that's why he'd been so insistent on monitoring my progress. I was now not allowed to go to the clinic for my weekly check ups without Alec. He and Kai had taken to picking me up from school, taking me to work, and back and forth to the library—I was beginning to feel like a prisoner.

"It's just until I can get a better read on the situation and on Patric." Alec was attempting to explain; after I'd thrown yet another fit that he'd come to escort me to the gym.

"God Alec, Jack's a frickin Bonder, I think I'll be ok!" Alec had successfully managed to isolate me from most of my counter-culture friends at the gym, but trying to keep me from training with Jack, well that was going to far.

"I don't know Jack, Ana, and what I do know is that Nathanial never trusted him," Alec spoke, cutting through my disgust. I used to think that Nathanial's distaste for Jack came from a place of jealousy, but of course, I now knew that that couldn't have ever been the case. People get jealous sometimes because they worry that the object of their affection may desert them for another. That would mean that Nathanial cared about me—he did not. Alec reached and touched my face. I knew he'd heard what I had been thinking. We pulled into the parking lot of the gym and I grabbed my bag while reaching for the door handle and Alec touched my shoulder. "I'm going to talk to a few friends of mine who are a bit more familiar with Patric and his history. I'll be back for you in one hour. If you are not in the parking lot waiting for me, I will of course come in and get you," He said this in a very quiet tone but I sensed an undercurrent of sternness.

"Yes sir!" I said, rolling my eyes. "One hour." I jumped out of the car and watched him pull out of the lot. The gym had become my salvation over the last several months since the attack. The loud music and the intense workouts helped to quell the massive, unyielding anxiety that now filled every waking moment of my day. I looked forward to seeing Jack, he was always so enthusiastic about us working together and it made me feel nice to have someone who thought I could kick ass all by myself. I walked into the familiar blast of cold air and the smell of metal and sweat. The music was blaring. Perfect.

"Hey beautiful!" Jack leapt down from the ring and trotted over to meet me.

"I don't know about all that, but thanks for the compliment!" I blushed. Beautiful was not a word that I used when describing myself.

"Put your bag down and let's get started. What do ya want to do today?" He winked at me.

"How about just upper body today. I was thinking back, bi's and tri's?"

"Sounds good, I'll start pulling weights." I watched him jog over to the free weight area, his dreadlocks swinging like woven ropes down his back. The workout was just what I needed and Jack was relentless with my reps and sets. Feeling my muscles contracting and aching, seeing the sweat pour off my head; for the first time since the night of the attack, I felt strong. Somewhere in my mind, I knew that this feeling was fleeting. Nathanial had bitten me, he had poisoned me and at some point my body would begin to feel his betrayal. I noticed Jack stare at me suddenly and I wondered if he had heard my inner monologue.

I checked the clock over the front desk and determined that I could take a quick shower before I had to be in the parking lot. Alec drove a Porsche and I never felt comfortable getting sweat and dirt on his nice leather seats. There really wasn't a designated changing room or showers for women as I was the only woman who worked out here. The guys knew enough to give me my privacy when I needed to clean up. Stripping down, I grabbed my towel and my shower kit, turned the water to HOT and stepped in. The water pressure was just hard enough to kneed out the tension and soreness in my shoulders and back. I let the steam from the water swirl around me and penetrate my skin. I was quick to wash my hair these days; I didn't like touching my mark anymore, I didn't like having to think about it. Rinsing out the conditioner, I wrapped my towel around me and stepped out into the hot steam. I dabbed the streams of water coming off my hair and moved out into the locker room. I must have really used a ton of hot water because there was a lot of steam filtering into changing area. I rifled through my bag and pulled out my underwear, bra, shirt and jeans. Dropping the towel I bent to hook my bra around my waist. I felt a warm rush of heat up the back of my neck and the hairs on my arm prick my skin. I wasn't alone.

"I've always thought you were beautiful Ana," a voice spoke hypnotically and quiet from the swirls of mist. It was Jack. My heart raced and some primal instinct told me that I was in danger. I yanked the towel up around my body, but when I turned around, his eyes were locked onto mine and he was so close that I felt the heat from his breath on my face. It was his eyes that surprised me. They weren't his usual greenish blue, but coal black and with what appeared to be the flickering of tiny fires deep inside. Something about his eyes conjured a memory in my mind; I had seen fire in eyes before, but where? My mind was racing as I tried to place the source of familiarity. My body tensed. I had always liked Jack, but not in a romantic way. It took a lot for me to be interested in someone, to feel safe and this felt wrong; it felt wrong in my entire body to be standing here with him. I felt vulnerable and I felt scared. "Ana," Jack spoke softly. He had reached for the towel that now hung loosely around my body. I suddenly realized that I could not move, not my hands, not my legs—nothing. This was familiar to me, but now I sensed I had something much greater to fear than when Nathanial had been angry with me for running away. Jack inched closer, sinuously and with great deliberation. I watched as he slipped the towel down off my body, letting it fall to the ground at my feet. His eyes pulsed with red flames and he was trembling. He brushed my wet hair back over my shoulder and I felt the heat from his skin as his

89

fingertips lingered along my chest. My heart pounded in fear and I all I kept thinking was, please, just make it quick, whatever you're going to do, let it be quick. His hands swept down my chest and across my breasts, lingering. I gasped as he moved down to my stomach. Memories flooded my mind; memories of horrors that no child should endure. I watched as his eyes pulsed harder and his breathing became ragged. Oh, god, please no, I didn't want this. Maybe if I was lucky, he would kill me, then we wouldn't have to worry about Patric or the stupid Vampires. Nathanial would never know or care—it would all be over. Jack's hand grabbed the back of my head, his fingers weaving into the wet strands of my hair. I felt him snap my head back, creating such a pain in my skull that I couldn't breathe. I watched as he bent his head close to my throat and saw him lick his lips. Something odd was filtering its way into my body. My skin felt as if it were filling with air, like it was swelling. A heat rushed into my blood and I sensed that my muscles were tight, even though I couldn't move them. An urge to lock my eyes on Jack seemed to snap the paralysis in my body and then, out of nowhere, I felt a jolt of movement from my limbs and I watched as Jack flew backward into the lockers, smashing his head on a corner of metal, his fall breaking his hold on me. I was shaking and I screamed as loudly as I could, but I didn't need to. Alec was already there. His eyes were wide and he was standing very, very still.

"Looks like Nathanial was right," he spoke quietly as he walked over to Jack and kicked him hard in the head, knocking him out.

"He's a Vampire." I didn't even realize that I had spoken. "It was his eyes, they had fire in them, just like Patric's."

The episode at the gym had shaken me to my core. How could I have not known about Jack? What had caused Jack to fly backward? Had it been Alec? Was it me? I was completely freaked out.

"He's a shape shifter Ana. It would have been impossible for you to know that he was a Vampire. He can take on the natural identity of just about anyone or anything, very clever really. Nathanial didn't know either, he just sensed something was off." Alec had tried to comfort me over and over again, but there it was, I had been betrayed yet again and tricked. Alec also wasn't prepared to answer any of my questions about who had caused Jack's fall and he was quick to shut down any considerations from Kai or me that I had somehow done it, mentally. It was frustrating. Alec thought there might be a connection between Jack and Patric, but it was hard to infiltrate the Vampire community as a Bonder. He was going through various back channels, but he was sure that at the very least, they knew each other. Seriously, I actually had stopped caring at this point. The episode with Jack seemed to have triggered Nathanial's poison and I was feeling sick, physically and mentally. I had developed a nagging cough and I was excessively tired. I was taking some time off from my job and trying to orient myself around a schedule of writing on my dissertation. I just wasn't feeling like myself. I was scheduled for my next visit to the clinic and of course Alec insisted that he go with me, especially now. It was odd how close Alec and I had become since Nathanial left. Kai was generous enough to share, what was now amounting to less and less time together, in order for Alec to figure some things out about Patric and my mark. If I wasn't feeling sick, then I was feeling guilty. Kai was my best friend and I was keeping the very essence of his happiness occupied with these ridiculous events of my life.

"They're not ridiculous Ana," Kai had said to me before leaving for the Clinic. *"I love you and Alec loves you and we are going to do everything we can to figure all of this out. I don't care how long it takes or what I have to do."* He'd spoken with a ferocity that was rare for someone so gentle as Kai, so calm. I desperately wished that I could believe him.

I didn't think it was a good idea for Alec to actually come into the clinic with me. If Jack was indeed working with Patric, then Alec or myself had basically attacked a Vampire and I was sure that Patric would not have a positive responsive to Alec's presence. Seeing as Patric might need me for something, I was betting that he was far more unlikely to harm me than he was Alec. I didn't win the argument and Alec led the way into the waiting room. As usual, the scent of incense permeated the air around us; I coughed and hacked, gasping for air. Alec put his arm around my shoulders and led us to the bench to sit down. I was finally able to stop the coughing by drinking a bit of water when a sudden pressure squeezed the deep recesses of my mind. *It appears the poison has begun to spread; it's a shame really, but I don't want you to be afraid Ana. I promised that I would do everything in my power to help you and I will, I want you to trust me.* I sucked in a breath and held my head in my hands. Patric was in my head.

"What is it Ana, what's wrong?" Alec spoke with alarm.

"It's ok, I just have a headache," I whispered. For some reason we had yet to figure out why Alec couldn't "hear" what Patric said when he spoke, but Alec knew that someone was in my head. He clenched his jaw and squeezed my hand. The voice continued… *Interesting that Alec can't hear me isn't it? Better for us I suppose. I want to apologize for Jack's actions at the gym this week; they were reprehensible. He shouldn't have approached you in that way, he shouldn't have touched you, but you would have to concede that your friend Alec's actions were a bit… hmmm, shall we say, overdone? Or maybe they were your actions Ana? I suppose that has yet to be determined. Rest assured, I have dealt with Jack and he is no a danger to you. Ana, I know that you are curious about me, that there's something in you that wants to know me and I want to know you… I can give you what you want.* I felt another squeeze of pressure and a whooshing sound in my head. He was gone. I exhaled loudly and turned to look at Alec. He was sitting so still, like an ancient stone carving and he was angry. I didn't have time to ask him if he'd sensed what had just occurred, Patric came out from behind the beaded curtain with his arms opened wide.

"Ana!" he exclaimed with such gusto that if you didn't know any better, you'd think he was actually a longtime friend.

"She's not well," Alec spoke in his usual acerbic tone. "She's gotten worse."

"Well, we can't have that now can we?" Patric chortled to me, but his eyes were on Alec. "Why don't you come on back and we'll take a look!" Alec shifted to get up, but I shot him a mental stabbing, telling him to stay where he was. Nothing was going to happen while he was in the waiting room. I couldn't handle all of the tension; it was making me nauseous. Reluctantly, Alec let go of my hand and sat back down. He wasn't happy. I followed Patric down the hall to his office, a surprisingly cozy space filled with candlelight and a glorious painting of the night sky on the ceiling. He gestured for me to lie down on the sofa and he knelt beside me. I tried to concentrate on the stars that glittered and winked down from the painting, tried to focus on the moonlight and the depth of space. I felt his eyes surveying me, probably wondering what I thought of his little dialogue in my head. Instead, I focused my mind on the vision of the night sky on the ceiling and I thought of Nathanial. I thought of his eyes, their deep blue and brilliant silver rims, and then I had to look away from the painting. I heard Patric laugh softly and I wondered if he knew just what memory had flooded my mind. "I do Ana, I do in fact know what you were thinking about. It's really quite sad, a terrible tragedy what occurred between you and my brother." At this new mention of his sibling, I guessed that we were now past all pretenses. "But I can't say that I'm terribly disappointed in the outcome, that would be lying, and like you thought, we are indeed past pretense aren't we?"

"What's wrong with me?" I wanted to shift the conversation; I felt something tugging in my chest when he spoke of his lack of "disappointment" for my situation.

"You're dying, but of course you already knew that. Nathanial's poison is probably the most concentrated there is amongst Bonders, it takes its time but, when it hits, it hits hard." He smirked, as if remembering some distant incident, something not quite pleasant.

"What do we do then?" I asked softy, I wasn't sure if I really wanted to know the answer.

94

"Well, I can continue to give you some herbs to quell the spread, but that's just a temporary fix, something to buy us some time. I believe Alec has already guessed what your options are, no?" Jesus, we were back to the whole donating blood thing, to me asking Patric for help, to having him be the one to save me, to having him complete the exchange that Nathanial refused me. I was so sick of everyone talking about my blood. "I'm sorry that you are frustrated Ana, but your idea of a 'donation' is a bit incorrect. Yes, an exchange between us can indeed spare your life, and yes, you have time to make that exchange to a point, but you should know that you are only going to get weaker, and the weaker you become the more difficult it will be for you to survive our exchange." He smirked at me again. "The longer we wait, the more likely you are to die." My head snapped up to look at him, how was it that I didn't know this? How was it that Alec hadn't figured this out? "Hmmm, it's interesting that Alec failed to mention this particular, um, 'problem'; perhaps he's wanting to protect you? However, I'm under the impression that you are a woman who appreciates knowledge, no matter how dire the circumstances." I closed my eyes and took a deep breath. So there it was, my paths laid out like train tracks, with the train barreling down upon me, on what could be the ending of my life. One of only two beings who could save me was gone, and now the only one left was a half-Vampire, with a bloodlust for power and revenge, and like Nathanial, he was in a position to determine if I was actually worth saving.

"Well, I wouldn't put it so dramatically, but yes, I would very much relish in returning the species to whom I have chosen to belong, to their former glory, and of course resume my position as their trusted leader. Is that really so bad Ana, to want redemption for my kind?" It really wasn't a question that required an answer so I just turned away, trying to stop the tears that I knew were coming. It was also not entirely correct. Patric wasn't a full Vampire, he was also a Bonder by blood and I found it odd that he seemed to refuse to acknowledge this fact. I wondered if he knew that I now had *his* symbol embedded in *my* mark; what that meant, I still had no idea. His head snapped up and he stared at me, his eyes pulsing and flashing. I met his gaze with a fierce determination. He recovered and I felt him shift onto the sofa beside me, placing my legs gently over his lap. "Now, let's take a look at that wound shall we?" He moved to take my left arm in his hand. It was a slow movement, hesitant and I snuck a look at his face. His eyes were burning. I felt his fingers glide slowly down the length of my scar from my palm to my forearm as heat radiated from his touch. Again, I felt the familiar pulling in my body that came when he'd first touched me, whenever I felt his voice in my head. It wasn't unpleasant, but I felt it moving into the darker places of my soul, places that I had not dared to let out, that I never explored. I watched him as he moved his fingertips to the center of the wound, the place where Nathanial had bitten me, and the place he'd torn open. Patric's eyes were on me and our gazes held steady. He pressed slowly down into my flesh and started to trace the tips of his fingers along my skin, caressing and stroking me and I felt a sudden chasm open up inside of me—so deep was the onset of my desire, that I lost breath in my lungs. The reaction was out of my control and yet it was from me, from inside of me. A wash of heat flooded into my chest and between my legs and I felt my body arch. Waves of want and of need began to fill the blood in my veins. Patric's eyes were ablaze, but instead of flames, I saw them change color so fast that I wasn't sure of what I was seeing. Colors I recognized, black coal, emerald green, stormy gray and finally a deep turquoise blue. I felt him press harder on the center of my arm and again, I was racked with a spasm of heat and uncontrollable desire. He was breathing in jagged, short breaths and his face was flushed with color. His body tensed and his jaw was tight as if holding something back, something violent. I felt a deep groan move through my throat and I fell back onto the cushions as I let my legs fall open. I wanted him to touch me; desperately, my body seemed to crave the heat from his fingertips, the feel of his hands moving deep inside. My body rocked and another groan melted from my lips. Patric gasped and I saw him shimmer in and out of form. He started to reach his hand down between my thighs and I opened for him. His eyes flashed, ignited and he groaned desperately as he began to rub me over my clothes; the fire from his hands warmed me and made me surge with moisture and longing. Our eyes locked as I whispered his name moaning; suddenly he pulled his hand away quickly, violently, and I was thrown back down as if someone had hit me in the gut.

"Get out of here, NOW! Get out of here Ana!" he spoke quietly, but with such fear and anger, that I moved as quickly as my dizzied, weak body would take me. I ran out of the office and pulled Alec up of the bench with unusual force. Stunned, he let me shove him out the door into the fresh air. I tried to quell the overwhelming emotions that were now flooding my body; I was beside myself, it seemed surreal and yet I distinctly felt that when Patric touched me, that I had wanted that feeling from him, that I desired him, desired to be close to him, to know him. It made no sense.

"Ana, what the fuck! What the hell happened back there?" Alec was turning to go back into the clinic, but I pulled at his coat and spun him around.

"Let's go now!! We need to go Alec!" I shouted at him. He looked me in the eyes and paused, probing my mind.

"Fine, let's go," he said quietly. I knew he was seeing what happened and I knew that I was in trouble, not with him maybe, but with myself. The drive back to their house was silent. Kai was waiting for us to return and seemed anxious, very anxious.

"Alec, I have some information for you, for us," Kai exclaimed. Alec grabbed my elbow and pushed me inside the house. "What is with you two?" Kai asked, sensing the tension between Alec and me.

"Later, what's the information Kai?" Alec's tone was short, something that he never, ever used with Kai. Kai looked from Alec to me and back to Alec before continuing.

"Well, it's quite a lot actually, you'd better sit down." He motioned for us to take a seat on the couch, I sat as far away from Alec as space would allow, something Kai did not miss. "Your horse friend from Argentina showed up here today, while you were gone."

"Carlo? Carlo showed up here?" Alec seemed stunned and slightly frightened. Odd. I had no idea who this "Carlo" was, but I knew that Alec was well connected with lots of people in the world.

"Yes, he said he'd been thinking about your visit, and what you'd described to him about Nathanial's, um," Kai glanced at me and paused, "um Nathanial's reaction to Ana and the attack carried out on Nathanial at the University."

"What about it, does he know something?" Alec was leaning off the edge of the couch, so much so that I thought he might just topple over onto the floor.

"Well, he said that it was the nature of the attack that got him thinking, the fact that the assailants had hit Nathanial directly in his weakest spot, his head. That doing this would completely immobilize his ability to defend himself—he didn't think this was mere coincidence."

"Wait, are you saying that Carlo thinks the attack on Nathanial was planned?" He was incredulous in his tone but I could see Alec's eyes churning; he was trying to process. I looked back at Kai, my eyes wide.

"Why would anyone want to specifically attack Nathanial?" I asked. I felt like I was missing some piece of the puzzle.

"Carlo also mentioned," Kai steamrolled on, "that he thought given what we know about Nathanial, his reaction was not one that seemed normal, it was out of control, like he was not himself."

"Like he was possessed," Alec whispered, the words falling slowly from his lips.

"Possessed?" I said, my voice high and tight. "How was he possessed, I mean by who?"

99

"Can you not think of anyone with the ability to possess someone Ana?" Alec asked me, while staring me straight in the eyes. A flash of me on the sofa, my body arching and heaving, Patric's hands on my wound, the rush of heat and desire...

"Patric," I said. "It was Patric?"

"Kai, did Carlo say what he thought the motivation was for Patric, I mean could he venture a guess?" Alec was grasping Kai's hands. Kai glanced at me and sighed.

"It's ok Kai, I can handle it, what did Carlo say?" I just wanted it out there; I wanted everything on the table, it was easier that way.

"Yes, he did have a theory, although he cautioned against acting too quickly on his assumptions. He said that Patric was a genius in tactical maneuvers and that we shouldn't be too hasty in planning anything. Still, it was his thought that Patric had managed to get to Nathanial *before* the attack, get in his mind and create doubt about Ana. He asked if Nathanial had ever shown any aggression toward Ana..." he trailed off and I knew we were all remembering the night at my house when Nathanial had almost attacked me.

"Ahhh, I can see where this is going," said Alec with a tremor of disbelief.

"What? Where is this going? I don't understand!" I yelled. I was tired and frustrated; the incident with Patric had left me feeling weak. I turned toward Alec and grasped his shoulders. "Tell me what's going on!"

100

"Well, from what I can ascertain," Alec continued calmly on as if my outburst had not happened, "by helping to evoke Nathanial's attack mode, Patric was hoping that you would be disgusted enough *not* to make the exchange for Nathanial, thus leaving him to die and leaving you exposed to have Patric enter your life as a friend or potential mate; someone who would be willing to protect you from Nathanial should he try to initiate the exchange by force, and that you would be someone who he could possibly convince to join with him. Patric grossly underestimated your compassion and your growing love for his brother and Nathanial's love for you." I didn't quite think the last part of that statement held true. Nathanial had never loved me. Alec turned to look me in the eyes and for a split second I thought I saw his gaze flash. He continued. "When his first plan backfired, he took things a few steps further. He forced you into a hastened exchange with Nathanial the night of the attack with Nathanial being in his most weakened and corruptible state. If he couldn't destroy Nathanial through *your* own decisions, then he'd have to go the long way around and attempt to corrupt you, feeding on your despair and sadness at Nathanial's betrayal. Ana, if Patric were the one to save you, for the two of you to be 'bonded' in a sense and your mark indicates that you have some connection to Patric already, perhaps through Nathanial, perhaps through them as brothers; if you were to survive an exchange from Patric, the fusion of your blood with his would allow him to be strong enough to destroy Nathanial...and anyone else he feels has wronged him," Alec murmured those last words quietly and his tone turned dark. "He wants revenge and he wants you to hand it down. Perhaps the attack was a mechanism to get Nathanial out of

101

the picture, to influence him to leave you to die…" Alec turned to look at me and I saw desperation in his eyes, a wave of nausea and bile suddenly hit my system. My head was reeling and I felt a sudden guttural wretch in my stomach and I heaved forward onto the floor vomiting. Sweat soaked my body and my neck was burning. I vomited once more, my stomach convulsing. Kai wrapped his arms around me and waited for my body to calm itself.

"I'm ok," I said weakly, I'm alright, just help me up please." I wiped my mouth with the rag that Alec produced and Kai sank down beside me hoisting me to my knees.

Once Kai and Alec laid me on the couch and cleaned up my mess, Alec continued to speak. His desperation heightened, like we were all on the edge of a cliff, waiting to jump. I closed my eyes and listened.

"Nathanial's strong now, for sure, but not nearly as strong as he could be if he had completed the transaction between himself and Ana," Alec was muttering to himself. "I wonder…." His voice trailed off and he looked at me. That was it, I couldn't take anymore, and I just wanted to sleep through this horrible, horrible nightmare.

"Can I please go home now, I just want to go home." I was crying, yet again.

Once home, I curled up with Kuckuc and Piyip and tried not to think about everything that had happened today, it seemed like enough to fill a hundred lifetimes. I lay back in my bed and closed my eyes, falling asleep immediately. At some point in the night I awoke, shaking and sweaty. I didn't think I'd been dreaming, but my mind felt confused and strange colors were popping in front of my eyes. I heard something shift in the corner of the room and immediately Kuckuc began to growl and snap viciously. I struggled to turn on my light. A soft golden glow pierced the blackness and I saw a figure standing against the back of my room. Kuckuc lunged, but the figure casually waved a hand and she submitted. It was Patric.

Chapter Four

Ana

"You have so many protectors Ana, I haven't seen anything like it before, amazing." He moved out from the shadows and I now could see him clearly. His hair was no longer in his traditional dreadlocks, but loose and wavy, it rippled down his back and moved as if it had it's own breeze. His face was smooth and his eyes were their brilliant turquoise, small flames danced around his irises. I was captivated at his beauty and the subtle sensuality he seemed to emit. "I didn't have a chance to give you your medications today. We got, let us say, *distracted* didn't we?" He emphasized the word "distracted" and I felt a slight pressure in my head, a vision of us on the sofa came rushing into my mind and I saw myself again, writhing at his touch. I shivered, but not out of fear. He took out a small vile of liquid and placed it on my nightstand, he was standing next to my bed. "Make sure you only do one drop under your tongue a day, alright?" It was odd having him act like a concerned doctor for his patient. "But I am concerned Ana, I'm concerned about your fate, I know you can believe that can't you?" I didn't know what I believed anymore, nothing made sense, particularly the absurd amount of desire I was now experiencing.

"Why are you here?" I asked. "I don't know what you want me to do Patric," I said his name, letting it fall from my tongue as if I was saying some sacred incantation. He didn't fail to notice. His eyes burned brighter as he stared into my face.

"Tell me," he spoke in a quiet, seductive tone. "What were you feeling when I touched you today, when we were together?" I looked down, feeling embarrassed and knowing that he could tell what I had experienced, why did he need me to confirm anything? He was standing next to me now and I could feel the familiar pulling toward him, in my chest and now in my stomach. He continued to speak, moving closer still. "Because I want to hear if from you, it makes it so much more real, if I can hear you explain." Tenderly, he stroked down my temple to my jaw and let his fingers linger on the pulse rapidly beating below my ear. He sighed contentedly. "Tell me Ana."

"I felt, I felt like I didn't want anything but you, that I didn't want you to stop touching me, to stop making me *feel* you…" I let my voice fade out to a whisper. At hearing my words, I felt his fingers tremble on my skin and I dared to look up. His eyes had turned black, the flames were ember-like, burning slowly, pulsing. I felt something in me begin to move. In rhythm with the strange movement of his eyes, my veins throbbed and his familiar heat began to caresses my skin. He moved to sit on the bed. He inclined his head in a slow, deliberate movement, watching me. His hair moved over my bare shoulders and his breath warmed the skin on my neck. My body shuttered and I took in a shaky gulp of air. Lips, soft and moist and full of fire, pressed into my neck. He pulled himself back, breathing hard. His eyes, urgently searching my face, changed color; they were intoxicating and I could see nothing else. Without thinking, I weaved my fingers into his hair, pulling him to me. I had no control and yet I knew exactly what I wanted at that moment. He moaned softly and I shivered as his tongue moved over my throat. I had never felt such longing, such a deep need, and the darkest places of my soul felt released into the

105

night. With each touch of his mouth, with each breath I felt on my body, I wanted him to move in me, to feel our bodies matching the pulse of his eyes.

"Ana," he groaned my name, his hands pushing up the fabric of my t-shirt. I felt him move his fingers between my thighs and I gasped in pleasure as he slid them deep inside. I grasped at his shirt, tearing it off. I felt disconnected from the woman that I knew, yet somehow I did know this person, this new woman who wanted things that I would never have had the courage to admit. She made sense. Digging my fingers into his skin, I moved my body underneath him, my hips grinding slowly against his. He was moaning and I felt his fingers probing and massaging me deeply. He was moving in a rhythm that my body craved. I cried out, groaning softly at his touch and he pulled his hands away, pining my wrists and hovering above me. He brought his face close to mine and I saw his teeth were barred, his lips slick. "What are you doing to me?" he asked breathlessly. "What are you trying to do?" His voice was urgent, desperate. Still hovering above me, he brought his mouth to mine biting down on my lower lip. He sunk his tongue deep in my throat and I pushed his hands back down between my legs; I wanted to come again. Gasping, he pulled away. "What do you want Ana, what do you want from me?" He was breathless, panting and I could feel how solid and tight he'd become; I saw how hungry he was for me.

"I want you Patric. I want you to feel me, to touch me... please," I said, my voice sounded distant and low.

"NO!" he said. "No, this can't happen, this shouldn't be happening!" He rolled so quickly off of me that he became a blur. My body shook, again like I was coming out of a deep trance, but it had not been a trance. I had wanted to be with him, to feel him touching me, those were my deep and true desires and I had no idea why. He was pacing around the room, running his fingers through his hair and pressing the sides of his temples.

"Patric, what's wrong, why can't this happen? I want it to happen, it's not you *making* me want you."

"Is it not Ana? Are you so very confident in your abilities to resist me, that you can honestly say that what just happened was of your own desires, your own need for me?" I knew it didn't make any sense, that I should want him so badly. We had only just met but still, I felt that I did know him, that he was part of those deep places in my soul that I had always been afraid to reveal. Even though I knew that I stilled loved Nathanial, I would always love Nathanial, but he didn't want me or need me and he had left me alone to die. I was disgusted with myself. I had had enough, I just wanted to give everyone what they wanted and then they could spend the next three hundred years trying to eviscerate one another—I was pretty sure that I'd be dead, so what did it matter? Patric's head snapped up. "Are you so willing to give yourself to me, that you'd be comfortable with the knowledge that our merging would essentially kill this man you claim to love so much or potentially kill you?" He was incredulous. I sighed loudly.

"Patric, I'm so tired. I'm so tired of trying to do what everyone wants, trying to save everyone from themselves and from each other; I don't know anything about this world you're existing within." I motioned toward him. "Yes, I love Nathanial, but he took what he wanted from me and he left me to die without a single glance back." Patric's eyes flashed and I saw him wince. "I know you don't really want me, not for any type of loving relationship, you need me to get your power back, to reclaim what you feel you lost, to right all of the wrongs you felt were set against you. We're not that different you and I, in our suffering I mean. Maybe that's why I feel connected to you. I know you want to kill Nathanial—that for some reason you hold so much hate and anger toward him, there's a part of me that also feels that way about him if I'm being honest, but I also know that there still might be a shred of doubt in your mind about whether that's the right way to feel, if hatred and revenge will really get you what you want." I was speaking quickly and the words were rushing out of my mouth. "I see us as two people, two beings, who started out trying to live up to their potential, trying to let everyone see that they were worthy, of power in your case, maybe love in my case. You saw a path that offered you the things you *thought* would show your quality to the world. I decided to commit myself to making others see the value in themselves, hoping beyond hope, that that would prove that I too had value. Both of our assumptions are wrong, don't you see? We're both wrong. You could choose to save me and choose to forget about those perceived injustices that occurred. Maybe you *could* care about me, or at the very least, we could start our lives anew—choosing paths with the right intentions, not for anyone else, but for ourselves. It doesn't have to be the way you think. It doesn't have to be about revenge or betrayal or even trying to prove our worth, our value, not if we don't want it to be." I was crying now, desperate, I felt as though I was begging for my life. I couldn't stop the racking sobs heaving

108

from my chest. "If you want to save me or if I am to die at your hands, then I want you to know me Patric. I refuse to be seen as a means to an end for anyone—no more, it ends now. If we're going to do this, then I want you to know the person who is sacrificing her life so that you can carry out your vendettas. Because when you do this, when you take my blood from me, I want you to be able to look into my eyes and see, really see what I am giving to you—it is a gift Patric and if you are to use it for violence, for power, for revenge, I want you to know that it will be *you* who made it so." I was shaking. Of course he could just decide to kill me right now and none of this would make any difference.

"I'm not going to kill you Ana," he spoke from the corner of the room, he was standing still and quiet, not moving, barely breathing. I nodded.

"Well, thank you Patric, thank you for that," I muttered, and I *was* thankful, perhaps there was still hope for us. He laughed darkly.

"Don't be so quick to thank me Ana, I haven't quite decided *what* I'm going to do with you yet." And with those words, he frowned, crossed the room, touched his lips to my forehead and disappeared.

Nathanial

It was cold. It was always cold and not just because I'd been trekking up and down the Sawtooth Mountain range during

109

the dead of winter, but because I was always trying to quell the icy waves that radiated from within me. I couldn't remember the last time that I had slept, weeks, months, maybe? I couldn't afford to sleep, not since the nightmares had started. They were always the same. I'd be hovering on the ocean waves. I'd look up to see a woman teetering on the edge of a cliff, looking down at me. I didn't know why, but I wanted her to jump, to come to me—for some reason, I knew that I needed her. She would whisper my name and the wind would carry it across the watery mists to my ears. Like a caress, I would feel it envelope me, breaking over my body as if a giant wave was crashing overhead. I would call to her, this woman whose name I knew from some distant memory. *"Ana,"* I would say. *"Jump, I'll catch you."* And she did, she always did. I would watch her fall through the clouds, arms outstretched, reaching for me. Then, the most hideous laughter would echo into the mists, sinister and compressing. I was laughing. *"You foolish girl,"* I would cackle. *"It's over."* She would scream, still reaching for me, and I would watch her plummet into the sea, to her death. It was the same dream, and every time, I would awaken, shaking and gasping for air.

For months I had been in Idaho working on the Nez Perce Reservation as an Archeologist and advisor to the tribal council. I had no memory of how or why I ended up in this particular location, I just remembered feeling a deep compulsion to come to this place, to be here in the midst of these grand mountains and sacred lands. Most of my work had me outside and very occupied. I was involved in overseeing various building and land restoration projects that were underway. This was one of many reservations that had not been spared during a particular nasty outbreak of

Bonder, Human, and Vampire violence a few years back. The land was scoured and various burial plots had been unearthed. My days were spent out on sites attempting to composite and recover broken artifacts and remains of the dead. It was long and arduous work, and there were many disagreements about the use of funds between the tribal elders who wanted the money to be spent in ecological and cultural restoration, and those of the newer generation who felt that development on the ruined sites would prove to be a more fruitful endeavor. Surprisingly, mediation was proving to be my forte, it had a familiar place in my mind, but like most things these days, I couldn't give context to the memory. My "new" skills had allowed for me to hold several productive meetings between both groups, and I had finished the day with a somewhat fragile agreement.

After such a long day outdoors and in meetings, I needed to clear my mind for a bit and I was returning to my cabin after a walk down to the river, when I noticed a figure standing on my porch. Immediately, I felt my teeth become slick and my limbs tensed, ready to spring. The reaction was sudden and instinctual and brought with it a surge of heightened awareness and extreme power. I was still getting used to this new side of myself. This, along with my current location and the nightmares, was just another of the great mysteries about who I felt I currently was. I walked slowly up the drive, feeling the crunch of gravel under my feet. I could sense that the figure was watching me, and my jaw clenched with tension. Upon closer inspection, I felt a flood of warmth radiate from the figure and I could sense his energy—he was a Bonder.

A flash of light and pain doubled me over, my hands pressed on my knees. I saw a picture of the figure on my porch, standing over a woman who was coughing and sputtering; she was waxy and pale and looked weak. The picture zoomed in and I could see swirls of coppery and auburn brown hair flowing down the woman's shoulders, it was limp and damp with sweat. I gasped as a realization struck me, she was the woman from my nightmare, the one I would watch jump to her death! The memory blackened and swirled and I was able to stand upright again. I turned to look at the Bonder who was clearly responsible for the vision. My self-control vanished, my teeth barred, I charged at him, leaping from the ground into the air. I slammed my body into his chest and tackled him to the ground in one fluid motion. I smashed my fist against his head, hearing the familiar crunch of bone into flesh. He remained on the ground, still and quiet, not fighting back. "Get up you fucking bastard, get up!" I growled at him and stomped my boot into his side, another crunch as I heard his ribs shatter. Still, not moving, I watched as his wounds already began to heal. I heard him take a deep breath and spring lightly to his feet, he was taller than me and there was something familiar about him. His hair hung in long, shimmery brown dreadlocks, his face was composed, smooth and ageless, his eyes a brilliant emerald green. "Alec?" I exclaimed. I knew this Bonder, but from where? I couldn't for the life of me place the details of our relationship and this was making me very uneasy.

"It's not important how we know each other Nathanial, at least not for the moment, there are far greater things that you should be concerned about other than me my old friend." Spitting a clot of blood from his mouth, he spoke calmly but his tone hinted at an undercurrent of urgency and desperation. He continued to speak. "I'll take it that there are many gaps in your memory as of late, am I right?" I felt my chest heave at his understanding. I couldn't really remember much of anything, yet I knew, somewhere inside me, that I was missing something that I needed, that I wanted very, very much. "I might be able to help you out with that," he spoke out loud to my internal ponderings. My eyes narrowed,

"Alec, why are you here?" I eyed him warily.

"Nathanial," he spoke solemnly, and I felt a sudden blackness creeping into mood. "Your brother has returned. Patric has returned."

Patric's face flashed in front of my eyes, this image I was able to conjure on my own—sometimes there are things one will never forget. I hadn't seen or heard from Patric for almost a century but he was always plaguing the deep recesses of my memories, tugging at some unknown source of anxiety I was always battling. Perhaps it had something to do with us being twins, brothers from two of the most honorable and powerful beings of our kind. Even after all of these years, I still could think of Patric as a Bonder, that was his true destiny, but sometimes even destiny can be overruled by greed and an unquenchable thirst for power. Before our parting, Patric and I had come to an agreement of sorts after the war; I still could remember bits and pieces from our conversation. I remembered that the meeting had been the first time I had shown any kind of Bonder aggression—I had bitten him. It was an odd occurrence in that I had yet to make the full biological transition into a Bonder, but my memories of those times were very, very clear…

I had gone of my own accord to visit Patric, hoping to gain a truce to his violent and disturbing rule within the Vampire ranks. The Bonders were losing, not for lack of strength or power but out of despair. So many Bonders had seen their Chosen Ones, their loves, slaughtered and mutilated. Humans had sided with us, but they of course were not immune to Patric and his cronies. Stories of rapes and beatings of Human women, the brandings of Humans from Bonds not yet fulfilled, ripped from their necks—killing them. So much hate and loss of life, it was easy to understand why despair was now our worst enemy. It was slow to consume and it crept into the collective will to fight, crushing and suffocating its one and only threat, hope. I went as one last chance, but also because something odd had been happening to me and I knew that if I could get Patric to "see" what I had been experiencing, it might just give us a chance for a peaceful settlement. It was a risky move because I had to work at only letting Patric see the vision I wanted, and try to keep him from witnessing those visions that I knew were on course for changing my life and his…

The details were eluding me, my memory seemed weak and I was struggling to recall what had transpired between my brother and myself.

"You showed him a vision of the two of you united, ruling over all of us, Bonders, Humans and Vampires, you showed him what he truly wanted." I jumped; Alec was leaning against the railing, watching me.

114

"How do you know this?" My tone was doubtful, but somehow his statement resonated with me, it made sense.

"You told me once, a very long time ago. You also were able to keep him from 'seeing' Ana, from knowing that you were now experiencing the first stages of becoming a Bonder—well, at least that is what you thought. Unfortunately, you, just like so many of us Nathanial, underestimated how powerful your brother was and he saw your destiny, he saw Ana." Alec said her name with reverence, as if she was someone to be praised. "She is. She just doesn't know it yet," he spoke quietly and sadly.

"I was never really planning on uniting with Patric," I mumbled. "It was a tactic, a move made out of desperation."

"Hmm, yes it was a tactic and I would like to be able to tell you that it was that vision and that vision alone, that made Patric so willing to leave per your request, but it wasn't. It was the vision that you were so desperately trying to hide from him, the vision of both of your destinies, the vision of the one person who ties the very bonds of your lives and your deaths, together…" he trailed off, staring into my eyes; I felt a jerk and a sudden crushing of emotion. My heart heaved and a desperate pain began to squeeze my lungs. I choked and gasped for air. Collapsing on the ground, my body shook with uncontrollable sobbing. Darkness was filling my mind and I saw figures moving in front of my eyes. I didn't want to look, but a voice vibrated in my head. *You need to see this Nathanial; you need to look.* I heard Alec's voice deep in my mind, commanding and stern. The memory, filtered and hazy, moved like a movie, slowly clearing. I saw a man, or what looked like a man, chained to the ground. Blood was everywhere, it leaked and oozed in clots and streams. The picture closed in on a woman lying over his bloodied body, she was screaming and crying. I could smell the putrid stench of death and earth. I felt myself heave on the porch. The vision continued. I saw the woman, her wrist slashed, placing the wound to the man's lips. I saw him lunge from the ground, manic and crazed. He pulled her forward, she screamed again as he tore at the wound in her arm, slicing it wide, her blood spilling down his chest. They fell to the ground together, struggling. I watched as he pinned her arms and I heard him laugh, a sick and corroded laugh, one filled with poison and with hate; it was a laugh that I knew. He turned and I saw his face, I saw his eyes, and I screamed.

Ana

For the first time in six months I was feeling really great. My energy had returned and I was able to get back to work and school full-time. Whatever new medicine Patric had been prescribing, it seemed to be working. Since the time in my room, Patric had been a constant presence in my life; we spent numerous hours together. He would watch me cook, we'd go for walks on the beach and just talk for hours, we'd hike with my wolves and enjoy the quietness of the woods and softness of each of our breaths as we moved amongst the trees. He'd insisted that nothing physical happen with us, and I found myself being a bit disappointed in our lack of intimacy. I supposed considering the circumstance, it seemed a bit odd

116

but for me, for the first time since Nathanial left, I felt the deep cloud of despair lifting and the chasm in my chest didn't seem so painful when I was with Patric... my blood didn't feel nearly as cold. He was actually quite funny and witty when he allowed for me to see that side of him, but he was also contemplative, and I found him studying me often when we were together.

This recent connection was something that infuriated Alec and made Kai just plain scared. Hours I had spent trying to convince both of them that I didn't think that Patric wanted to hurt me, at least not yet, and that he seemed committed to saving my life or keeping me healthy until he could figure things out. Moreover, if it was my blood that was destined to restore Patric to power, then didn't it just make sense that I should try to befriend him, and that I should try to convince him to spare my life because he needed me? For some reason, I trusted Patric. I trusted that he was not going to take what he wanted by overpowering me; I needed to live in order for him to be strong. Alec of course was disturbed by this new found trust I had established, but what bothered him more was the very fact that Patric had *not* tried to take my blood by force, that he was waiting. Waiting for what? Well that was for Alec to care about. I was just glad to get back to some semblance of normalcy—like working out.

Since the whole Jack episode, I unfortunately had to find another gym to join. I managed to find a small, low-key place out from the city center. It was a bit of a drive, but the time in the car always proved calming and centering. Plus, I could think about Patric. Even though I was extremely busy now that I was healthy enough to resume my normal activities, I still found it hard to concentrate sometimes. I was always thinking about him, always picturing his face. Sometimes when I would dream, I would revisit that night in my room, feel his mouth on mine, the fragrance of sandalwood and vanilla that penetrated his skin, and I wouldn't feel so alone, so devastated, but I was also having nightmares, well the same nightmare actually. The one with Nathanial, the one where I'm standing on the edge of a cliff, watching him rise on the waves, listening to him mock me in that cold laughter as I fell through the mists. Between my fantasies of Patric and my nightmares of Nathanial, I wasn't sleeping very well.

Coming out of the gym, I headed for my jeep parked in the grass near the inlet. Dusk was settling into the horizon, and I kicked myself for not stopping by the clinic to get a new vile of medicine for the week. I was almost out, and I feared missing a dose would send me into a regressive state of health. The medicine that Patric was currently giving me, was, if I was being honest with myself, the most delicious medication I had ever tasted; it was nothing like those horrible cough and cold concoctions that most Healers and doctors usually dispensed. This stuff was like liquid crack—I actually had to work really hard at not giving myself an overdose. It was subtlety sweet and had the texture of honey. I could always taste hints of vanilla and some spicy notes of cinnamon or allspice. Smelling the vile always sent a rush of warmth into my veins and I felt instantly energized and calm at the same time; it was totally addictive. I took out my phone and called Patric, hoping that he could hang out a bit longer at work so that I could come by. I waited for him to pick up.

"Hello Ana, I was just thinking about you," he spoke softly. My heart thudded frantically in my chest, it always did that when I heard his voice.

"Hey Patric, I'm really sorry to bother you, but I'm almost out of my medicine and I just wanted to stop by and see if I could get another vile." My voice was shaking with excitement, another one of my bizarre physical reactions to him.

"Hmmm, well I'm not at the Clinic, I'm actually at home. Can you come by the house to pick it up?"

"That won't be too intrusive for you?" I asked. Patric was a very private person and in the months since I'd met him, I had yet to see where he lived.

"Not at all, like I said, I've been thinking about you. Let me give you directions." After jotting down what appeared to me some of the most complicated directions I'd ever tried to map, I jumped in my car and headed toward the mountains. My phone vibrated and I saw that Alec had called and left me a voicemail.

"Ana, it's Alec, I wanted you to know that I was going to be traveling for bit longer, I'm trying to find out how many followers Patric has managed to herd in since his return. I'll know where you are, so please try to keep yourself out of danger." I rolled my eyes. He continued. "Also, as a favor to me, someone who I assume you love and care about, I would appreciate you keeping your interactions with Patric to the bare minimum; i.e., seeing him only for your medications. Call me if you need anything." A stab of guilt washed over me. I was pretty sure that being alone with Patric at his house was exactly what Alec had in mind in terms of me *not* doing anything dangerous. I sighed. Well, I had trusted the universe with my fate so many times before; I might as well keep going!

The route to Patric's house was long and curvy and full of steep switchbacks. I could hear the rushing of water below me as I climbed higher into the mountains. I passed the turn off once and struggled to find a place safe enough to back my jeep up and turn around. Recognizing the hidden drive on my second attempt, I turned into the tree-covered path. It was dark, darker than it actually was outside. The canopy from the trees made the blackness seem denser and heavier and I felt a rush of relief when I rounded the corner and saw the lights from his cabin; they glowed and pulsed and I suddenly thought that someone could be hypnotized by their vibrations. I saw that he was already waiting on the porch, leaning casually over the railing, a glass in his hand. I felt breathless and giddy. Sheesh, what the hell was wrong with me?

I walked up the wooden stairs and he turned to look at me. I couldn't help but stare. His hair was twisted into a low ponytail and it hung in a luminescent wave down his back. He was wearing the same loose white shirt I had first seen him in, unbuttoned to reveal the smooth plains of his throat and chest, his turquoise amulet startling against his coppery skin. His pants were also loose in their fit, some kind of cargo type style and they seemed to glide away from his body in one fluid piece of fabric. I looked at his eyes, they were their usual turquoise, but this time the flames seemed to penetrate outward and I thought I could actually feel their heat.

"Ana," he spoke quietly as he approached me. "How are you feeling?" His fingers reached to touch my throat, he traced down along my exposed collarbone. I shuttered as the familiar heat surged through my body, and I sighed contentedly.

"I'm good." That was all I could manage to whisper. He smiled and gently laughed.

"Well, there's no better news than that, is there? Shall we go inside?" He held the door open for me and I crossed the threshold into his home.

Quiet music greeted me as I followed him down the long wooden hallway. The melody was a bit dark but also sensual in its tone and it suited my mood. The cabin was beautiful, of course. It mimicked something out of the old lodges, built as outposts for hikers and backpackers many ages ago. Hardwood floors peeked out from soft, furry rugs and a creek-stone fireplace ignited the dim living room. On the far side of the space was a giant picture window that offered a view of the mountains and the distant volcano, with its constant stream of red-orange lava, filtering down the side like a great gash in the flesh of the rock. The moon hung in its fullest glory, bathing the glass in a deep, penetrating light. "Wow, looks like I picked the wrong profession," I mused. "Maybe I should have become a Healer, this is such a beautiful place Patric." I had wandered over to the giant window and was gazing out at the moon, as I so often liked to do.

"Hmmm...I'm glad you like it." His voice was soft and I turned to look at him. It took me a minute to locate his position. He was standing across the room in a darkened corner, watching

121

me. My heart pounded in my chest. We stared at each other for what felt like an eternity. I was suddenly struck by his fragrance. He seemed to be emitting it like a signal of sorts. I felt my mouth begin to water and my body ached with such an overpowering desire that I had to bite my lip to keep from groaning out loud. It wasn't an entirely unpleasant feeling, but it was definitely a new experience. My lips felt moist and I tasted Patric on my tongue. I looked at his face. He was still, but breathing rapidly. Then as quickly as it had come on, it faded. My breath returned to normal and I felt my heart rate slow, but the desire remained. Patric moved from his corner out into the light of the fire, his gaze had not lost any of its intensity and I struggled to regain my composure. What had just happened?

"Tell me Ana, how *exactly* have you been feeling?" His breathing was still intense and heavy, but he looked like he had gathered himself from whatever had just occurred between us.

"Uh, well, I guess, specifically, I've had a lot more energy lately, a lot more…" I was stumbling over my words. He glanced at me and moved to sit on the leather sofa in front of the fire. Taking a deep sip from his drink, he surveyed me over the glass and motioned for me to join him.

"Anything else? Anything beyond your energy level, I mean?" Blood flooded my cheeks. I wasn't sure if I really wanted to talk about the fact that I was having trouble concentrating because I was fantasizing about him all day. That was embarrassing, especially since I still wasn't sure exactly what the nature of our relationship was, boundary wise. I was sure that he still hadn't figured out what "he was going to do with me," I thought, recalling the initial discussion we'd had in my room that first night he'd come to see me. I stared at him. He was facing me with his back against the soft armrest, his shoulder casually draped along the spine of the sofa. I sighed.

"Well, I've had a bit of trouble concentrating, I mean it's not interfering with school or anything, and it could just be that I have late onset ADD or something." I laughed nervously. He lifted his chin and his eyes locked with mine. He knew that I was trying to hide something from him. I wasn't very good at keeping him out of my head, not nearly as good as I was with Nathanial, but I could do it sometimes if I concentrated really hard.

"I've been thinking about you quite a bit as well, Ana." Damn! He'd gotten in. Probably because we were on his turf, I thought to myself. I heard him softly chuckle. "Perhaps, or maybe because we most certainly have some deep connection to each other. Something that I never anticipated," he spoke those last words as a whisper, almost to himself as he fingered his amulet.

"Is that such a bad thing?" I asked in a voice that flowed with that undercurrent of desire. It surprised me, I wasn't usually the sexually aggressive kind but with Patric, it seemed that everything that I thought I knew about myself went out the window. He leaned toward me and again I was hit with his scent, more potent this time, maybe because he was so close. I swore that I thought he was acting on his own to allow the fragrance seep into the space between us, but I couldn't be sure. Immediately, my mouth began to water again and my throat constricted. I felt myself leaning closer to him, trying to get nearer to his skin, to his scent. He laughed and stood up. The scent was gone and I felt frustrated, although I couldn't place the source for my sudden angst.

"Let me get you your medicine." When he spoke, I thought I heard his voice tremble for just a moment. He left the room and I watched him climb a set of wooden stairs. He stopped halfway up and turned to look at me. Even from a distance, I could feel his eyes; they were burning and pulsing. For a split second, I felt the urge to go after him, to follow him up the stairs but it passed, and I exhaled the breath I had been holding. I heard the floorboards above me creak and shift under his weight as he traveled from room to room. I sat staring at the fire, trying to get a handle on my feelings for him, trying to understand what was happening between us. Then it hit. The scent was back, but somehow it was different, more powerful and it seemed to be filtering into places that only served to bring me deep arousal. It kicked me in my gut and I felt a sudden urge to leap up from the sofa and run upstairs. I was breathing hard and a deep, red haze swam before my eyes. I licked my lips and I could taste the sweetness of vanilla and the spice of cinnamon, but I also tasted fire, smoky and seductive it licked at my lips and made me groan with need and *hunger*. I tried to clear my head, tried to shake off what was now becoming an impossible urge to control. I thought I heard quiet laughter from upstairs and I became angry. Did he know what was happening to me, was he responsible for this sudden desire I had, this need that was rising like a flame inside my chest? I was annoyed and I started for the stairs. What the hell was going on? I climbed slowly up, again trying to gain control over this sudden onset of craving and sheer passion. I got to the top of the stairs and saw a stream of moonlight coming from the last room at the end of the hall. I shook my head again, the urge was getting worse. The door was cracked and I pushed it open. Patric was standing in the middle of a large bedroom; it was dark except for the moon and the stars filtering through the glass of the window. He was holding a vile and he was smiling, but he also looked— it couldn't be; he looked scared. I moved toward him and he took a step back. Did I frighten him? That didn't make any sense. The urge that had come on so strongly was diminishing, but what was left was something so powerful, it made me gasp. Desire. Desire radiated from every pore in my body and my bones ached with longing for him. I wanted to feel him touch me again; I wanted to come by his hands and I couldn't explain any of this. I also couldn't move; I was paralyzed by my needs. His eyes locked onto mine and I could see that the colors were shifting again, gray to black to turquoise.

"Ana." His voice was a whisper and a groan. I stepped toward him and he froze. "Ana, this can't happen, it shouldn't happen." He sounded like he was pleading with me, trying to get me to turn around, but I looked into his eyes and saw that they were now full of deep, pulsating fire and hunger—hunger for me. I moved toward him again, slowly closing the distance between us until I was close enough to touch him. "Ana…god I want to feel you," he whispered.

"I want that too," I said softly looking into his eyes. I reached out to stroke his face. He closed his eyes and I heard him sigh. "Please Patric," I spoke softly again. I let my hands glide down his throat and over his bare, smooth chest, touching briefly his amulet as it hung solidly over the planes of his tightened muscles and the back of my neck grew warm. The vile he'd been holding slid from his fingertips onto the soft rug below our feet and he reached to stop my fingers now tracing over his abdomen.

"You don't know what you are asking, you don't know what you are doing to me, what you *have* done to me Ana." His voice was fierce but also soft and urgent. The grip he had on my fingers slackened and I let my hands continue to trace over his stomach unbuttoning his shirt, always watching his eyes. He shuttered as the tips of my fingers moved below his waist and he groaned softly. I moved to undo the button on his pants but he stopped my hands and looked at me, questions filling his eyes.

"It's ok Patric, I want this to happen; I want to be with you," I crooned softly. And I did, I had not wanted anything else more than I wanted him, at least not since Nathanial. He touched my lips and closed his eyes. I moved him back toward the edge of the bed and gently pushed him down. He sighed, and I knelt down by his legs and finished unbuttoning his pants. I moved to pull them down over his hips, and I felt him shutter and sigh. I let my lips run over his stomach and his chest, tasting the sweetness of his skin, feeling my throat contract at the very scent of him. He groaned and whispered my name. To me, it sounded beautiful, for the first time in my life, it sounded special.

"You are special Ana," Patric spoke gently and so much of me believed him, so much of me wanted him to be right, to be speaking the truth. I could feel the pulse in his groin and the scent became overwhelming. I moaned and pressed my lips to the throbbing spot and traced my tongue on his skin, my teeth grazing his flesh.

"God Ana, what are you doing?" he groaned to me, and his voice made my body ache with pleasure. I felt his hands weave themselves into my hair and press down on the top of my head. We were both breathing hard. He guided me down between his legs and my body trembled with the desire that I had to taste this part of him. His hands pressed down harder on my head and I took all of him into my mouth. I heard him gasp at the contact of my lips and tongue, and my throat exploded with thirst. I felt his muscles contract as he pushed me further, deeper. I worked him with my hands and my mouth bringing him close to his release, and then calming him down. He was thrusting against my mouth and my body shuttered as heat rose deep between my legs. The pulse of him was proving too much of a distraction and I let my mouth return to the throbbing source of his scent. He was breathing hard and groaning loudly now and I felt the movement of his hips rise to meet my mouth again. I felt my teeth digging, trying to tear into his throbbing flesh. "Ana, god! Please, I want this, I want you." His body was shaking, his voice speaking in between jagged breaths and I heard myself groan. I felt Patric heave his hips, bringing them crashing against my lips. Flames were rushing into my body and my teeth became slick. I was moaning and Patric was saying my name, over and over. "Ana, Ana, please, oh god, Ana!" He was so close and I wanted to take him, I wanted him to come as I took his blood and I pressed my teeth deeper into his flesh feeling my own release heighten. Then I felt him seize. "Ana Stop! Stop!" He grabbed at my shoulders and yanked my mouth away from his groin. "Stop!" He was panting and his face was flushed with color, his eyes ignited. "Stop!" He spun me so quickly to the side, that I saw stars burst in front of my eyes. My head was throbbing and I felt delirious with my need for him, but I also felt shocked at what had just happened. My emotions had come on so suddenly and with such ferocity that I had no control and really no desire to stop them. I had wanted to be close to Patric; I felt a deep need for the intimacy and the connection—whatever that was, I didn't know, but clearly that's not what he wanted or needed from me.

"Oh, Patric! I'm so sorry, I'm so sorry!" I moved away from him, cowering on the bed. What was happening to me? Had I almost bitten him? " I could have hurt you! I'm so sorry. Please Patric, don't be angry." Panicked now, I gathered myself up and moved towards the door. It swung shut, sending a gust of wind across my face, blowing my hair back. I turned and saw him sitting on the edge of the bed, he was still breathing hard and his eyes were beating in rhythm with my heart, fast. Slowly he moved from the bed to stand in front of me, I felt fear begin to ice my veins, freezing my blood. I couldn't take my eyes off of him, he looked so beautiful, so terrifying. He took a measured step toward me and I noticed that he wasn't blinking. The force of his eyes paralyzed me against the door as I watched him inch closer. I tried to calm my rapid breathing, but the closer he came, the harder it was for me to fill my lungs. Still, somewhere under the fear, under the complete and indescribable terror that I was now feeling, I wanted him. He was close enough now that I could smell the intoxicating fragrance coming off his skin. It washed over me and I felt the paralysis diminish. His lips were parted and he moved to put his hands against the door on either side of me.

"Ana," he said softly moving his body so that our hips were touching, grinding himself slowly against me, he moaned. "Ana, you have no idea what you do to me do you?" He pressed his lips to my ear and whispered, "I don't know how to *not* want you," he said the word "want" in such a way that made my blood unfreeze and flood with intense heat. He was tracing his lips down my neck, stopping to feel the rapid beating of my pulse. I felt him smile as his tongue moved along the length of the vein. He shivered; I shivered. He pushed back from the door, breaking the spell, leaving me quivering and breathless, yet again. He turned his back to me and bent down to pick up the vile that had fallen. "Take this," he said, his arm outstretched, offering the medicine to me. I peeled myself from the door and hesitantly crossed the room toward him. I felt the hot rush of embarrassment flood my face as I took the vile. His fingers lingered on the wound across my wrist and the wave of desire that I always felt with Patric, found its way back into my body. I sighed.

"I'm so sorry, Patric, really I am…" I shook my head, letting my words trail off. How could I possibly explain what had happened, what was happening inside of me when I was near him; it was unexplainable. He rubbed his face in his hands and took a step back from me.

"Ana, I think it's a good idea to keep a bit of distance between us for a while, I just…" He was searching for words, a very rare occurrence for Patric. I interrupted him before he could continue.

"I understand, of course Patric, whatever you think is best." I could feel the familiar pricking of tears stabbing at the corners of my eyes. I just wanted to get the hell out of there as quickly as possible. It was all too much.

"Go," he said softly. "But, the minute you feel ill, or the medicine doesn't seem to be helping...you need to call me. Do you understand?"

"Ok." I bent my head and looked down at the floor.

"Ana, do you understand what I'm saying? This is very serious and your condition is not something to take lightly." He hooked his finger under my chin and brought my tear soaked face up into the moonlight. I saw him wince and trace the tear tracks down my cheek. I brushed his hand away and took a step back from him. Rejection, swift and devastating, entered my conscience and I felt anger rushing out toward him, toward his refusal of me. I saw his eyes widen at his revelation of my feelings, and he was stunned into silence.

"Yes, Patric, I understand very well about the seriousness of my condition, and yes, I will call you if I need you." My tone was even, emotionless. I turned on my heel and walked abruptly from the room.

Nathanial

What had I done? I felt sick, my stomach heaved and I pressed my head into my hands. I'd left Ana to die! She was dying at

130

my hand. After everything she had done for me, after she'd let me into her world, after I knew how little she valued her own life, and how she'd placed mine on a pedestal—I had handed down the death sentence to her! And Patric, dear god, he'd come back, he'd come back for *her* and somehow he'd managed to infiltrate her Bond with me, carving out his own claim on her life, her heart. It was Ana that he'd seen in my vision, the dream I had desperately tried to keep from him. He'd seen the two paths for her, all dependent on who got to her first, who infiltrated her life first. He had felt what I had felt for her, made those desires, that passion, his own memories of her. He had hunted her, waited for her, and spent his exile thinking of her and following me—Jesus, I led him straight to her, and now she was with *him*. He could save her, he could give her his blood, he could spare her life but he hadn't. He was letting her linger, get weaker. The weaker she got, the less likely she was to survive the transition, even with his blood flowing through her. I shuttered at the thought of their mingling, of any part of him being in her. I heaved again and collapsed back against the bed.

"It might not be too late Nathanial," Alec spoke from across the room. He had been the one to figure all of this out, he'd come to help me remember, to convince me to return to Indonesia. He'd been with me for weeks now, trying to fill in the gaps in my memory.

"How do you know?" I spat bitterly, a metallic taste coated the inside of my mouth—adrenaline.

"Because I know Ana, I have acquired quite a connection with her since your...departure." I glared at him. "Sorry," he said

131

abashedly. "I won't lie to you though Nathanial, there are very deep feelings that she has for Patric, feelings that I cannot unravel. Perhaps, what's an even bigger mystery is the depth of feelings that he has for her. It's odd considering his position in all of this. Ana could be disposable to him, he could take her blood, get the power he so desperately desires, and then he could take her life, it wouldn't make him that much weaker if she died, but of course keeping her alive would allow him full access to his powers, but he hasn't done either or those things and I don't know why. He's planning something, but I also think that perhaps your brother, in all of his infinite wisdom, failed to account for any shred of humanity left lingering within in himself. Perhaps, it's just enough to be awakened through his desire for Ana." Fear crashed over me, fear and something else, jealousy. I was jealous of my brother. He had Ana wanting him and he wanted her, corrupt and destructive as that want might be, still, it was there. "I think it might be within your interest to return with me to Indonesia Nathanial." Alec's tone simmered with that of the General he used to be. "I think that seeing first hand what is happening between Patric and Ana, well perhaps, it might give you the impetus to act."

"And do what Alec? What is it that you propose I do? Fight Patric for Ana? I'm stronger since, since…" I couldn't bring myself to say the words. "I'm stronger now, but that wanes, the transaction was never completed and my powers will eventually level off. Patric doesn't have those conditions, it wouldn't be a fair fight," I said.

"Maybe, but I think you are forgetting one very crucial detail about your relationship to Patric." I was sure that I wasn't missing anything, he was my brother and I knew him better than I knew myself. "True, but did you know that brothers who are Bonders, and that is truly what Patric is by birth right, a Bonder, that what happens to one, affects the other? That your weakness is his weakness, your strength, is his strength. Didn't you ever wonder why it took you so long to go through your Bonding ritual, why it was only coming in intervals throughout your life? It was because Patric was struggling with it himself, trying to decide if there was a better, more lucrative path that he might take. His indecision and ultimately his choices, affected what you became as a Bonder. When he agreed to leave, his fall from the ranks affected his internal powers and yours, you were both left weakened, although it didn't seem to disrupt your life's path too severely. Perhaps, it is within the true nature of the soul, that therein lies the strongest powers…"

"Alec," I said disbelieving. "How is it that you know all of this, how is it that I missed it?" I couldn't comprehend what he was saying, and yet it fell into place in my mind. How quickly Patric had agreed to leave, because he saw what was before him, what he could be and do, *if* he found Ana.

"I've spent months crossing the globe, finding people who remembered Patric, who remembered the war, who remembered your parents. I'm still piecing things together, and I sense that there's something that I'm still missing, something very, very important, but I just can't connect things, there are too many gaps yet." He moved toward me and I rocked back onto the bed.

"How is she? How's she feeling, I mean." I had to ask, although fear was creeping into my mind.

"Well, that's also an interesting mystery. By all standards, because your particular brand of poison is probably the strongest known of our kind, Ana should be near death by this point. And she was, she had a month or two there when I thought things were beyond saving. Then, Patric changed her medication—an act that makes me suspicious but I can't figure out why. Anyway, she's actually thriving now, health-wise," he said those last words as to emphasize that he was not so sure about her mental health. "Yes, I am not sure how she is holding up psychologically and I get the feeling that her thoughts are becoming more and more consumed with Patric." I do not, however, think that he has possessed her. I think her thoughts of him are of her own volition, mostly. Ana's tendency has always been one to try to see beyond the pretenses that beings tend to put forth and with Patric, I think that she's been trying to understand him, understand his journey. I think she feels connected to him," Alex said. Another wave of jealously tugged at the corners of my heart. Alec moved to stand up and stretch. "Patric is smart enough to keep his distance from me and to keep me out of his head, so I have no idea what kind of treatment he's giving to her, but her condition definitely has my hackles raised, it just doesn't make any sense." He looked as if he wanted to discuss something else and I felt a darkness drifting into his mind, something about Ana, about what he thought she could do or have the potential to do; he was struggling. He stood suddenly, breaking my hold in his mind. "Now, I think we've discussed enough, for the time being, what is your decision Nathanial, are you to accompany me back to Ana or not?" I got the impression that I was not actually being given an option. "You can always act of your own accord Nathanial, but let me just say this. I know that you love Ana and despite her compassion and desire for Patric." I cringed. "Despite that desire," he continued, "she still loves you, conflicted as it might be, it's there. You can decide to save her life and we'll just have to figure out a way to deal with your brother and his ill-conceived notions that you'll join him in resurrecting the Vampires—we'll have to deal with that later. You made a tactical error in planting that vision in your head for him to see, but perhaps we may be able to use what I think amounts to his longing to have his brother by his side, and perhaps we do have a weapon, the problem may be that he does as well…" My heart stopped. Ana, I thought. His weapon was Ana.

Chapter Five

Ana

It felt good to be out on the water. I needed to be outdoors more and more as of late and rowing had always served as meditation for me. When I graduated with my second Masters degree, I treated myself to my used jeep and a sculling boat. Since Nathanial, since Patric, since everything had happened, I couldn't remember the last time I had been out on the lake. The night at Patric's house had proved to be quite a disturbing event in my life. I still couldn't explain why I reacted to him in such a violently passionate way. Since leaving his home, I had stayed up nights trying to place the source of my longing for him—was it love? In my despair of losing Nathanial, of what I was sure to be my impending death, had I found solace and love with someone who was destined to also betray me? How did that work? Even with many of my thoughts still occupied with Patric, I had listened to his request; I had put as much distance as I could stand between us. Actually, for almost two months, I had gone out of my way to avoid him. If I needed refills of my medication, I would plan my visits to the Clinic on days when I knew he wouldn't be there, days when he was out at the commune or treating people on the outer islands. Funny enough, since our agreement, I had lots of time in my schedule open up. Alec was still traveling and Kai and I were able to rekindle our friendship over good margaritas and beautiful sunsets. I had taken to working more shifts at the Preserve, and interacting more with the few female friends that I had. My life was probably the closest to normal as it had been before Nathanial and Patric, but of course there was always the bitterness of that life waning; death, waiting for me like some cloaked figure, watching for those last beats of my heart, if that was to be my end. I tried not to let despair hinder my routines. I was, in fact, feeling ok. Every once in a while I would have a massive coughing jag and it would leave me sweaty and nauseous, then it would pass and I would continue on with my day. I was determined to live my life, not for Patric, certainly not for Nathanial, but for me.

As I heaved the oars into the water and felt their drag work against the currents, I suddenly had the feeling that I was being watched. Chills ran up and down my back, even though I was sweating heavily. I felt the prick of the tiny hairs on the back of my neck stand on end, and I absently reached to touch the base of my head. Of course my mark was still there, but it had undergone a bit of a transition. I'd felt it when it happened, the sudden pressure and tightness on my spinal cord and heaviness in my brain. The metals had separated. Now, instead of the woven lines of silver jewels and midnight blue and the deep turquoise line running through their connection, the silver and turquoise had split from the dark blue, leaving a deep fissure down the center of the main imprint. The newly joined lines were now wrapped around each other in a rock solid bond of metal and stone. The symbolism had not been lost on me.

I steered the boat into the center of the lake and looked back toward the trees. The sun broke through the clouds and in a flash of light and shadow, I thought that I saw a gleam of silver and bright blue bouncing off the water. I looked again toward the woods, but couldn't see the source of the fractured light.

I felt a slight tugging in my head, a familiar pressure that came when someone was trying to break through. I breathed steadily through the surge of heat and braced myself for what I thought was coming. Nothing, the pressure ceased and there was nothing. Ugh, I needed to get off the lake. I'd been out exerting myself for a bit too long today and I was beginning to feel the effects. Kai and I had plans to meet at a local bar and have a nice dinner and some drinks; the thought of seeing my dear friend made me smile and row that much quicker back toward the shore.

****

It was late when I arrived home from my adventures with Kai, after one in the morning. We'd had a nice time dancing and laughing, but I couldn't help still feeling as if someone was watching me. The smell of hookah and cigarette smoke was on my skin and in my hair and I knew that I was going to have to take a shower before I could go to bed. I sighed, I was tired and really just wanted to go to sleep. The breeze blew as I walked up to the door and I sucked in my breath. The fragrance of lemon, of honey and the woods, was on the wind. No! I thought, my mind racing. No! It couldn't be him; it had been more than six months; why would he come back? The wind shifted and it carried another familiar scent, this time hitting me so hard that I leaned forward and grasped my knees. Spice and sandalwood, vanilla and musk—my heart stirred and I felt such a combination of desire and despair that I wanted to cry. I struggled to get into the house away from the wind and into the scent of my own home. Kuckuc greeted me immediately; she was waiting up for my return. Piyip too was up and they both seemed anxious. They circled me, whining and howling as they ran their noses over my legs. It must be the hookah; it was probably too potent for their acute sense of smell. I rubbed them both under the chin and told them to settle down; all their nervous energy was not helping to quell the anxiety I had carried with me since the lake.

I climbed the stairs to my bedroom and stripped off my smoky clothes stuffing them in the bottom of the hamper. I turned on some quiet music and started the shower. It took three washings to get the smell out of my hair and repetitive scrubbing and shaving to remove the hookah from my skin. I needed to remember that the next time Kai has the bright idea to smoke the stuff. I slathered on my favorite smelling moisturizer and started the arduous task of untangling my hair. Ten minutes later I emerged from the bathroom and saw him sitting so still, on the edge of my bed.

"You've been avoiding me Ana. Did you think that I wouldn't know what you were doing?" His tone was icy and I stared at him unblinking, still unsure of what I was actually seeing. "You've been practicing at keeping me out of your mind as well, haven't you? Visiting with friends, working, studying. It makes it nearly impossible for me to be able to get to you." I started to speak, but he held up a finger to silence me. "I realize that it was I who suggested that we take some time apart, and I realize that our *incident*," he spoke the word slowly, as if remembering what happened between us, "was somewhat unsettling for you and for me, if we are being completely honest, but I truly did not think that you would go to such lengths to put so much distance between us." I wanted to speak, but I had no idea how long his little rant was going to continue. "It's hardly a rant Ana." His tone wavered on sarcastic and impatient. "I'm merely stating what you already know to be true." His eyes turned to me and his voice hung heavy and dark in the room.

"May I speak?" I folded my arms across my chest and glared at him. I made sure that my tone denoted that I was not actually asking for his permission. He waved his hand at me and he sat back against my pillows, like an adult waiting to hear the excuse of some rebellious teenager. He raised his eyebrows at my unspoken comparison. "Patric, seriously, are you going to come here with that ridiculous attitude and try to get me to feel bad about my behavior toward you—really? That's how you want to play this?" I was angry now. We were both responsible parties in what transpired, but it was *he* who wanted distance from *me*, not the other way around. I wasn't going to stand there and let him use his self-perceived "power" to get me to feel guilty about anything. He started to speak, but I cut him off. "And by the way Patric, how was I supposed to know just exactly what you meant by 'distance', I mean for all I knew, that could mean days or weeks or months. I cannot, unlike you, read minds." My emotions were so close to the surface now, I could feel the anger filtering into my body. "I mean I know," I continued, pacing around the room, "that our relationship is not exactly conventional and I know that you, for whatever reason, are struggling with your feelings for me, but between the both of us, I have been the more honest of the two. At least I told you that I was confused, that I felt something so deeply for you, but I didn't know what that meant." I felt my voice rise. "You, you have been fighting with your feelings ever since I met you and look where it's gotten you. Do you feel good, does it feel right for you to be away from me, how's that working out for you Patric?" I turned to face him, my face flushed and my heart racketing in my chest and I felt that sudden odd skin swelling that I had had when Jack tried to attack me. My blood felt hot, boiling hot. I took a deep breath. "I get that you have this, this decision to make about me, about what it is exactly you are going to 'do with me'." I quoted him from the last time he was in my room. "But are you honestly going to tell me that what you feel for me has not gone beyond whatever your plans were going to be, whatever it was that you hoped to fulfill?" I continued to glare at him. He was furious. A low growl was emitting from his chest and I thought I heard him snarl at me. I laughed bitterly. "Oh honestly Patric, do you think after everything that I've been through, and I don't just mean with you or with Nathanial, do you honestly think that you can scare me? Because you know what, I don't care anymore, I don't care what your decision is and I don't care about what happens to me. You want to know why? Because it's no longer about me, or what I can do for you or for your stupid brother; you are going to do what you want, that's always been your plan, and no matter what I tell you, no matter what I say about how I feel towards you, you've already made your decision haven't you?" I was standing next to him, watching as he tried to quell the rapidness of his breathing. I ran my fingers through my hair and moved to sit down near his feet. I looked at him, waiting.

"Yes." His words sounded muted and quiet. "My decision has already been made Ana, but what happened between us at my house, what *keeps* happening between us, that decision, it just doesn't seem to matter anymore." He sounded upset and confused. He put his face in his hands and sighed. "When you touch me, when I feel your skin and taste you on my lips, I am so many things at once." My chest contracted at his words and I sat still, listening to his desperation. "I am both damned and redeemed, I am at my strongest and my weakest, I am both sinner and saint and I need to be with you Ana," he was whispering and his eyes were on me, searching my face. "The things that I want from you, the things you *make* me want from you—I need to be with you before...before..." He couldn't make himself continue and his breath sounded urgent and frantic. I closed my eyes and breathed in, tasting the fragrance that was coming off of his skin. I was no longer angry. "Ana." He reached to touch his fingers to my lips, parting them. "Ana, please." I opened my eyes, what was he asking? What did he want? "You know what I want Ana, you've always known." His fingers traced down my throat making my chest shudder. "Please," he whispered as he bent his head close to my neck. "Please," he murmured, and I felt his lips press themselves to my pulse, his nose skimming the flesh. I heard him sigh, exhaling his breath into my skin and a strange sensation began to rise suddenly in my body. I pressed my fingers to the back of his neck, under his hair and pulled his face to my throat. His body quivered and weaving his fingers into my hair, he pulled my head back, exposing my full neck. My breath was coming quickly and so was my passion for him. His tongue moved up and down my throat, over and down my collarbone to my breasts. I felt him graze his teeth across my nipples, sending shocks of pleasure rippling through my body. His hands gripped my shoulders and he pulled me over

142

on top of him. He pushed my thighs apart so I was straddling his hips and he pulled my shirt over my head, running his hands down my bare back and across my stomach. I groaned from his touch. His hips ground roughly into mine and I could feel the strength of him; it wasn't close enough for me. I needed to feel him, to have him against my skin. Sensing what I wanted, he flipped me onto my back and proceeded to undress us both.

"Is this what you want Ana," he asked, panting as I pressed his hips hard against me, wanting him to understand what I so desperately needed. I held his face in my hands and looked him in the eyes; they were the deepest, clearest shade of turquoise that I had ever seen. I gasped at their beauty and at how close he was to entering me—the throbbing heat was intense and I could feel him slide himself deep inside, the fire from his body ignited my blood. He groaned and we were moving together, pulsing and moaning in our primal need for each other. He was slowly thrusting and I felt the room change and swirl around us. I tried to breathe as I pushed him deeper unable to feel him enough. His breath left his lips in a quiet moan and he moved his head toward my throat. Patric's mouth was moist, his tongue licking forcefully against the throbbing of my vein, but then he suddenly stopped moving. He pressed my hands over my head and brought his face close to mine. Releasing one of my arms, he took his fingertip and slowly caressed my cheek. I saw that his teeth were barred, sharp and glistening, and his eyes were now black fire. I didn't want him to stop; I wanted to feel every part of him inside of me, I wanted him to keep going.

"Patric, please don't stop. Please, I love you, don't stop," I begged him, my words filling me with their truth. I had come to love Patric in my own way, gently and quietly over time, over walks on the beach and hikes in the woods, over dinner and late night phone calls; I loved him for what I wanted him to be, for what I saw he could be and I loved him because in spite of the choices he was making, he had helped me to heal. Without knowing it, Patric's presence had made my pain from Nathanial more manageable and he helped me to hold myself together when all I wanted to do was fall apart. A stunned look crossed his face as he stared down into my eyes and I again I touched his cheek. "I love you." I felt him slowly thrust again, pulling himself in and out, raising the intensity of the passion that I was feeling. I moaned loudly and brought his mouth back to my neck. I wanted him to do this, I needed him to do this. He moved again, faster now, so that the vibrations of his grinding between my thighs, served as a distraction. He pressed his mouth to my throat at the same time he pushed himself deep inside me, hard.

I felt a sharp tear in my throat and a quick burning sting and then he began to suck on the fresh wound, groaning and grunting in his pleasure. That feeling, the feeling of him taking the blood from my veins; it was overwhelming and I wanted him to never stop. My back arched and my soul shuttered with such intense desire, that I couldn't call out, I was gasping for air. His face was buried in my neck and I could feel the blood trickling down my skin. His tongue was quick to catch the falling droplets and I felt him lapping up the streams of liquid from the puncture. He sucked hard, moving his tongue in the same rhythm in which he was still moving inside of me, thrusting deep and slow as I found my voice. A scream rose in my throat, not of pain, but of the most delicious pleasure that I had ever experienced. As he drank, I felt him erupt inside of me, so powerful was his release that he held me down, pinning my body to the bed, unyielding in his pulses, they came fast and rough. My arms still restrained, I felt a rush of heat and a surge of desire flood between my legs, my body quivered. He was breathing hard watching me and shimmering in and out of form.

"Ana, open your eyes. I want to see you; I want to see you feeling me." He was breathless and begging in his tone, and I groaned deeply as I felt his hands move, they slipped down between my thighs, gently rubbing, and bringing me to my full release. "God, your taste; the way you feel, I can't stop..." He grunted and snarled pushing forcefully against me as he drank. He withdrew himself and let me feel just how hard he was as he ran himself between my legs, rubbing and teasing me. I groaned loudly as he bent his head back to my neck. His lips were still lapping up the blood that was now flowing freely, and I felt his tongue turn coarse and prickly as he sealed my wound. He licked his lips and brought his mouth down on mine, kissing me deeply. I could taste the salt from the blood, but I could also taste something sweet in the after flavor. He entered me again, moving slowly, moaning softly.

Finally, I felt that he was finished, he was satiated and he rolled off of me, lying back with a deep exhale. Our bodies still, we listened to each other's attempts at calming our breathing and at quieting the desire that I knew we were both still experiencing. Minutes, maybe hours passed, then I heard him shift his weight next to me. Propping himself up on his side, he let his eyes roam over my naked and.bloody body.

Slowly, he ran his tongue down over my stomach, his eyes watching my response to him. He gently moved his mouth between my legs. He paused at my groin and I felt his finger push inside of me reaching and searching, and I moaned with pleasure listening to him laugh softly.

"Hmmm, still so sensitive…god I love that," he whispered and I turned my face toward him and saw that he was still watching my body responding to his touch, to his mouth on my thigh. Then, as his eyes blazed, I let my legs fall open, wanting to accommodate his need and mine. With his finger still in me and with his other hand, he pressed my legs open wider, exposing the pulse in my groin. Massaging me slowly with his fingers, I felt his lips press into the flesh and then the familiar sharp pain and desire, the deep sucking of my blood into him…I groaned again as Patric came deep and fast empting himself and me.

I was bloody and sweaty and the fragrance of our mutual physical passion lingered in the air around us. I was sure that this wasn't the most attractive appearance that I could have hoped for, but that was the consequence of making love with a Vampire, even one that was half. Throwing his head back, I heard Patric laugh, a deep hearty laugh, and one that I had never heard out of him before. He pulled me next to him on the bed, entwining me in an intimate embrace, both of us breathing softly into the fading darkness between us.

"Actually Ana, your current state couldn't be more appealing," he said softly and he reached out to touch my newly acquired bite marks. I watched as his face darkened and his eyes blazed.

"How do you feel?" I asked, trying to roll over on my side to get a better look at him; I was worried that his mood had so quickly shifted from laughing to what now looked like a deep sadness and longing. His fingers lingered on my inner thigh and I saw him lick his lips.

"Resurrected." The word hung in the air as it fell softly from his lips. He did look different. His hair was darker and richer in tone, and his eyes reflected deep pools of blue and liquid amber, blending into each other, adding yet another mystical quality to his already unearthly physical traits. His skin was flushed with color, his lips full and tinged with the subtlest of pink hues. I couldn't help but stare. He was watching me and again I saw a shadow move across his face.

"What's wrong," I asked, concerned that I had done something to offend him, that he was angry with me somehow. I reached to touch his face and he held my hand.

"What has happened here, what we've done, it doesn't change the course of my plans Ana. I wish I could say that things are different, that things will be different for us, but they aren't. I won't save you." He was looking up at the ceiling. I turned my face away from him and looked out the window. The sun was just beginning its journey into the morning sky and it shone down on Patric and me lying on my bed, the warm pulse of him still inside of me.

"I know Patric, I know and it's ok." And it was ok because I truly felt the honesty of that knowledge. "I love you, for all of your failings and in all of your missteps, I really do love you in some bizarre way, so for me, that's actually enough." I was amazed at how casually I was speaking, it was jarring. "I feel pretty lucky, really. I got to experience the love of Noni, of Kai, of Alec, of all my friends, my wolves—maybe even from you and Nathanial, although I know that you'll never admit it." The tears were rolling down my cheeks, but I wasn't crying from sadness or despair, I was crying from total and complete happiness. No matter what happened, it was going to be ok, and it was at that moment that I was fully able to grasp just what Noni meant about living your true Life after your soul is gone. I had so much love in my soul, that my Life was going to be glorious in its return to the earth and if I was lucky, in its return to all of the people who were kind enough to love me back. I sighed into the dim light and I felt deep silence move around me and I knew, that Patric was gone.

Patric

I felt strong. Control and energy coursed through my veins. Physically, I could *feel* that I moved differently, stood taller, walked with a longer, more sinuous gate. Mentally, my mind was sharp, every detail in my memory, every image that my brain processed was clear, focused. I was so close now, so close to achieving my deepest desires. My heart was racing with the anticipation, but I was going to have to wait a bit longer, to practice patience. Everything was now dependent upon him, upon his love for her and his promise to me. My new mental clarity, the extreme focus I was now able to have, allowed for me to put her away, to not conjure her face, to not remember holding her in my arms. My body's physical memory however, was proving difficult to quell. I craved her, my blood nourished by hers; I needed her. I was going to have to work very hard at not allowing too much contact with her. Keeping her alive, hovering on the brink of death was crucial for the full execution of my plan. She couldn't know this yet; it would be necessary for me to monitor her condition. I needed to know how her body was processing what had happened between us. I had given her part of me, but not the part that could save her, and mixed with Nathanial's blood and his poison, her system would most likely begin to weaken very quickly and shut down. However, I was confident that I could watch her unnoticed. I would leave medicine for her at the Clinic, to be dispersed by my assistant, which would limit her access to me. I laughed at my use of the word "medicine". It wasn't of course a real medical treatment that I had been giving Ana for months now; it was something much, much better in its capacity to revive the body, to heal her physical wounds, to keep her alive until he could save her.

I marveled at how well things had gone so far. Occupied by thoughts of my own intelligence, of my own grand superiority, my mind slipped and I saw her, a clear vision that left me breathless in its sudden arrival behind my eyes. She was kneeling down by a box, in which she was placing in photographs. There were more images scattered around her, as if in some sacred circle and she traced her hands over each one and smiled. I scanned the floor around her and noticed four pictures placed separately from the rest, isolated in their importance, I guessed. Intrigued and unable to resist her face, I focused my mind closer in and could see very clearly the pictures that she valued above all others. The first was of a young woman, maybe seventeen, her arms wrapped around an old woman with long, white hair. Mountains rose up behind them, giving way to a horizon painted by a bright, red sunset. The rays shone off the girl's hair, setting it ablaze. She was beaming and her smile wide, reaching her eyes, made them glitter. The next photograph showed the same girl, now clearly a woman, in between two other people. One person I recognized immediately as Alec, whom I had known and hated for quite some time. The other person was a shorter, darker looking man, ethnic in descent, with dark curly hair and even darker eyes. They were holding her around the waist and squeezing her close as they laughed. Next to that photo was one that made my blood boil. The same woman was standing on a cliff, overlooking the sea, a turbulent sky as her backdrop. She was facing away from the camera, turned to the side, her hair blowing off her back and shoulders. She was gazing up at a man with long, straight, black hair, holding onto her outstretched hands, locking his fingers into hers as he faced her. Even from the photograph, I could feel the intensity of their bond, it radiated out from their bodies, and it was in the air around them, light and pure.

Anger and jealousy flooded into my heart and for a moment all I could see was a deep black in the space where she was sitting. Clearing my mind, I turned to the last photo, the one she was now gently touching and I gasped without restraint. A photo of two people, her face turned toward the lens, the other face turned toward her. She was smiling a soft and beautiful grin, her lips full and her eyes deep and clear. But it wasn't her face that garnered my attention; it was the other face, the one turned toward her. The person's gaze upon her was so intense, so completely unaware of the world around him that I almost felt embarrassed to be looking so closely at such an intimate moment. I could feel the desire, the need

150

filtering out from the eyes that looked at Ana. I could feel such a complete sense of love that it overwhelmed me. I knew those eyes, in their purist form, in the form they had from birth. They were my mother's eyes—a color so rare and brilliant in their translucency, with the irises housed in a deep, penetrating turquoise. I felt myself begin to choke and gasp as I tore my mind's eye away from the scene, away from her. Coming out of my trance, I clutched at the pain in my chest, it was squeezing, compressing everything that I knew to be real. Falling to my knees, I cried out in despair as I saw yet another flash of her face, her body moving under mine, whispering... whispering that she loved me. I felt my chest grow warm, then hot and I grasped my amulet as it became suddenly fused into my flesh. I looked down to see a single jewel, a star now embedded in the center, Ana's star from her mark. My heart shattered and I collapsed, face down into the earth.

Nathanial

I stood near the vast picture window, looking out toward the volcano. Turning my face up to see the moon and the stars, I was feeling anxious, jittery. My journey back to Indonesia had been long and tiresome. I had been gone for more than six months. Alec had advised me against going to see Patric so soon after my return. He thought I should take some time to observe Ana from a distance of course, to get a grasp on the reality that was now hurdling toward both of us. Clearly, Alec lost the argument. I had been waiting for my brother for over an hour, and now I could sense that he was getting closer to home. He would know that I was here, that I was waiting—he always knew.

"I'm glad to see that you haven't forgotten just how tuned in to you I am, Nathanial." I heard snickering behind me and I whirled to see Patric standing over at the bar, pouring himself a drink. I hadn't heard him come into the living room. My eyes surveyed him quickly. Physically, he looked better than I had ever seen him, his face clear and smooth, and his hair dark and glossy—a shade lighter than my own. I could see the tensed veins and tendons of his musculature, his limbs looked solid, chiseled. I let my gaze flow to his eyes, and immediately he looked down. "Well, I think that there will be plenty of time for you to provide some sort of assessment of me later," he said as he took a slow sip from his glass, and licked his lips. "But I'm guessing you are here for much more important things, no?" He was still standing back from my position at the window and his face remained cloaked in shadows. He turned his back to me and wandered over to the fire that was now ignited in the fireplace. I stared at him. He passed his hands over the flames, watching as the tips of his fingers slowly began to morph and shift into small fires of their own. He took another slow sip from his drink and I waited for him to speak. "Hmmm," he mused softly. "Where should we start Nathanial? Perhaps I should first ask you how you are doing, physically I mean." Immediately, I knew that he could sense my weakened state, nothing that would necessarily hinder my health in any severe way, but it was nonetheless uncomfortable for me and he knew this. He laughed quietly. "Yes, I suppose 'uncomfortable' would be an accurate enough description of your current condition, but you appear to be managing quite well. Your memory has returned, yes? Your

152

General friend proved quite a guide for you in being able to recall those horrible, horrible events, so I suppose that was helpful to you, otherwise you wouldn't be here." His voice was flat, monotone and dark. "Good thing I was able to get past his heavy mental armor, at least enough to lead him down the right paths, and propel him to find you…" He turned to me, laughing at my complete surprise. "Oh come on!" he chortled, "Alec is smart, but you didn't honestly think he was going to be able to piece all of this together on his own? There's too much history involved, even for a quasi Bonder General to decipher." He passed his fingers back over the flames, chuckling softly. What the hell was he talking about? There was nothing quasi about Alec. Patric shook his head as if I was missing something. He continued. "Of course, I kept the most crucial piece of information from him, he needn't know everything." He paused, gazing into the fire. "Odd really," he turned toward me, "the closer I became with Ana, the easier it was for me to get into Alec's head. It was as if our connection, Ana's and mine, was actually helping to enhance my mental abilities. You really did choose an exceptional woman to Bond and of course I don't have to tell you that she has many other talents beyond just her providing 'mental' advantages." He licked his lips slowly, and sighed softly. "Nathanial, I really should give you your props—well done!" Rage shot from my body and I lunged at him. Smashing the glass from his hand, I grabbed him around the neck and jarred my knee into his groin, bending him forward.

"SHUT UP YOU FUCKING BASTARD! SHUT UP!" I was growling and snapping at him as pure, white-hot anger, hatred and jealously flooded my blood like fire and ice. He placed his hands on his knees and laughed. He licked the blood trickling down from his hand and smiled at me. I felt nauseous.

"Well," he said breathing hard, "it looks like sharing our sexual experiences with Ana, are going to be off limits." He threw his head back and laughed again, "It's good to know where the boundaries are my brother—it's always good to know." He moved back over to the bar and poured himself another drink. I couldn't do this, I couldn't be here listening to him; it was all too much. "Oh come now, you just got here, and we have so much to discuss, I promise that I won't make you listen to or see anything that will piss you off, ok?" He took a long swig from his glass and finishing the drink in one hit, he poured another. "I'm sorry, where are my manors, a drink?" He held out the bottle of scotch. I turned away from him, growling my disgust. I focused my attention on the moon, thinking of her.

"You possessed Alec?" I was reeling from this information and I wanted an explanation. I was also eager to shift the conversation away from Ana.

"Possession is not quite the right word, more like 'heavily influenced'. The inclination to figure out why I had returned was already there, I just helped to nudge him in the right direction, well, the direction that I wanted him to go." Patric smirked and placed his glass on the bar. "It's quite easy once you practice a bit, and of course, the fact that he has a great love and friendship for Ana, that just made it easier to keep him obsessed with finding answers."

"Alec said he had help, friends' of friends who remembered things, who were skeptical about the attack on me—did you get to them as well?" Disbelief colored my tone.

154

"No," he spoke dismissively. "They had the accurate information, I just wanted Alec to draw the right conclusions from that information—really it's just about how best to use your energy." Smiling, he moved across the room back toward the fire. "I am very sorry about the attack Nathanial." His voice was quiet now. "It's not something that I'm proud of, not something that I had wanted you to experience." I could barely hear him. "But I just couldn't see any other way. I was sure that you had forgotten our little agreement, sure that you were trying to create a life without me…I couldn't have that now could I? I mean, a deal's a deal. Still, if it helps, I made sure that Alec would see the attack. I made sure he knew what to do. I didn't want you to die Nathanial." I snorted loudly. His head snapped up to look at me. "I never wanted you to die." Frustrated and angry, I spat back at him,

"Not because you *love* me Patric, not because you feel some spiritual bond to me as my brother, my twin; you didn't want me to die because my death would have leveled your entire plan for return, you need me and *that* is the *only* reason that I'm still alive." My tone was venomous and filled with hate. "That and because Ana fulfilled her side of our exchange without ever knowing what was going to happen to her…" I said more quietly, the pain in my chest no longer allowing me to continue.

"Well, what's done is done Nathanial." He moved back from the fire, his tone composed and casual. "You survived and now you are here and we should figure out, together, what our next steps are going to be. Ana is going to need you and you have some decisions to make, especially now, with things having taken such an interesting turn." I glared at him, what

155

was that supposed to mean? What turn had things taken? What was he talking about? He grinned, his face twisted and sadistic in his knowledge.

"I suppose I could just show you, it's much easier and so much more fun, edited of course, since I did promise to spare you from seeing anything that might make you upset…although I can't make any guarantees of course." He was smirking at me. "Care to have a look?" I exhaled, defeated; I waved my hand for him to proceed.

"Make it quick," I growled.

"Sure, sure." He laughed. I closed my eyes and felt my mind go blank. I waited for the familiar pressure that was an endemic part of Patric's talents. The haze in my mind began to swirl and rearrange itself into a composed scene. I was seeing Ana's bedroom, I'd know it anywhere. From some deep place inside, I heard myself recall the space as "our bedroom". I heard laughter in my head—Patric. The swirling haze moved the scene to the bed, the image was blurred, Patric's doing I was sure, however, it wasn't hard to see what was happening. I saw him above her, moving slowly, caressing her face with his hands. Her back arched, and I watched her mouth move in a silent groan. I was suddenly thankful that Patric had sparred me the audio track to this little fantasy. *More like reality, Nathanial.* I heard his voice in my head and I felt my lips pull back over my teeth. More laughter. The scene swirled again and I saw that their movement had stopped, that Patric was holding his face close to hers, they were speaking to each other. She brought his face to her throat and I saw her body shiver, then I saw the blood, seeping like some dark, red ocean current, onto the white fabric of the bedspread. I heard myself gasp, and cry out. NO! NO! This was all wrong, this had not happened. He wanted me to see this, to think that she had obliged his deepest desires. For some sick reason, I had the need to look, to see up close what was happening. I forced myself to control Patric's memory and I zoomed in on their faces. I saw my brother lift his eyes to stare at Ana, there was something in his body, and something in the way he held her that captivated me. I felt Patric struggling against my control over his memory. I moved my mind's eye closer, focusing on the vision of my brother. Something was off, something was different, but I couldn't place it. Closer yet, I dared to move and then I saw something that I had not seen since our time as children, since we would spend hours together playing and running into the depths of the jungle, climbing onto our father's lap, laughing and kissing him; I saw Patric's eyes, the clear turquoise blue of our mother. I saw them looking at Ana, memorizing her face, seeing into her soul, I saw them, saw him, loving her. Suddenly, a terrible pain ricocheted through my mind, piecing my brain and sending the vision of Patric into total blackness. Gasping, I pulled myself up off the wooden floor where I had collapsed and whirled to face him. His head was in his hands and his breathing was labored and raspy. My mind couldn't comprehend what I had just seen, what sudden change had occurred in my brother.

"Get the hell away from me Nathanial, get-out-of-my-house," he said each word, slowly, deliberately, as if it was suddenly laborious for him to speak. I moved toward him a fraction of an inch in some deep compulsion to comfort him—could that be right? Watching my brother in his complete and utter despair, did I want to reach out to him, to have him tell me how

157

he'd loved her, how she'd changed the very core of who he was, of who he wanted to be? Did I want him to know that I understood his feelings, that I knew about the love he had for Ana, the desperate desire he had to be with her—she had been mine and I had betrayed her, we both had. I reached toward him, and then pulled my hand back. I turned slowly away from the fire and from my brother and walked out of his house, without glancing back.

Ana

"Stop moving Ana, I can't get to your vein!" I kept yanking my arm away from Alec each time he approached me. I didn't mind needles, I just didn't want them anywhere near my veins. He came at me with the syringe and I felt Kai gently squeeze my hand.

"God Ana, for someone who has bigger muscles than I do, you sure are a big baby!" he scoffed at me. I jerked my head to the side and mouthed a *"fuck you"*. He stuck his tongue out at me. I felt a quick prick and whipped my head back around just in time to see Alec stepping back, smiling as he admired his work and Kai's ability to distract me.

"There, that ought to do it, the nausea should subside here in a bit." Alec patted my head and turned to throw out the needle. In the last month, my condition had pretty much deteriorated, most likely from what had transpired between Patric and myself. He hadn't given me any of his blood needed to complete the exchange and according to Alec, it would have to be a significant amount. Of course I had told Kai about what I'd done, who in turn told Alec, who then proceeded to badger me for hours on end about what, in my right mind, had I been thinking. Alec was convinced that Patric had managed to possess me into giving him my blood—to seduce me, and Alec wouldn't listen to my explanation that I thought that I did love Patric in some weird way and that I had truly hoped that he would make a different choice; that he didn't have to love me or even care about me, but that maybe he would be able to resurrect some connection he had to Nathanial and he would pick a different path—he didn't have to save me, but maybe he would choose to save himself, save himself from bitterness and greed, and save himself from losing a sibling that he was lucky enough to have in his life, they could try again, recover and heal as brothers.

Alec was incensed with Patric and had taken to picking up my medicine from the clinic himself. He had also taken to treating some of my more mild symptoms, utilizing his rusty medical training. He actually was a very skilled doctor and I trusted him implicitly. I had not heard from Patric since our night together weeks ago, and I figured that now that he'd gotten what he needed to carry out the rest of his plans, well, that I most likely wouldn't see him again anytime soon. Patric made his choice and it wasn't the one that I had so stupidly hoped for. Over the last several weeks, I had a sense that both Alec and Kai were keeping something from me, trying to protect me from some knowledge that they both possessed. I had been feeling so ill lately that I didn't have enough energy to really consider what was going on with the two of them. My physical health had taken such a sudden and severe turn, that Kai and

159

Alec had moved me into their home so that one of them could monitor me at all times. I was not pleased. I missed my own home and my own bed. I missed the trees in my backyard and the cliffs leading to the Preserve. Alec and Kai had a sprawling beach house and while I enjoyed being so close to the ocean, seeing the constant waves crashing onto the shore just made me really, really sad. The tides always reminded me of Nathanial, and the frequent storms that seemed to be constantly churning on the horizon, reminded me of Patric—I couldn't win.

Every once in a while, when Kai or Alec would open the windows, I would smell the two fragrances that I had come to know so well, the scents that now were running through my blood, coursing in my veins, honey and lemon, woods and musk; sandalwood and vanilla. Together they proved to evoke powerful and visceral memories for me, memories that were no longer separated and distinct parts of my life, but entwined, merged together, bonded. Whatever medicine that I was still receiving from Patric seemed to be keeping my deterioration in a somewhat uncomfortable, but stable state and every time Alec returned from the Clinic, I knew he saw the questions in my eyes, my desire to know if he had seen him, if they had spoken, if he had asked about me. Alec never answered, whether it was because he had not in fact seen Patric, or because the more probable was true, that he had seen Patric and Patric had not bothered to ask about me at all. Yet still, here he was, making sure that I had some treatment to help me, something to keep the worst of the pain away, something that showed that perhaps he still thought about me, about us and still cared.

"Ana, Kai and I need to make a quick run out to see some colleagues of mine. It's a ridiculous fundraiser that the law firm is hosting. We won't be long, just an hour or two. I'm putting your phone on the coffee table and here's the remote to the TV. Call if you start to feel bad, alright?" Alec was speaking so fast that I could barely follow what he had said—he was terrified of leaving me.

"That's totally fine Alec, no worries, I'm actually feeling much better…" Alec's eyes narrowed and he gave me the *"you're such a bull-shitter"* glare that he was now becoming famous for these days. I flipped him off, turned on the TV and heard him laugh as they left the house.

Actually, It was kind of nice to have the place to myself; Kai and Alec had been so vigilant in their care for me that I hardly had a moment to spend with myself. I nestled into the sofa and pulled the blankets up around me. Piyip was sleeping on the outside deck and Kuckuc was up to her usual pacing around my feet. That's all she was capable of doing lately, I could sense her concern for me and I tried to soothe her anxiety by stroking her head and whispering her name gently in her ear. I flipped through the channels, finding nothing of particular interest and finally settled on the BBC news. My ill health had kept me spending most days and nights sleeping and I felt a bit out of the loop, information-wise. Lots of uprisings around the globe seemed to be the main concern, nothing new there to report, I thought to myself, but then the anchor shifted his attention to a story in West Papua New Guinea. A mass slaughtering had occurred out in one of the indigenous communities. One hundred Bonders and humans had been slain, mutilated and their land burned. I struggled to sit up, rousing Kuckuc off of my lap.

The footage showed bodies lying bloodied and strewn across the streets of the main village. Children, women, men, young boys—no one had been spared. I forced myself to look away from the carnage. The anchor reported that authorities were still trying to decipher if the attack had been between the Bonders and the humans, or was there some outside instigator that attacked both groups. I didn't have to decipher anything, I knew exactly who was responsible for such violence and malice, just who had been waiting for centuries to retaliate for their fall from power and who now had a strong enough leader to initiate such terror; Patric and his Vampires, it had begun.

I felt a sudden wave of terror and guilt encapsulate my body. I heaved forward, sobbing and hyperventilating. This was all my fault. How was it that I too was not responsible for such destruction when I had freely allowed for the most vengeful, the most corrupt being to return to power? How could I have believed that my love, that any love really, would make him reconsider, would allow for him to find redemption and forgiveness in the possibility of a different life, perhaps a life with me—how could I have been so manipulated and so very, very, stupid? Ugh, I felt nauseous again and rested my head back against the pillows trying to control the urge to vomit. I tried breathing slowly through my mouth, hoping that I could wish away what I knew was coming. I launched myself over the side of the couch and heaved the contents of my stomach onto the carpet, narrowly missing Kuckuc. She began to bark and Piyip darted in from the deck, hovering over me; they began to howl. Cold, damp sweat broke out over my skin, leaving me both hot and chilled. I stayed lingering over the couch just in case another wave hit. I felt the nausea subside and I slowly raised myself back into a lying position against the cushions. Again, I started breathing through my mouth, trying to calm the racing of my heart. The sweat evaporated and the hot flash quelled. God, I was exhausted and I felt like crap. Every bone in my body ached, my veins ached, if that was even possible and my head hurt. I closed my eyes and fell asleep.

I awoke some time in the night, under the covers and in bed, having been placed there by Kai or Alec, I was sure. The window was open and I could hear the soft, rhythmic lapping of the waves as they pulsed onto the shore. I sighed and realized that my mouth was extremely dry and my tongue felt swollen. I wanted some water. I slowly swung my legs around to the floor and steadied myself against the sudden onslaught of dizziness that rocked my head. Moving at an incremental pace, I made it to my bathroom and noticed that my door had been left cracked. I should just get Kai and Alec a baby monitor, it would probably be a ton easier I mused. As I went over to shut the door, I heard voices, they were quiet in their volume, but I could tell that the tones were urgent and desperate. At first I thought it was just Kai and Alec arguing over what the best course of treatment for me might be, but I quickly realized that there were more than just two voices speaking. There was a quieter and gentler voice filtering down the hallway, a voice that sounded the most desperate, the most urgent and the saddest. I sucked in a giant breath, my heart seized and I felt my blood turn icy. I *knew* that voice, I had listened to that voice for months, I had memorized the quiet confidence, the soft tone, I had heard it murmur my name in the darkness of our room; it was Nathanial's voice. I exhaled loudly and immediately the voices stopped.

"Ana, are you alright?" It was Alec. He had heard me, they all had. I heard shuffling and chairs being pushed back. Alec was coming down the hall toward me. "Ana, what's the matter, are you feeling sick?" He was standing in front of me, blocking my view into the hallway. Adrenaline pumped into my veins and I pushed him aside. "Ana! Wait a minute Ana, just wait a minute please!" He grabbed for my sleeve and I whipped my arm around, shaking free of his grasp.

"Get off of me Alec!" I charged down the hallway and into the living room and then my legs just stopped moving. I felt Alec stop himself from running into the back of me as he put his hand on my shoulder and I reached back to touch him, to let him know I was ok. Nathanial was standing by the open window with his back to me. His hair, shinier and blacker than I remembered, blew over his shoulders as gusts of wind swirled around him. "Nathanial," I whispered. I didn't know what to feel or what to say. His name on my lips seemed to make my legs quiver and I felt Alec, still holding my shoulder, move his arm around my waist, trying to hold me steady. "Nathanial, please look at me." Again, my voice came only in a hush. I watched him as he slowly turned from the window to face me. He was more beautiful than I had ever seen him. The blood that he had received from me must have transformed his appearance, enhanced it so he looked like himself, but more otherworldly—enchanting and intoxicating. As these thoughts filtered around in my mind, I saw that Nathanial had bowed his head, the fall of long, black hair mimicking a dark curtain that shrouded his face. Had he heard what I'd been thinking, of what my assessment was of him? Could he read minds fully now?

"Yes," I heard him say so quietly that I found myself leaning closer to him, moving to close the distance between us. Just as I started to take a step toward him, my body filled with an intense anger and an intense love, but both were housed in such deep pain and anguish that I had to stop moving and grasp the back of the sofa to keep from lunging at him. Nathanial's face snapped up and he stared at me, unblinking.

"Ana," I heard Alec say as he rushed back to my side. "Just calm down, you don't need to be getting upset, you don't have the energy for this." He was grasping my waist tightly. I took a deep breath and stepped back into Alec's arms. I cocked my head to the side and spoke directly to Nathanial, trying to keep my tone even.

"So I'm guessing that Alec here tracked you down, told you what happened with me and your brother, made you feel incredibly guilty for not being strong enough to find your own way back to me, and so now here you are trying to decide if you are, yet again, going to spare my life." My words were coming so rapidly and I could no longer keep the tenor of my voice calm. "It's like we've come full circle. Almost, but not quite because you see," I said, my tone was quiet and possessed, with a sinister undercurrent that I had never experienced from myself. "I'm actually worse off than I was before I met you and you are, well quite clearly, you are better off—thanks to me of course." My words dripped with sarcasm. "And let's see, your brother who was worse off before meeting me, well, he's now also better off, thanks to me." Anger rose again in my chest and I could feel the volume of my voice ratcheting up higher; I was yelling at him now, screaming actually, my blood beginning to boil and my skin starting its now familiar swelling, "SO LET'S TALLY THAT UP SHALL WE? NATHANIAL—BETTER! PATRIC—BETTER! ANA—DYING! Oh and let's not forget that I am also once again, having to put my life in your hands or the hands of your brother, two people who don't have the best track records for unselfish behavior!" I was now right in front of Nathanial, breathing hard and glaring at him. "You, my friend, have gotten yourself into quite a dilemma haven't you? Oh you *could* spare my life, but then, as we all now know, that would mean you would have to work with Patric—that would be a bummer! Or, you could choose *not* to save me and to let Patric find another way to return to power, and maybe we could all just put our faith in Patric and hope that he can find enough decency to want me to survive and for him to save me himself." I was holding Nathanial's shoulders and shaking him, "Ah, but here's the kicker Nathanial, here's the genius of your brother that you failed to overlook—yet again. By not replenishing what I gave to him—willingly I might add," I turned to glare at Alec, "by not helping me in return, your brother has left me in such a weakened state, that even if he *is* the one to try and spare my life—I wouldn't survive the transaction! You have to hand it to him, to Patric I mean; he's a fucking genius isn't he? Either way he's gotten what he wants." I looked at Nathanial, his eyes bright and wide. "Perhaps, Patric and Alec both have overestimated *you* Nathanial." I let my grip on his shoulder slacken and I turned to look at the moon, almost talking to myself now, fire burning underneath

166

my skin. I was so furious, but not just with Nathanial but also with myself, for being so stupid with my heart, for wanting to believe that even if someone was so broken and lost, that they would have the strength to redeem themselves, that if they knew that someone loved them, that someone was trying to understand their journey, that maybe they would find the courage to remember themselves. I shook my head. It didn't matter; nothing I did mattered. Nathanial was staring at me, his eyes wide and turbulent. I pressed my fingers to my temples feeling my anger and my ignorance rise violently. I looked at him, realizing everyone's mistake. "See, they both were counting on something that I know you never had, they're counting on this, this *thing*, for two very different reasons. Patric's counting on it so that he can use it to manipulate you into keeping your promise, and Alec, well he's just hoping that you'll use it because he doesn't want to see me die. Can you guess what it is Nathanial? Can you guess what it is Alec and Patric *think* that you have, and that I *know* you don't?" I was holding his face in my hands, forcing him to look me in the eyes. "No? You don't know? Well, let me enlighten you; it's *love* Nathanial. Alec and Patric are counting on the fact that you *love* me enough to save me yourself. It was a fatal error in judgment because we both know that you never loved me, not truly, not the way that I grew to love you." I pushed his face away and turned my back to him. "So now here we are, all of this trouble spent on tracking you down, all of the plans Patric so meticulously set out—all of these things based on one, small, stupid and wrong assumption. It's really funny how such a collective of brilliant minds with centuries of experience can make such a crucial mistake. It actually makes me feel better about all of the crap that I've screwed up in my life—I

167

mean if you guys can do it...well..." I laughed bitterly at the room. "It doesn't matter what you decide Nathanial, because like I told Patric, I truly do not care. Do what you want; save me, don't save me, because it really does not matter. What's happing here, what's happening out there in the world, what Patric wants, it's much bigger than me, much greater than my single journey on this planet. I've reconciled things within myself and I'm ok with what's happened, with the decisions that I've made. I'm glad that I loved Patric and," my voice fell to a whisper and I felt my breath catch in my chest, "and I'm glad that...that, I loved you. It's over, just do what you are going to do." I waved my hand toward his shadow, and then a sudden lashing of nausea hit me, doubling me over onto my knees.

"Ana!" I heard Nathanial shout. I heaved and vomited violently onto the floor. I felt Nathanial wrap his arms around my back and sweep my hair from my face.

"We need to get her back in bed," Kai and Alec were telling Nathanial. I felt his arms move under me, scooping me up and pressing me into his chest.

"Good god, Nathanial, I don't need to be carried, put me down for Christ sake." I tried to sound militant in my orders to him, but my body and my voice were weak, and I ended up sounding like a small child having a ridiculous tantrum in the arms of their parent.

"Shut up," he said quietly in my ear and proceeded to carry me back to bed.

Her breathing was labored and she was making soft wheezing gasps from her throat. I had seen her deterioration in my mind; it had been quick, soon after seeing him for the first time in so many months—an emotional trigger most likely, but I was waiting, waiting for him to come to me, and in his complete desperation, to tell me that he was ready. I smiled at my perfect execution, at how everything had fallen into all the right places and I was finally going to get what I had spent years trying to achieve; it was all right in front of me—in front of us, I mused. I heard Nathanial snort at my correction. "Oh, come on, it's not so bad, at least she'll live, at least we're giving her a chance to continue her life."

"*We've* given her a chance? *We?*" Nathanial moved to face me. "*We've* done nothing of the sort, *we* made her suffer, hurt, *we* made her feel unloved, unwanted…" He trailed off in his own disgust.

"Well, I choose to see it differently." I laughed softly. "I mean, if it hadn't been for me, she would have been a goner long before now, and you would never have known until it was too late of course." I saw him whirl around and blur over to my position near the window, forcing me to stagger back a few steps.

"Excuse me? Just what the hell are you talking about; 'if it wasn't for you', what did you do that hasn't left her destroyed, still loving you, still wanting you to have a better

life as she suffers—what could you have possibly done?"
Nathanial asked and I laughed again, and patted his shoulder.

"Nathanial, how exactly do you think she's being kept alive,
kept mostly healthy up until our little tryst that is? How do
you think that works? It most certainly didn't come from you,
we both know that." He snarled at me and I smiled at him. "So,
how was I going to keep Ana well and alive until you could be
found after your 'episode' and reminded about your promise
to me? What is it that I could have possibly done?" I raised my
eyebrows at him, letting the information sink in.

"No, no, you didn't, you couldn't have, she'd be...she'd be..."

"Like me?" I asked enjoying his utter disbelief. "I made sure
not to give her enough of my blood to initiate any
transformation, Bonder or otherwise, but just enough to keep
her alive, a little trick that I learned during my self-imposed
exile. Plus, I'm only half; I'm not the best person to actually
change her Nathanial," I said. I saw Nathanial's eyes widen; he
looked frightened and sick.

"Patric! Do you realize what you've done? Do you realize how
stupid you've been?" He was speaking violently and his body
was shaking. I couldn't place the source for his anger or his
fear. He was pacing around the room manically. He stopped
to kneel by Ana, and I watched as he took a damp towel and
brushed it against her skin. She murmured and turned toward
him. I had to look away.

"What's the problem Nathanial?" I was trying to sound casual,
but something in his voice was sending terror right into my
heart.

170

"The problem is, Patric," his jaw was clenched and he growled, deep and menacing, "The problem is—"

"She can't have both Bonder and Vampire blood in her system," a quiet voice spoke, interrupting Nathanial. It was Alec. He moved from out of the shadows in the room and crossed over to stand next to Ana's bed. His fingers traced along the bite marks on her neck and I suddenly felt a deep longing, a pull to be with her, to touch her as well. He looked up at my face, sensing my desire and I saw his eyes darken. "Humans can't handle both types of blood Patric, their system becomes overwhelmed and it will crash, killing them, even in small dosages," he spoke softly to me, like I was a child hearing the worst possible news.

"What?" I whispered. "What are you saying?" I asked warily.

"He's saying that you've effectively killed her, you stupid, fucking bastard!" Nathanial grabbed my shoulders and threw me across the room. I heard Ana moan and I steadied myself.

"Outside, both of you!" Alec commanded. "Kai, can you come in here please?" Kai entered the room, his eyes were flat and hollow, and they were also red and swollen—he'd been crying ever since I had arrived. "Sit with her ok?" I watched as Alec gently touched Kai's cheek and exited the room with us behind him. I collapsed onto the couch, not comprehending anything, my resilient high just moments before had now turned into a crushing weight of despair of confusion. Alec moved to the window and I craned my neck forward, trying to listen. "She's far too weak now, too weak I mean, to be saved by you or Nathanial," Alec spoke as he turned the full force of his eyes upon me and I had to look away. "She'll never

171

survive the exchange if you are to be the one to save her, to give her your blood or Nathanial gives her his. She's too far-gone health-wise. By keeping her alive with small dosages of your blood Patric, she now has that blood flowing through her veins and if mixed with Nathanial's," he motioned toward my brother, "well...the probability of her living through such an assault on her body, it's just highly unlikely. I've never known any Human to be able to possess both Bonder and Vampire blood, even if that Vampire is truly only half." He looked at me again, as if reminding me of my past and current betrayals. Anger erupted inside my head. How could I have had such a miscalculation, how could I have not foreseen such consequences? I was being torn apart. My mind was forcing me to acknowledge the inevitability that my plan for a full return may now be in jeopardy, but my heart, my heart was aching with the even more probable likelihood that Ana would die regardless of whatever action we decided to take. I was split into two halves—irreconcilable in my anger and in my love.

"You don't love her!" Nathanial spat towards me, clearly hearing what had just played out in my mind. "You god-forsaken bastard, you never loved her!" His words slapped me across the face and rage erupted from deep within my soul. I turned toward him in malice and despair. Lunging, I dug my fingers into his mark over his heart, making him scream, paralyzing him. Keeping my fingers pressing down on his chest, I dragged him down the hall into Ana's room.

"DO IT!" I yelled at him! Digging my hands into the metal carvings in his flesh, he screamed again. "DO IT NOW! If you don't, I WILL KILL HER IN FRONT OF YOU, NOW DO IT!" I kicked him in the stomach, doubling him over. He tried to move away from me. I swiped him across the head, "DO IT!" I yelled again, gasping in my fury. From the corner of my eye, I saw Alec blur to Nathanial's side. I turned on him and pushed my fist, hard into the center of his chest, sending him hurdling back against the wall. I grabbed Nathanial from the waist and threw him toward Ana in the bed. She was choking and her chest was rising and falling rapidly.

"Alec?" I heard my brother cry out. "Alec what can I do?"

"DON'T ASK HIM!" I shouted at my brother. "You'll do what you promised me, what you *owe* me—you'll do what I tell you, you spineless thug!" Again, I swiped him across his face, splitting his lip. With the amount of Ana's blood in my system, I was stronger than he was and he knew it—he wasn't fighting back, the sorry sack of shit!

 "Alec?" I heard him say again, "Can we do anything, after the exchange? Is there anything we can try to do to save her?" I whirled around to stare at Alec, a strange feeling seeping into my chest upon hearing Nathanial's plea.

"I don't know Nathanial, I'll try…" Alec's voice trailed off.

"Alec, you must promise me, you have to promise me that you will do everything in your power to try to save Ana, please, you must promise me Alec!" My brother was holding out his arms toward Alec, begging; he was pathetic.

"I will do everything I can to save her, everything that I know, that is my promise to you." I looked at Alec and I saw that he was not staring at Nathanial while making this declaration, but at me. His eyes turned clear and I felt a deep pressure rise in my heart. I stepped back from him and turned to grab Nathanial's left arm, placing my nail over the vein. I heard Kai gasp and run from the room, coward.

"Wait!" Nathanial spoke to me. "Let me tell her what's happening, she has a right to know Patric." I didn't think Ana was in any condition to know what was going on, but I humored him. Still holding his wrist in my hand, I pushed him forward and closer to her. I watched as he bent his face towards hers, as if to kiss her, it made me sick

"Hurry up!" I growled at him.

"Ana," I heard him whisper, "it's going to be ok, I'm going to help you now ok? It won't hurt at all." I snickered. "I need you to do what I say, I know you're weak, but you need to do exactly what I say! Do you understand me?" God, he was speaking to her like she was a child.

"She understands Nathanial, now do it!" I was getting tired of these games, this needed to happen and it needed to happen now. Nathanial rose up from his position on the bed and I pulled his arm back toward me.

"I don't need your help, Patric." Nathanial's voice was trembling and dark.

"Fine, then get on with it!" I snapped. I saw Nathanial look once more at Alec, then he turned to me. For a brief moment our eyes locked and for the first time in many centuries, I saw my brother, my twin. I saw him in all of his despair, all of his panic and fear and I saw his strength and his weakness and I remembered in that brief moment, that we had been bonded as children, we had been bonded by our mother's love for us, in her complete and ultimate sacrifice—we lived and she perished. I heard myself gasp at this understanding between us and I felt my hold on my brother slip—just briefly. I heard Ana moan, breaking the spell of our gaze and bringing me back to my rage. "Now or I- will- kill- her!" I said quietly. With one more brief glance in my eyes, Nathanial lifted his fingernail to his wrist and slashed across the flesh, spilling crimson liquid down his arm. I watched him move closer to Ana and place his wrist to her lips, speaking quietly to her. Her body began to pulse and quiver as his blood entered her system. She heaved herself into the air sending Nathanial flying backwards, his blood splattering across my face as he crashed down beside me. She screamed, pain and agony shattering across the night sky and I saw Alec and Kai running to her side, trying to hold down her thrashing limbs. Blood was pouring from her mouth, from her eyes and I noticed from somewhere else— somewhere from below the sheets, dark red was beginning to creep across the lower part of her body. I stood unmoving, mesmerized by the amount of blood that was now oozing from her.

"Alec!" I heard Nathanial scream out next to me, "Alec, her legs, something is wrong with her legs!" Ana screamed again and I felt myself reach up to hold my ears, the sound was deafening and full of so much pain that I couldn't bare to listen to it anymore. I grabbed Nathanial up off the floor, blood streaming from his wrist. I wrapped my arm around his neck, choking him.

"LET'S GO!" I shouted at him, squeezing him harder. My mind was racing, the exchange had been made and it wouldn't be long before Nathanial would feel the effects, before I would benefit from his new strengths and powers. I felt him struggling against me, trying to get to her. I slammed him across the head, knocking him out. Wrapping my hands around his waist, I hoisted him up onto my shoulder and shimmered away from the scene, away from Alec and Kai, away from the impossible amounts of blood, away from the only woman that had ever been courageous enough to love me—away from watching her die.

Chapter Six

Ana

I sat in the sand, watching the tide come in and the sun sink, its red fire painting the deep white-blue horizon. Somehow, beyond all reason, I had survived. My body proved just strong enough and Alec, with his unparalleled skill, had worked tirelessly to revive me. Together, both had been enough to save my life—but I felt broken, shattered from the inside.

In the almost four months since my near death, I had spent every waking moment on the beach, searching the waves—for what, I didn't know. I knew Nathanial was gone. I knew Patric had betrayed me, had used me, and he was gone. I knew that they were both together now, planning and waiting for a war that couldn't be stopped. It had already begun. More attacks were being reported in the U.S. and across the globe. Familiar scenes of brutality and corruption, fear and cohesion—they were filtering their way into every part of daily life, slowly corroding the fragile balance between Bonders and humans. Like a cancer in every cell of our social and cultural autonomy, the rise of the Vampires, their monolithic need for revenge and control, threatened to destroy the collective body from the inside out. I felt sick. Not physically sick, but the kind of deep mental fatigue that seeps into your soul, your core. A sickness that makes you question your very presence on the earth and makes you wonder if letting go, if *not* holding on, if that's the better choice.

I knew that my moodiness was not going unnoticed by Alec or Kai, and Alec particularly had taken to staring at me when he thought I wouldn't notice. He sensed my malaise. Fortunately, I was able to get back to work, and therefore I had an excuse to get out from under Alec's penetrating gaze. Lately, my job was requiring me to evaluate various animal attacks on indigenous people from the outer islands. This was not my favorite type of work as it required long trips out to villages to assess what was left of a body or bodies, and so many times I spent my hours consoling the families of children who were the main victims of these brutal attacks. Wolves or rogue and rabid primates were usually to blame, and helping the people to initiate practices that changed their daily lives so as to decrease their chances of a run-in with these animals, always proved challenging.

Today was no exception. I had taken a small plane out to West Papua and was due to meet up with a team of wildlife biologists and anthropologists to examine what appeared to be a mass grave of human remains. My supervisor, Caleb, a Bonder himself and someone who had shown me the kindest of support and friendship during my past ordeals, was nervous in sending me to meet with such a group. Apparently, my fellow colleagues were a collective of Bonders and Vampires who had somehow been able to put their differences aside to work on this particular case. Caleb was suspicious of such an alliance and managed to call me five times before I departed, each call getting more panicked and slightly manic in his anxiety. Bizarrely, I was not nervous at all. After everything that had occurred, after losing so much and regaining some semblance of a life, I just didn't have nearly as much fear in my heart as I usually did. To me, the scariest thing in the world was to love someone or in my case, love two people and then lose them both. To rebuild from that, well, really nothing seemed so scary anymore.

I exited the plane to a greeting of the most extreme heat and humidity that I had ever experienced. Immediately, I felt my shirt become one with my skin, as sweat seeped from my pores. My body felt constricted and suffocated by the wall of hot moisture and I was thankful that I had opted for a cotton tank and cargo shorts, but with this kind of heat, it just wasn't going to matter. Had it always been this hot here? I remember coming out to West Papua a few years ago, around the same time, and I distinctly remember that it was never this oppressive. Perhaps climate change was a real problem, I laughed to myself. I gathered my backpack and headed to the car rental to check in. Caleb had secured me a nice open-air jeep, but I was now wishing that he had opted for an air-conditioned sedan. Sighing loudly, I hauled my pack into the back seat and pulled out the directions to the village and headed out away from the landing strip.

The drive proved as scenic as I had remembered, but there was a distinct smell of burning wood in the air. Heavy, black smoke swirled up over the hills and in the trees alongside the road. It made the air foggy and dense and I noticed small particles of ash begin to accumulate on the windshield. I didn't think that the indigenous populations in this area were fans of slash and burn agriculture. In fact, on one of my first trips here, I had interviewed several tribal leaders about their sustainable practices. It seemed odd that they would have made such a leap and started to burn down their own vital forests. I made my way to the lodge where I was scheduled to

179

stay and where I assumed that I would meet my team. The lodge had just recently been built to support an increase in ecotourism to the island and it was definitely impressive. The foundation was erected into the surrounding forest and appeared to utilize natural materials from the local environment. Bamboo and red clay added a slightly African and South American feel, while beautifully landscaped walkways provided local flowers and plants, all of which enveloped the acreage with a lush, fragrant and tropical energy. Well, if I was going to have to deal with Vampires, at least my housing arrangements were going to be posh. I pulled into the enclave at the entrance and parked my jeep under several large palm trees. Just as I managed to make it up the creek stone walk way, my phone vibrated in my pocket. My first guess was that it would be Caleb, checking of course to see whether or not I had been attacked on my way from the airport to the lodge. Surprisingly, it wasn't Caleb, it was Alec.

"Ana." His voice sounded tense and I rolled my eyes.

"Hey Alec, what's going on?" I tried to make my tone light.

"I just wanted to make sure that you got to your destination alright. I thought we'd agreed that you would call us as soon as your plane arrived and I know for a fact that you arrived at the airport over an hour ago." Frick, I had forgotten to call. He sounded like an angry father, scolding a teenager who'd missed curfew and didn't check in. "Well, I actually don't have any children, so forgive me if I have taken to view you as my daughter or sister—I am over three hundred years your senior, I think that deserves a bit of respect, don't you?" Ugh, I hated how tuned in to me he was since saving my life; it was annoying. "I suppose I could have just let you die, but I'm guessing that Kai would have most certainly divorced me, and then where would I be?" He was trying to sound casual, but I knew that he was really upset.

"I'm really sorry Alec, you know how nervous I get trying to navigate directions, I just got a bit consumed with making sure I found the place. I've arrived and I haven't even checked in yet, but I was going to call as soon as I got to my room, I promise."

"Hmph, fine. Listen there's another reason that I called. I spoke with Caleb this morning." I knew this wasn't headed in a good direction. "He seems extremely concerned about cohort sent out to the island. I've been following the case in the papers and it's being called a 'historic collaboration' of species, mainly referring to the team of Bonders and Vampires. With all that seems to be going on as of late, with all of the increase in attacks on Humans, I just want you to be wary." I tried to interject, but reading my mind, Alec plowed on. "It makes both Caleb and me suspicious. We think that perhaps the Vampires are trying to assess whether or not people suspect that they are behind some of these attacks; the Bonders may also be part of the cover-up. I'm just not sure what's going on and I want you to be cautious in your recommendations to the team. You are going to have to use all of your diplomatic skills here Ana."

"Are you done?" I asked, laughing. "No, seriously Alec, I understand your concern and it's valid, really. But I'm actually just down here to tell the team if I think the attacks were animal induced and make recommendations to the local population about their interactions with the wildlife—I'm the least valuable person here!"

"Perhaps." Alec sighed. "But nonetheless, I just want you to be aware, and Ana," he paused for such a long time that I thought the connection had been cut. "Ana, you are anything but invaluable—you need to remember that please." His voice had an undercurrent of such emotion, that I felt my chest contract.

"Thank you Alec, I promise I'll use caution, it'll be ok, I'm only here for the week anyway…" I trailed off.

"Call me or Kai this evening and check in ok?" Alec asked, a slight edge to his voice.

"Will do! Love you!" I shut the phone and headed to check in.

****

After finally getting the key to my room, which actually turned out to be a private villa right on the beach, I was going to have to take Caleb out for a really nice dinner when I got back, I unpacked and surveyed my surroundings. My room was spacious with dark, hardwood floors and soft throw rugs scattered deliberately in the right places. I had a huge picture window that overlooked the ocean and the rising moon. I was also equipped with a stone-carved fireplace in the bedroom. I was really, really impressed. Suddenly, a wave of great familiarity crashed over me. This room, the layout, the furniture, it was all familiar, right down to the dim lights that washed the space in a soft, pulsating glow. Had I been here before? There's no way, I would never have been able to afford a place like this by myself, so why did I feel a sense of intimacy with the room? I didn't have time to ponder what was amounting to a very disturbing feeling now creeping into my chest. I was due in the main lodge for a dinner meeting with the team and I didn't have time to ponder my surroundings. I showered and changed into what I had hoped would be somewhat casual attire—my favorite turquoise cotton dress. I wanted to make a good first impression, but I also didn't want to look like I belonged on Wall Street instead of out in the field. I wore my hair twisted into a bun at the nape of my neck, covering most of my metal imprinting and pulled some loosely curled pieces around my face. I opted for a pair of casual sandals instead of pumps, checked myself one last time and sighed, it would just have to do.

Someone arrived in a golf-cart to take me up to the restaurant and I was thankful that I wouldn't have to walk, my hair with this humidity, would not be a pretty sight. My driver was chatty and I was happy to have the conversation. For some reason I could feel a sense of anxiety begin to filter into my chest and I used the dialogue on the way over as a distraction from my mounting unease. There were lots of cars being parlayed into various spots around the lodge, and the restaurant seemed to be catering to a large crowd this evening. I stepped out of the cart, tipped the driver and entered the huge lacquered doors to the dining room. I noticed immediately that there were two different dining levels, one huge outdoor deck area, and a dance floor that seemed to be accommodating the ever-growing crowd. I gave the hostess my name and she nodded motioning for me to follow her. Walking through the restaurant, I could see that the place was set for partygoers and business people alike. There was a good mix of tropical and reggae music that seemed to shift in rhythm and beat with the volume of the diners. I was so caught up in the atmosphere that I failed to notice that the hostess had led me to the outside deck where I quickly noticed a huge round table set up in a quiet corner allowing for a direct view of the now setting sun. I also noticed that the table was almost full. All of the attendees had their backs to me as they focused on the blood-red sky and the turquoise waters. I felt another wave of panic wash over me as I followed the hostess to my seat. The panic quickly turned to an intense feeling of self-preservation as I realized that the entire table, with the exception of two empty seats, was a tribe of Vampires. Immediately, I cleared my mind. An odd side-effect of having both Nathanial's and Patric's blood in my veins was that now I could keep anyone out of my head space with greater ease and with much more strength than I could do before. I hadn't yet been able to practice with Vampires, but I guessed that I'd find out soon enough if the enhancement was indeed a good one. I approached the table.

"You must be Ana," a Vampire asked as he shook my hand. I noticed that he was dressed very casually, but impeccably of course, his hair loose and flowing down to his waist. As he leaned over to take my hand, his shirt fell open at the neck and I caught a glimpse of something lying against his bare chest—a necklace of sorts. Unlike Bonders, Vampires were extremely rugged in both their physical looks and the way they dressed. Most of them opted for expensive distressed jeans, layered shirts, motorcycle boots and all usually sported some perfectly shaped five o'clock shadow on their face. They did wear their hair long, but I had seen some with shorter and more textured styles. Like Bonders, Vampires were exquisitely handsome, but their ruggedness seemed to give them a more organic and primal sexuality than Demons. The Vampire that I was currently staring at smirked, and I quickly looked away.

"Yes, I'm Ana, I didn't catch your name?" I put on the most casual and confident persona I had, I was good at acting; so apt was my skill that I was the best mediator in my entire organization.

"Devon, my name is Devon and this is Andres, Stephen and Christopher." He motioned to each man in turn. I noticed that every man's chest, with the exception of Stephen, also seemed to house some sort of necklace like Devon's, but I couldn't make out the shape or style and I didn't want to look too closely. I shook all of their hands and smiled appropriately. Frick! I was the only girl, at least so far. I sat down and turned to Devon.

"So, are we waiting for two more?" God, please let them be women, even Vampire women would be better than the current scenario.

"Oh, yes." Devon looked at me out of the corner of his eye as he sipped his drink. I swore that I could have seen one of the other men smirk at Devon's tone, like they all knew something that I didn't. I hated that feeling. I was suddenly thinking that Alec and Caleb had been right, this wasn't the most comfortable group to be around if you were a human. I had thought there were supposed to be Bonders as well. Where the hell were they? "We have one Bonder in our group, he'll be joining us shortly," Devon answered my unspoken thought. Holy shit, so my newly acquired mental ability was not going to work on Vampires, at least not these. Devon laughed and he turned to look at me. "We've heard quite a bit about you Ana and it's nice to finally meet you and you most certainly do not disappoint," he purred, as his deep gray eyes roamed over my neck and chest and I saw them darken slightly. How had any of these guys heard of me? I've never worked with any of them, at least any that I could remember.

"Your reputation precedes you," Stephen spoke softly and I noticed that he had a thick Irish accent. He leaned across the table and smiled shyly. He had the most devastatingly beautiful eyes, sea blue and crystal clear. I saw Devon shoot him a quick glance and he immediately moved back in his chair.

"As a mediator, he means," Christopher chimed in, he sounded the more outgoing of the group, but I sensed something dark in his voice. "You're one of the best, Caleb tells us."

"Well, I don't know about that, Caleb tends to over exaggerate things a bit. I enjoy my work, so perhaps that translates into being ok at what I do." I laughed.

"Nonsense, you're too humble, we know that your compassion and communicative abilities have navigated some very difficult cases and that's nothing to downplay." Again Devon turned to me, speaking as he poured me a glass of wine. Something about the way they all kept saying "we" was making me slightly uneasy. Devon caught my eye and winked. Good god, it was going to be a long night.

While we waited for the other members of the team, I learned that Devon and Andres were wildlife biologists. Christopher worked as an environmental attorney and Stephen as a professor of natural resource management and he played the guitar. All were compatible areas of study with my own, with the exception of my lack of musical ability, and I hoped that there wouldn't be too much disagreement between us when it came time to make recommendations. We were waiting on the anthropologist and a doctor, who Devon explained, had been called to the scene at the discovery of the mass grave. They were all extremely polite as Vampires went, and they managed to ask me more questions than I had ever been subjected to in my entire life. The discussion proved a distraction because I did not notice when our other two guests had arrived. I did, however, smell them.

I knew who was approaching before I even looked up from the table, their fragrances blurring together in a swirl of memory and emotion. Honey and lemon, woods and musk, vanilla and sandalwood, I felt my heart freeze. Everyone at the table rose at the entrance of the additional arrivals and I stood, preparing to face the two people who I had loved, the two people who felt my life was so expendable, that they both had betrayed me. Rising from my seat, I turned as Nathanial and Patric walked slowly toward our table. My mind was quick to assess both of their physical appearances and I was quite surprised at how different they both looked. Nathanial, who at least for as long as I had known him, wore his hair long and loose, always a satin ribbon of black cascading down his back, now had his hair intricately twisted into thick dreadlocks coiling and weaving down to his waist. There seemed to be strands of the finest silver intermingling amongst the deep black, like some shimmery, metal roping. My eyes locked with his, and I saw that they were still the reflection of the night sky that I had loved so much, but there was something different, something off; they looked flat, dead and cold. I didn't have time to assess any further as my attention was immediately drawn to Patric who was laughing. His appearance had also undergone a bit of a transformation. His hair was still long, still flowing over his shoulders, but it was extremely dark in color, almost the same shade of Nathanial's, but with hints of copper and red, the contrast set the strands ablaze against his dark skin. I let my eyes find his, pools of deep black, not the turquoise of his mother, were gazing at my face, roaming over my body and I felt the familiar pull and pulse emitting from their fiery centers. Someone touched my shoulder; it was Devon.

"Patric and Nathanial, this is Ana. She'll be the sound voice of reason for our little case study here on the island." Devon laughed and ran his hand down my bare back, sending chills along my spine. I thought I saw Patric's eyes darken at Devon's touch, but I couldn't be sure and I tried to bury every single thought that was now racing through my mind. They don't know that we knew each other I thought, and my brain was racing to figure out what to do, how to act. Immediately, I stuck out my hand toward Nathanial.

"Nathanial, it's so very nice to meet you." Upon touching him, I felt the back of my neck grow warm, then hot and I felt a tearing in my chest. Swallowing the upsurge of emotion, I retracted my hand and met his eyes.

"Ana," he said to me, quiet and strong his gaze did not register any familiarity with me, not a flicker of emotion or memory crossed his face and I felt my stomach drop to the floor. I quickly broke his stare and turned toward Patric.

"It's nice to meet you as well Patric." There was a brief element of surprise that crossed his face. Perhaps he hadn't anticipated that I would still be alive or perhaps it was that he hadn't *counted* on my survival. Either way, he recovered quickly. His hand grasped mine and I felt his fingers gently caress over the scar from Nathanial's bite. Heat rose inside my body and lingered across my abdomen, the familiar pull toward him was stronger than I had ever felt and I could sense that he knew this. Christ, this was so not good. He pressed gently on my scar and let his hand fall away. Another surge of heat moved up my back and heightened at the base of my neck. Bizarrely, at that moment, I was glad to be sitting between Devon and Christopher; I wanted as much distance between myself, Patric and Nathanial.

"Please, please, sit everyone, let's enjoy some drinks and just relax a bit shall we?" Patric motioned for everyone to take their seats and I was glad to have the stability of the chair to hold my weight. My world was crashing down around me and it was all I could do to not crumble right along with it. Patric ordered several bottles of wine for the table and I watched as he managed to send our server into a delirious flirtatious mood, winking at her and slipping what looked like a hundred dollar bill into her hand. Nathanial was watching me watch Patric and I turned away. I noticed that Stephen was staring intently at me and I bowed my head; I was sure he could sense

189

the rising despair in my heart. I swallowed and tried to regain my composure.

"Ana, how rude we are, we should really order you some food, you must be starving!" Devon grasped my hand and I heard Patric and the other Vampires laugh. Did I miss something? Stephen, sensing my lack of understanding, leaned across the table and whispered,

"Food isn't exactly to our liking now is it?" he said as he winked at me and I saw his eyes flash as our gazes met. I suddenly caught on. Of course, Vampires didn't eat human food, they drank human blood, and I was pretty sure that I was still mostly human. I gave him a shy smile and nodded. I was not even close to hungry. In fact, I was wondering if I should get the hell out of here, feign an illness, call Alec and have him meet me at the airport. I just wasn't emotionally equipped to handle any of this. Suddenly, a deep pressure resonated within my head, squeezing all thought and the capacity for thought right out of my brain. I knew what was coming—Patric. *I really don't think leaving is a viable option at this point Ana do you? I must say, that I'm quite surprised that you managed to survive such a physical assault on your body. I greatly underestimated Alec's medical skills—he's quite a Healer isn't he? I would also like to recommend that when Alec does call, and I think he should be contacting you in just a few moments, that you do not let him know that Nathanial and I are here with you on the island, at least not yet. I fear that it would just upset him too much and he's likely to overreact.* I knew that his tone was not one open for negotiation, and that he was essentially *ordering* me not to leave and not to discuss anything with Alec. I felt a sudden surge of hatred and stubbornness at his bravado and immediately shot a wave of emotion directed right at the voice in my head. I looked up in time to see him flinch in pain at my sudden attack; I smirked at him and reached down to pull out my vibrating phone. It was Alec. I excused myself from the table and felt six pairs of eyes follow me to the other side of the deck. "Hi Alec!" I forced myself to sound casual, the only reason why I listened to Patric, was to protect Alec, he'd been through too much of this crap already and I wanted to keep him away from both Nathanial and Patric and whatever they were planning.

"Ana, how are you doing, is everything going alright down there?" He sounded tense and I wondered what he had seen in his mind.

"Yep, everything's fine, I'm at dinner right now with the rest of the team; I'm the only girl and the rest are Vampires, not the best of luck." I chuckled. Dead silence. "Alec? Are you there?"

"Yes, I'm here. I thought Caleb said that there would be some Bonders also with you? What happened?" Christ, he was already suspicious.

"Um, I think that we are still missing a few from the team, maybe they'll be the Bonders. Look Alec, I've kinda gotta get back to dinner ok? I'll call you tomorrow after I return from the village. Tell Kai that I love him!" I didn't give him a chance to respond and I shut off my phone. When I returned to the table, Patric was staring at me. I was sure that he had heard my conversation and was probably not pleased at the mentioning of the Vampires. Screw him, I thought. I didn't owe him anything. Both he and Nathanial already took what they

191

wanted from me, they both left me to die, what could either of them possibly do to me now? Kill me? I noticed that Stephen's head snapped up upon hearing my thoughts. Fine, I didn't care; a few months ago I was ready to do it myself and would have if Alec hadn't read my mind at that exact moment and put my ass in counseling. I heard a low growl coming from the table and I looked up to find Nathanial glaring at me; what the hell was his problem? I took my seat and noticed that I now had a plate of rice and chicken and a ginger ale at my place setting—my favorite meal.

"I took the liberty of ordering you some food Ana, I hope it's to your liking." Patric looked at me and smiled stiffly. A memory of cooking in my kitchen when he was there with me suddenly flooded my mind. That was after Nathanial had left me but before I had discovered just how strong my feelings were for Patric; the scene penetrated deep into my heart, making my breath come in short, quiet pulses. Patric always used to make fun of the fact that I ate the same thing everyday and that I should mix it up a bit more...like with blood, I used to joke back, if only I had known what was to come. I looked up to find him staring at my face, a look of complete peace falling over his eyes. Did he remember? Was he sharing the same memory? Unlikely I thought, as I tried to swallow away the emotion that had just welled up in my chest.

"It's fine, thank you Patric," I murmured and began eating. The conversation shifted from my need for sustenance, to the current scene in the village.

"Another body was found just this morning, the medical examiner is keeping it blocked off until we arrive tomorrow,"

Andres reported and I didn't fail to notice how he had referred to the body as "it". I met his eyes across the table,

"Was the body a *woman* or *man*?" I asked pointedly.

"Neither, *it* was a child." He smirked at me. I could already see whom I was going to have a problem with tomorrow.

"I hear the body was pretty mangled, it took a while to make an identification." Stephen had turned toward Devon and I could hear every word that he spoke. My throat turned dry, and I had to work hard to swallow the bite of chicken in my mouth.

"Well that's a shame. Although, I must admit that I will be intrigued to see how our ecologist and our biologists are able to identify the source for the trauma," Patric said this while he poured another round of wine for the table.

"I don't think it's necessary for Ana to physically see the body, Patric. I'm sure photographs will be quite suitable," Nathanial spoke quietly, but with a dark and commanding tone.

"Nonsense!" Patric exclaimed, taking a long sip from his glass. "Ana is a woman of Science, surely she can separate out her compassion from what is needed in terms of evaluating the evidence." Patric laughed, but I noticed that he was staring defiantly at Nathanial as he spoke. I looked away from them both. Nice, they were arguing over what they thought was best for me as if they owned me. My imprint began to burn and Nathanial caught my eye. I stared at him; I was so pissed. I felt my skin grow warm and swell slightly, I reached around to my neck to wipe a bead of sweat. Devon, who had managed to turn his chair so that it was now facing inward towards me, whipped his head around to look in my direction. I heard him take a deep breath and lean in towards my back. The table erupted in laughter, all except Nathanial and Stephen. I missed something, yet again. Devon purred over my shoulder.

"Well, if you are going to sit there and tempt all of us Vampires with your delicious fragrance, then I think you at least owe me a dance?" He laughed as his fingers traced down my arm. I heard Andres chuckle, but noticed that he had pushed his chair as far away from me as possible. Devon's offer made me hesitate, but not for the reasons that I would have thought. I wasn't hesitating because I was afraid of Devon, but because I wasn't sure if I was allowed to be with another man or being after having completed my exchange with Nathanial. Didn't that make us now Bonded? I had heard that sometimes Bonders go their separate ways from those with whom they have chosen, they live different lives, take new lovers, but they are still always "together". I suppose if I were a male Bonder, that would be the best scenario to have; you get all the power from the exchange without all of the commitment— not a bad deal, I mused to myself. Nathanial glared at me from across the table. Apparently, I wasn't doing too well with the whole closing my mind thing. "Ana, what do you say, how about a dance?" Devon was staring at me, his gray eyes locked with mine. Screw it! I wasn't with anyone, and I didn't belong *to* anyone, and I hadn't been out on a date since meeting Nathanial almost a year ago. I at least deserved a dance with an extremely handsome Vampire. I nodded to him and took his hand. I heard the table erupt in a bunch of "you go man" and "I'm next." Nathanial had turned to look out at the water, but I distinctly felt Patric's eyes on me as Devon led me to the outer deck where the other diners were dancing. The music was slow and reminded me of some sort of sensual trance beat that you would hear in an underground club. I liked it. He took me around the waist and I moved my hands to his chest. Well, I could've done a lot worse. Devon was beyond beautiful. The smoothness of his skin reflected the color and tone of deep, crème coco. His hair was shimmery and dark brown with bronze flecks that caught the light. The highlights offered a startling contrast to his eyes, which I noticed kept changing color, from deep smoky black, to a piercing gray, still with the familiar trait of small embers set ablaze deep within his pupils. He smiled at me and I felt him pull me closer so that I could feel his hips against mine. Actually, the intimacy was nice and I felt myself being drawn into the beat of the music and how strong Devon felt with his arms around my body. The feeling of loneliness quelled for a moment offering me a brief space of reprieve from the despair in my heart.

"Hmmm, well this is better than I could have imagined." He bent his head close to my ear, murmuring. "God, your scent is driving me crazy—in a good way." He laughed softly and I felt him run his fingertips slowly down my back. Chills erupted on my skin and he laughed in my ear. He was an excellent dancer, his body was sinuous, graceful yet commanding and I was happy that he knew what he was doing. "I've seen you in his mind you know. Patric I mean, I've seen you through his memories." I pulled my body back and stared at him in complete shock. Devon smirked and pulled me back against his chest. "His powers may be quite extraordinary, but apparently even Patric can't hide how much you affect him, what you do to him—physically, emotionally; it's really quite intriguing." My heart was racing, thudding against my chest and I was sure Devon could feel the hammering pulse. "Listen to your heart, my god, that's incredible. It's so strong, so full of life." He moved his face close to mine and I felt the warmth and smelled the spicy fragrance of his breath on my neck. My body was responding in an odd way, I felt the sudden pull that I usually felt with Patric, happen with Devon, and it began to move through my bones compelling me to gently press my hips against him. This couldn't be me doing this, this had to be coming from Devon, from his abilities to seduce as a Vampire, otherwise what the hell was wrong with me? He pulled his face back and chuckled at my sudden engagement with him.

"Hmmm Ana…Patric was right, you are quite a temptress aren't you?" He laughed again as his eyes roamed over my face, urgent and full of desire. They paused on my neck, just below my jaw and I heard him gasp. His fingers immediately went to the small puncture marks now embedded in my flesh. "What's this? Ana, did you give your blood to one of us?" Devon was searching my face, looking incredulously into my eyes. A sudden sadness overwhelmed me and I felt the tears begin to well up in my throat. God not here, not now. Suddenly, I felt Devon move away from me, but it didn't seem as if it was of his own volition. He was stiff and he seemed to be trying to fight against some invisible tether pulling his body away from mine. I turned to look at our table and found Patric standing and staring at Devon; he had seen Devon's touch on my neck, his recognition of the permanent reminder that I had of my sacrifice, and Patric was angry. I looked at Devon.

"It's fine, it's not a big deal; it doesn't matter anymore…" my voice faded and I could feel myself unraveling. "I'm really sorry, I need to go back to my villa now." I tried to smile at him and we walked back to the table, Devon's hand still around my waist, he was looking at me with wonder and with questions. I knew that it was a very rare occurrence for a human to ever volunteer to give their blood to help a Vampire. Vampires hated humans, and we were, by evolutionary standards, usually just their prey. Perhaps no human had ever fallen in love with a Vampire, had ever wanted them to see another choice, another possibility for a different life. Perhaps the other humans were all considerably smarter than I was. Clearly neither the Vampire nor the Bonder that I had helped had ever considered a life with me. As these thoughts filtered into my head, I saw both Patric and Nathanial turn to look at me, both of them sharing a visible shadow of pain in their eyes. Hmph! It didn't matter now anyway, it was what it was. "Well everyone, it's been an interesting evening, but I think I'm going to head back for the night. Thank you all for your company," I said. For some reason, I noticed that Devon was holding my hand, it was a weird sensation and I felt him squeeze it once, before letting it go.

"Goodnight Ana, I know that I speak for all of my brethren when I say that I'm greatly looking forward to working with you tomorrow and throughout the week," Stephen spoke as he took my hand to kiss, his clear blue eyes connecting with mine. Briefly, I thought I saw a glimmer of some emotion, something just beneath the surface, but I didn't know what and it was gone as quickly as it had appeared.

"Thank you Stephen, you are good for my ego." I tried to laugh softly and turned back toward Nathanial and Patric who had formed somewhat of a blockade to my exit. I nodded at them and moved right in between their shoulders, knocking them back just a bit, with the force from my own. Fuck them both, I thought as I wound my way off the deck and back into the restaurant.

I stayed awake that night, replaying the events from the evening. Well, at least I knew the reason for my familiarity with my room. It was almost an exact replica of Patric's living room and his bedroom. How nice of him to reacquaint me with those memories, I thought bitterly. The room aside, I was having a difficult time placing my anger at seeing Nathanial tonight. I knew that he had essentially "saved" me by completing the exchange and that when he left me the first time, that he had been possessed by Patric apparently, but still, he left me for months, even after Alec tracked him down, he didn't come to me, he didn't even try to explain anything. I wanted him to be stronger, to be able to reconcile what had happened, I wanted him to want to be with me, to want to make things right. Instead, he saved me because he was scared, scared of himself, and he was bullied into keeping his promise to Patric and instead of refusing him, he accommodated Patric, gave him what he wanted and it wasn't to save me. No, Nathanial knew that it was an almost certainty that I would die having both of their blood in my system—so why bother? It's not like he came to see if I had survived. By completing the exchange, Nathanial ensured that he was going to be at his strongest, his most powerful. Even in my most dire circumstances, he, yet again, got what he wanted and still, he chose to leave me. As for Patric, well I was just really pissed at myself. If I was truly being honest, I knew who he was, what he had wanted from me, and from Nathanial. I supposed that I just wanted to believe that I could love him enough to give him another chance at a different life; it was a bad habit of mine, believing in people, wanting to save everyone no matter what the cost. Maybe, for how ever long I had left to live, maybe I should start concentrating on saving myself for a change, giving myself the space to see choices, to make decisions that were solely for me and not to help anyone else. Could I do that? Could I be that selfish? I didn't think Noni would be too happy with such a turn in my personality, but maybe it was possible to find a balance, to look down from the cliff to see what danger was below, but to also gaze out toward the horizon, hopeful in all that you still couldn't see, couldn't know. Perhaps then, maybe it was safe to jump.

I awoke the next morning, fatigued and unsettled. I noticed a distinct fragrance filling my room. I rubbed my eyes and tried to clear my head from the cloud of restless sleep that I had just endured. Something was different. My entire bedroom and most of the living room were covered in Frangipani flowers, their sweet, exotic perfume mixing with the salt air that permeated through my open windows. Warily, I rose from the bed and made my way toward the kitchen where I noticed a silver tray with coffee and an assortment of breakfast items, was sitting on the counter. Had someone come into my room during the early morning? Surely I would have heard them. I was a light sleeper and especially last night, I was struggling with a massive bout of insomnia. A thick, antique looking piece of parchment was attached to the dome of the tray and I noticed the note was in handwriting, intricately scrolled and elegant:

Ana, I hope that in sleep, you found yourself transported by your deepest dreams and desires. The Frangipani flowers reminded me of you. Thank you for your company last night, and I look forward to seeing you in the morning.

Truly yours,

Devon

Uh wow. I was at a loss for words and thoughts, but I did find myself smiling. I wasn't exactly scared of Devon, after Patric, most people, most beings, seemed rather tame, but there was a definite undercurrent of awe that I had for him, for his sheer power and commanding force of presence, it was slightly intimidating. That was nice of him, but I also felt wary by such a profound display of interest. I was always suspicious these days. After breakfast, I gathered up my pack and headed out to my jeep, knowing that whatever happened today, that it was sure to be at the very least, interesting.

****

I arrived in the village at ten-thirty, thirty minutes ahead of schedule, I was hoping to have a few moments to myself to look around, but I had no such luck. I pulled in behind a large, black Land Rover and saw immediately that the Vampire clan was hanging out waiting for me, but I didn't see Nathanial anywhere. Stephen greeted me and opened the car door, taking my pack and helping me to step down, it was bizarrely chivalrous, but I appreciated the gesture nonetheless.

"Are you ready for today?" Stephen seemed a bit too excited to be examining dead bodies for our afternoon entertainment

200

and I took his oddly placed enthusiasm as inherent to his Vampire conditioning.

"Um, well, I don't actually like this part of my work Stephen; for some reason, I just find it really difficult to know that someone has suffered and died. I guess I just get too attached to the presence of souls in the world…" I trailed off, guessing that he was not in any need of so much personal information from me. He turned to look at me straight in the eyes.

"Yeah, I can see that Ana, I can see that in you. Of course this would be difficult for you, I'm sorry. My comment was inappropriate," he said sounding genuinely sincere. He stood staring at me for a moment and I thought I could actually see the oceans begin to churn and shift deep within the currents of his eyes. What the hell was going on here, first the flowers from Devon, now Stephen was being considerate and apologetic; these were not the kinds of Vampires I was used to being around. I heaved my pack over my shoulders and we headed off to join Devon, Christopher and Andres. I noticed loud construction noises coming from the forest, they seemed completely out of context for such a tranquil community. I gazed into the trees, trying to find the source of the commotion but was distracted by a hand on my back. Devon had wandered away from the group and I guessed he had noticed me peering into the woods.

"See something?" he mused, as his gaze lingered across my face.

"Oh, I was just wondering what all of the industrial noise was? Are they building something?" I met his gaze as steadily as I could.

"Yes, they're clearing the trees for development. They're logging trucks you hear." His stare remained unwavering against mine.

"Logging? I thought logging was forbidden on this island, it's a nature preserve. How can they be logging here?" I was caught off guard. I had worked with several environmental groups years ago to help get the indigenous land marked as a wilderness sanctuary—it was protected under law.

"Yes, well, it's amazing how much you can accomplish when you have the means and the power to help people rearrange their priorities." I caught a hint of darkness to Devon's tone and I turned back to look at him.

"What company is this? It has to be a multimillion dollar investment to clear this land and to buy off all of the politicians to make this happen." I knew most of the logging companies in the area and none of them had that kind of power or money.

"Arias Development, they're funding the logging and mining efforts and the development plans for more lodges and hotels," his tone was even as he spoke, still gazing at me.

"Arias," I said more to myself than to Devon, how did I know that name? "Arias?" Devon turned back to me and as I focused on his clear gray eyes, it hit. Arias! That was Nathanial's last name.

"And Patric's," Devon murmured quietly, he'd known what realization I had just come to. He raised his eyebrows at me and laughed. "We should go, the others will think that I'm trying to possess you," he said softly, gazing once more into my face, I felt a surge of longing when I looked at him; I didn't know why.

"Devon wait," I said as he began to turn back toward the cars. "Thank you for the beautiful flowers. That was, that was truly an unexpected joy to have this morning and very kind of you to... to spend money on me." I hated people buying gifts for me, it seemed ridiculous and it made me feel awkward. Devon turned back and closed the distance between us in one step. He was staring at me with the same look of incredulity that he'd given me after seeing my bite marks.

"Hmm... if I had known just how much you were going to appreciate such a simple gesture, I would have opted for something a bit more lavish." He laughed as he reached his hand up to push an errant strand of my hair out from my eyes. At his touch, I felt both sadness and a strange new desire rush into my body; god, it would be nice to not always be a walking paradox. He winked at me and we walked back to meet the now fully assembled team, Nathanial and Patric included.

So, Patric had a stake in this entire "animal problem" here in the village. The land was now technically his and if people were found murdered by, say Vampires, well then he'd be up against one hell of a law suit; somehow, I thought that even if that were in fact to be his fate, I was certain that Patric would find a way around the legal system. I was guessing that he was just wanting to avoid any extra nuisances, like a murder trial; he had better things to be doing. Suddenly, the part that I had to play in this entire case became crystal clear. I was to recommend that the deaths were animal related, I was to steer the authorities away from any conclusions that would make them think that anything other than a rogue wild animal could have caused these horrific series of events. I was going to have to lie and I was going to have to lie better than I had ever done in my life. The sudden impact of what I just determined, hit me like a lightening bolt out of a clear sky. I leaned against the back of the Land Rover and tried to steady my now shaking legs. Immediately, I noticed that Nathanial had not missed what was now a mounting panic attack. His eyes found mine and I saw them get clearer and more blue as he stared at me. He of course was in on this whole charade, how could he not be? I forced myself to look away from his face not hiding my disgust, and turned to follow Stephen and Devon who were headed into the woods down a trail.

Getting to the main village proved to be a bit of a trek. The trail wound in steep grades that plummeted down into deep ravines. I was a skilled hiker and perfectly capable of handling myself over rugged terrain, but for some reason, Nathanial seemed keen to stay beside me, matching my strides step for step. He never spoke to me, he never looked at me, but a few times out of the corner of my eye I thought I caught him staring at my face. I contemplated engaging him in conversation but thought better of it. I truly had no idea if he even remembered me. I knew his physical transformation was obvious, but I was unsure what he had managed to deem worthy enough to keep as an emotional tie—it most likely wasn't me.

"That is a complete untruth Ana, and to hear what you have been thinking, to listen to what thoughts have been in your mind as of late; I can't even get my head around any of it," he hissed at me, not in an evil way, more frustrated it seemed. I stopped walking and turned to glare at him. "Keep walking," he ordered me, and I noticed that he looked immediately to our front, checking to see if anyone else from our party had stopped upon hearing Nathanial's whispers. Still glaring at him, I stomped off taking the lead down a fairly steep patch of terrain. So now he decides to talk to me, now, in the middle of what I was sure to be one of the most bizarre situations in my life, now he chooses to acknowledge my existence. Well fuck that! I wasn't having any of it. I didn't want him to talk to me, I wasn't interested in anything he had to say, or explain. I was tired of everything being on everyone else's terms—no more. I'd talk to Nathanial when *I* wanted and no sooner.

Finally we emerged from the depths of the forests and made our way into the heart of the main community. I knew something was wrong the minute we stepped onto the dirt road. People were everywhere, hoards of them were gathered around in small groups, their arms around each other. There was no sense of energy or vitality. It was as if someone or something had shrouded each person behind a dark veil, impervious to light or hope. A deep sense of foreboding fell over me as I watched the faces of women and young fathers, tears staining their cheeks. God, this was horrible. As we entered the village center, a woman rushed to meet us. She had been standing with an intimate cluster of people, her family I guessed. She approached Patric and he immediately embraced her as if he had known her forever; I knew that type of embrace.

"Ana, this is Cora, she's the mother of the child who was found yesterday. She knows why we are all here," Patric spoke in a soothing tone, so much so, that I could actually feel the dread in my body, beginning to dissipate. The rest of team stepped forward at Patric's beckoning. I took three amulets from my pack. They were gifts to them for all that they'd endured and I moved to stand in front of Cora. Taking her hand, I placed one amulet in her palm, placed one around the neck of her eldest son who had come to see us, and I gave one to her husband. I grasped her hands in mine and pressed them to my heart. She shuttered and then began sobbing, falling into my chest.

Upon my recommendation, Cora's husband escorted us to see the body and we started down the dirt path towards the elementary school. Stephen and I walked with the husband Ahmed and we talked about his daughter, Maria. She was ten, loved soccer and painting. She would spend hours alone in the forests writing poetry and stories. He never worried about her going alone into the woods until the trucks arrived to begin the clearing, that's when the first of the bodies had been discovered over a month ago. He trailed off in his memories and I stayed silent, I wanted him to have the proper space to feel what he needed to feel at that moment. We continued down the path and as we rounded the bend, Ahmed halted in his tracks. I put my hand on his back and asked him to point in the general direction; he was shaking. I looked back to see Nathanial coming up ahead of the group. I found his eyes and I let him sense what I wanted him to do. Immediately, I felt Ahmed's body relax and his face became calm. I guessed that no matter the distance, Nathanial and I would always have that inner dialogue with each other. I

206

hugged Ahmed close to me and I fell in step beside Nathanial and Stephen as we walked toward Maria's resting place. Yellow plastic tape was crudely marking the spot of the attack and I could see the small body quite clearly, she looked as if she had just fallen asleep on the spot. I found that the closer we got to her, the more difficult it became for me to walk. The rest of the team passed me in my hesitance and began to gather around the site, however Stephen stayed behind, keeping his distance, but standing next to me. Patric stepped away from the group and motioned for me to join him. His eyes surveyed me as I forced myself to move forward. I felt the heat from my imprint move into my head as the distance closed between us.

"Ana, would you please have a look for us?" Patric asked me quietly. I noticed that when he looked at me, I saw a flash of brilliant turquoise appear in his eyes. I had forgotten how beautiful his eyes were in their natural state. Just for a moment, I thought I saw sadness move over Patric's face when our gazes met, but just briefly, then it vanished. I nodded to him and moved through the team toward the body. It was worse than I could have imagined. There was so much blood. The dirt surrounding the girl was caked and dried into dark, reddish brown pools. I knelt down at her legs and moved to pull my gloves out from my pack. I felt everyone's eyes on me as I lightly pressed my fingers across her legs. I was looking for scratch marks or bite wounds. Maria's legs were bloodied, but I couldn't tell from where the blood had come. There were no open wounds in her flesh, yet massive amounts of the seepage had poured from somewhere below her waist. Out of the corner of my eye, I saw Patric move to the front of the group so that he was standing directly in front of my position over the body. Was he seriously trying to intimidate me? This was not the time. I moved so that I could kneel at Maria's head, placing Patric directly behind me. Of course he immediately shifted to the side, never losing sight of what I was doing. I cradled the girl's head in my lap and began to examine her hair and her skull. Again, there were copious amounts of blood down her face and her neck. He skull was in tact, so that mostly likely ruled out a mauling of sorts. The community had a very small and very endangered population of big cats, but they were usually frightened by any human interactions and rarely attacked. I stroked the girl's hair, moving the matted and clotted strands away from her face. Her eyes were still open. They were staring up at me, big and brown, they reminded me of my own eyes, but Maria's were fixed, unmoving—dead. I couldn't stop looking at them and a wave of complete and utter despair threatened to overwhelm me. My hands shook as I continued to stroke her hair. I wasn't a mother and it was never something that I had thought about becoming, ever. Still, having this beautiful girl's head resting peacefully in my lap, I thought of her as my own, my daughter. I saw her as a possibility, as a precious part of her own mother's present and future. I also conjured images of my own parents and wondered if they would be sad if I died, probably not.

"Ana," a voice quietly sounded from the group. I looked up to see everyone staring at me, watching me stroking the dead girl's hair and brushing the dirt from her cheeks. My team looked confused and concerned at my sudden display of emotion, and I heard the voice again. "Ana, are you alright to continue?" It was Stephen. He had moved to stand next to Patric and he knelt in the dirt beside me, his marine blue eyes

roaming over my face and hearing my most intimate thoughts.
I had forgotten that he was even there, that any of them were
there. I looked over at Stephen and Patric and nodded. I
took a deep breath and turned back to my examination.
Maria's head was bent toward my left, so I gently moved her
to my right and swept the dark clumps of hair from under her
chin, and that's when the violence that had befallen this child
reveled itself. Her throat was torn open, a massive chasm in
her flesh that reveled her slashed tendons and bones. The
wound was so deep that her head lulled to the right, barely
still attached to her neck. I felt myself begin to gag. I had
thrown up the first time I'd seen a human who had been
attacked by an animal. The body was so mangled and the guts
had been spilled everywhere, that I just couldn't stop my body
from reacting. This was different. Yes, the physical violence
was horrific, but the sheer brutality that happened to this
child, this girl, and what she must have suffered during the
attack—it was just too much. I was trying to breathe. I looked
up to find Stephen staring at me, the oceans in his eyes taking
in my emotional tenor. He looked devastated. Our gazes held
and I found myself concentrating on the swiftly moving marine
tides that seemed to beckon me to be swept away in his stare;
I swallowed and tried to regroup.

"Ana, what do you think, what are your first impressions?"
Patric said as he knelt down next to me, his eyes roaming over
my face. I gently placed the girl's head back down in the dirt
and I moved again over to her legs. The injury to her neck
most certainly explained the source of the blood by her head,
but I was still confused as to why there was so much blood
that had accumulated near her legs. She was wearing what
many of the children wore in developing countries, donated,

more Westernized clothing. Maria's body was clad in jean shorts and a long, sleeveless tunic that hung down to her upper thighs and covered the edge of the cutoffs. I moved the shirt up a fraction and saw that her shorts were also soaked with blood. I glanced up at Patric, he was on edge, I could tell. I pushed up her shorts as far as they would go toward her groin and I heard myself gasp. There was a gash on the inside of her left upper thigh, it was long and deep and had torn open the flesh to the muscle and tissue beneath the surface. This was no animal attack. I knew those exact pulse points from voluntary, personal experience; no child, no child should ever have been subjected to that ritual, to such careless violence.

I heard voices and looked up to find that the local authorities and Ahmed had come to join the group. I stood up and brushed the blood and dirt from my pants and moved away from the body. I knew that Patric was waiting for me to speak, but I was going to let him wait just a bit longer, I needed to calm myself. Whoever did this, whatever Vampire, they'd been messy. Ironically, this made things a bit easier for Patric and his company. No animal attack was ever neatly done. Had the Vampire or Vampires taken their time, had they left small, barely noticeable wounds, well that would be extremely difficult to pass off as a rogue animal. I peeled off my gloves and shoved them into my back pocket. Patric and the team were talking with the local police and I shepherded Ahmed away from his daughter's body.

"Ana, could you come over here for a moment please?" Patric spoke from the circle of people. I motioned for Nathanial to come and stand with Ahmed; out of all of the men in the group, I knew Nathanial to be quite a compassionate person, at least before things went horribly wrong, before his change, but I figured he could dig deep and find some source of sympathy for this father and do as I asked.

"Miss, we understand that you've checked out the body?" one of the police officers said, folding his arms across his chest and standing with his legs in a wide stance. I guessed he was trying to exert some sort of leadership, testosterone type position amongst all of the men surrounding him—god, if he only knew. The men in the circle could kill him before he would even be able to shift his weight.

"Yes, that's right. I've checked over the body. I'm not a medical examiner though, so I can only give you my opinion based on what I know from previous animal attacks. I'm not an expert in any sense of the word." I was surprised at how strong and confident my voice sounded.

"We have experts miss, we're just trying to get a few more opinions about the attack, see where we need to be placing our efforts," he explained, his arms still crossed. I felt Patric move next me, and my mark begin to burn into my skin. Good god, he really needed to back off, I could handle this; I knew what he wanted me to do. I glanced over toward Ahmed. Nathanial had his arms around the young father and he was whispering something to him. Ahmed was nodding and burying his face in Nathanial's chest. I watched as I saw Nathanial press his lips to Ahmed's forehead. I cocked my head to the side as a rush of emotion coursed through my body. That was the Nathanial that I remembered, the man that I knew, the man that I had once loved.

211

"Ana." Patric placed his hand on my back and I realized that he too had been watching the display of emotion from his brother. We looked at each other and I swore that I saw my exact feelings, reflected on Patric's face. That was the brother he had known, the twin that he possibly still loved. It made me sad to think about just how wrong things in Patric's life had gone, just how poorly he made decisions. I was sure, absolutely sure, that Patric, as a child, would have never wanted any of this, not for himself and not for his brother. I felt as if everything in the world at this one moment, with me staring at Patric, and with us both standing there loving Nathanial; that everything was hovering on the edge of a knife, waiting for us to fail, to fail each other and ourselves.

I told the detectives what I thought had happened, that Maria had been attacked on her way to school, most likely from a rabid animal and that the bite marks were similar of those associated with a large predator and Devon agreed with me. I had no idea if that was enough of a lie to please Patric, but I honestly didn't care. We had several more bodies to examine and I just wanted to get this entire, god-forsaken day over with. Six hours later, we had made it back to the center of the village. I was exhausted, emotionally drained and the heat was really taking its toll. I headed straight for my jeep and released my pack from my sore shoulders. I grabbed some water and leaned against the back of my car, trying to relax my mind a bit before driving back to the lodge. I was a horrible driver when I was upset, and extremely prone to accidents if I was mentally distracted.

"Tough day," Devon said as he approached my jeep.

"Yep." I took another sip of water and stared at him.

"Listen, Patric wants us all to meet for drinks this evening at his villa and discuss some of our findings today."

"You mean he wants us to make sure we all have our stories straight." I glared at him. Did these people think that I was stupid? Devon laughed and moved to take my water bottle out of my hand. He ran his fingers around the rim of the container where I had just been sipping and he raised his hand to his lips, licking his finger. I looked passed him and noticed Stephen off to the side, watching us.

"Spicer than I thought," he mused as he raised his eyebrows at me. "But incredibly mouthwatering nonetheless." Laughing, he reached to give me back the water bottle. "I'll save you a seat on the couch." He winked at me and headed back to the Land Rover. I knew that the invitation was not optional. I sighed and opened the car door. Just as I was pulling on my seat belt, Nathanial appeared at the window.

"Ana, I just wanted to tell you, to warn you actually, that you need to be very aware of your associations with certain members of this team." He was barely audible and I had to lean in toward his face to hear what the hell he was saying. Suddenly his fragrance hit me, stirring vast waves of memory and emotion. I looked at him unblinking. "I think you know to whom I am referring. Devon is extremely attracted to you and his thoughts have, shall we say, not been the most gentlemanly, since your arrival."

"Well, that's very nice of you to be concerned Nathanial, but I think that I can handle Devon." I didn't need or want Nathanial to express any trepidation for my safety; I was no longer his concern. Nathanial flinched and sighed deeply.

"Ana, don't be fooled by appearances among this group. Patric looks every bit the leader, but Devon's powers rival Patric's and besides myself, Devon has the longest relationship with Patric," he paused and looked back toward his car before continuing, "Patric has not been quite so savvy as myself, in covering up his memories of you, of your time together. That's a perceived weakness in a Vampire's mind, especially if the memories are of a Human." Wait, so Nathanial has been covering up memories of me? What the hell was going on? "I can't explain everything right now, I just wanted to warn you that Devon is a predator in the truest sense of the word and he's stalking you Ana. I can't…I won't be able to protect you…" his voice was choking up and his eyes were pleading with me.

"Nathanial! Let's go!" Stephen shouted out of the window as their car drove by. Nathanial looked at me, and I saw him turn his body in such a way that blocked the group in the Rover from seeing me. He bent his head low, and I saw his hand move to touch my face. He paused just before the caress and his eyes locked with mine.

"Ana," he whispered as I felt his fingertips trace along my cheeks. My heart hammered against my chest and I closed my eyes, they felt wet. When I opened them, he was gone and I saw the back of the Rover rambling down the road in a swirl of dust and wind. Frick! I was so screwed!

I had a few hours before I was due at Patric's, so I decided to head out into the main village to hunt for a coffee and of course, I needed to call Alec. After settling into a small makeshift café, I pulled out my phone. I decided to call Kai instead of Alec, there was too much that had happened and I was less likely to be able to divert things from Alec than Kai. Kai picked up on the first ring.

"Ana, Ana, my beautiful friend—how are you?" Kai yelled into the phone. Gracious, he must have started drinking early, I laughed.

"Kai, how much hookah have you been smoking, why so excited?"

"What, I can't be happy to hear from my best friend? You should be honored by my enthusiasm!" He laughed into the phone.

"I am always honored by your undying and manic displays of affection for me—what are you up to today?" I was intentionally trying to keep the conversation focused on Kai.

"Mom is here and she and Alec are in the middle of debating the teaching of local indigenous languages in the public school system. I think she's kicking Alec's ass, but that was over an hour ago. How did things go today for you?" His tone was still light, but I could sense his urgency to know about my day.

"Ugh, it was just awful and traumatic, but mostly it was just exhausting…" I heard a rustling on the phone and some static. "Kai?"

"Yeah, I wanted to go out to the beach for a minute. Listen Ana, Alec knows that Patric and Nathanial are there with you—" I cut him off.

"What! How the hell did he find out Kai? How could he possibly know that they're here?" I was dumbfounded.

"Ana, Caleb was forwarded a memo by someone with a list of names for the team, some sort of check list or something for the local authorities; he had to check your name off and yours was the last listed. It was all I could do to stop both him and Alec from getting on a plane and pulling you out of there. He's really, really pissed at you for not telling him. Ana, are you ok down there? I just can't believe this is happening." I waited for him to continue but when he fell silent, I started to speak.

"Kai, listen, there's really too much to discuss right now, and I'm pretty sure that Patric will know if I say anything, in fact, I'm pretty sure that he was the one to send the memo to Caleb, he likes taunting Alec. I'm ok, and I..." I heard the phone shift and the sounds of arguing. Crap!

"Ana, it's Alec. I can't even begin to tell you just how much danger you are in right now, and that's not counting the danger that you are in with me!" I decided that now was probably not the time to tell him that I was also currently being stalked by a ruthless Vampire who I seemed to have some sort of attraction to—better to wait with that information. "Stalked! Did you say that you were being stalked? Did I hear you right?" Frick, he was way too good.

216

"Alec!" I interjected. "I know that you're angry, but really, that's exactly what Patric wants, he wants you to come down here, he wants you to confront him. I can't talk to you about anything it's not smart ok? You have to understand." I was pleading with him. I knew that Patric would be able to know what this conversation entailed, and I didn't want to give him any incentive to retaliate against Alec.

"Nathanial is there?" Alec asked and I hoped he'd sensed what I had just mentally said to myself.

"Yes, he's here, look, I'm due back for dinner in an hour and if I don't show up, well that's really not going to look good. Alec, I'm leaving in a few days and hopefully we can sort all of the mess out when I get back. Truthfully, I'm pretty sure that Patric actually needs me down here, so the chances of him or any of his clan trying to kill me, seem pretty remote." Of course, since my discussion with Nathanial this afternoon, I couldn't quite buy that analysis myself and neither could Alec.

"Ana, you have no idea what you are up against down there, these are not your typical rogue Vampires, they are lethal, violent and they have no regard for Human life. Your relationship with Patric can only serve to harm you, his feelings for you will not protect you—he will not protect you Ana. I know that it's in your nature to believe in the humanity of all souls, to want them to choose better paths for themselves, but Ana, Patric chose his path a very long time ago and as beautiful and extraordinary as you are, you cannot save him—he won't let you."

"I know Alec, I know this," I murmured, the truth of his words sinking into my gut, crushing my heart. "Alec, do you know a Devon Batayo, he's from Trinidad?"

"Batayo? Hmmm… Devon Batayo. Ana, is he there with you? Is he the one that's stalking you?" Alec's voice was flat and even.

"No, no he's not, I was just wondering if you knew of him, that's all…" I trailed off, my ability to lie had reached its pinnacle for the day and Alec knew it.

"Ana, don't you dare lie to me, don't you ever lie to me. I don't have time to go into his history, but you need to be very, very careful. Devon is a lot more than he appears." Wow, had Alec spoken to Nathanial today? "Why? Did Nathanial say something to you about Devon?" I sighed

"Alec, I can't do this right now, ok?" I was getting more and more nervous the longer Alec spoke.

"Fine, but know this Ana, Devon was the one who turned Patric, who changed him into a Vampire and by any standards in this world, Devon owns Patric and I am sure that he is wondering just how Patric became so powerful all of sudden." I cringed. It was my blood that was responsible for Patric's sudden increase in mental and emotional strength—it was my fault. "Ana, it's not your fault, listen to me, this is very important. If Devon finds out, if he's already found out that you gave your blood to Patric, that you are the reason for his new powers, that Patric took blood from a Human, had a relationship with a Human and did not kill you—Devon is likely to retaliate and I have no idea how he would do that." God, this was unbelievable, I couldn't escape, I couldn't have a moment of peace; I was going to be hunted until someone actually finished the deed and did leave me to die. "Ana, I don't care what kinds of feelings that you have for Patric or Devon; you need to stay close to Nathanial, do you hear me?"

"Alec, Nathanial said that he couldn't, that he wouldn't be able to protect me…" I had said too much.

"What? Ana, Nathanial warned you about Devon? What did he say?" Again, Alec's tone had turned slightly stoic and monotone.

"Alec, I have to go, I can't talk to you anymore, don't call me ok, just, just…I have to go!" I slammed the phone shut and felt my body begin to tremble. Christ! What was I going to do? I was alone on this frickin island with a hoard of Vampires, one of whom seemed to be stalking me, and a Bonder who may or may not be working with his psychotic brother. What did a girl have to do to have a normal relationship, a normal life? I finished my coffee and headed back to my room; I had a feeling it was going to be a very long evening.

****

I decided against driving over to Patric's myself and settled for walking along the beach down to his villa. I didn't know what I was expecting to gain from my stroll, perhaps just some quiet moment of peace before all hell broke loose—I wasn't sure. I paused just before arriving to the walkway and tried to take a few breaths. If I could just keep things low-key and placate Patric, if I could keep my temper in check and if I could keep my strange attraction to Devon under control, I might just have a chance to get out of this place with my life and my heart in tact.

"Ana, are you alright?" It was Nathanial; he had been sitting on the bench in the front garden, watching me. He was so quiet, as usual, that I failed to notice him there.

"Yeah, I'm ok. Thanks." I turned and smiled at him. I noticed how handsome he looked. He was dressed in fluid white pants, sandals and a deep gray shirt that allowed the copper in his skin to shimmer. He was beautiful; he had always been beautiful.

"I could never hold a candle to you, Ana." I watched as his eyes took me in, and I could see the familiar glimmer of the stars reflected in his gaze. I sat down next to him on the bench and rested my chin in my hands. It was a casual enough gesture, but it seemed significant somehow. I don't know how long we sat there side-by-side, neither of us talking. Maybe we didn't have anything to say, or maybe, as it was in my case, I had too much to say. I watched Nathanial close his eyes and take a deep breath in. He stood and turned to me offering his hand. "We should go. Patric has never been one to appreciate late arrivals." He laughed darkly. I rolled my eyes and wove my fingers in his. Immediately upon our touch, the metals in the back of my neck seared my skin and I thought I felt them shift. I sucked in a sharp breath and pulled my hand away to touch my neck. "What's wrong Ana? Are you in pain?" Nathanial asked, worry coloring his tone.

220

"Nah, it's just this stupid imprint thing, ever since I've been down here it's been quite active, shall we say." I laughed and turned my head back and forth, trying to dissolve the tension from the burn. Nathanial moved behind me and I felt him gently sweep the tresses of my hair so that they fell down my chest. His fingers moved tenderly over the mark and heat began to move through my spine.

"Hmm, I don't think that I've ever seen that before," he spoke under his breath.

"What, seen what?" I was concerned that there was something wrong.

"It appears that you now have three separate divisions of your imprint Ana—quite extraordinary actually, but then again, *you* are quite extraordinary," he whispered into the back of my neck, causing chills to erupt on my skin. I reached around and moved my fingers against the space where I knew the imprint to be, I felt myself graze Nathanial's fingertips in the process. Sure enough, I could now feel three separate pieces of metal and stone on the back of my neck. The long turquoise strand was to my right, the knotted emblem of silver and jewels in the center and the midnight blue portion, was now to my left. At that moment, I had never felt more alone in my entire life; hell, even my imprint had shifted to show the division in everything that I had loved or tried to love—it was a bit pathetic. "Imprints move and shift like tides Ana, but they are always controlled by the gravitational pull of the moon— your gravitational pull is like the moon, like my moon…" Nathanial whispered in my ear. Strange time to be offering an astronomy lesson I thought, and I turned toward him, questions in my eyes. He laughed softly at my expression. The laugh was a familiar one, a sound that I used to look forward to hearing upon his arrival home from his classes, but that was before, before he left, before Patric, before any of this mess happened and now I was just hoping that whatever outcome, whatever was going to transpire, that it would be over soon; god, I hoped it was going to be over soon. I'm not sure what compelled me, but tentatively, I found myself reaching to touch Nathanial's face. It was an odd impulse considering how angry and hurt I was, but I felt that I *needed* to touch him, to make sure that he was real, no matter how much he'd changed his appearance, no matter what path he'd decided to take, I needed to touch him to remind myself of the man whom I had consciously decided to bind myself to, and to whom I was still Bound. At my touch, I felt his body tremble and saw that his eyes were on fire, not the same fire like Patric's or Devon's, but a deep smoldering fire that pulsated from within Nathanial and not out towards me. Instead of pulling me in, the fire lifted me up and I felt calm and buoyant, but I also felt a deep longing, a deep need to keep his eyes on mine, to keep him there with me, to have him to hold onto for just a little while longer.

"Nathanial! We're waiting on you, what's the hold up? Oh Ana! I didn't see you there! Wow, you look nice." It was Stephen. His voice seemed to break the spell between Nathanial and myself. Ice replaced the fire in his eyes, and I felt him immediately step away, creating a chasm of space between us. I swallowed hard, fighting back the tears and emotion that were threatening to spill over. I waved at Stephen and followed him up the path to Patric's.

Of course Patric's villa was the most beautiful and the most romantic place I had ever been. If he were a normal man, it probably would have been a great place to come as a couple, I mused as I stepped into the living room. I heard Nathanial snort behind me. I noticed that a long table had been set in front of the fireplace, which had the perfect amount of slow burning embers to create gentle warmth and a soft glow into the room. The table was lavishly set, with handcrafted stoneware and baskets of fresh bread, fruit and cheeses. I thought it an odd selection considering the majority of our party did not eat and Nathanial rarely touched any food, as much as I could remember.

"It's all for you," Nathanial whispered, as he took off my sweater and draped it over his arm. Lovely, I thought. What was it, some sort of last meal before Patric or Devon decided to kill me off? How thoughtful. I really would have preferred pizza. I sighed and moved deeper into the room with Nathanial behind me.

"Ana, I'm so glad that you are here," Patric exclaimed, grasping my hands. I shot him a look that said, *"It's not like you gave me any choice."* He caught my eye and smirked. Pulling me closer to his chest, he bent his head toward my ear, as if he was going to kiss me. "No Ana, I didn't give you a choice and I'm glad that you've managed to get over your stubborn streak and try to at least enjoy yourself." His lips brushed over my cheek and I felt him squeeze me harder around the waist. I pulled out of his embrace and glared at him. Laughing, he placed his hand on my back and led me over to the table where the other Vampires and Nathanial had gathered.

"Ana, we've been waiting for you." Devon stood at my arrival and motioned for me to take the seat next to him. Whatever, I thought. At least I had a good-looking, homicidal stalker. I thanked him and took my place at the table. Taking in the scene, with the fire and the ocean and full moon outside, with Patric and Nathanial, Devon and the rest of the team all looking so exquisite, so unearthly in their beauty, I couldn't help but think that I was placed in some sort of campy vampire movie. The bizarreness of the whole situation, of _my_ whole situation, suddenly struck me as hilarious and I had to bite down hard on my lip to keep from laughing out loud.

"I wish you would let me in on the joke," Devon purred beside me. He was fixing me a plate of food and pouring me a glass of wine. I looked at him and shook my head. For some reason, my sudden internal laughter had given me a rare injection of courage and I met his eyes.

"May I ask you something?" My voice was amazingly holding steady.

"Of course, you can ask me anything Ana." He winked and took a sip from his glass.

"Are you happy Devon? What I mean is, when you think about your life, about everything that's happened to you, when you think or remember times when you were really and truly happy; would you say that that feeling is what you are experiencing now...in your life at this moment in time?" I had no idea where I was going with this, but for some reason, I really wanted to know if he felt good about where his various paths had led him, it seemed important to me. I saw his eyes widen and he raised his eyebrows at me. I couldn't tell if my questions had made him upset or if they just surprised him. I could hear other conversations around the table, so I felt safe enough to engage him without everyone hearing our dialogue. However, I did notice Stephen turn subtlety in his chair to glance at me. I took a bunch of grapes from my plate and waited for him to respond.

"Well, I don't think that we, we meaning those of my species, I don't think that we are that introspective Ana. Happiness is a Human emotion, a Human construct that provides you with reasons to question things, to question people; it serves no purpose for me to ponder such Human conditions for my own life." He surveyed me over his glass and I could see that he was trying to figure out why I was taking him down this road. I wasn't letting him off the hook. He was trying to sell me something and I wasn't buying. I nibbled on my grapes.

" Mmm… I understand that you have problems with us humans, but you didn't actually answer my question. I didn't ask how you *viewed* happiness, I asked if you *were* happy, and correct me if I'm wrong, but were you not human at one point?" That got him going. I saw his normally clear gray eyes, turn coal black. I took my chances and plowed ahead. "I'm not trying to upset you, I'm just trying to figure out if you are pleased with how you turned out, if you are happy with the paths that you took, with the decisions that you made, because I'm not. I mean, I've really let myself get pretty screwed over quite a bit in my life and yet I keep trying to save everyone. I keep thinking that there is redemption and resiliency even when we've gone down the wrong road, when we've hurt others and hurt ourselves. I keep thinking that if you just hang on, if you just don't let go, that maybe there will be that one person, that one being who will remember that *you* believed in them, that *you* carried them when they couldn't walk, and that maybe that one individual will remind *you* to not let go, to not look down and they'll carry you, they will help you to find yourself again..." I felt the tears coming now and I couldn't stop them. Devon was staring at me so intensely, that I had to look away. He wasn't moving. I wasn't even sure if he was breathing. I felt blood rush to my face and shook my head. "I'm sorry. I'm sorry, it doesn't matter if you're happy, and whatever that means to you—it's ok; I shouldn't have asked you anything. God, it's been a long day." I felt someone watching me, watching us and I looked up, fully expecting to see Nathanial or Patric gazing at our end of the table, but it was Stephen who was staring. Our gazes met and I saw his jaw clench and his eyes became stormy with emotions I didn't understand or recognize, but I found that I couldn't look away from him.

"Ana." Devon leaned in breaking Stephen's hold on me, and placed one finger under my chin, he lifted my face so that I was looking into his eyes. "You really do care about everyone don't you? It truly matters to you if Humans or Vampires or Bonders, if we live and have peace in our souls, if we find a path that brings us happiness as you refer to it, where we can rejoice in who we are and find a hand to hold as we try to decide who we are to become. What an odd gift, to have so much compassion that it serves as both your greatest strength and your greatest weakness. How to reconcile those two halves—I do wonder if it is possible..." His musings were cut short by Patric, who apparently also had been watching and most likely listening to our conversation, and had decided that he had had enough.

226

"I think it's time to discuss the events of today, shall we?" I saw Patric shoot Devon a look so dark and foreboding, that I felt it reverberate in my own head. Devon leaned back away from me and waved his hand for Patric to continue.

For the next hour and a half, I listened as Patric and the rest of team decided on a formal recommendation to the authorities about the most recent murder. We were going to have to examine the rest of the bodies throughout the week and then make an official plan for wildlife management in the community. I didn't see any particular need for me to participate in the conversation, so I just focused on my food and wine. I was also focused on Nathanial, who seemed to be watching every move I made. I wondered if he had heard my conversation with Devon. I saw Patric leave the table and return with what appeared to be an extraordinarily expensive bottle of wine. It was larger than the other bottles, now empty and strewn across the table, and it didn't appear to have any sort of label. I heard quiet laughter filter from Andres and Christopher as Patric began to decant the wine. As with so many times thus far with this group, I felt as though I was missing something. I distinctly saw Nathanial shift uncomfortably in his chair as Patric moved around the table, pouring wine into everyone's glass. When he got to me, he hesitated and I looked up at him. "I don't really need very much, I'm a bit of a lightweight." I laughed, trying to break the source of his sudden immobility. Loud chuckles erupted from around the table at my joke and I saw that Patric had collected himself enough to pour my glass. He took his seat at the head of the table and raised his glass.

"A toast, a toast to old friends, to brothers and to the luck we are all experiencing by having such a beautiful and elegant woman in our company." His eyes locked with mine and I saw him wink at me as he raised the glass to his lips. He closed his eyes and his body begin to shimmer, in fact that was the reaction from every one of the Vampires around the table upon drinking their wine—everyone except Nathanial and Stephen who had yet to take a sip. Immediately, I felt wary and on edge; what was going on? I put the glass to my nose and sniffed. Initially, my physical reaction threw me. My mouth began to water and the scent was something so indescribably delicious that I was at a loss for words. The fragrance was familiar, something that I had smelled before, but so much more potent. Suddenly, I noticed how quiet it had become and I looked up to find everyone at the table staring at me, waiting.

"What is this?" I asked, even though I was pretty sure no one was going to volunteer any information.

"Just a little something to help enhance your evening," Andres spoke from across the table.

"Of course it's not nearly as exciting as a Bonder's choice for a good time is it Nathanial?" Christopher leaned in toward Nathanial and raised his glass towards him. I saw Nathanial bow his head and look away. What the hell were they talking about? "I've always been fascinated by the whole 'blood exchange ritual' that you guys have, I mean we all have our tools I suppose, but you Bonders really know how to do it right," Christopher said laughing. He couldn't be talking about the Bonding ritual, the one that I had gone through— his tone didn't see appropriate and besides, Vampires knew all about the human and Bonder relationship, that was one of the main reasons that the Vampires hated Bonders so much, their close ties with humans.

"That's some dark shit, good shit, but dark," Andres said, his voice sounded amped. I looked at Devon, hoping that he would take an opportunity to enlighten me.

"Ahhh, Ana is lost boys. Perhaps Nathanial can explain about the 'blood exchange', catch her up." Nathanial glared at Devon. Clearly he wasn't about to offer up any information about the topic at hand. "No? Well, I will be happy to fill you in Ana, being Human, I'm actually surprised that you haven't already heard about this…" Devon took another sip of his drink and I saw everyone move their chairs closer to our section of the table. Jesus, what was he going to say that was so interesting? I had yet to hear anything vaguely intriguing from this entire group except about Stephen being a guitar player. "Well let's see." Devon moved his chair so that he was facing me, but with an obvious gap between us. "You of course know about the traditional Bonding ritual, I believe that you have gone through that yourself, yes?" He turned to leer at Nathanial. "Well, there's actually another ritual of sorts that Humans and Bonders have been performing for centuries, one that we Vampires are a bit intrigued with, I must admit." He raised his eyebrows at me, as if daring me to ask him to continue. I waved my hand at him and he laughed. "So you know that the blood exchanged between Bonders and Humans is actually quite a small amount, as taking blood goes, but you can actually accommodate much larger doses, if the Human is healthy. Larger amounts of blood exchanged by both parties… hmmm, how do I say this in a respectful manner? If large amounts of blood are exchanged between the participants, then their respective sexual experiences with each other are, shall we say, immensely more pleasurable. I hear it's the equivalent of being reborn; not that I would know, Vampires have their own mechanisms for achieving extraordinary heights of pleasure, but perhaps Nathanial can share in his experience." My head jerked toward Nathanial. Had he done this with people? Had he done this with human women after we had slept together, after he had left? What was this "blood ritual" and why had he never told me about it? I had told him of everyone that I had slept with, all five of them, including Patric. Why didn't I know about this? I felt embarrassed, almost like I had just found out that someone had cheated on me, not that it mattered. Nathanial leaving pretty much ensured that he could be with whomever he wanted and I certainly hadn't remained monogamous.

"I think that's enough," Nathanial said quietly.

"Hey, we're all adults here, well actually Ana is a mere child compared with all of us, but technically she's an adult, right Ana?" Christopher said, cutting across Nathanial.

"Ok, so Bonders and humans have some weird sexual rituals that they do, it doesn't seem all that different than having sex while you're taking Ecstasy," I said casually. My curiosity was peaked and for some stupid reason, I wanted to hear more.

"Hmm, perhaps," Devon purred. "Again, I wouldn't know. This, however," he pointed to his glass, "a little of this manages to get us Vampires going quite a bit, sexually, I mean. Wouldn't you agree Patric?" I looked over at Patric, who was sitting still and tense, his eyes locked onto Devon. "I mean sex and violence go hand and hand and when you can experience them both at the same time, well, it's quite a turn on, for us at least. Personally, I enjoy the taking while the actual sex is happening, definitely a delicate skill to have, but if you can get it right—god, it's amazing. Right Patric?" I heard Patric growl, at least I thought it was coming from Patric. He had stood up from his chair and his body looked as though he might launch himself across the table at Devon. I heard another growl, this time coming directly across from me—Nathanial. I looked back and forth between all three of them, something wasn't right, they knew something...my heart froze and I realized that Alec had been right. Jesus Christ, he knew. Devon knew about Patric and me! He knew that I had given him my blood. He knew that we had been intimate, that Patric had left me, a human, alive, and that he had continued to keep me alive, he knew everything. Suddenly, the whole plan fell into place. Somehow my brain clicked and I knew why I was actually here. Patric had not invited me, he had not been the one to send the list of names to Caleb, he had not decorated my villa; hell, he probably didn't even care about my conclusions about the murders. In fact, remembering Patric's initial physical reaction upon seeing me for the first time, I didn't think that he even knew that I was going to be here. It was Devon; Devon had set things in motion, had lured me down here under some bogus pretense; Devon was dictating Patric's behavior toward me. I was here as a warning aimed at Patric and possibly Nathanial; they were all playing roles for the sake of the team.

Patric needed to be seen as the one in charge, as the leader that he was, but now Devon had the trump card, the one weapon he knew that allowed for Patric to have such an

231

increase in power and in coercion; Patric had my blood, my blood that gave him the strength to return to power, to take his place with the Vampires. Devon had turned Patric into half of a Vampire and had allowed for him to live, as long as he converted fully to the Vampires credos. Devon's blood ran in Patric veins, my blood ran in Patric's veins and now Devon wanted the same thing for himself; he wanted me. My conclusions were coming faster, my brain working to understand, to make the connections. The only way for Patric and Nathanial to loose the powers that I had given them was if I were to die. In death, most if not all of their powers would lose their potency, returning them to normal, still extraordinary, but normal as half- Vampires and Bonders go. Patric's fall again would free Devon to take over. With my blood coursing through Devon's body, and with me dead, it would be an easy usurping of the power structure that Patric had established. Clearly Devon thought himself much more powerful than Patric, that even in my death, Devon would still be strong enough to take Patric down, that he stood no chance against a full Vampire like Devon. It was a beautiful plan even I had to admit, but still, if Devon killed me, wouldn't his powers also be limited? Perhaps it was an issue of the extent to which they would be limited? Would it be more or less than Patric and Nathanial's? I wasn't seeing something, my mind was trying to fill in gaps with knowledge that I didn't have. I felt dizzy and my neck was beginning to throb. I had been so tuned out, my mind desperately trying to sort through what was happening, that I failed to see that Stephen, Christopher and Andres, were attempting to keep Nathanial and Patric from lunging at Devon.

232

"Hey, hey boys, let's try to keep things friendly shall we. A lady is present," Stephen chortled but his voice had turned dark and his eyes were now black. Nathanial yanked his arm out of Christopher's grasp and he held out his hand to me.

"It's late, and I think that we've had enough discussion for the day. I'll walk you back Ana. Let's go." I knew that Nathanial had heard everything that my mind had just navigated and I was sure that he could sense the panic beginning to flood my body. I nodded and turned toward the rest of team.

"I have had a bit more difficulty than the rest of you with today's events. I suppose it's just comes with being the slightly weaker species." I looked down at Devon as I said this; he met my stare and smirked. "Thank you for hosting me Patric, and I do promise that I will be in better control of my emotive tendencies on tomorrow's expedition." I laughed, trying to hold my emotional state together. I moved to walk past him and to follow Nathanial out the door, when I felt a sudden and familiar pressure in my head. *I have never thought of you as weak Ana. A hopeless romantic perhaps, a classic martyr, definitely, but never weak. He knows Ana. Devon knows about us. I'm sorry, but I will not protect you; it would potentially cost me my life and really, my life with a few less powers is still a life—helping you to stay alive, it would only serve to compromise everything that I have already put in place and my memories, my thoughts of you, they have already proven to be disabling to my plans; I can't have that, I'm sure you can understand. I do wish that things could have been different for us Ana, and I really do hope that you survive what is to come and not just for me and my ambitions, but because I will always care about you—more deeply than you will ever know...* The pressure subsided and Patric's voice was gone. We stood staring at each other. I subtly nodded and looked into his eyes. A brilliant flash of the clear turquoise that I had loved, appeared and I felt the point on the right side of the back of my neck grow warm, then turn ice cold. I knew that it was over. Whatever had transpired between Patric and myself, it had completed its journey. He wasn't going to help me, he wasn't going to protect me from Devon; he was going to let the natural course of things happen, he was going to save himself.

Nathanial and I walked in silence on the beach, back toward my villa. I couldn't begin to talk to him about what we both knew was happening. Saying things out loud just made it seem that much more real and that much more terrifying. How was I ever going to be able to fight off a Vampire, much less one so powerful and skilled as Devon, there was just no way. Upon hearing my thoughts, Nathanial took a deep breath and exhaled slowly. We approached my front door and I turned toward him. "Do you want to come in? You don't have to talk or anything... we could just sit and not talk..." I rambled; it was so weird having him beside me again. He smiled down at me and I felt him take the key from my now shaking hand and unlock the door. I heard him snort upon seeing the familiar décor of my room.

"Unbelievable, he's a class act." He motioned around the space dramatically. I suddenly became quite uncomfortable with the knowledge that Nathanial had seen through Patric's memories that we had been together. I felt embarrassed and slightly ashamed. He turned around to face me. "Ana, I do not blame you for what happened between you and my brother.

For all intents and purposes, I betrayed you, I left you to die and Patric was the one to save you, to put some of the pieces back together, but he also used your vulnerability, your compassion, your love." He turned away from me as he said this. "He manipulated you and seduced you into thinking that he could be saved, that he may want to make a different choice, if you just gave him what he wanted." I didn't think it was actually that simple.

"Nathanial, I loved your brother, in some strange way, I loved him and he wasn't the only instigator in that relationship. He tried to push me away, and time and time again, I came back; I felt compelled to come back. I think all three of us were somehow destined for each other, why else would I have three imprints on my neck? Do you think that's just a coincidence? It doesn't matter anyway. He's done with me now, he told me that he won't protect me from Devon, he can't be seen saving a human for the second time." Suddenly a thought occurred to me. "Nathanial, Devon never finished telling the story about the 'blood ritual', there was something else he was going to say before he got sidetracked. There was also something strange with that wine that Patric brought out—I noticed that you didn't drink any, why was that?" I eyed him warily; Nathanial was never terribly good at lying to me. He shook his head and sighed.

"Ana, I really don't think that you need to be hearing about dark, underground sex rituals right now, and as for the wine…" He rolled his eyes at me, exasperated.

"I'm not interested in hearing about the sexual stuff, Nathanial, I have a pretty good imagination—no, there was more to the story wasn't there? And what about the wine? You're acting like I should know what's going on there." I moved to stand in front of him, blocking his view of the ocean. "Nathanial tell me," I pleaded with him.

"Nothing about the way the wine smelled to you or your physical reaction to it, nothing about those things struck you as funny?" He raised his eyebrows at me. I pursed my lips, trying to remember why that stuff had created such a powerful physical response in me, why it seemed familiar. Then it dawned on me. I had a bit of Patric's blood in me; Patric was part Vampire and had Vampire blood in him, and Vampires, even half-Vampires craved one thing above everything—human blood. I gasped. Oh god, was I turning into a Vampire? That couldn't be right, I would have known if that was happening, Alec would have known.

"You're not a Vampire," Nathanial said darkly. "But you do have some very minimal side-effects from Patric giving you his blood."

"Would one of those side-effects be the attraction to human blood?" That seemed odd, I had been around Kai since Patric had been giving me my medicine—his blood, and I had been around my students and my co-workers and I hadn't ever had that kind of reaction like I had tonight.

"That's because it's not human blood that you actually crave." Again, he spoke in a dark tone.

"Well, what is it then?" I didn't get it.

"It's Patric's blood that you crave Ana; it was his blood, mixed with a bit of human blood in that bottle."

"Wait. Vampires drink each other's blood?" That was a bit of new information.

"Not a lot, it's more of a symbolic ritual, a bonding of sorts. The leader offers his brethren his blood for them to take as their own. It's the Human blood that offers the 'enhanced experience' for Vampires, not Patric's."

"Why didn't you drink it?" I asked, still a bit shell-shocked.

"I prefer to limit the amounts of blood, Vampire or otherwise, that I consume, Patric and I already share a bloodline don't we?" I guessed that that was a rhetorical question.

"Ok, so what's to the rest of the blood exchange thing?" Nathanial sighed and I could tell that he was hoping that I would drop the subject. It wasn't going to happen.

"Fine, fine, you want to know, I'll tell you." He put his arms up around the back of his neck and turned away from me. "If a Bonder so chooses, he can allow a Human to take more of the Bonder's blood than is necessary to…to have their 'experience'; the amount can be gauged of course depending on the individuals and what it is they want to explore sexually. By doing this, the Human *may*, they *may* become more like a Bonder and gain some of the similar powers we have in physical strength and mental prowess as well as an extended life span, even more so than originally gained from the initial Bonding. However, the chances of the Human surviving having that much excess blood in their system is slim to none and I haven't known too many Humans who have lived through that experience." He was pacing back and forth across the room, casting rapid shadows against the wall from the firelight. He looked manic.

"Oh." That was all I could manage to say. My thoughts had turned toward my initial reaction when I first heard Devon speaking about this ritual. "Nathanial, may I ask you something?" I knew that I didn't want to know the answer, but for some reason I needed to ask.

"What Ana." He stopped pacing and moved to stand in front of me.

"When you left, you know after…" This was harder than I thought. "Did you, did you find someone else to be with, I mean while you were gone—or that you are with now? I know that considering my behavior, that I probably don't have any right to ask you that, but…" I couldn't go on, my voice had started to shake and I moved to sit down on the sofa.

"Is that what you wanted to know?" He shook his head at me and sank down beside me. "I thought you were going to ask me to… well, to try and make you more like me." Well, that actually was going to be my next question, but not if he would make me more like him, but if he thought that performing that ritual might give me a chance against Devon. "Give us a chance, Ana, might give us a chance against Devon." Nathanial's face was gazing into the fire.

"I thought you said that you couldn't protect me, aren't you working for Patric now? He'd know what you were trying to do, he'd have you killed Nathanial." I still wasn't sure if I could

238

trust him. I didn't know exactly what his role with Patric was and I had no idea how he felt about me. He still hadn't answered my question. He turned his gaze away from the fire to look at me.

"No, I was never with anyone else after I left. I am not with anyone else now and there will never be anyone else Ana." His eyes were burning again and this time I did feel their pulse pulling every part of who I knew myself to be, towards him. He broke his trance on me and he leaned his head back against the sofa. "Tell me something," he asked softly. "You're attracted to Devon are you not?"

"Maybe a little, before I knew he wanted to kill me," I said. Nathanial laughed quietly.

"Fair enough, but I saw the way you were dancing with him, the way he was touching you, the way you were moving your body…" his voice became considerably softer as he spoke. "You liked the way he felt didn't you?" I had liked the way Devon had touched me, how he moved next to me; it was pointless to lie.

"Yes, I liked dancing with him, but I think it really came from a place of just wanting some normalcy—even if that meant accepting a harmless dance from a Vampire."

"There is nothing harmless about Devon, Ana, and nothing harmless in the way he was touching you, or in his lust for you. Let me ask you something, and I want you to answer me honestly, because I will of course know if you don't," he paused to look sternly at me. I nodded. "If Devon came to you and he gave you a choice, if he said that he could take your

239

blood by force and effectively kill you or you could give it to him willingly, but by doing so, you would have to join Devon in trying to overthrow Patric; what if he promised you that my life would be spared by volunteering your 'donation'—if that's part of his plan; what would you do?" He was staring at me, searching my eyes for some hesitation that he would never find.

"Nathanial, I don't trust Devon at all, but honestly, if it meant saving you, if it meant even a chance at you keeping your life, I would do whatever he wanted." I was surprised at how easily my response came. I didn't even have to think about what I would do, of course I would save Nathanial and perhaps try and save Patric too, I couldn't deny that I would never want to see Patric killed. Nathanial's eyes were locked on mine and he looked at me incredulously.

"Even after all of this time, even after you still have doubts about whether or not you can trust me, even after Patric said that he would not protect you, even after you are still not sure whether or not I would protect you; still, you would choose to spare my life to possibly try to save Patric, to give your life for mine. How can that be Ana? Since I've met you, since I've come to know you, that is how you have always felt, that it is the other lives that matter more; it was mine the night of the University attack, it was Patric's in your hope that he would be able to chose a different path, and I even think it's Devon's, with your nonsense about his happiness." I raised my eyebrows at him; he *had* been listening to our conversation at dinner. "It was impossible not to feel your despair Ana," Nathanial answered my unspoken thought. "I can't wrap my head around it, honestly."

"Well, you don't have to wrap your head around anything, Nathanial," I said stubbornly. "I'm not a puzzle piece that needs a proper placement; it's just who I became, and I'm sorry if I don't fit comfortably into who you think I should be." I felt defiant and I felt as if he was criticizing the one aspect of my personality that I actually liked.

"Ana, I'm not criticizing you. I'm just saying that it's preposterous how little you value your own life, your own contributions to the world and how much you put other people on pedestals—" I cut him off.

"I'm not putting Devon on a pedestal or even Patric for that matter. I just thought that perhaps no one had bothered to ask either of them in a very long time, if they had ever been happy, or what they wanted for themselves when they were children. I just thought that maybe it would be nice if someone reminded them that perhaps this is not what they had hoped their life would be, and that maybe, just maybe, if given another chance—they would make a different choice. I'm not saying that I'm the person good enough to give them that opportunity, I'm just saying that I don't mind being the person who asks." I was infuriated.

"Ana, that would make a very nice speech, if your questions didn't seem to get you into so much trouble." His head still leaning against the back of the couch, he turned to look at me.

"And what the hell is that supposed to mean?" He was picking at a wound and he knew it.

241

"Ana, come on. I know that you can stand here and 'declare' that you had feelings for Patric, possibly even say that you loved him and that you initiated the relationship, but do you honestly and truly think that what happened between the two of you, that that was coming from you?" He leaned toward the fire.

"Of course it was coming from me Nathanial, whom else would it be coming from?" I was thoroughly confused.

"My god Ana! Seriously, have you learned nothing? Patric is not who you think he is, he's not who you want him to be and he outsmarted you. He used you. He knows you. He knows that your compassion and your desire to help people, it's your Achilles heel. He's a master manipulator. So much so, that you thought everything you were feeling towards him was coming from you! The physical relationship that the two of you had Ana, that was a direct side-effect of the blood he had been giving you; that's what it does, it makes you *want* people—it made you *want him*. He also got into your head. I mean didn't you ever wonder why you were so suddenly transfixed by Patric, how it happened so soon, that your feelings and thoughts for him were bordering on the obsessive? Tell me Ana, does that sound like you, like who you truly are—are you obsessive in your relationships?" I couldn't speak; I was stunned. That's not what happened. I did care about Patric, I had trouble placing why or how I had come to feel so strongly about him, but still, I knew that I cared for him deeply, and he had cared for me. He had kept me alive—Nathanial cut through my thoughts. "He kept you alive Ana so that he could *use* you to get me, not because he cared about you. He kept you hovering on the brink of death;

he twisted your own good qualities into behavior that was not, that is not you. He knew exactly what he was doing and now of course, Devon knows what he was able to do. Devon knows that Patric got so deep into your head that you allowed him to take blood from you Ana, Christ!" Nathanial turned toward me as he stood, his hands on his hips, the fire blazing behind him.

"No," I whispered, shaking my head. "No. Patric said that he cared for me, that he was sorry that things couldn't have been different for us, he did care for me, I'm sure of it, and besides, how do you know all of this—you weren't even here, you left, you left me to die…" I trailed off, my head hurt and my heart hurt.

"I know Ana." Nathanial moved to stand in front of me, his hands resting on my shoulders. "I know, because Patric told me what he had done, he was proud and he wanted the others to know just how easy it was to coerce weak and foolish Humans, his words, not mine." He sighed loudly. " I do think though, that somewhere deep inside Patric, that he perhaps did care for you, that somehow during the course of your relationship, that he came to…he came to possibly feel something for you; was it love, I don't know, but yes, there was something there, but it was not enough Ana, it was not enough to bring him back, to save him." I wanted him to leave, to just get out. I didn't want him to look at me, standing there like he felt sorry for me, like I was some stupid and small child who needed their parent to tell them that it's ok to make mistakes. I wasn't a child and I could be accountable for my own decisions. He didn't know me. "I've known you your whole life Ana," he whispered. "I'm sorry if the things that I've said this evening have hurt you, I would never *intentionally* do that to you." He emphasized the word "intentionally" as if reminding me that he too had been a victim of Patric's psychological warfare. I didn't care, we weren't alike and Nathanial should have been stronger than me anyway; he's not even human. "You're right Ana, I should have been stronger. I have no excuse for what happened to me, I was a coward, but you should know that I fought hard to regain my memories of you, of us; that I pushed back against Patric and I fought for my place in your life, in your heart." He brushed his hand over the left side of my chest, but turned away from me and exhaled loudly. "I can't say what I want, I can't tell you what I'm feeling." He sounded frustrated. " Patric can't know what I want, how badly that I need you, that I want you Ana. What Patric knows, Devon knows…it's too risky right now; I'm sorry." His eyes were pleading with me, searching my face for some sort of understanding of his position. I wanted none of it.

"Can you please leave Nathanial, because you know what, I'm really not interested in what's 'too risky' for *you* at the moment. I'm just going to sit here and hope that I'm not brutally attacked by a blood thirsty Vampire this evening. So you'll have to forgive me if I can't indulge your problems with you and your brother at the moment," I spat at him. He winced at the bitterness of my words.

"Devon won't attack you tonight Ana." He moved away from me and towards the door. "He's a planner and he knows that you require a more sophisticated form of seduction than most of his prey, but you should be aware that Devon's ability to play with your psyche, it makes Patric's talent seem inconsequential—harmless even. You need to keep your guard up tomorrow. Patric knows that it was Devon who managed to get you down here, and he's aware that Devon wants to take him out; neither one of them play fair and while Patric can't and won't cause you any physical harm, mainly because it would affect his powers, he's most certainly not going to protect you from Devon, that would make him appear weak to the rest of his brethren." I knew all of this already. Nathanial nodded. "I'll do what I can to keep you safe Ana, but I have to maintain a united front with my brother; I'm bound to my promise to him, at least for the time being." He bowed his head and I saw a shadow of desperation linger across his face. I turned back toward the fire and the door quietly shut.

Chapter Seven

Ana

I just wanted to go home, to get out of this horrible place. Of course I knew that going home wouldn't mean staying alive, but at least I would have Alec and Kai, at least I could be in my own bed with my wolves and my friends. I didn't want to think about Nathanial or Devon or Patric, or what anyone was planning —I just wanted everything to end, to stop time and erase the inception of my own life, to be in nothingness, to just cease the wound from bleeding. A memory of ten years ago made me slam on the brakes of my jeep. So powerful and visceral were the feelings that I had to close my eyes. I saw the scene playing out as if I were watching a film of myself, slowed down so that my mind could let me focus…

I had been sad, very, very sad. Memories of abuse, of severe trauma had begun to surface and I was having a difficult time regaining any sense of who I was. I was away from Noni, studying abroad; I was lonely and stressed. I saw myself sitting on the beach in Bray, Ireland. Looking out at the cliffs. I watched myself pull out a bottle of pills; they were sleeping pills that I had been taking for my insomnia. The film showed me pouring fifty or so caplets into my hand. Even though my mind knew that I was watching a memory, and my subconscious knew that I had not killed myself, I could feel my heart begin to pound as I observed myself staring at my hand, staring out at the ocean. I knew what I had been thinking. I could make it all go away and the pain would just stop. I hadn't killed myself, obviously. I had decided to give myself another chance, that I couldn't do that to Noni and that perhaps I could hold on for one more day. The film went black and I leaned my head back against the seat, breathing hard. A thought occurred to me, a thought so dark and penetrating that it troubled me to even have it in my presence, and yet, there it was, waiting for me to acknowledge it like some small child, desperate for attention. It was an option, a way out, a possible solution that no one had even considered, until now. Nathanial wasn't going to attempt to turn me into something close to his species; Patric or Devon didn't want to turn a human into a Vampire, all three of them needed me to become better versions of themselves, to gain the upper hand, but what if I leveled the playing field, what if I made everyone even and no one was that much stronger or better than the others, what if I made it so that they would have to fight each other with the powers that they each naturally already had, those given to them by birthright or by some dark ritual, as in Devon's case. What if I did the one thing that they all had missed? All of them, in their infinite collective wisdom, had assumed the most obvious of the scenarios, except me. I saw another play that could be made; sure it rang of martyrdom, but it also made sense. Within my musings, I began to feel a great peace and renewed strength. I had a trump card as well and I was going to use it.

Nathanial

Something was wrong. I knew it the minute I saw her get out of her jeep. For days I could sense that Ana was upset and distressed, but something about the way she felt today, sent terror into my very soul. She didn't look at me. She didn't look at anyone. I watched as she grabbed her pack and walked toward the team; she seemed defiant and rigid. She smiled at everyone, but I could see that it was forced and the smile never reached her eyes. I could barely see her face because she was wearing a hat pulled down low; I was unsettled by her appearance, by her energy. Something was very, very wrong. I tried to scan her mind, but I was met with such a deep blackness, it was impenetrable. Had Devon gotten to her? I knew that I shouldn't have left her alone for so many days, I had broken her down and she was vulnerable, exhausted. I glanced over at Devon, he didn't seem on edge or particularly anxious. I probed as far as I could into his mind; his thoughts were, of course, on Ana and his little fantasies were becoming quite detailed. I felt a shot of pressure to my head and I looked to find him quietly laughing at me. He winked and turned to move over near Ana. I watched her body language with him, she seemed relaxed and she was smiling and showing him some of her notes, but something was off, I just felt it. Unfortunately, I didn't have time to analyze her further as the Medical Examiner had arrived to take us out to the site that was now beginning to resemble a mass grave.

We took off through the forest and I noticed immediately that Ana fell in step next to the M.E. She was asking questions about the site, about how long the guy had been in West Papua, about his conclusions. I saw my brother move to her side; apparently Ana's skill at banter was making him uncomfortable. Suddenly, I saw Patric stumble back a few steps as if he'd been punched. I looked at Ana and saw that she'd hadn't missed a step; she and the Examiner were still talking, but I was sure that the sudden balance problem that Patric had experienced, had indeed come from Ana. I frowned. Maybe she was just angry per our previous conversation. I know hearing that Patric had used her, had manipulated her, this had not settled well in her mind. Perhaps she was determined to retaliate a bit, but I had not seen Ana ever have a physical ability to move someone away from her...that was a talent shared by demons and Vampires. I frowned and moved to get closer to watch her.

Getting to the site proved to be an enormous challenge, not for myself or for the Vampires, but for the two Humans we had with us. Ana was an exceptionally skilled hiker, but the dense forests and steep ravines were making things difficult, even for her. Twice I saw her about to step off a ledge and for sure, tumble to her death, and twice I saw my brother reach out to grab her, both times pulling her back close to him and twice I saw her jerk her body away so forcefully, that it threw him off balance. She was definitely angry, but the violent nature of her response seemed out of place with her normal demeanor. Patric shot me a look and I was sure that he was trying to see if I had shared anything with her, anything that could jeopardize his strategy or anything that could make him seem weak. He couldn't get in. I had become quite versed since my last mistake with Patric, at allowing for him to see what he wanted and to never see what I was truly thinking and feeling; it was excruciating work, but essential. I rushed to catch up with Ana. I noticed something glistening on the ground at my feet, diverting my attention; the reflection was so brilliant that it blinded me for a brief moment. I kneeled down to the dirt and saw the source of the glare. I felt my chest heave as I picked up the small star-like jewel that had embedded itself in the earth. It was a single piece that had fallen from Ana's imprint, from her metal symbol, the one that represented her soul and her life. I took the lone star and looked down the trail at her figure and gasped. Tiny spots of fractured light were scattered along behind her. They dotted the thick dense green of the ferns, pulsing and shimmering and there were hundreds of them. What was happening? I tucked the one jewel that I plucked from the ground, into my breast pocket and hurried to catch up with the rest of the team. Something was terribly, terribly wrong and I felt ice move through my own imprint, chilling the place over my heart.

We arrived to the site and immediately began to rifle though the remains. Christopher and Andres were looking at photographs from the M.E., Stephen and Patric were in the ditch turning over bones and dirt and I noticed that Devon and Ana had wandered toward the migration gaps in the reserve's fence. They weren't out of eyeshot, but having Ana so isolated from the rest of the group was not an ideal situation. I was about to follow them when my brother motioned for me to join him over at the main site. I looked one more time at Devon and Ana as I watched them cross through the fence and out of view. Over the course of two hours I managed to identify the remains of five children under the age of ten, six women under the age of thirty and two men, also possibly under the age of thirty. Every five minutes I would glance up towards the fence to see if Ana and Devon had returned; I was getting anxious and it was becoming more difficult to maintain my focus and my composure. During one of my quick checks down the road, I noticed something odd. I wasn't the only one who was staring at the fence line. Patric's attention was focused on the spot where Ana and Devon had disappeared and I could see his eyes scanning the vast and dense jungle for any glimpse of their figures. He seemed nervous. He turned and noticed me staring at him and he immediately looked away. God, he was always at war with himself.

Finally, at five-thirty, just as we were wrapping up our assessment of the site, I saw Devon and Ana emerge from the forest. She looked normal, of course I wasn't sure what else to expect. I knew that Devon wouldn't try to kill her now, not while there were so many of us here, plus, he liked the chase. It would have been too easy, too quick and Devon was extremely patient. Still, I was worried. I knew how seductive Vampires could be and I knew that Ana was feeling somewhat rejected and definitely used; any woman, even one as strong and confident as Ana, could fall victim to the charms of an extremely attractive Vampire; my chest contracted and I felt a sudden surge of anger envelope my body. Ok, so maybe I was a little more than worried about Ana and Devon, maybe I was a bit jealous. I hadn't liked at all the way I had seen her dancing with him, in fact, the whole image had made me so sick with jealousy, that I had forced myself to look away from them, from her body moving against his, from the way his fingers caressed her skin…ugh! Maybe Patric wasn't the only one fighting a war with himself.

As they got closer, I could see that Devon had his hand on her back and they seemed to be having an intense but jovial conversation. She was nodding at him and he was laughing a bit at whatever she was saying. Again, I saw that I was not the only one to notice their return. I saw my brother look once at their image and then I saw him bow his head and turn away. I

251

fingered the tiny star-like jewel in my pocket and moved down the trail to greet them.

"Ahh… Nathanial, it seems that both Ana and I concur that an animal, possibly another rabid animal has managed to cross through one of the migration gaps. Actually, it was Ana who so aptly provided such a stellar analysis, but she's gladly letting me share some of the credit." He turned and put his arm around her shoulders and pulled her into his side. I saw her smile gently and move to walk around me. She didn't look at me, she didn't acknowledge me, and I suddenly felt very, very cold.

Ana

Today had been the easiest day by far and I was sure that it was in large part to do with the fact that I now had a plan, a plan that I was in control over and that I would initiate. It had been fairly simple to fall into a role today, although being alone with Devon had proved somewhat of a challenge. He wanted to apologize for the events of the dinner at Patric's and say that he was sorry that the conversation had turned to a very disrespectful discussion about sex and women. I had waved him off and told him that I wasn't so much of a prude or Nazi feminist that I couldn't tolerate "men being men" or Vampires being Vampires, I had joked. Then things took a bit of a turn. Just recalling our conversation made my heart race a bit…

"So, aren't you even the least bit curious about the whole 'blood exchange' ritual?" he had asked as we walked deeper in the forest.

"Well actually, I was more curious about your reaction to the whole thing, I mean it seemed like you and Stephen and Christopher, all of you guys seemed jealous that the Bonders have that as part of their... um, their sexual arsenal, I guess." He had laughed and snorted at my misinterpretation of his reaction.

"What, me jealous? Ana, a Vampire is never jealous, especially when it comes to sexual gratification. The Bonders may think that they have the market cornered, but like with so many things about that species, they are misinformed my love, completely misinformed." He had moved closer to me and brought the rhythm of our steps to a halt. "Although I have to say, that I was a bit surprised that you and Nathanial had not shared in such an experience. I mean if we were together, like you and Nathanial had been, well I'm sure that we would have been able to explore many a ritual for ourselves, don't you think?" He had smirked at me and I had felt my face go flush, but I hadn't let him make me unsteady. Apparently, the mounting courage that I was experiencing from having made my decision had proved quite helpful today. I bit my lip as I continued to remember how I had totally disarmed Devon. I had leaned forward, moving almost so that our bodies were touching, almost, but not quite.

"Devon, Devon, Devon..." I had said, slightly mocking him. "Why don't you just get it over with? What exactly are you waiting for? Unless it's really not me that you want, unless you

253

have some other reason for why you appear to be so interested in me. I mean normally, I don't quite go for the hypersexual males, the ones who I know have made promiscuity a life-long hobby, but really I'm long over due for a one night stand, but of course you already know that don't you?" It had been my turn to smirk, as I saw a flash of bewilderment appear in his eyes. I had moved back several feet and had turned to continue down the trail. *"Come on you wuss, let's go!"* I'd laughed at him, as he remained standing in the same spot—motionless. My comments probably were not the wisest route to go, but for some reason I was feeling a bit reckless. Maybe I had hoped that Devon would just kill me, that by doing so, that he would have taken the decision out of my hands, and Nathanial and Patric would just have to figure out how to take Devon down on their own. Or maybe, I was still in the mode of not wanting to think that Devon was purely evil, that maybe he did have some shred of humanity in his heart—although my gut was telling me that that was highly unlikely. Or, maybe I just wanted to prove Nathanial wrong, to let him see that even though I knew that I was being used, that I still could make the decision to allow for that to happen, that my choices were still my own and if I wanted to sleep with a Vampire who was waiting for the perfect opportunity to kill me, well, then I could do that too. Maybe it was all three.

Devon had been silent for most of the hike back to the team so I had taken the opportunity to continue on my reckless streak. I had to be careful though, I hadn't wanted him to know that I had figured out that he could use my blood to harm Patric, or that I knew that he had been the one to turn Patric into a Vampire. I had worked very hard to bury any thoughts that would tip Devon off, it was hard, but I knew that I could do it…

"Seriously Devon, all joking aside; you and I both know that you are not remotely interested in having any kind of serious relationship with me. You don't even know me and on top of that, you hate humans! Are you in that much of a need to scratch another notch on your headboard that you feel compelled to spend energy trying to seduce me?" Again, the directness of my comments had stopped him in his tracks. "I mean, I'm pretty sure that you could have any woman you wanted, and some who I would guess, if you drugged them enough, may even offer you a bit of their blood to boot; why are so interested in me?" His normally composed façade had slipped just a little, and I could see his clear gray eyes darken.

"Yes, I suppose that I could have any woman I wanted, mostly by sheer force of personality and my uncanny ability to make Humans do what I want." His voice had been even, but it was tinged with a bit of the same darkness that had appeared in his eyes. "I think that you could be very important to me, your ability to, let's say, ward off my internal assaults on your psyche… well, that's positively irresistible to me," he'd purred and began to slowly close the distance between us.

"Humph, you just like the chase Devon, this right here, this is what you like." I'd rolled my eyes at him and walked back through the migration gap, thankful to be out of the darkness of the forest. I had been able to see the rest of the team down the road and I had waited for Devon to catch up. He emerged from the trees and blurred to my side and placed his hand on my back.

"Don't you like a good chase Ana, the anticipation, the energy, the predation factor is arousing, no?"

"How nice Devon, we women always like to be associated with someone's predation games, it's great to be debased to sheer animal instincts. On behalf of women everywhere, let me thank you." He had laughed at my sarcasm, but he wasn't finished. I had seen that Nathanial was making his way down the path to meet us and I wasn't in any mood to talk to him. In fact, I had been ignoring both he and Patric all day.

"Aren't you just a little bit curious about what it would be like if we were together? I mean I know that you've had your 'experiences' with Bonders and of course there was Patric." I'd turned to him, there was no use trying to lie to Devon. He'd winked at me. *"But don't you think that being with someone who actually can show you how it's done, to really be able to indulge your desires, to want you in ways that you didn't even know were possible; aren't you the least bit tempted?"* He had bent his head low, trying to see my eyes. I hadn't wanted him to be able to see them because I knew that they would have betrayed me, that he would have seen the truth—that I *was* tempted.

My recollections came to a halt, as I pulled my jeep back into the lodge. My mind was swimming and I just really wanted a nap. Alec had called twice since I had left the site, but I wasn't in the mood to talk to him, plus, his hackles were always raised since I had thought about killing myself several months ago. He was sure to see through my façade and I wasn't about to let me ruin my plan. When I thought of Alec, of course I thought of Kai and how much I would miss them, how much I would miss Noni, but I knew that in time they would come to understand, to forgive me. Oddly, the issue of taking my own life was not proving disturbing to me. It's not that I was necessarily comfortable ending my time on the earth, but I had always felt that me being here was a fluke; I had never thought that my birth had been a particularly good decision on the part of my mother, that the events that followed in my childhood were too horrible to endure and that she really should have terminated the pregnancy. Besides all of that, I knew beyond a shadow of doubt, that I would do anything to save Nathanial, that I would go to whatever measures necessary to allow for him to continue his life, to allow him to be able to make better choices. I loved him desperately and I knew that a world without him would not and could not be a good world. I had never felt that way about myself and neither had anyone else for that matter. I just couldn't see any other option and perhaps I was also looking for an excuse; an excuse to end a lifetime of pain of feeling unworthy and unsafe and a lifetime of never being able to keep the people that I loved and needed close to me; they always disappeared.

My conversation with Devon and my internal musings about my life were still on my mind as I dressed for dinner and suddenly a completely different option entered my thoughts, one that I also had not considered, a scenario that might make things a bit easier for the people that I loved. Maybe I could ensure that both Nathanial and Patric also had a little something to help them win against Devon…I needed to think this through a bit more. I was sure that Devon would bide his time a little longer, heighten his arousal. I just needed to figure out what to say, how to ask for what I wanted. I was going to have to play the part first and worry about the consequences later. Before I left for dinner, I phoned the front desk and asked for the lodge doctor to be sent over to my villa, it was imperative that I took care of this first and extremely crucial step.

I was late getting to the restaurant, but it appeared that my team had managed to entertain themselves in my absence. Several human women had joined our little group and the table had gotten significantly more crowded. Of course the only seat available was next to Devon and for me, tonight, that would work. I waved at him and he stood to pull out my chair. Only he and Nathanial were unaccompanied by women and I noticed that Nathanial wasn't at the table but leaning against the railing, watching me. I was wearing a flowing skirt that was cut a bit more above the knee than I was actually accustom to displaying. I had chosen a silk camisole and my favorite sandals, and by the looks of both Nathanial and Devon, it was working for me.

"Well, I must say that I'm not at all ashamed to admit that I like you so much better when you aren't so covered up." Devon laughed as he kissed my hand. I smiled at him and turned to look at Nathanial. I caught his eye and the intensity of his gaze made my resolve waiver. I forced myself to look away and to blink back the tears that had suddenly appeared. Did he know? Could he sense what it was that I had planned? Would he forgive me? I couldn't spend lifetimes pondering questions that I would never know the answers to; I had to keep moving forward, not looking down. The servers arrived and we all managed to pull ourselves around the table. I had a middle seat, with Devon to my left and Nathanial directly to my right—at least I wasn't surrounded by scantily dressed women flagrantly groping the people next to me. I ordered my meal and a glass of wine. I saw Nathanial raise his eyebrows at me; I'm sure he was remembering that I hardly ever had wine with my meals out. I felt Devon's hand on my leg and I turned to look at him. He was facing away from me, talking to Stephen, but I distinctly felt his fingers begin to caress my skin. His touch was hot, not warm like Patric's or even Nathanial's had been, but hot, and just when I thought for sure he was going to burn my skin, a sudden coolness swept up my leg and into my abdomen where it began to spread. It was an odd sensation. I was reminded of an ocean breeze that washes over you, whispering lightly and filtering itself through you, to your very core, but there was also a darkness to the touch, something that hinted at hungers I knew nothing of, at least not yet. The music was loud and there were so many more people dancing this evening than the other night. I quickly scanned the table and noticed that both Patric and Stephen were gone, as were their lady friends and Christopher and Andres were continuing their discussion with Devon. I supposed I could talk to Nathanial, but he seemed quite content to just sit and stare at me, it was uncomfortable. Finally Devon turned. He brushed my hair back over my shoulder and held out his hand for me to take.

"I think dancing has become our set routine now don't you Ana?" I saw him look over at Nathanial and wink. I had to hand it to Devon; he definitely had balls. I took his hand and let him lead me into the crowd. He didn't waste anytime pulling me in close to him, not like the last time we had danced, he had been a bit more cautious. I didn't mind; if I was going to do this, I was at least going to do it well. I wrapped my arms around his waist and moved my hips closer to his, slowly pushing him against me. "I see we're feeling a bit more daring tonight aren't we?" he murmured against my neck. I slowly turned my face to his so that our lips were barely touching. He put his finger to my bottom lip and smiled. "I don't kiss Ana." His eyes were bright and clear and full of veiled emotion. "At least not on the mouth." He laughed softly and I felt his fingers move down my back. I shivered and he pulled me closer to him, his hands now on my hips, pressing me harder against his body.

"Hmmm, well if you don't kiss, then what *do* you do Devon?" I knew that I was treading in very dangerous waters, but I had to test his limits, if he had any. He pulled back and gave me a look filled with so much violent passion, that I felt transfixed. I had never seen anyone look at me that way, not Nathanial, not Patric, not one man that I had ever been with, had ever looked at me the way Devon was looking at me now. I saw his eyes flash and he grabbed my wrist and dragged me through the crowd to a darkened corner, a very darkened corner. He pushed me up against the wall and brought his face close to mine. He was composed on the surface; his face was smooth and his tone was calm, but there was something underneath that terrified me, something very dark and filled with violence.

"You're playing with fire Ana. Patric has you conditioned into thinking that he knew what he was doing, that he had the nature of our species all figured out; he was so, so wrong." His hands were on my shoulders and I could feel him press me further against the wall and move to trace his fingers along the bite marks on my neck.

"Oh, I don't know Devon," I said. Bizarrely, the seductive nature of my voice didn't sound unnatural to my ear. "I think

Patric might have known a little about what he was doing." I took his hand and pushed it up my thigh to my groin where Patric had placed his other two marks. He laughed.

"Mmmm, I see, you're a bit of a hellcat in bed are you?" Keeping his hand on my upper thigh, he took his free hand and covered my mouth, all the while pressing me with an absurd amount of strength against the wall. "Let's just see how you do with a small dosage, shall we?" He deepened the pressure of his fingers to the bite marks on my groin and I felt myself start to scream. The hand over my mouth moved to smother my voice and I felt weak. It wasn't that his touch hurt, it was more that I felt the most intense desire that I had ever experienced in my life. So powerful was the heat and the rush of lust that I felt for him, I guess one could say that it *was* almost painful. He moved his hand away from the bite marks, but not off my thigh. I gasped, trying to regain breath. "That's one. Shall we see if we can go for another?" Again he moved his hand and I felt him press harder on the wound. Another rush of heat came so fast that again, I tried to scream out. I was breathing so hard that I thought I might hyperventilate. He was taking the breath right out of me and yet all I could do was groan in pleasure. "That's two." He removed his hand again. "I can go slower Ana, I can go much, much slower. Do you really want to play with the adults, because I can do this all night, I'm just getting started," he whispered in my ear and I felt his fingers begin to massage the punctures in my flesh. He pressed deeper and I heard myself groan and felt my legs begin to open to his hand. He laughed again. "No, I don't think we're quite ready for that yet do you?" He was moving his hand slowly yet still pushing down, still massaging me. I shuttered and gasped as I felt him shift his hand away and just

261

barely brush his fingers between my legs, feeling me. I groaned again. "That's three." He dropped his hand from my mouth and my thigh, but still he kept me pressed up against the wall. He brought his lips to my ear and whispered, "I can show you things Ana, things that you won't let yourself want. I can show you things that I know you desire, that I know are in the deepest places of your soul and that you refuse to let out. I don't mind chasing you Ana, it's an amazing turn on, but now that we've had this little experience, now that you've let me get this close to you, to *feel* you, well it's going to be a bit difficult for me to control myself now I'm afraid. I can wait a bit longer, possibly, but I really would rather not. For some reason, I'm extremely attracted to you, more than most Humans and that just seems to be adding to my whole problem with self-control. What should we do about this?" He pulled back and looked at me. I was trying not to faint.

"Ana, are you alright?" I looked past Devon to find Nathanial standing behind him; my eyes widened, I didn't recognize him. His face had changed, it was dark and his hair was now free of the dreadlocks, it was blowing behind him despite the fact that we were inside and there was no wind. He looked bigger somehow, taller and more muscular. His eyes were black, jet black and his skin seemed to glow. The usual copper sheen was now emitting what looked like tiny embers, or small flames beneath the surface. Nathanial looked as though he had stepped out from a fire and he was burning. Devon's eyes grew dark upon surveying Nathanial; apparently I was not the only one surprised by his suddenly altered appearance. "Ana," Nathanial said and he held out his hand to me. I looked at Devon and he smirked and released me. I peeled myself from the wall and moved toward Nathanial, but I didn't take his

262

hand. I nodded toward him and walked back through the crowd. The rest of dinner was a blur. I couldn't concentrate and I felt slightly woozy. Nathanial's confrontation with Devon and me had only seemed to make Nathanial watch me that much more intently and while his appearance had returned to normal, well his skin had returned to normal, he still looked taller somehow and extremely strong and his eyes were still jet black. I couldn't help but think that perhaps I was just slightly in over my head, and that maybe I actually had no idea what real Vampires could do or what sort of transformation Nathanial had gone through in his time with Patric. What I did know was that there was definitely something more going on, something a bit older and deeper than the current well of knowledge that I was drinking from, and that perhaps my original plan was the better of the two options. Although, if I was being completely honest with myself, *if* I had to die, I was thinking that Devon would at least make it an interesting experience, I mean what a way to go. I felt my cheeks grow warm as I recalled just how it felt when he touched me. Hmm, perhaps no more wine for me with dinner, I mused.

I left the dinner party in full swing and headed back to my villa. Before the evening out, I had spoken with Alec and told him that I was flying back tomorrow, earlier than expected. I was planning to feign some sort of committee meeting for my dissertation so as to not tick off Patric. Alec agreed vehemently and was due to pick me up at the airport in the morning. Since I didn't think that I would actually be able to get out from under Devon, I figured that if I was going to make any of this happen, I wanted to do it at home; I wanted to be able to see Kai and Alec, to call Noni maybe, if I didn't chicken out, and to just be somewhere that I had always felt was a part of me. I walked into the hallway and immediately noticed that the fire had been lit, a possible service of the lodge I had hoped. Of course no such luck was going to befall me because as I came around the corner, Devon was sitting on the couch looking relaxed and amused at my surprise.

"Patric had it wrong you know," he spoke softly and as if we were picking up from a previous conversation. "About vampires I mean, about how Human blood affects us, well maybe it's not so much that he got it wrong, as it is that I just didn't tell him." I sighed. It figured that Devon would be one step ahead of me; still, I was pretty sure that he had no idea what I was prepared to do. I stepped out of my sandals and walked over to the kitchen. I noticed that on the counter was a note from the lodge doctor confirming that my deliveries had been made. I quietly slid the note down into the drawer and went to grab a ginger ale from the fridge. My hands were shaking; at least that part was finished, I had done what I could to help and I just hoped that this would all be over soon. I popped the can open and went to sit next to Devon on the couch. Surprisingly, I was feeling calmer than I would have thought. I took a sip and turned to him, pulling my legs up under me.

"Care to elaborate at all?" I asked. He turned to me, his eyes stormy and dark in their tint and I thought I could see clouds moving swiftly, deep inside them. He looked me over and smiled.

"Patric is a lousy Vampire, I'm not even sure if he would have been a very good Bonder had he chosen that course, but that's neither here nor there. He's weak, he's emotional and he's overly confidant, three very bad traits to have as a leader." He paused and looked back into the fire.

"Is it that you don't like *him* or is it that you don't like what he stands for, because sometimes they can be different things. Sometimes who a person or a being is, can be at odds with what they are trying to accomplish…" I stared at him, waiting.

"Ana, it's the oddest thing with you. You have the tendency to anthropomorphize my species. The ability to like or dislike, to feel love or hate, compassion or empathy; it's not part of who we are—" I cut him off.

"But you hate humans, you hate Bonders, you fought wars with both groups because you hated them, that's an emotion, hate is an emotion Devon." He turned back toward me and pursed his lips.

"We do not hate Humans or Bonders, we find both species to be inferior and not of much use to our endeavors on their own. However, we have managed to find some relevance for those groups, particularly Humans, due to their fragile nature and bizarre capacity to trust. Both Humans and Bonders are easily manipulated because both groups feel that they are immune to such 'sins of the soul', if you will. Vampires have no pretense; we have never tried to hide who we are or what we want." I wanted to debate that matter further, but I remembered that he had started this whole thing saying something about Patric. I shrugged at him.

"Ok, fine, you are what you are and humans and Bonders are weak and fragile and corruptible; we're pathetic and disposable, I get it. What's the problem with Patric? He always seemed pretty smart to me." I sipped my drink.

"Well, you just proved my point. You trusted that he was what he appeared, a strong, smart and calculating Vampire, but he's not. He's only half-Vampire and his Bonder genes have proven to dominate most aspects of his personality, to his disadvantage I might add. Bonders are somewhat trusting in nature, like Humans, and Patric is no exception. He trusted me to guide him, to teach him about his new life, and I did. I could also see that Patric was ambitious and was easily seduced by power, sex and money. He gorged himself on temptation and worried about the consequences later. But, I also saw that he was an excellent communicator and that both he and Nathanial had abilities that allowed for groups to want to listen to what they were saying. Patric has some value, but just barely. He learned what he needed to, in order to become successful amongst our species and I was quite comfortable to allow him to take such a position; we needed a passionate leader, someone who was young enough to the cause to not have any bitterness about our current status, and just reckless enough to carry out some of the more violent retaliations. I became his closest advisor, he trusted my guidance." Devon moved back against the couch and leaned in toward me, his eyes roaming slowly over my body. I felt my face flush. He smiled and touched my cheek sending a wave of burning heat deep into my skin.

"But there were things that you withheld from him right?" I was trying to keep the conversation on track, for some reason I felt that Devon was giving up a crucial bit of information, but I didn't know why.

266

"Yes, I didn't tell him everything about his transformation, about how things would affect him differently. I saw myself in the perfect position to take over from Patric and it's not good strategy for the opposition to reveal all their secrets, is it?" His fingers traced down my cheek to my bottom lip. He pulled back and returned his gaze to the fire. God, was I going to have to pull this out of him or what, he was dragging this out on purpose.

"So human blood affects him differently then? In a bad way?" I asked quietly, not wanting him to sense my impatience at his intentional lagging.

"No, it's not necessarily bad per se, but it certainly does not affect him as positively as it does full Vampires like myself." He smirked at the fire. "My abilities that I can acquire from Human blood are not diminished in their death; the host can die and I still benefit from having their blood in my system. Patric is half and really a full Bonder by birth; if his host dies, then of course any 'enhancements' that he acquired from taking Human blood become quite diminished." Oh shit! I felt the sudden impact of what Devon was saying. I was too late and I was trapped. There was no way that Devon was going to let me walk away from him tonight, he was going to kill me and then kill Patric and Nathanial. The only thing I could be sure of was that both Patric and Nathanial had received the packages and that they would know what to do and what was going to happen. It was a bummer that I didn't have an opportunity to tell them this new information that Devon was now reveling. I just hoped that what I left them; I hoped that it would be enough.

I heard the ocean crash onto the shore and saw the moonlight illuminate the small bluffs that surrounded my villa. My deck was situated so high in the forest that you could step out and be level with the cliffs on either side of you, it was an amazing site. I had no idea why my mind was turning to my outside surroundings, except that I started to formulate yet another plan, one that just might actually work, but it was dependent upon the trust that I had for two people, that they still loved me. I turned to Devon and he was watching me. Immediately, I closed my mind, except I reached out to one person, the one person who I had shared many a private dialogues with, the one person who I hoped would finally see the true value in who they were and finally realize that I did love them, that I would of course always love them and that choice, was in fact, my own. "Devon, I need some air, this is just a lot to take in right now." I tried to hold my voice steady as I stood up and moved toward the open doors leading out to the deck. Devon stood as well and followed me silently outside. The wind had picked up and it blew my hair back sending it swirling up around my face and neck. There was a gentle fragrance on the air, subtle in its notes, but familiar all the same. I smiled as I breathed in woods, honey and vanilla, musk and sandalwood; I felt a calm suddenly pulse through my body. I turned my back to the opening in the railing and felt the wind begin to churn against the nape of my neck. I reached up to feel my imprint and sucked in a sharp breath. The metals were no longer divided but locked together in one symbol again, an unending connection of silver and stone, moonlight and starlight; they were as they should be—bound.

"Ana." Devon had moved to stand in front of me. He looked so beautiful and so utterly terrifying that I couldn't breathe. I turned away from him and gazed up at the moon, my feet moving back just a bit from him. He reached his hand out to touch my neck and I felt the strength of his grasp. I was sure one twitch and he could sever my spinal cord. I was betting that Devon enjoyed a bit of torment before going in for the kill. Again, I moved my heels back a few centimeters until I felt the edge of the deck. I looked at the moon, then back at Devon. He was breathing hard and his eyes had gone dark. I saw a shadow move behind him, the moon playing with the light. I stood still, my body tensed. I saw a flash of brilliant blue and silver dance across the night as a figure stepped from the shadows. Patric. Patric had come; he had heard me. Now, all I could hope for was that my belief in his love for me was not misplaced.

Patric put his finger to his lips as he moved closer to Devon. I felt Devon's grip on my neck tighten and saw his head begin to bend in toward my own as if in some tender kiss, when suddenly his body went rigid, stiff. He managed to spin around, dropping his grip from my body. I heard Patric growl, or maybe it was Devon. In one silent moment, Patric and I locked gazes and I saw his eyes, his beautiful, beautiful turquoise eyes. They were pleading with me, asking me to hold on. I let him see what Devon had told me, but more than that, I wanted to tell him to fight, to fight for himself and for Nathanial and for me, and that in my heart, he had been redeemed. I smiled at him. It had to be this way; Devon would make sure that I died and I wasn't going to be taken down like that, not in such a cruel way and for such horrendously selfish reasons; at least I could give Patric a chance, even in my death, Patric still could possibly have the upper hand. He might be just a bit stronger with my blood, with my love, and by being who he was all on his own… and maybe, just maybe, it would be enough.

"NO ANA, NO!" Patric shouted, making Devon turn one last time toward me with his fangs barred and his claws ready to slash my throat. I glanced briefly up at the moon one more time, stepped backward off the deck, and fell into the night.

Chapter Eight

Nathanial

I heard Patric yell, his scream carried over the cliffs and into the wind; it was guttural and the very sound of it made my heart crack. I looked up to see the villa erupting into flames. Blue fire danced back and forth on the deck and I knew that Patric was fighting; not for himself, not even for me but for the woman he loved, for the woman he had just watched jump to her death to save him, to save both of us. Ana. I saw her body fall to the earth, slow in its movement over the cliffs. I saw it break upon the water, shatter into a million pieces and remain still as the waves left her upon the sand. I looked up once more at the villa. It was burning, now fully engulfed, embers shooting into the night sky, like an explosion of stars. I could no longer see my brother or Devon and I had no way of knowing if either of them was still alive. I blurred to Ana's side. Kneeling down in the sand, I saw her, for the first time I truly saw her. Her face was pale, yet somehow it still glowed. I looked up to see the moon, now directly over her body. Her hair was wet and as the waves moved over her head, the water swirled and swayed the curls and strands around her face, as if she were standing in the current of a breeze. She was broken. I couldn't move and I felt a sudden coldness filter through my soul, freezing my heart, numbing my mind. Burning clay and wood filtered into my lungs, choking me. I couldn't breathe, I couldn't think. I pressed my head down onto her still chest, and placing my body next to hers, I begged for death. I didn't know how long I stayed by her side, my head

271

against her body, my hands caressing her face. The world seemed to spin slowly, covering us in a black veil. There was no light, no moon, no stars, no fire, no burning, no ocean, no wind—there was nothing.

"Nathanial," a voice spoke, breaking through the darkness. "We need to take her home." I pulled my head from her chest and saw Alec standing on the shore next to us, his face bright against the darkness that surrounded me. "Patric is dead. Devon's been wounded, but he escaped. I can't get a read on the others that were with him. We need to go Nathanial." His voice was flat, even. I looked at him, desperate, not wanting to move her, not wanting to be moved from her. I watched as he knelt down in the sand next to her. He moved his hands gently underneath her waist and picked up the crumpled pieces of her body; he held her next to him. My legs wouldn't work and I couldn't get up out of the sand. I felt the waves lap around my body as the water began to soak my skin. "Nathanial." Alec looked at me and I felt a sudden steadiness begin to rise in my body. I moved slowly, but I finally managed to stand next to him, next to Ana. I placed my hand on his shoulder and I felt him shimmer us away from the beach, away from the cliffs, away from Patric and Devon, away from this horrible, horrible nightmare.

We arrived back at Alec's beach house to a terrible storm and the violent wind threatened to rip Ana away from his chest. He carried her through the viciousness of the storm and laid her in the bed she had occupied before, when she was dying the first time. He moved his hands over her and I saw that immediately upon his touch, her hair and clothes became dry. He tucked the blankets up around her and smoothed back her curls with his fingers. I stood standing at the door, again paralyzed in my despair. Alec turned to look at me. I didn't want to see his eyes. Coldness again burned itself into my heart. The sharpness of the pain created a chasm of heat, erupting and scorching my skin. I grabbed my chest and fell to the ground, writhing. I felt something sharp dig into the space over my heart. I moved my fingers over my skin and my hand grazed against something small, but very sharp, it had pierced my flesh. I dug my fingers into the skin and pulled out the source of the burning. I saw Alec blur to my side. I looked into my bloodied hand and saw the single jewel-like stone nestled in my palm. It glimmered and I felt its heat radiate through my hand and into my chest. The warmth was soft and light and it quelled the icy burn that was coursing through my veins. It was the star that I had picked up on the trail that day; it had fallen, one among many stars that had left Ana's imprint. They fell because she had already made her decision. For her, there was no going back.

"Nathanial, what is that?" Alec whispered beside me, his gaze focused on the now shimmering source of light in my palm.

"It's Ana," I replied as I crossed the room to stand next to her. I sat down near her form and slowly moved her head so that it faced away from me. I swept her hair back and found her imprint. The metals were merged but all the colors were now black and there was a thin layer of ice that had filtered down to the skin surrounding her mark. I let my fingers feel the coolness on her neck and my body began to tremble. Alec moved next to her on the other side and he was frowning.

"What?" I asked him. "What's wrong?"

"Did that come from Ana's imprint?" He was motioning to the still glowing star in my hand. I had forgotten that I was still holding it.

"Yes, it fell, they all fell actually. This was the only one that I picked up." I was still trembling and I sunk down onto the bed, holding Ana's hand in mine—it was cold.

"May I see it please?" Alec asked with a sudden sternness to his voice. Reluctantly, I placed the tiny jewel into his outstretched palm. He held it close to his face and turned the piece in every direction, watching as the facets captured the little amount of light in the room. He walked over to the window and waited for the turbulent clouds to move across the moon. I watched as he held up Ana's solitary star to the sky. I saw Alec's hand shake as light radiated through the window. The jewel shimmered and began to glow so brightly, that I had to lower my eyes. Heat filled the room pulsing and moving through my body mimicking the rhythm of my heartbeats. Then it was gone. Alec turned away from the window and held out his hand for me to take back the glowing piece. He was still frowning. "Remarkable," he murmured. "I would have never anticipated this at all," Alec spoke under his breath.

"What's remarkable Alec?" I felt an odd emotion begin to flood my body and my limbs began to tense.

"Nathanial, how much do you know about imprints? I mean, how much do you know about their connections to the Humans who bare them?" What the hell was he talking about? I did not have the mental capacity for a history lesson right

274

now. Ana was dead, Patric was dead, and I was just trying to figure out a way around my own immortality.

"Nathanial, Ana is rare, not just in herself as a person, but she is a rare choice as far as Bonding goes. She had the capacity to not only be Bonded to you, but also to your brother, something that I have never, ever seen in our ritual." I traced my finger down the now onyx stone that ran through our entwined metals, Patric's stone.

"So?" I said, my tone slightly acerbic. I forced myself to take a deep breath, tempering my emotions slightly.

"So," Alec continued, his voice soft and his eyes roaming over Ana's face. "So, she survived the mixing of your blood and Patric's blood, she Bonded herself to two beings, she has you and Patric coursing through her veins and an imprint that I have never seen the likes of in my three hundred and fifty years. She believed enough in Patric's love for her and for you, that she willingly sacrificed her life; she sacrificed her life for a Bonder and a half-Vampire—Ana, a fragile Human…" his voice trailed off as he moved to stroke her face.

"Are you saying that she's not dead Alec? Are you saying that we can save her?" I was desperate, manic in my emotions. What was going on?

"I don't know, this is all so beyond anything that I have come to understand…I'm just not sure about anything anymore," he spoke with such awe as he looked at Ana, with such astonishment; I didn't understand his emotions. I didn't want to allow myself to hope, to think that maybe we could save her and that I could bring her back to me—that it wasn't over. I tried not to think about any of those things as I felt her cold fingers in mine, saw her pale, smooth face, watched as her chest lay still and the pulse in her neck stay silent. I couldn't allow myself any shred of hope, yet….

"I need to think about this Nathanial, I need to see if there is anything we can do. I won't promise you that we can fix her, that we can bring her back; I won't promise…" He looked once more at Ana's lifeless body and left me alone with her. There was ice inside of my soul. I could feel it begin to creep in and surround the very core of who I was, of the *man* that I was with her. I took the jewel from my hand and moved her head to the side one last time. I pressed the piece into her imprint and watched as it embedded itself into its rightful place. I shuttered and turned her back to face me. I leaned my face close and gently pressed my lips against hers, breathing in her now faded scent. I parted her mouth and exhaled my breath into her, hoping that it would find its way to her heart and to her soul.

I stayed with her through the night, listening as Alec paced back and forth in the living room. Night gave way to the dawn and the moon set as the sun rose, painting the sky with flames. I watched the light filter through the open window and move across Ana's face, setting her hair ablaze against her now pale skin. I turned my eyes toward the horizon, wishing that I could be with her, that she was somewhere that I could not follow and I became suddenly angry. Angry that I didn't do more to protect her, angry that I had been such a coward, angry that I breeched her trust, I was just angry. I hadn't even allowed myself to think about Patric. He had come to save her just like she had always known he would. He came to me with his package that she had sent, those two containers of her blood; he had figured it out, while I just sat there in disbelief, not wanting to understand, not wanting to think about how she had planned this all out so quickly. She trusted Patric's love for her, buried and twisted as it was; it surfaced, pure and real, in the end. A whisper, so soft and light, that I was sure that my mind had produced the voice itself, came from behind me. I whipped my head around and found Ana's shimmering brown eyes staring back at me. I was sure that I had snapped. That in my utter and complete despair, my mind had shut down in order to protect itself from reality. I moved slowly toward her bed, not trusting what I was seeing and not trusting myself.

"Ana." I could barely speak her name. She licked her lips and looked up at me. She coughed; the sound was raspy and tight. Despite my complete shock, I found myself smiling, but immediately I stopped. I thought about her fall, about how her body had broken and shattered on the rocks and how she couldn't be alive, there was no possible way. I looked at her arms and legs and my heart seized. "Ana, can you move your legs or your arms, can you move anything?" Fear swept through my body as I waited for some movement to come from beneath the blankets. I watched in awe as she slowly flexed her legs up and down. She gasped in pain and I rushed to her side. She tried to move her arms over her head, but again she gasped. Her eyes found mine and I could see tears beginning to spill down her cheeks. She could move, but it was apparent that her body had experienced a massive amount of trauma and she was in pain. "Let me call Alec." I turned to head toward the door, but Alec was already coming down the hall.

"Nathanial, what's going on?" His eyes flashed with alarm.

"She's survived Alec, but she's hurt, her body is hurt." I couldn't say anything else, I still hadn't gotten my head around what was happening; it didn't seem real.

"What did you do? How did this happen?" Alec charged into the room, the abruptness of his reaction seemed to jerk me out of my trance.

"I…I don't know," I stammered.

"Well, you had to do something! Did you give her any of your blood Nathanial?" Again, Alec's reaction sent my head spinning trying to decipher what, if anything, I had done and I certainly didn't give Ana any of my blood, it wouldn't have helped, she was too far gone.

"I didn't do anything Alec, I've just been sitting here all night watching her. I…" Suddenly I remembered that I *had* done something, something that seemed so ordinary and so right. I moved over to Ana's bed and asked her to turn her head to the side, facing the window. I saw questions fill her eyes and I nodded for her to trust me. Slowly, she moved her neck and winced in pain at the extension of her muscles. I took a sharp breath in as I saw her imprint. No longer black and icy, her entwined metals were now fully restored and more brilliant than when they first made their appearance. The tiny jewel that I had retrieved and placed back into her neck, had multiplied so that now millions of tiny facets of light sparkled and pulsed outward. Patric's turquoise stone was glossy and marbled with a thin silver pattern, looping and twisting itself down the length of her neck. My midnight blue metal on the surface looked the same, but as I examined the pattern closer, I could see movement within as tiny silver crystals passed back and forth deep inside, like a small universe full of stars.

"Well, if it was anyone other than Ana, I wouldn't believe it." Alec laughed to himself, but the sound was tight and sharp.

"What do we do now?" I asked. I was sure that she would need some sort of hospitalization and physical therapy; I felt overwhelmed and I was having problems processing the whole situation.

"Ana, can you talk?" Alec was leaning his face close to hers. I saw her gently nod her head up and down. She licked her lips again and tried to speak.

"Patric." Her voice came out soft and raspy, and I felt myself moving closer to her head in order to hear. "He came to help me, did he..." She started to cough loudly and I rushed to help Alec sit her up. There was a bit of blood coming out of her mouth and I looked at Alec, hoping he would know what to do.

"She might have broken a rib or punctured her lung. It's hard to say; I'm going to have to examine her." He was gently pulling her into a sitting position on the bed. "Nathanial, get my bag from the living room please." I blurred to the front room and grabbed the large leather medical bag from the sofa, knocking something round and silver off the coffee table in my haste. I reached down to pick up the object and frowned, it was Alec's wedding band. Suddenly my body tensed and my instincts told me to take a quick survey of the room. Everything looked in the right place, all of Alec's books and journals, his photographs and papers, they all seemed to be where he usually kept them—neat and organized on shelves and in paper trays. I scanned the room once more and realized what actually was missing; Kai's things were absent. No photographs of him and Ana, of his mother and friends, none of his books for school were on the shelf. My mind was processing things very quickly. What had happened? Had they had a fight? Had Kai moved out? That would be an odd scenario for a Bonded pair, especially one as united as Alec and Kai, to break-up emotionally or physically. I frowned, a growing unease spreading into my mind.

"Nathanial, my bag?" Alec called down the hallway. I pocketed his ring and made my way back down to the bedroom, still frowning. I tossed him the bag and went to sit beside Ana on the bed. I watched as Alec placed the stethoscope over her heart. "Take a deep breath for me ok?" he asked her quietly. Her body shuttered from the effort, but at least she wasn't coughing up blood anymore. He moved to her back and I saw her wince at his touch. I moved to take her hand, but stopped myself. I could sense that Ana had her wall up and she wasn't ready to let me in, not yet. Alec took out a syringe and a vile full of medication, for some reason my hackles were raised; the last time Ana had been given any sort of "medication" had been from Patric. "Relax Nathanial, it's only pain medication," Alec replied, responding to my wariness. "She going to need physical therapy for her back and her legs, but I don't see any permanent damage that's been done; remarkably, she's pretty well healed." I saw him studying her face, his gaze intent and penetrating. Something about the way he was looking at her made me uneasy. Perhaps I was just feeling a bit possessive, even though I had no right to feel that way about her anymore. I brushed her hair back as she fell asleep, murmuring about Patric and fire. I motioned for Alec to follow me out of the room. "I'll make a call in the morning, I have a colleague who's an excellent P.T. He's close to the University and he owes me a favor. He'll be a big help in getting her up and walking again," Alec muttered, and I watched as he paced nervously around the room.

"Alec," I said quietly from my position on the couch. I reached into my breast pocket and pulled out his wedding ring and placed in on the table. He turned to look at me, then at the ring and I saw his eyes grow dark, darker than I had ever seen them before. "What's going on? Where's Kai?" My feeling of unease was quickly heightening as he continued to stare at his ring. He slumped down into a chair across from me and put his head in his hands.

"He's with his family. We had an argument and he left. He said he needed to be away from me for a while. He's only been gone a few days." He reached across the table to pick up his ring. "I must have dropped it, it must of have fallen off…" he murmured, almost to himself as he fingered the thick band of silver and onyx. This was the first time that I had been able to study Alec since seeing him on the beach. It had been months that I had been with Patric, and Alec and I were not in contact with each other. I scanned his appearance and noted some distinct differences. His hair, which he usually kept in tight dreadlocks and pulled back, was now loose with the locks flowing down to his waist. The color looked darker, as did his eyes. Normally clear and bright green, they seemed dimmed and shrouded, and I thought I could feel some sort of vibration coming from within their depths. Perhaps Alec's physical appearance was simply a translation of what he was feeling emotionally; maybe he was depressed.

"You've changed quite a bit as well Nathanial," his voice broke through my ponderings. "Apparently the combination of your bloodline and the completion of your 'exchange' with Ana has offered you immeasurable strength and power...how are you adjusting?" He was offering a diversion to my questions about Kai but I wasn't willing to play along.

"I'm fine Alec. What happened between you and Kai?" My tone was colored by a sternness and directness that I rarely ever used and especially with Alec. He laughed softly.

"You're really coming into your own aren't you Nathanial. It seems your time with Patric has managed to bring out your, can we say, 'darker' side. I'll be honest with you, I'm partial to it; it suits you." He looked away from me and I watched as he pocketed his ring. This was an odd conversation, and it looked as though Alec was not prepared to discuss what had happened between him and Kai. "No, I'm not," he said, turning his gaze upon me. "And I don't think we need to tell Ana anything other than Kai has returned to take care of his mother and that he has asked not to be contacted. I also do not think she needs to know about Patric or Devon, she has to stay motivated and committed to her recovery and fear and grief can only serve to debilitate her further. Are we agreed?"

"I'll agree to the business about Kai, but don't you think she has a right to know that my brother died trying to prevent her from killing herself? And I also think she needs to be aware that Devon may still be after her, even if he defeated Patric; Devon wanted Ana from the start and apparently he's still

282

convinced that her blood will allow for him to gain an excess of power. He knows she's special, she's a commodity to him, and I'm guessing the first Human to outsmart his attempts to seduce and kill her. I'm sure he's not happy about any of that. Devon is a predator Alec, he's always enjoyed the chase, and unless you can assure me that either Patric managed to kill him on that deck, or that Devon has moved on to bigger things and has forgotten about Ana, then I don't want her guard down." Alec turned to me and smiled.

"You're right Nathanial, Ana is a commodity. For some reason, her humanity has allowed her to host blood that is so powerful, so full of life, that she's desired by Vampires and Bonders alike. I've never seen anything like that. A Human with the ability to offer other species the potential to become greater than they could ever imagine; couple that with her willingness to sacrifice her own life to save others...well you can most certainly see why she's so desired." I snapped my head up to stare at Alec. His voice was steady, but there was a definite current of excitement and desire as he spoke about Ana—I didn't like the way he sounded. He seemed to catch my unease and managed to compose himself again. "I agree with you then, we'll tell her what we know about Patric and Devon, but Kai's off limits—agreed?" He stood up and stretched.

"Fine. Tomorrow I would like to move her back home, I think it would make her feel better to be back in our—in her house." I corrected myself. Alec laughed darkly at my mistake.

"Go slow Nathanial. Ana won't be used to this new, darker persona you've adopted and I sense that your old abilities for unending patience may not be what they once were." He patted me on my shoulder and went off down the hall to bed. I spent the night in Ana's room, watching her sleep again. The conversation with Alec had left me quite unsettled. The whole of the situation with Kai was odd and the fact that he didn't want Ana to know about Patric or Devon was even odder. Maybe he wanted to protect her. Alec had always shown Ana the utmost respect and I knew that he loved her very much, but his demands to keep her in the dark seemed out of place with the nature of their relationship.

"Nathanial." Ana was awake and starting at me. I moved to her side and sat on the edge of the bed.

"What's wrong, are you in pain?" I scanned her body, looking for anything that seemed out of place.

"No, I'm alright. I just wanted to say that I was sorry that my plan didn't work; I just couldn't see another way to get out of what was happening. It was all so horrible and unbelievable. I had hoped to give you and Patric a chance against Devon. I thought even just a little blood, even if I died, might have been enough to help you both survive…" She was working herself up into a panicked state and she started coughing.

"Shh… Ana, you don't need to get upset, you need to rest." She put her hand up to stop me from talking.

"I'm ok, I'm fine." She took a shaky breath in and leaned back against her pillows. "Listen, I don't know you anymore, I mean I don't know what you want and I didn't know what Patric wanted, but I figured that I could hedge my bets that neither of you wanted Devon to be running the show, plus for some reason, he was obsessed with me and he was going to kill me and I really didn't know if Patric was ever going to be able to beat him; I just wanted to end things on my own terms you know—I didn't want Devon to win." I zoned out after she said that she didn't know me anymore. Had I changed that much? Was I that different from before, from when we were together? "Nathanial, is Patric dead?" I snapped myself back to reality.

"What?" I asked.

"Patric, is he dead?" She was staring at me, her eyes clear and bright, the flecks of gold glimmering from the moonlight.

"Alec thinks so," I said quietly, not wanting to look away from her beautiful, beautiful eyes.

"But you don't? I mean do you think he's dead?" She sat up and leaned toward me. That was an interesting question. As twins, Patric and I had always been very in tune with one another. Physically, we could usually sense when one of us was in pain or had been injured, but as our relationship began to sever, those connections were diminished. Still, I wondered why I didn't feel something from his death, some sense of loss or detachment of a part of my core. Perhaps our relationship had been beyond repair and I was to never feel my brother's presence again. "Nathanial?" Ana was staring at me.

"I don't know Ana. It seems pretty unlikely that Patric could have survived a fight with Devon. Devon is an old world Vampire and his powers are dark and have a long history. His fire is fatal to both Bonders and Vampires alike."

285

"So you think that Devon escaped, that he's still out there? I mean can he be killed?" She sounded exasperated.

"Yes to both of those questions. Alec thinks that Devon escaped, although we are waiting on confirmation, and yes, Devon can be killed, but it would take someone who also can yield a power dark enough to rival his own." I inclined my head, wondering what she was thinking.

"Hmmm, do you know anyone like that? Do you know anyone who could take him out?" I had my own inclinations, but I wasn't ready to commit to that knowledge.

"Maybe, I don't know. Bonders also have a very long history and we have our own old world demons, but they are rare and hard to find." I moved to sit along side of her on the bed, I wanted to be closer to her; I needed to be closer to her.

"You look different." She slowly turned her head to face me. "You also smell different." She wrinkled her nose.

"I didn't know that you could smell me before." That was odd for a Human to be able to acknowledge a Bonder's individual scent; that was for our own purposes, it's how we identified with each other, how we knew one another. We didn't use scent like Vampires, not to lure or seduce, our fragrance merely reflected our moods and emotional climates.

"Yes, you always smelled like my favorite tea, chamomile, honey, lemon and sometimes you smelled like the woods, depending on your mood." I raised my eyebrows at her; how had she come to know this?

"What do you mean?" I was stunned at her level of intuitiveness. Scent also helped us as Bonders particularly, to come to know the person who we Bonded ourselves to—their scent became part of us, part of our skin and our blood, part of our soul.

"When you were trying to calm me down from something, I would smell the sweeter of your scents, the honey and lemon, and when you were…uh…when you were, when you wanted to…" She was struggling with her words. She sighed. "When you were wanting to be intimate with me, you would smell more like the woods and the trees, like a soft musk, or patchouli oil…" I saw color flood her cheeks and she turned away. I had to take a breath. I had no idea that she had been that attuned to me, that I had become so much a part of her. She was right of course, that was the nature of my species. Our scents mimicked our desires. I always desired Ana.

"What do I smell like now?" I was afraid to ask, afraid that my scent would give away my feelings, what I wanted from her, what I had no right to want. She took a deep breath and parted her lips.

"It's the musk scent, but it's more potent and spicier than it was before." She was staring at me, her voice quiet. I leaned my face closer to hers, inhaling deeply, not wanting to stop breathing her in, I moved closer to her face. "Why do you look different Nathanial?" She broke my movement and looked up at the ceiling.

"It's part of the transformation," I said evenly, not shifting my gaze from her face; I wanted her to look at me, I wanted her to see me staring at her.

"Do you feel different?" she asked, still looking up.

"Yes. Very different." And I did, I felt everything stronger than I had before, everything was more potent to my senses, sight, sound, smell, touch, taste; they were all jarring to my nerve endings as if some electrical current had been turned on and up. My muscles surged with new strength and agility and my mind was constantly moving and assessing. I could see things that were buried deep in someone's mind, things that were expertly packed away. I had learned to control the emotions of others around me. That talent I got from Patric. He had shown me how to tap into the emotional conscience of someone to make them feel things, to make them want things. I couldn't manipulate them into doing anything per se, but I was able to tap into their own desires, to let them see what it was they were afraid to indulge in or ask for; that was a trick of Vampires, but Patric had managed to harness it for himself and then show me. I wasn't sure if Ana needed to know all of that, it might make her more wary of me than she already was.

"You like the way you are now though, I can tell. You like what you can feel now, what you can do." She turned her face back to me and I saw that her eyes were roaming over my body.

"You might like it too if you just gave it a chance." I smirked at her. She rolled her eyes and leaned away from me. I didn't like that. I moved closer to her. "I'm taking you home tomorrow," I said quietly, bending my head close to her ear. I felt her shiver at my breath on her neck and I smiled.

"Ok, but I don't think it's a good idea for us to be living together again, at least not right now." My chest heaved, but I composed myself. Alec was right, I was going to have to be patient with Ana, I needed to regain her trust and prove to her that I was the best choice for her, despite her attraction to Patric and even Devon, that I could give her what she wanted, what she desired and that I would protect her, fight for her, love her.

"Well, I have a nice house that's been a bit neglected in the last year. I think that will be a suitable accommodation for me, for the time being." Again, I leaned in toward her neck and whispered those last words in her ear.

"Hmmm, ok." She yawned and closed her eyes, breathing deeply. I settled in next to her and laid my head on hers, kissing her forehead gently.

"I love you Ana, I never stopped loving you and I will spend the rest of my life showing you just how much you belong with me." I closed my eyes and fell asleep, my fingers entwined with hers.

Ana

"Two more Ana, two more, c'mon, let's go, two more!" Adam was yelling at me as I stood at the Smith Machine trying to crank out two more reps for my physical therapy session. For two months, I had been working with Adam, a colleague of Alec's, on getting my battered body back in working order. It was excruciating. Adam had me working out three hours a day, four to five days a week. Luckily Caleb, my internship supervisor, was kind enough to keep my position open until I finished my P.T. and my dissertation, so according to Adam, I had plenty of time to be in the gym with him for hours on end. I hadn't seen Alec for weeks. Nathanial mentioned that he was visiting Kai and trying to figure out if Devon had survived the fire and Patric's attack. I was trying to push the whole thing from my memory, but Nathanial had insisted that I spend a bit of time in counseling, sorting through why I felt it necessary to commit suicide. He was nice enough to find me someone who was not anti-Bonder or anti-Vampire and who seemed willing to help me navigate through my constant need to make everyone happy. Between all of my physical work and all of the mental exercise, I was exhausted. Whatever time I did manage to have, I needed to put toward my dissertation. I was scheduled for my defense in less than a month and I needed the prep time. Then of course, there was Nathanial. He was back teaching, but he was also spending quite a bit of time renovating his house. He had respected my request that we not move back in together, that I needed some space to figure out how I was feeling about him and how I felt about this new Nathanial that was now in my life.

He had changed. I had noticed the difference upon seeing him the first time down in West Papua and then again, when I was with Devon at the restaurant and things were not quite going in my favor. Nathanial had looked so remarkably powerful, so completely in control, that his appearance and his reaction to Devon had frightened me. His transformation into a full Demon and I was guessing, the source of his mystical and powerful bloodline, had totally altered who Nathanial was. Still, there were moments when I caught a glimpse of the quiet and contemplative being who had occupied a part of my life for a while; it was mainly when I found him staring at me,

290

intensely. I knew that he was hoping that we could resume, at least our friendship again, but any inclinations that he might have for something more, was not even in the picture for me— at least not right now. My feelings for him were confusing and I still felt hurt and betrayed by his decisions. It was going to be a very long road back to rebuilding those crumbled foundations.

"Ok Adam, that was five reps, not two, do you think I can't count?" I grunted and racked my weights, sweat dripping down my face.

"I do think you can count and I do think you have a hundred calve raises left before you can get out of here; now get to it sweetheart!" He winked at me and went to greet his next client. I sighed and went to the back of the gym to finish up. Ten minutes later, I limped out of the gym and headed to my jeep, gorging myself on water. Nathanial was leaning against my door, grinning at me. The redundancy of the scene was not lost on me. The last time we were in this situation, we had been together and I had been kissing him. We were headed to the University to go by his office...I made my memory stop there. My heart always hurt when I thought about that night, when I thought about the things he had said and how he had looked. I sighed and waved at him, walking slowly forward, my legs aching. He was staring at me again, and I wondered if he could read what memory I had just halted; I wondered if he had remembered the same scene, only so different this time. I thought I saw him wince as I approached.

"You look tired," he said to me as he swung my bag over his shoulder, composing himself.

"What else is new?" I laughed and leaned back against the car.

"Well, how about dinner? I'm preparing your favorite, well, I'm preparing the one meal that has enough food in it that you'll eat everything on the plate." He laughed and rolled his eyes. I was a health nut, but I also had a ton of food allergies, and Nathanial was always intrigued by how well I could manage eating the same thing everyday and not get bored, something that Patric had also not failed to notice. I felt my heart seize a little as the thought of him crossed my mind. It was funny; I was more angry and untrusting of Nathanial than I was with Patric, mainly because Patric had never promised me anything. He had never said that we would be together, that we had a future or that he would even protect me from anything. I knew what I was getting with Patric and I loved him anyway. Nathanial was different. We had stayed up late at night, talking through some of our feelings, not everything, but we had agreed to take things slowly, to get to know each other in a new way, as a Bonded pair. He knew that I feared the final exchange, that I was worried that he might leave and that I would die; he knew, and even if Patric had gotten a hold of his mind, he still didn't fight, he didn't return and it took Alec to convince him to come back to save me. Nathanial had to be *convinced*. Maybe that was why I was having a hard time with him. Certainly he was more powerful because he had completed his part of the deal, but in all actuality, Nathanial was already pretty strong after he took my blood; completing the exchange on his part, was just a bonus. I think he could have survived quite nicely with the enhanced abilities that he was already experiencing.

"Ana." Nathanial cut through my recollections. "You don't have to come if you don't want to, of course I'll understand." He stepped in front of me and lifted my face up towards his. Nathanial's eyes pulsed outward, again, something new to his whole demeanor. The color had changed a bit as well. He used to have deep midnight blue eyes, the night sky is how I had always thought of them, now they reminded me of a stormy horizon, dark bluish gray and turbulent, churning and shifting; they were hypnotic in their rhythm and their depth, I found myself feeling transfixed by their beauty and power.

"No, I want to come, that's so nice of you to have cooked, I know you have a lot going on," I stammered, bending my head and looking at my shoes. He laughed and tousled my hair.

"Good then. I'll see you in a few." He turned to get into his car. I'd always thought it was funny how Bonders and I guessed Vampires, chose to drive everywhere. They could easily shimmer, transporting themselves anywhere on earth and yet they opted for something more human than was necessary…maybe they desired the normalcy of life just as much as someone like myself did.

"Wait Nathanial, I need a shower, big time. Maybe an hour or so?"

"I have a shower Ana—a perfectly restored one actually. I'll see you back at the house." He winked at me and climbed into his car and drove off. Frick! I felt weird about doing my freshening up at his house; it seemed so, so…well, it seemed like something that couples would do. I sighed loudly and checked my bag hoping that I had brought some extra clothes with me. Frick! I had not. Well, let's hope that Nathanial actually owned a t-shirt and sweats; I had never seen him in lounge wear.

Nathanial's house was about twenty minutes from the gym and I took the time to try to call Kai. I had been calling everyday since I had heard that he and Alec were "having problems", as Nathanial had put it. Every time I called, I got Kai's voicemail. I must have left over a hundred messages by now. Kai had been gone for two months and he had yet to return any of my calls. I was thinking of asking Nathanial if we could take his boat out to the island where Kai's family lived; I was feeling anxious the longer I went without talking to him. Maybe I would ask Nathanial tonight, he seemed to be in a mode of trying to accommodate me as of late—feeling guilty I suspected.

I drove the winding road along the coast out to Nathanial's home. Like Patric's, Nathanial had a cabin of sorts but it was styled with a very traditional Indonesian/Bali type feel. Patric's house was reminiscent of a ski lodge, where as Nathanial's taste was more along the lines of a beach bungalow, tropical and warm, with lots of open space and light. The house had a very indigenous feel to it, with Mayan and Aztec art and woven fabrics draped expertly around the living space. The tropical and the cultural mixed quite well and made the space seem almost Zen-like in the blending of the two styles. I liked it so much that I was thinking of asking Nathanial to redecorate my place. I grabbed my gym bag and made my way up the walk admiring all of the flowers and plants he had landscaped. He was sitting on the steps, watching me as I approached. "Wow, maybe you should quit teaching and do some sort of landscape architecture. You have a great eye," I called to him.

294

"It's ok, but you like it?" he asked as I sat down next to him.

"Yeah, I love it. Where can I get one of those blankets?" I pointed to this beautiful Mayan quilt that he had hanging over the porch swing.

"That was my mother's. She made it for my father as a wedding present," he said, turning his gaze to my face. His stare was so penetrating that I had to look away.

"I can't sew," I said laughing. "I usually just round up the stapler and see what magic I can perform with that, not exactly a nice way to present a wedding gift I suppose," I said feeling sort of bummed at my complete lack of domestic skills.

"It's not the object itself that matters Ana, it's the intent behind the object that holds the true nature of the person who gives it." Again, he stared at me as if trying to look into my soul.

"Hmmm…" was all I could manage to say. I suddenly realized that I was sitting very close to Nathanial and I still had not taken a shower. I remembered how potent my scent could be when I was sweaty. "Ugh, I should really take a shower, Adam kicked my ass today, as usual. Um, do have any sweats or a t-shirt I could borrow? I didn't bring a change of clothes." I felt heat and blood rush to my face. His eyes roamed over me slowly.

"I think we can rummage up something that will do. I'll have a look while you're in the shower." He stood up and offered me his hand. Grateful for his support, I put my hand in his and let him pull me to my feet. His skin was hot, burning almost. The

295

force of his pull had managed to bring me within inches of his body and I could feel the heat from his skin filter over me. His hand still in mine, I felt him pull me closer, threading his fingers into mine, his grasp firm. I risked looking into his eyes. They were startling. I saw clouds move within their depths and the moon seemed to be reflecting its light out toward me, pulling me towards him. "Nathanial." I swallowed hard and dropped my hand from his, stepping back.

"I know, Ana. I know." He moved away from me and turned to go inside the house. I shuttered as I watched him disappear inside. Sadness and desire filled my heart and left my bones feeling weak and my muscles tense. I swallowed again and stepped into his home.

Nathanial was right; his shower was unbelievable. It was huge, the size of both of my closets combined. He had installed dark red, ceramic tiles that had smaller, intricately woven designs in turquoise and silver. The shower itself was hand-polished silver and stone and I couldn't for the life of me figure out how to turn the damn thing on. It had a million knobs and buttons and three or four different showerheads. After successfully managing to ignite some sort of steam vaporizer and unscrewing one of the knobs, I gave up, wrapped my towel around me and yelled down the hall. Nathanial came into his room, an apron around his waist and looking alarmed. I saw him take a quick survey of the space and then look at me, his eyes slowly taking in my dry appearance.

"What is it, what's wrong?" he asked warily. I thrust out the knob that I had broken.

"Uh, how the hell do you work this frickin shower? I mean I know that you like nice stuff, but seriously, when the utility of the thing is more complicated than the actual construction—you've screwed up," I said exasperated. He smirked at me, rolled his eyes and walked into the bathroom. I watched as he turned the main knob to the left and pressed a big red button situated down below that I had failed to notice. Immediately, hot water came pulsing out in a waterfall like stream. He stood back still smirking, but this time his eyes roamed over my barely towel-clad body. Again, I saw his eyes churn and the gravitational pull they seemed to emit was making it hard for me to keep the space between us. "Thanks," I said, trying to steady my breathing.

"No problem." He tapped the tip of my nose and sauntered out of the bathroom. The shower was great and had I not wanted to hold up dinner, I probably could have stayed in there for an hour. I wrapped my hair in a towel and saw that Nathanial had laid out a pair of baggy, dark grey sweats from the University and a white t-shirt. Excellent. I found an extra pair of underwear and bra in my bag and changed quickly. I could smell onions and garlic sautéing and hear music filtering its way down the hallway. I suddenly realized just how hungry I was and cleaned up the bathroom as fast as possible. I came around through the living room and into the kitchen. Nathanial was at the stove, his hair pulled back into a long dark plait, his turquoise and silver bracelets jangling against the motion of his wrist. He was wearing dark, worn jeans and a fitted black t-shirt that seemed to mold itself to the contours of his muscles. His physique was no longer the long and lean composition of when I first met him, instead his muscles were full and chiseled and I could see the tendons flexing with every subtle effort he

297

made. I had to admit, I was a bit jealous. I had been working out for years and still hadn't been able to pack on that much muscle, but I also had to admit that his whole look was more rugged and weathered than it had been and I really liked it. He looked up and caught me gawking at him.

"What?" he asked rather amused. Blood flooded my cheeks and I shook my head.

"Nothing," I said, obviously embarrassed by my detailed examination of his appearance. He chuckled. "Can I help with anything?" I was desperate for some preoccupation.

"You can make guacamole if you want. You always do a nice job." He handed me an avocado and cleared a place on the counter next to him. He looked at the towel wrapped around my head and smiled. I set to work, happily chopping and mixing and listening to the music he had chosen. It wasn't his usual selection of violin or cello compositions, but some sort of dark Goth rock, slow and very sexy in its lyrics and rhythms. It was my kind of music, but never would I have associated the genre with Nathanial. I snuck another glace at his face. "Something on your mind, Ana?" he asked causally and I swore I heard him laugh under his breath. I had been doing really well at keeping him out of my thoughts, but sometimes I was sure that he'd gotten in, that he had seen what I was thinking about him, that he knew that I was battling with both my desire for him and my wariness to trust him again. I looked away, not answering and finished making the guacamole.

We ate outside and Nathanial lit an impressive fire in the stone fire pit, it was like being at a campsite, but with comfortable seats, the ocean and really good beer and food. I wasn't a beer drinker, but Nathanial insisted that I would like *this* particular selection, and I did. It tasted more like mulled apple cider than the disgusting pilsner stuff I usually was coerced into drinking by Kai. That reminded me, I was going to ask Nathanial about using his boat to visit Kai. I surveyed him over my glass. He looked pretty relaxed. I felt my mind slip a bit.

"No," he said. He'd gotten in and knew what it was that I wanted. Frick!

"Oh, come on! Please? I haven't seen Kai in ages and he's not returning my calls and you haven't heard from Alec. I'm worried Nathanial. He's my best friend and I'm worried." I knew that I sounded like a child, whiny in my tone. I watched as he sipped his beer and picked up his bowl of food to eat. I stared, waiting for him to continue.

"Is there something else?" he asked. Clearly, he was done talking about Kai.

"That's it? You're not going to even think about it? I mean you like Kai, aren't you worried at all about him?" I was getting annoyed. He took another sip of his beer and leaned back against his chair.

"Of course I like Kai Ana, that's not the point." I was about to interrupt him but he held up a hand, stopping me. "The point is, that Alec has asked us not to bother Kai at the moment, that they are trying to work through some very serious issues and that Kai has asked us to respect his privacy." He moved to pick up his fork.

"That's bullshit and you know it. Kai is my best friend, and we've always helped each other work through every issue, with boyfriends and fiancés and, and...you." I remembered how Alec and Kai had worked so hard to keep me sane after Nathanial left, at how even though they both hated Patric, that they tried to understand what I needed, or at least what I thought I needed; Kai never judged me for my decisions, he was just always there. I felt tears filling my eyes as I thought about how much pain my friend must be in and how badly I wanted to go to him and help. I wiped the moisture from my eyes and glared at Nathanial.

"You can glare at me all you want Ana, I'm not changing my mind on this." He handed me a napkin to wipe my face and moved to stoke the fire. I watched the flames licking and winding their way across his skin and I gasped. His arm was on fire! Had he not noticed the flames burning his flesh? Had he not felt the heat scorching his skin?

"Nathanial!" I shouted. "Your arm, it's on fire!" His snapped his head up to look at me, then back down to his arm. In a blur of movement, I saw him retract his arm from the fire, leaving the flames searching for something else to burn. I moved to examine his arm, taking it in my hands. Nothing, there was nothing wrong with it, no burned flesh, no blackened skin, nothing but the deep glow of his copper sheen. I ran my fingers gently up and down the length of his limb, not believing. He trembled at my touch. "Are you hurt, is something hurting Nathanial?" I asked, still stroking his arm. I felt a sudden wash of heat flow through him as I sat running my fingers along his skin. He trembled again and I looked at his face. His eyes were closed and he was breathing deep and

300

slow. "Nathanial, are you alright, are you hurt?" He didn't look injured, but what the hell did I know about Demons and their potential for injury. He took another breath in and opened his eyes. They were midnight blue and the silver starlight had returned, they were shining at me, their gravitational pull was too much and I felt myself lean closer toward his face. I moved my hand up his arm to his shoulder, feeling his muscles tense at my motion. He placed his free hand on my leg and I felt his fingers press into my skin as he moved slowly up to my hip and lower back, pulling me forward. My face was even with his and he released the arm that I had been touching, placing his hand on the side of my face. He was so controlled, so calm, nothing like the last times we had been intimate, everything had seemed so new to him, he was overwhelmed. But now, as his hands moved down my back and across my neck, Nathanial was not overwhelmed, he was powerful and I could sense the tension in his muscles as his arms caressed over me. I didn't understand what I was feeling. I knew that I was not ready for this, allowing him to be so close to me again; I just wasn't prepared, not emotionally or physically. This was a very different man that was now holding me, he was darker and more powerful, but he was also more seductive and sensual than he had been before, so much so, that I was finding it very difficult to reason with myself to stop what I knew was coming.

He moved his hand to my throat and I felt him trace over Patric's scars. I couldn't breathe. His fingers wove into my hair and he pulled my head back. I closed my eyes as I felt his mouth drift over my throat, his tongue tracing up and down my exposed neck. This was not Nathanial. He was usually gentle and always worried about my experience. Tonight his movement was rough and he was completely in control, dominating even. I tried to move myself back from him, attempting to breathe, but his arm encircled my waist and he shoved me against his chest. My face was inches from his and he pushed my wet hair back forcefully, as he shifted me onto his lap. This was not good; I didn't want to be here, feeling him like this, wanting him like I did. I wasn't ready. His grip on my body was so tight that I couldn't push myself off.

"Ana, look at me," he spoke with such command and deliberateness, that I had no choice but to look. As our gazes locked, I felt something happen inside my body, something that seemed to come from Nathanial, but he wasn't touching me where I was having this odd sensation. It felt similar to when Devon had gotten a hold of me, but this was different in its intensity, it was deeper somehow and much more sensual. I couldn't tear my eyes away from Nathanial, he wasn't blinking and his body had gone still, but mine was moving. I was pressing my hips against his, wanting to feel him on me. How was he doing this? By all standards, this couldn't be happening. It was as if he was inside me thrusting, but he wasn't. A voice inside my head was telling me to resist him, to stop what was happening, that it was dangerous, that my heart was in danger of breaking all over again. Another wave of desire threatened to erupt inside of me and I closed my eyes not wanting to want this so much.

"Stop, Nathanial." I heard myself murmur with as much conviction as I could muster. "Stop, please. I can't do this, I can't." My voice was getting stronger and I could feel the power in my limbs returning. I shoved him away and disentangled myself from his arms. "Stop! I can't do this. Who the hell do you think you are?" I was shouting at him now. I stood up and moved away from his position in the chair. "You can't do this to me, Nathanial. I won't let you do this to me again." I felt the tears flowing down my face. "You've changed, but I've changed too. I'm not the same person Nathanial. I've been living half a life since you left, and now you want me to act as if nothing ever happened! I just can't do this—I won't be that weak! I won't fall back into your arms just because you want it to be that way; I won't do it!" My chest was heaving and I was shaking. He leaned forward and moved his fingers across the flames in the fire. I watched in awe as they lit up his fingertips and he tossed them back and forth between his hands.

"A little trick I learned from Patric," he said quietly as he tossed the flames back into the fire. "I'm sorry Ana, I really am. I shouldn't have gone that far and that fast with you. I know you're not ready for us to have that kind of relationship yet. That was wrong. Can you forgive me?" He stood up and walked over to where I was standing. I had put a chair between us, still not trusting Nathanial or myself. He held out his hand as if to make a truce. I glared at him and he smiled. "Please?" he asked again. "I swear, I won't touch you ever again, at least not until you ask me to." He winked at me and I shoved his hand away. "Come on Ana, don't be mad." He lowered his voice and made his tone soft, he was almost purring. "Please. I don't want you to be upset, please?" He reached for me again. I took his hand in mine fully intending to just shake him off, but he pulled me out from around the protection of my chair and positioned me so we were standing eye to eye. He wove his fingers around mine and I felt the back of my neck grow warm as our hands entwined. I sighed and looked at him.

"Everything I said is true Nathanial. You can't just expect to come back all changed and with your weird new powers and seduce me; I'm not ready for that—" He cut me off.

"I know Ana, you have a right to feel everything you do towards me, every right. We'll slow things down ok? We'll go slow…" he murmured as he pulled my body closer to his. Still holding my hands in his, he took a step in, closing the remaining distance between us. "We'll go slow Ana…" he whispered as he brought his face close to mine. "Slow," he said again, his lips barely skimming my mouth. "As slow as you want." I felt his mouth move gently as his lips parted mine. He breathed into my mouth and I tasted him, his new scent, familiar but more potent, stronger and more intense, like everything he did now. Desire rocked my body and I ran my tongue along his bottom lip, wanting to taste more of him. He laughed and stepped back from my body. "You're quite the conflicted woman aren't you?" he said, still laughing.

"And you're a tease." I glared at him. He laughed harder and pulled me into his chest, hugging me.

"I thought you wanted to go slow. Did you or did you not just make quite a display about how you were not going to be seduced by my 'new weird powers'," he said, miming back to me from my little rant.

"And I meant every word, but you are making things difficult for me on purpose. You would never have behaved in such a domineering way before!" I said, breaking his grasp on me. He shrugged.

"I don't think you'd be so opposed to my behavior if you just gave it a chance, but you tend to be a bit of a control freak no?" He pulled the wet strands of my hair off of my face. I shoved his hand away.

"What the hell does that have to do with anything?" I said, stepping further away from his reach.

"All I'm saying is that I think you might like having someone else take care of you for once, take care of your needs, fulfill your desires, even the dark ones you don't want anyone to know about," he said laughing but his tone was hypnotic and even.

"You know who you sound like Nathanial? You sound like Devon!" And he did sound very much like Devon. Nathanial shrugged again.

"Well, there are some benefits to hanging out with Vampires. Devon doesn't have much value, but some of his talents are quite practical." He laughed. I rolled my eyes and turned to go back into the house. I grabbed my bag and headed for the door.

"Thank you for dinner, but let me assure you, this will be the last time that I come over to your house unaccompanied." He was following me down the path to my jeep.

"Hmmm…I actually don't think that it's such a bad thing that you feel you need to be chaperoned in my presence; it speaks to issues of your self control," he said casually, opening my door.

"God, when did you get so fucking cocky Nathanial; it's not attractive," I huffed at him and slammed my door shut. He leaned in through the window.

"Call me when you get home please." He kissed the top of my head and stepped back from the car. I rolled my eyes, put the jeep in reverse and barreled down his driveway.

I made it to the bluffs before my house in record time. I wanted to stop and collect myself a bit before continuing home. What a bizarre night this had been. I couldn't reconcile all of the changes that had occurred with Nathanial and I couldn't ignore just how much more he was reminding me of Patric, particularly in the area of his physicality with me. Maybe they were more connected than I knew. I stepped over to the edge of the cliff and watched as the clouds flew across the night sky, passing over the moon. I breathed in the salt air and wrinkled my nose. Something smelled bad, rotten. I looked around to see if there was a dead animal near by or in the road. I couldn't see any source of the assaulting fragrance. I heard the tides crash on the rocks below and I moved closer to the edge scanning along the shore. Maybe there was something below, decomposing. It was too dark at the moment and I couldn't see much. I waited for the clouds to pass by. The moon's light broke through the blackness and again I stepped to the edge and scanned the beach. My heart stopped. Someone was below, lying face down in the sand, the waves lapping up over the still body. I ran to the gate that led down to the shore and jumped over the fence, running at top speed down the bluff.

It was dark and I kept losing my footing on the rocks. I had to slide on my butt over the steepest part of the bluff, but I made it to the shore. Leaping down from the last little cliff, I hit the sand and sprinted to the dark figure lying in the water. The smell was horrible and I had to stop to gag into the sand. I stumbled over to the body and knelt down beside it. Holding my breath, I dragged it free from the tides and up onto the main beach. Decay had set in and the body was bloated. I had no idea what the hell I was doing, but for some reason I felt compelled to turn the body over. I thought it might be a man, but the shape was too distorted to tell. I turned my face away from the corpse and took a deep breath in, holding it. Quickly, I shoved my hands up underneath the waist and heaved the body over on its back. Immediately I saw that it *was* a man and his throat had been slit wide open, almost decapitating him. There was no blood thank god, but maggots and other insects had eaten away at the flesh and it hung in shreds and chunks away from the wound. Something hit me in my gut and my chest began to shake. I tilted the head up towards the moon and I heard myself scream, a gut wrenching, earth-shattering explosion that came from my soul. I started vomiting violently in the sand as I held Kai's body in my arms, his eyes fixed and dead.

307

Chapter Nine

Nathanial

Ana had spent hours with the police, with the EMTs; she tried to call Kai's family, but they were unreachable. I knew she was in shock and I was worried that the gravity of the situation would hit her and send her reeling. I had been able to reach Alec, who was traveling abroad looking for Devon. He hadn't said a word when I told him; he was his usual stoic self and Ana and I were at my house awaiting his arrival. I heard her throwing up in the bathroom again and I went down the hall to my bedroom. She was hovering over the sink dry heaving. I grabbed a washcloth and ran it under the shower, soaking it in cool water. I brushed her sweat soaked hair back from her neck and pressed the cloth to her skin. Her body jolted forward and she gagged again.

"I just can't stop picturing his body Nathanial, his head and his throat…I just can't stop…" She heaved again, gasping and choking.

"Shhh Ana. Shhh, it's ok. It's ok," I said, moving the cool cloth to her mouth. I had tried to calm her down myself, but my abilities to navigate her nervous system were locked down due to her extreme emotional state. I couldn't navigate around her grief and shock.

"Nathanial," a quiet voice spoke from somewhere in the bedroom. I looked up to see Alec standing in the doorway to the bathroom, watching us. Ana's head shot up and she moved away from the sink and into Alec's arms, sobbing.

"Oh Alec, I'm so sorry, I'm so sorry, what are we going to do?" Ana buried her face in his chest. Again, my instincts were somewhat heightened in Alec's presence. He had closed his mind and I couldn't get a read on the tenor of his emotions or his thoughts. I did not fail to notice the lack of comfort that Alec was giving to Ana. Out of our whole group, Ana of course, was the most affectionate and over time I knew that she had gotten Alec to be a bit more emotive with his gestures, but that was not case tonight. In fact, I watched as Alec pushed Ana away and stepped back. Perhaps he too was in shock.

"We're not going to do anything Ana," Alec said, using his commanding tone.

"What?" Ana sniffed and wiped her face.

"I said we're not going to do anything. There's nothing we can do. What's done is done." I caught his eye and his face looked blank, smooth and expressionless. Definitely shock.

"We have to do something Alec. Someone murdered Kai, someone killed my best friend and your husband and we have to do something!" Ana was yelling at him. "Why are you just standing there, why are you not calling people, why are you just staring at me?" She started pounding him on the chest, her body heaving. Alec grabbed her wrists and moved her away from him. Ana turned to me, desperate. "Nathanial?"

"She's right Alec, I don't think Kai's murder was a random killing by Humans, the wounds are too distinctive." I surveyed him as I spoke. He was standing very still.

"You have a theory?" he asked raising his eyebrows.

"Don't you?" I said, disbelieving that he didn't see where I was going with this.

"Devon is too occupied to bother with incidental Human lives Nathanial." Alec had turned his back to me.

"Wait, you think that Devon did this?" Ana asked, looking at me, but my mind was already analyzing what Alec had just said. I put my hand up to stop Ana from continuing and moved over to where Alec was standing.

"Do you mean to tell me that you know for a fact that Devon is alive Alec?" My voice was even and controlled as I spoke, but I could feel my body tense. Why hadn't he shared this information with me sooner? Alec turned toward me and I could see that his eyes had gone black. He smirked at me.

"Of course he's alive. You didn't honestly think that your brother was powerful enough to take a Vampire like Devon out, did you?" Alec's voice was cold. "In fact," he continued, "if Ana's little stunt had worked, then we'd be dealing with two less Humans, instead of one." I heard Ana gasp as the words fell from Alec's lips. In a blur I was on him, slamming his body against the wall, shattering the wood. He waved his hand sending me stumbling backward, but not throwing me off balance. I rocked backward on my heels and sprang forward grabbing him around the neck and tossing him to the floor. The tiles cracked under the force.

"Stop it! Jesus Christ, stop!" Ana yelled. Suddenly, I was watching Alec's body being flown through the air, his back breaking upon the floor harder than when I had first thrown him. I turned to see Ana standing so still, her arms to her sides and she was rigid, tense. I gawked at her. Had she just thrown Alec across the room? I heard him grunt, breaking my gaze on Ana and I yanked him by the hair, standing him up. He growled at me and wiped the blood from his face. I noticed that it was oozing black, not red and a realization hit me, but before I could get my head around anything, Alec looked at me once, then at Ana and I saw his eyes widen at her stance, and quickly he shimmered out of sight.

"Nathanial, what was that all about?" Ana was standing in the middle of the room, but she was swaying, her body about to crumple. I blurred over to her and caught her just as her knees buckled. I swept her up and carried her over to my bed.

"I don't know," I said, more to myself than to her. I was staring at her, trying to understand what I thought had just happened.

"What's wrong with Alec, why would he say those things?" She was looking at me, her brown eyes flooding with tears. "Did he crack or something?" I glanced down at her. That was a possibility, but a very remote possibility. I knew my theory was much more likely.

"We can't worry about Alec right now," I said quietly to her. "You need to get some rest, the next few weeks are going to

311

be very difficult." I smoothed her hair back from her face and stroked her cheek. She nodded and closed her eyes, breathing slowly. I stayed with her until she fell asleep. I sat, trying to navigate just exactly what kind of change Ana had managed to undergo during my absence and what is was that Alec had become. I had too many questions and not nearly enough answers to quell the raging anxiety that was now coursing through my body.

****

The weeks after Kai's death proved just as trying as I had predicted. Things had continued to get worse. Authorities discovered that Kai's mother and sister had also been murdered, as were his uncle and stepfather. They had no leads, but of course I knew that they would never find the killers, unless they were prepared to arrest a coven of Vampires. Alec had not reappeared and the longer he stayed away, the more ill at ease I became. Amazingly, Ana's boss at the NGO, Caleb, became an excellent source for information. He was an old world Bonder, an extremely powerful demon that had racked up many histories with both Devon and Alec. He had volunteered to make contact with some of his connections and try to sort out what exactly was going on with Alec and confirm whether Devon or Patric were actually alive. Ana was holding up better than I had anticipated and she was managing to still go to her physical therapy sessions and to continue to prepare for her dissertation defense. The unease over Alec had me guarding Ana with more than my usual attention. I didn't think that Alec would ever hurt Ana, at least that was what I kept telling myself, but things had taken such a disturbing turn, I didn't know what to believe anymore. I had made plenty of allies in my time with Patric and even before that stint, and I was sure that should the need arise, that I could manage to gather quite a force that would be willing to fight. I was hoping that would not have to be the case.

I was waiting for Ana to come over after her P.T. session. To my utter surprise, she had asked to stop by; usually I was the one having to initiate any extra contact beyond keeping tabs on her. She had complied with my requests to call me upon her arrival to a destination and if she changed plans or changed a set location to go with friends, that she also let me know. It was ridiculous, but necessary. I was outside planting some flowers when I heard her jeep coming up the drive. She drove like a maniac and thanks to her skidding out all the time; I had to replace the gravel every other day it seemed. I laughed as I heard her tires tossing up rocks and dirt as she approached. I pushed the shovel into the dirt and leaned on the handle, waiting for her to get out.

"Hey!" she called, gathering her pack and gym bag from the back seat. Hmm, did that mean she was staying for a bit? I was hopeful. I waved and motioned for her come over.

"How was the gym?" I asked, her scent penetrating every pore in my body. It was always worse after she worked out; it had always been like that with her but now, now with all of these changes in me, I seemed to have a much more primal reaction to her and her fragrance. I steadied myself and flexed my muscles.

"It was ok, Adam wasn't there and I had this weird chick who kept hitting me on the ass after every set. I mean, I went through a whole experimental phase in college, but I'm really not into women right now," she said as she smiled at me.

"Really?" I said, raising my eyebrows at her. "An experimental phase? That sets up a whole different picture of you in my head." I winked at her and she rolled her eyes.

"God, what is with you? Even Demons have a thing for girl on girl action. I'll never understand it, perhaps I have to have a penis to see the appeal?" She yawned, flexing her arms and I could see just how much more muscular she had become since returning to the gym.

"Am I lucky enough to have you for dinner tonight?" I was trying to keep the desire out of my tone.

"Is that alright? I mean I don't want to mess up your plans or anything." She frowned at me.

"What?" I asked

"Hmm, I was just wondering? Are you interested in dating? I mean, like are you going out and meeting women when you are… when you are at work or whatever?" She was biting her lip. It was an odd question, but perhaps there was something more within the subtext of her query. Usually the only questions Ana asked me these days pertained to Alec or if I had heard from Caleb. Neither of which I was able to provide her with information. I placed the shovel down in the dirt and started back toward the house. She fell in step beside me.

"Why do you want to know?" I glanced at her from the corner of my eye.

"I don't know. It's not like I don't think you should, you know, have fun with someone; I was just wondering." She held the door open for me.

"Are you trying to feel less guilty about having been with Patric?" I laughed and turned on the stereo. It was the wrong thing to have said. She was glaring at me, her hands on her hips.

"YOU LEFT ME!" she exclaimed. "Your brother was the only reason I was still alive when you came back and Alec is the only reason that I survived after you disappeared with Patric. If it weren't for Alec and Patric, your poison and your blood probably would have just killed me!" Color rose high in her cheeks and I could see the vein in her neck popping out.

"Ok, ok," I said, raising my hands in surrender. "Ana, I told you that I don't blame you for anything that happened between you and my brother; I understand why you did what you did, you have nothing to defend. I'm sorry I made you upset." I walked toward her and put my hands on her shoulders. Her emotions were so close to the surface these days. I knew she was trying to move through her grief over Kai, her confusion with Alec, and her fear of Devon; I also knew that there was some deeper emotion that she was experiencing for me, one that she wasn't ready to bring out just yet. "Now, do you want to take a shower and I'll start

315

dinner?" I couldn't help but notice just how hot her skin felt. I could literally feel the heat rising out through her shirt and into the palms of my hands. I moved back from her, staring. She was breathing deeply as she grabbed her bags and headed down the hall.

I moved to the kitchen and began preparing some eggplant and pasta, still puzzled. I heard the shower run and I turned up the stereo. My mind returned to her original question about me dating. Truthfully, I had absolutely no desire to be with anyone but her. I had been in the presence of other women during my time with Patric and I had borne witness to some very dark behaviors from his Vampire coven, but all of my passion and my love was for Ana, it consumed my every thought, my every physical need, except when I was thinking about Alec and Devon and my brother. I had hoped that I would have heard from Caleb this week, but so far, nothing. I sautéed the eggplant in garlic and olive oil and added Ana's favorite heirloom tomatoes from my garden—my mind drifted. I wanted to know why she was so curious about my liaisons during my absence. I knew that the discussion about the exchange ritual that Devon so tactfully brought up at dinner, had her wondering about me and about the whole process. It was something deep in her memory and I had seen that she'd wanted to ask more questions than I was prepared to answer, at least at that time. Now, I had no problem discussing the matter further with her, but I thought it best that she be the one to bring it up. Besides, she'd already asked me if I had been with anyone when we were on the island after that horrific dinner. I wondered if she had forgotten our conversation, or if there was some other question she really wanted answered and she just couldn't bring herself to ask. I heard the shower turn off and I started chopping spinach for a salad. Ana appeared in the kitchen wearing my sweats and t-shirt, her hair full and curly, tumbling down her back. She took a seat at the bar and started slicing up tomatoes; she was staring at me. "Yes?" I asked her, smirking.

"Nothing, it's just, I know that when we were in West Papua, you told me that you weren't with anyone, you know, then, but what about since then, I mean since we've been back. Have you seen anyone that you like?" So she did remember our conversation. Good grief, she was frustrating the hell out of me, I wished she'd just come out with it already.

"Ana, we've only been back a few months, how fast do you think I operate? Besides, I've been with you almost every moment of everyday since we've returned." I eyed her.

"Not every moment," she said quietly, still slicing. "You go to class and you teach and you have students and colleagues that are interesting." She kept her head down.

"No one provides me with more interesting entertainment than you, my dear." I laughed and ran my finger down the bridge of her nose, touching her upper lip. "Do you want to eat outside?"

"Yeah," she said as she carried out two glasses and a bottle of wine to the deck. I wished she would just ask me what she wanted to know. I was prepared to be honest with her and let her in—it was time. I brought out our plates and took my seat next to her on the sofa.

"Thanks for cooking again." She smiled and poured me a glass of wine.

"Thanks for wanting to come over," I said, toasting my glass to hers. We ate in silence for a while before she put her plate down and turned me.

"Why didn't you ever ask me to do that blood ritual thing with you? We were intimate loads of times and you never once brought it up? Is it reserved for special people or something?" She was biting her lip again. So that's what it was, she thought I had been holding out on her, sexually. I sipped my wine and settled back against the cushions.

"No, it's not reserved for special people Ana, I just thought that perhaps it was a little more than you were used to and I didn't want to frighten you with such a request. You have to admit, it's a bit dark in nature, no?" I stared into the fire, thinking.

"I'm not a prude Nathanial, I've experimented with lots of things before," she said defiantly.

"Oh I know you have." I laughed and turned to look over my shoulder at her. She rolled her eyes.

"So, you've never participated in that, with someone? I mean in all your years, you're telling me that you never once had that experience with someone, just to know what it was like?" She twirled a lock of hair around her finger.

"I'm not as promiscuous as some of my brethren, and I'm actually quite protective of my blood supply," I mused. This was true. Giving Ana my blood in order to complete our exchange had been the first time that I had ever allowed another person to take from my body—at least from what I could remember. Something tugged at the recesses of my mind, but I quickly withdrew from my inner ponderings to focus on the conversation at hand.

Unfortunately, for both of us, my blood exchange with Ana had not been a pleasant experience; it had been a violent matter and not at all the sensual coupling that I would have hoped for her and for me. The nature of our current conversation was making me rather aroused and I needed to get myself under control. I had promised that I wouldn't touch Ana unless she initiated things first. I took another sip from my glass and turned to find her staring at me rather intensely. I moved myself against the seat and stared back at her. "What?" I asked her softly. "What is it Ana?" Her face blazed against the fire and I could feel the heat from her body moving over my own skin. My mouth watered and an acute desire began to rise in my bones and in my blood. I knew she wouldn't ask for what she desired and I knew what she wanted; she wanted me, but she was terrified to let herself give in, to let me take control. I could see it in her eyes and in her mind. I put my glass down on the table and stood up, moving back into the house. I went to the safe in my bedroom and removed a small chalice that my father had left to me before he'd passed, and the vile of blood that Ana had sacrificed for me. I stared at them both for a long while before taking them back out to the deck. Ana was staring into the fire, the flames setting her hair blazing in red and gold light. I sat back down and poured us two more glasses of wine, giving her a bit extra. I removed the stopper that contained her blood and poured the entire contents in to my glass, swirling the liquids together. She watched me, her eyes on my face. I looked at her and then took my chalice and decanted the bottle pouring my blood into her glass. I took my finger and mixed them together, watching as her white wine turned a deep red.

I motioned for her to take her glass and follow me into the house. I moved to stand in front of the fireplace and ran my hand over the logs, setting it ablaze. She looked startled and almost dropped her wine. Her hand was trembling. I reached out and wrapped my fingers around her glass, steadying her. She looked up at me and I thought that I saw small flames appear in her eyes. I stepped back from her for a moment, shocked at what I thought I had just seen. I looked again at her face and there they were, the glow of tiny embers igniting in the depths of her gaze. I locked my own eyes upon her and brought my glass to my lips, letting the sweetness of her blood make my mouth water and my heart race. It was intoxicating and I drank it down in one swallow, feeling the heat spread through my body and her life course through my veins. This was so much more than I had originally taken from her and the effects were immediate. Power coursed through my muscles and the need to dominate her, to revel in my most demonic nature, rose to the surface. I brought her glass to her mouth and watched as she slowly drank, I could see her swallow and I knew that in seconds, my blood would be running through her body and I felt a wave of desire so intense that a growl begin to rumble in my chest. Again, I put the glass to her lips and she drank more deeply, moaning. I took both glasses and placed them on the table behind me. I had to go slow with her; this had the potential to become very violent and rough if I was not careful. She was standing with the fire behind her and it looked as though she herself had been set ablaze. I moved toward her and she took a step back, clearly uncertain about what she was experiencing. "Ana, it's ok, you're safe, you're with me now." My body tensed as I approached her. "Let me show you what you want, what you need," I whispered, stepping closer to her. She looked at me, her eyes still burning. I reached out and touched my fingers to her neck and she shivered in pleasure at my touch. I smiled and pulled her closer to me. The contact our bodies made, sent a wave of passion and lust within me so deep, that I grabbed her around the waist and pushed her back up against the wall. "Ana," I whispered, and pinned her arms above her head. "Look at me." She opened her eyes and I could see just how much I was affecting her. I pressed myself against her, not breaking our gaze. "Let me show you what I can do to you," I said breathing softly into her face. Without touching her, I let my mind move inside her head, making her feel me penetrate deep inside her body. She groaned and tried to bring her mouth to mine. I smiled at her. "Not yet Ana." I put my finger to her lips and took her hand, leading her down the hall.

All of my senses were in overdrive and every look she gave me, every touch of her skin to mine, sent the most primal urges spiraling through my body. I needed to be in control of myself, in control of my need for her. I moved to sit on the bed and motioned for her to be next to me. I stared at her, letting her mind filter what I wanted her to see, what I wanted to do to her. I watched as she stood and removed her clothes, her eyes never leaving mine. I pulled her down on the bed onto her stomach. I moved next to her letting my fingertips trace down the length of her spine, watching as her back quivered under my touch. My lips moved across her skin, my tongue tasting every inch of her. My mouth was full of her, but I wanted so much more. I let my teeth gently graze the back of her neck, pressing them deeply into her flesh, testing her tolerance. She groaned and moved her head to the side, exposing more of her skin. I laughed and flipped her over on her back.

"What?" she asked, her voice more seductive than I had ever heard it. My body contracted as it tensed in my need to possess her.

"You don't seem to mind things being a bit on the rougher side do you?" I purred as I let my fingers trace over her breasts, watching her body respond. She moaned softly.

"Is that bad?" She opened her eyes searching my face. I knew that the blood was making her want things that she wouldn't normally crave; it was part of the whole experience and I wanted her to feel safe asking for anything.

"No Ana, it's not bad; I just want to make sure that we go at your pace. I want you to trust yourself with me, to trust me with your desires, your needs." I moved my hands down between her legs, caressing her slowly as I felt the heat from her arousal; I licked my lips.

"I do trust you Nathanial. I crave you, please..." Her hips were moving as my hand continued to massage her. My desires were overflowing and I wasn't going to be able to hold on for much longer. In a blur, I was on top of her hovering over her body, barely letting our hips touch. I bit down on my lip, drawing blood. I pressed my mouth to hers, biting down hard on her lips, letting her blood mix with mine. She ran her tongue over the slice in my flesh, groaning. "Why do you taste so good?" She moaned and brought her mouth back to mine, biting me. I laughed and pulled gently away from her.

"Easy now, don't get in over your head." Honestly, I didn't mind her biting me, I wanted her to taste me, but I also knew that such an action awoke a very dark part of my soul, a very demonic part.

"Please Nathanial, your taste, your scent; I want you," she whispered as she ran her lips down my neck, suddenly she spun me on my back. The movement happened so fast that I was completely caught off guard. She was straddling me and unbuttoning my shirt, well actually she was tearing it off. I could feel my eyes darkening and my muscles flexing; I hoped that I wouldn't hurt her and that she wouldn't be too roughed up. Her teeth grazed over my stomach and I grabbed her wrists and switched our positions pinning her under me once again.

"My turn first," I said, my full demonic nature coming to the surface now. I reached over across her body to my nightstand and removed a single black silk scarf. I ran the fabric over her body before bringing it up and binding her wrists together, tying her to the iron rods of the headboard. I pressed my finger to my bleeding lip and ran it across her mouth, letting her taste me. She ran her tongue over the tip, pushing my finger further into her mouth; the wetness of her lips and the pressure she was using as if she were going down on me, became almost feral and I growled as my groin warmed and I started to thrust myself against her. She groaned again and I could feel how hot she'd become and I smirked at her. "Be patient, please." I taunted her as I moved in position over her body. I felt lust raging in my veins, lust for her body, lust for her blood, lust to be inside of her, to hear her moan in pleasure; I wanted to be in control of what she was feeling and how intensely she felt it. I wanted to be everything that she needed.

I began running my mouth down her stomach, watching her body arch and hearing her groan. The incredible urge to bite into her flesh, to taste her, was enveloping me. I didn't want her blood in the same way that Patric had wanted it or in any way that a Vampire would want Human blood; I didn't need it to feed or for nourishment. I didn't need it for power or strength anymore, it was a primal desire; for demons, blood was a tool for the most intense arousal and I wanted *her* to take from *me*, to have my blood for *her* pleasure. It was mutualism in its most animalistic nature. I watched her moving under me and I quietly whispered in her ear what I wanted. I pressed my lips to hers and felt her bite down again, drawing more blood. I shuttered in pleasure as I felt her hips grind hard against mine. I ran my tongue down her throat and I held her shoulders back as I let my teeth puncture her skin. It was barely a scrape; I was adept at cutting skin to draw blood, without creating a wound. My tongue tasted her and I growled from somewhere deep inside. Roughly, I forced her legs open and pushed my fingers inside her. She gasped and her body arched clenching around me, holding me deep. I growled again and moved my face to her stomach, biting into her with savage passion. Heat rose deep and strong within my body, igniting me from the inside and I brought the flat plains of her stomach to my lips, my cock contracting in pleasure. She was moving under me, her hands twisting and turning above her. I laughed and reached up to untie her. I wasn't nearly done with her, but I knew that her urges were about to boil over. I wanted her to be satisfied. "Will you be needing this?" I swept the scarf across her face.

"Is that what you want?" she asked, pushing me down hard on the bed. When had she gotten so strong?

"I think that might be fun," I replied, still in awe of the force she was using with me. She took the scarf and wove it around my wrists, binding me tightly to the bed. I leaned up to watch her unzip my pants and slide them off to the floor. She ran her hand up and down my thighs, pushing my legs open wide. Suddenly I knew what she was going to do. I had never experienced that kind of pleasure before and I was unsure how my body would react. I was already feeling a bit sexually violent towards her, in a good way, but this was new territory for me, again though, something familiar began to pull from the depths of my mind and again, I pushed it back. Ana spread her legs over my thigh and rubbed herself against me igniting another deep growl from my chest. Not having the use of my hands posed an interesting dilemma. I was fighting the urge to break my bonds and push her down on me, but she was in control and I was at her mercy; not such a bad deal I thought as I felt her tongue trace up and down between my legs. I grunted and again she moved her hips against my thigh. I could feel her pulsating on my skin. This was amazing, how she was teasing me, getting closer then pulling her mouth away; it was making me delirious with pleasure. Her teeth skimmed the inside of my thigh and I felt a trickle of blood run down my leg. My god, she knew what she was doing. I was

stunned and breathless as I felt her lips taste my blood. She
moaned loudly and spread her legs wider, massaging herself
against me. This was too much and I snapped the scarf in two.
I pressed her head down hard between my legs. I gasped at
the feeling of her mouth, her tongue, and the violent sucking
motion... I pushed her down harder and faster, not wanting
her to stop. I was growling so loudly now that I was drowning
out Ana's own groans. I laughed in my delirium and I brought
her face back up toward mine. I spun her hard onto her back
and held her down as I shoved myself inside her. I felt her
contract as she held me firmly. I was throbbing and pulsing
savagely, but I wanted her to come first; I wanted to watch.
She arched her back and ground her hips against me. I pinned
her hands down and thrust as deeply as I could, keeping our
friction in the perfect spot. She screamed out in pleasure as
she opened her legs wider to me. I pushed once more and the
world stopped; I came so violently that I was sure that I had
died. So intense was my pleasure that I found it impossible not
to come again, and again. She was groaning softly. I could still
taste her on my tongue and still feel her blood coursing
through my veins. I moved my hips against hers, grinding
deeply. I felt something shudder in her body and she rocked
me faster against her. She moaned loudly and I held her down,
I wanted her again but I knew that she would need to recover
from this and I needed to check her over. I slowed our
movements until I was barely thrusting inside of her. I watched
her body come down from the pleasure she'd experienced,
and I panted in a great effort to remove myself from her.

I rolled off of her gasping for breath. I moved to sit back
against the pillows, pulling Ana with me and I stared at her.
She was not the same woman that I had made love to at the

326

beach. She was different, stronger and more powerful. She had always been a very tough person, a very commanding presence, but this was different. I wasn't sure if through her grief or her fear that she had managed to find her true self, to let me be in control and for her to control me. I didn't know what to think at the moment. I felt high and extremely aroused. "Ana let me look at you." I moved to sit up so I could examine her body. I was still trying to get my physical wants under control. She was very red in some areas, mainly the areas that I bit her and she had some bruises beginning to appear on her skin. I traced my fingers gently over her. She shuttered and turned to look at me. The embers were still there in her eyes, burning into me. I couldn't look away; she was taking the breath out of my lungs with her gaze. Her lips were bloody as were mine. Forcing myself to move away from her body, from her skin, I got off the bed and headed toward the bathroom.

"Where are you going?" she asked, her tone still seductive. I shook my head and exhaled trying not to breathe in the scent of her orgasms; I could taste them on my lips and I wanted more, much more.

"I think we need to clean ourselves up a bit. I'll be right back." I laughed. I dampened some washcloths in the bathroom and looked at myself in the mirror. My skin was glowing; the copper sheen that normally illuminated the surface was now a full-blown luminescence that reflected every ounce of light in the room. My eyes were shifting color from gray to blue to black and back to gray and my cheeks looked flush with color. I wiped the washcloth over my lips tasting the blood in the process, her blood. My muscles tensed again and I quickly

327

rinsed my mouth with water. I ran a second washcloth under the faucet and brought it back to the bed with me. Ana was now under the covers, her hair spread out over the pillow. She looked radiant. I crawled over to her and smiled as I pressed the cloth to her mouth.

"Thanks," she murmured. I pulled the covers back gently and swept the damp fabric across her neck and stomach. She trembled under my tender caresses. How was I going to do this? I wanted her again; so heightened was my desire that I felt myself begin to trace my fingertips along her lower abdomen. I breathed deeply and managed to stop myself, pulling the covers back up around her chest. "Do you want me to stay?" she asked softly.

"Good god yes." I laughed at the absurdity of her question.

"Just checking. I wanted to respect your space." She smirked at me and pulled the covers back. I stood naked in front of her and I felt her eyes roam over my body. I shook my head sliding into the bed along side her. "What?" she asked turning to lay her head against my chest.

"I'm just not sure how I'm going to manage to keep from attacking you on a daily basis; I want you again right now," I said earnestly. She moved her face close to mine.

"Really, even after all of that, you want me again?" she purred in my ear. What was she doing?

"Ana, seriously, we could end up never leaving this room if we continue down this path and I'm sure at some point all of the screaming would draw attention from the authorities." I was joking, but only partially. She moved herself on top of me. Dear god, she was going to be the one to steal my soul and corrupt it beyond repair. She pushed me inside of her and I gasped at the suddenness of the movement. She laughed and kissed me gently, deeply.

"Nathanial." She was staring at me, her eyes still on fire.

"What," I said breathlessly, my hands running down the length of her spine.

"I love you so much. I never stopped loving you. I was going to tell you that night that we went to your office. I had wanted to tell you the first night we'd spent together on the beach. I'm sorry about Patric. I did love him, but in a different way, I can't explain it…" Tears were streaming down her face. I reached to stroke her cheeks, gently moving my hips against hers; I was having trouble concentrating with our bodies in such a desirable position. I pressed her harder against me and she tossed her head back, groaning softly.

"God Ana, I love you so much, I love you and I want you. It's going to be ok. I know you're scared and I know that you miss Kai, but we're together now and we'll figure all of this out, I promise. Jesus, I love you." I brought her face to mine and kissed her and I didn't stop kissing her for the rest of the night.

I rose before dawn, leaving Ana sleeping soundly, the first time since Kai's death that I had seen her rest a full night, well almost a full night. I felt my mouth water as I thought about our evening and what we had experienced; she was mine, finally, Ana was mine and it would always be that way. She was my Bond and her heart and now her blood ran in my veins. I dressed quickly and headed out to the kitchen to make her coffee and breakfast. I had just started the espresso maker when I heard a soft knock at the door. I looked at my watch; it was six-thirty, very early for a visitor. My muscles tensed as I approached the door.

"Nathanial, it's Caleb." I exhaled and opened the door. Caleb hardly ever shimmered and I was grateful that he seemed to be respectful of matters of privacy. He looked different today. I was used to seeing him dressed in shirts and ties and now he looked a lot like Patric. Caleb's hair was coiled into dreadlocks that hung down to his waist and he was wearing a long, dark green leather overcoat, jeans and boots. He looked rugged and weathered. I eyed him closely and wondered why he and Ana had never gotten together. "Because I love her like a sister Nathanial," he said, exasperated at my thoughts. "And because she's the best intern that I've ever had, and because she's always loved you, and because I actually don't have the time or energy to deal with the hassles of Bonding, that's new world crap—take your pick." He pushed his way past me and into the hallway, shedding his coat.

"You know something?" I asked, leading him into the kitchen.

"Where's Ana?" he replied, concerned.

"She's sleeping, at least for the time being," I mumbled. Ana had amazing hearing and was the lightest sleeper I had ever known. It was only a matter of time before she heard our voices. Caleb eyed me, and then nodded.

"Well, Devon is alive. He managed to live through what were some very dark powers of fire wielding by your brother. I'm not sure exactly how Patric managed to harness such an intricate and ancient ability, but he did nonetheless. The only thing is that Devon also seems to have harnessed a bit of that same ancient power and your brother was just a fraction of a bit less experienced." He stopped, looking at me.

"So Patric is dead then?" It seemed pointless to ask.

"Well that's an interesting question. According to Devon's cohorts, Patric is dead, but I have several Bonders who say otherwise. There are rumors that Patric is wounded, but alive—where he might be, well that's still undetermined." I put a cup of coffee in front of Caleb. He nodded and took a sip.

"And what of Alec?" My mind was moving so fast, trying to process every detail. Caleb sighed and leaned forward.

"Nathanial, no one has seen him. It's the oddest thing. Everyone I asked said that they had no recollection of ever having crossed Alec's path, even people whom he had worked with for years. I showed them pictures, past and present and not a single person recognized his face. It's almost as if he never existed." Caleb's voice became muted and dark. I felt the hair on my arms stand on end.

"I don't understand, I've known Alec for hundreds of years; how can it be that not a single person remembers him or knows his face? There has to be someone." I was uneasy.

"I don't know. I got the impression that there may have been some memory modification going on; that perhaps the individuals did remember him, but their mind was not allowing them to confirm the recognition. It's just a theory, but it's all I have." Caleb took another sip from his coffee.

"Are you telling me that you think Alec has managed to get to every single person that he's come across in over three hundred years and modify their memories of him? That's absurd, no demon could do that; it would take lifetimes." I was in disbelief.

"No *one* demon could do that, but if you had hundreds or thousands, you could get pretty far. Then of course there's my other theory..." he trailed off, staring at me.

"What, what's your other theory Caleb?" I felt suddenly sick.

"What if Alec isn't a demon at all Nathanial? What if he's something else entirely?" Caleb looked out the window.

"What, what else could he be?" I wasn't seeing it, I didn't understand.

"No one remembers him, no one even recognizes his face, he shows up here just before you do, he attaches himself to Ana's best friend, he gains Ana's trust, her love, her friendship, he goes to find you when you leave, he somehow knows about Devon and Patric showing up in West Papua and tells me, he appears on the beach with you after Ana falls; didn't you ever ask yourself how he knew to be there? He tells you that Patric is most likely dead and he makes every effort to save Ana after he brings her back to his house..." My heart froze and ice flooded my veins. The vision of seeing Alec's blood, his black blood, flooded my mind.

"He's a Vampire." My voice was barely audible. "A shape shifter…he's working with Devon to get to Ana; it's been her all along." I understood now. They had hoped that Patric would have been the one to bring her to Devon, but my brother, in his undying quest for power, decided to betray Devon and take Ana's blood for his own. As soon as Alec found out what transpired between Ana and Patric, they knew that they had been betrayed and that Patric was making a bid to prevent Devon from taking over—Patric was getting stronger, while Devon had to wait, wait for the perfect opportunity. That's how he knew that Ana was planning to leave West Papua. She had called Alec and told him to meet her at the airport. Alec contacted Devon and that's when they decided to make their play for Ana, to bring their plan together. They had not anticipated Ana making the ultimate sacrifice for Patric, to try to keep things as even as possible to give him and me a chance against Devon. That's why Alec had reacted in such a bizarre way, why he seemed so intrigued that Ana had not died and that they still had a chance to obtain her; that's why he left so quickly after she was recovered. He was going to tell Devon that she had survived and that they needed to regroup. Caleb was nodding, his mind following my every thought. "He betrayed us, he betrayed her," I said quietly. But something was still bothering me. "Why didn't Alec just escape with her once we brought her back; he had ample opportunities to fight me, why the hesitation?" I was speaking out loud, but not expecting Caleb to answer.

"I don't know, you're a much more formidable opponent these days Nathanial. Perhaps Alec didn't want to risk a fight with you, at least not yet. Or perhaps they are hoping to use you somehow, to have your powers on their side would allow the Vampires to tap into some very dark and old world weaponry. Or…." his voice cut off and the color faded from his cheeks.

"Or what Caleb? Or what?" my voice rose slightly as I spoke and my heart pounded against my chest.

"Or they are going to offer you a choice Nathanial, a choice that no one would ever want to make. Ana or your brother, one life for the other, you join them and one of them lives, the other dies. You don't join them and they both die and they take Ana's blood for their own, guaranteeing that Devon will be strong enough to defeat you and the rest of our species. They want you to be the one to deliver the blow; it's the ultimate torture mechanism. They hate us Nathanial and they have never played by the rules. They are psychotic and they want to exercise the most horrific revenge. This would be it don't you think?"

"You think they're keeping Patric? You think Devon didn't kill him on purpose?" I was frantic, my body was shaking and I had to grip the side of the counter to keep from screaming.

"That's exactly what I think and I also think that Alec will be back for Ana. There's nothing we can do. He'll always be able to find you and he knows this. He's waiting, dragging it out, that's what Vampires do." Caleb rubbed his face in his hands.

"Nathanial," a quiet voice spoke from the hallway. Ana. She had heard everything. Caleb's head shot up. Tears were in his eyes, but he looked determined. He reached to touch my shoulder.

"I'll do whatever you want Nathanial, whatever it takes. Perhaps we can at least get an early warning on when they are planning to strike and whether or not your brother is actually still alive." He stood and walked over to Ana. She was standing so still. I watched as Caleb pressed his lips to her forehead and held her face in his hands. He looked at her once, and then shimmered away.

Chapter Ten

Ana

Getting my dissertation done was slightly anti-climatic, considering what was waiting for me around the corner, but Nathanial made it very special. As a gift, he redecorated my house in a similar style to his own, but he incorporated things that Noni had given me and pieces that Kai and I had found on some of our adventures. He even made a beautiful doghouse for Piyip and Kuckuc. He and Caleb were also throwing me a party. It was weird just how normal things were, how the three of us seemed to be going about our daily lives, but knowing that at any moment, everything could change. I never asked Nathanial what he was thinking about or what he was going to do, but he did make me promise him that I would not pull another stunt like the one I did with Devon. I swore on whatever life that I had left, that I would be with him until the end—until whatever end.

I was trying to decide what to wear to the party when I heard Nathanial coming up the stairs, Kuckuc nipping his heels. He leaned against the doorframe, his eyes moving slowly over my body. I probably should have put some clothes on before he arrived. I was standing in my bra and underwear; his desire was something that seemed, despite our impending doom, not to have diminished, but it wasn't just *his* desire, I was finding it harder and harder to resist him. I craved him desperately, all the time. He moved into the room and I turned to face him, my dress in my hand. He stood in front of me and took the dress, dropping it to the floor. I pulled him to me and put his hands around my bare waist. It wasn't close enough. It was never close enough these days. I moved my hips against his and pushed him down on my bed. He laughed but his eyes had turned dark and I felt his muscles tense as he dug his fingers into my back.

"Are you sure you want to do this? Your hair looks nice and I'm guessing you won't have time to take another shower before we have to leave." He ran his fingers through my perfect spirals. They had taken me over an hour to do, but my need for him was far greater than some stupid hairstyle. I pressed my hips into his groin and moved slowly up and down. He moaned and grabbed the back of my head, exposing my throat. I felt his lips on my skin and I pushed him back down against the pillows. I tore off his shirt, trying hard not to detach any buttons. I let my tongue run over his bare chest, tasting his skin, smelling his blood. Since we had our little exchange a month ago, I had wanted nothing but to taste him ever since. Every time he kissed me, every time he touched me, it was all I could do not to bite him. Nathanial seemed to think that having a bit of Patric's Vampire blood in me, made me crave the arousal that came from having *Nathanial's* blood in my system, more than most who go through the ritual. I didn't actually care why I was craving it, I just knew that I wanted him and I had to try very hard not leave constant bite marks in his flesh. I moved down his stomach to his inner thigh. His body trembled and he pulled me back up next to him. I pouted.

"What?" I said. "You don't want to?" I was already worked up and it was going to be hard to just stop now.

"God yes, of course I want to Ana, I always want to." He was laughing and stroking my bottom lip that I was pushing out. "But, since this is your special night, I think things should be all about you." In a blur, he had flung me on my back, his body pressing down hard on mine.

"Hmmm, what did you have in mind?" I purred, kissing him deeply.

"Something new I think. Something that I've been saving for such an occasion." He kissed me back. Something new? I was pretty sure that we had done just about everything both legal and illegal that two people could manage, as well as some things that only a Demon and a human could accomplish. I smiled at him, curious. He was looking at me like he always did when we were intimate, like I was the only being in the whole world that he wanted, that I was everything, that I was him and he was me. He ran his hand over my chest, gently pushing me back against the bed. "Relax," he murmured. I felt him move down to my waist and fall to his knees pulling me closer to the edge of the bed. I propped myself on my elbows, we had done *this*, lots. I gasped as I watched him bite his lower lip and draw a deep, wet, red line. Perhaps this *would* be new. I felt myself groan at the very sight of his blood. "Lie back," he whispered, but his tone was commanding; I was happy to oblige. Suddenly, my groin tensed as his fingers tore my panties off and I felt his mouth on me. Before I even knew what was happening, I was climaxing violently. He moved his blood soaked lips rhythmically between my legs and again and again I came, each time more violent and more passionate than the one before. I had no control over what I was feeling; he was dictating everything that my body did and how intensely it did it. He was so strong and so controlled, that I didn't have a chance to stop him, even if I wanted to—which I didn't. I felt something warm and wet move down my upper thigh and I realized that he had bitten me. I heard him growl low and deep and move his mouth back down between my legs, his body shimmering in and out of form. His tongue plunged deeper and I couldn't breathe; I was sure that I was going to ignite into flames. What was he doing to me? It was too much, and it was bordering on painful, if it hadn't felt so damn good. I groaned loudly and I heard him gasp and pull me down closer to his face. His hands moved over my waist and held me firm in his grasp. I hadn't realized that I was thrashing about so much, but I was. He was breathing rapidly and I opened my eyes to see that he was watching me, his own eyes on fire. I saw him bite his lip once more and run his mouth fully over the very tip of me, sending me into convulsions. I screamed his name and I shoved his mouth, sucking and pulling, inside of me. He shuddered and I heard him come, his passion exploding. I wasn't far behind, but he was slowing me down, teasing me. "God Nathanial, please," I gasped, my back arching.

"Please what Ana?" He laughed darkly. I felt the tip of his tongue slide between my thighs and he held it there, held me there on the brink of imploding. He moved it once and my body rocked up in the air, I was screaming and gasping in pleasure, in desire, in lust. He moved it again, and I came undone.

Ok, so I had gone a little bit further with her than we usually did, and she was slightly freaked out, but actually handling things quite well. I thought given her recent cravings, that I could show her some of the things I had observed by being with my brother's coven, things that only Vampires did with their prey; she seemed to respond well. I smiled to myself as I helped her out of my car and up the walk to Caleb's house. Her legs were still shaky and she seemed a bit off balance. I took it as a compliment. We arrived about twenty minutes late, not too bad considering what we had just done. There was a large crowd waiting for us on the back deck. I knew that Ana didn't want any of this to happen without Kai and it took everything in my arsenal to get her to agree to celebrate such a wonderful accomplishment, that is what Kai would have wanted her to do.

I had decided to keep Ana in the dark about the nature of Kai's murder. Caleb and I were pretty sure that Alec had committed the crime himself and that he might also have been the one to kill the rest of Kai's family. She didn't need to know that—it was too much. I also didn't want her to know what Caleb had found out about Patric and his powers or about mine and how they could possibly affect Ana. There was something very dark at work, something very ancient and Caleb was keeping his suspicions to himself at the moment. He did however, ask me to watch Ana, watch her face or her body when she became upset or angry. It was an odd request, but I trusted Caleb, as much as I could trust anyone right now, and

I did what he asked. I hadn't seen anything out of the ordinary as of yet except the time with Alec, when he'd been thrown across my room and then the unusual heat coming from her skin and then the flames that I had seen in her eyes...so maybe there were a few things that I had observed. Of course, I actually didn't know what I was looking for exactly so it was quite possible that I could have already missed something or I was making the previous actions seem more than they truly were. Regardless, Ana seemed normal or as normal as Ana could be.

I watched as her friends surrounded her in hugs and kisses and took her onto the deck. She looked so beautiful and so happy, but I could sense the familiar undercurrent of deep sadness that was always with her since the day we met. I caught her eye and she smiled at me. I grinned back at her and walked over to where Caleb was standing at the grill.

"Anything?" he asked, referring to Ana I guessed.

"Not really. What is it that I'm supposed to be looking for Caleb?" I reached over to help him wrangle the now out of control flames from the grill.

"I'm not sure yet, I just know that there's something different about Ana, something that has yet to reveal itself. I'm also hoping that it will be the one thing that may give us a chance against Alec and Devon, but..." he trailed off as his gaze followed Ana across the deck. She passed in front of us, and suddenly the fire from the grill shot up into the air, igniting the night in red flames.

"Jesus Caleb, do you know what you're doing?" A tall man stepped out from behind us having noticed the massive fire that almost sent Caleb and myself up in smoke. Caleb laughed.

"No, not really. I've never been one to handle fire very well." He winked at me and handed the man the tongs to the grill. "How about a drink Nathanial? I'm guessing Charles can take over from here?" He placed a hand on the man's back and motioned for me to follow him over to the bar.

We chatted over beers for quite some time when suddenly, out of nowhere, I heard a scream. My head snapped around and I saw the man that we had left to the grill, burning. Flames were consuming him and his screams were piecing the night. I tried to blur to his side, but something happened in the split second that I had moved through the space. He had stopped screaming and was standing very still, the flames still consuming his body. Caleb was at my side immediately. I didn't understand what was happening. Were we under attack? Out of the corner of my eye I saw something move slowly. Everyone had stopped to stare at the burning man, but someone was moving through the crowd. It was Ana. I could see that her eyes were softly glowing and her gaze was locked upon her friend. I moved to grab her, fearing for her safety, but Caleb touched my shoulder, holding me back. I heard gasps from the crowd as they saw her inching closer to the man, Charles. I wanted to call out to her. I looked desperately at Caleb.

"Watch the fire Nathanial," he said softly, still holding me back. I followed his gaze and stared, awestruck, at what I was

342

seeing. The flames were moving away from Charles. Ever so slowly, they inched out from his body, calmly, quietly. He wasn't moving, and it appeared that he was still burning, but as I looked closer, I could now see that the flames were *surrounding* his body, not burning it, not touching him. Ana was now directly in front of Charles and she was standing still, her eyes focused only on him. I saw her exhale and wave her hand subtlety in front of her body. Instantaneously, the fire moved through the air, landing in a cloud of smoke and flame into the pool. She ran forward just as Charles collapsed in her arms.

"NATHANIAL!" she screamed and Caleb and I moved to her side. The man's skin was hot, but it was looking more and more like a bad sunburn rather than something that should have killed him. I knelt down beside her and ran my hands over his body, cooling his flesh. "He'll need a doctor. Can someone call an ambulance?" Ana yelled into the crowd. She wasn't looking at me, but she was looking at Caleb. Their gazes were locked and I saw awe cross over his face. She finally tore her eyes away as she took a blanket that someone had handed her and draped it over Charles. He was shivering. "It's ok Charles, it's ok. You're ok," she was whispering to him. The EMTs arrived quickly and they left with Charles in the back of the ambulance. The crowd was buzzing over what had just happened, but I saw that Ana was still on the ground, shaking. I knelt down beside her but she wouldn't look at me. "I think I'm ready to go home now," she said, her voice quiet and cold. I signaled to Caleb and he blurred over to us.

"I'm taking her home. I'll contact you tomorrow," I spoke to him verbally and internally. I asked him if this was what he was talking about, if this is what I was supposed to be aware of? He nodded, still looking at Ana in awe. I shook my head, not believing what I had just witnessed; I grasped her hand and pulled her to her feet. She swayed and I put my arm around her waist.

The car ride was the quietest that we had ever had. She kept her face turned toward the window, still refusing to look at me. As soon as I had stopped the car in her driveway, she jumped out and slammed the door. I wasn't about to leave her alone tonight so I followed her inside. Immediately she ran up the stairs and I heard the shower start. I went into the kitchen and poured myself a scotch, drinking it down in one swallow and pouring another. I climbed the stairs to her room. Waiting on her bed, my mind began to analyze what I had just witnessed. Rapidly, I began to check off what I knew about demonic powers, about Vampire powers and about Humans. Collectively, I knew a lot, but the one thing that was practically screaming at me, was the knowledge that no Human, no Human, was ever in possession of a demonic power or a Vampire ability; moreover, not only could a Human never have those abilities, not even after they completed a blood ritual, but no Human could ever obtain the ancient and dark power of fire wielding, it wasn't possible. There were only a few demons and Vampires who had managed to acquire that power and even *they* could not harness it extremely well. Devon, maybe was the exception, maybe, but Ana...? I couldn't get my head around it. The scenario was improbable. How could she have acquired such a skill? My powers were mostly mental and I could heal the body if the trauma wasn't leaning toward the fatal, and I could summon an already burning fire, I just couldn't wield it. Patric's powers were also couched in the psychological and some physical and Patric had always hated fire, he was frightened by it as a little boy...just like Ana had been as a child. I had also witnessed him creating fire from nothing. I had seen him do it in the months that we were together. Maybe... I heard the shower stop, interrupting my thoughts. I sipped my drink and waited for her. What the hell was I going to say? I couldn't help her. Hell, I didn't even know what she had actually done. She came out of the bathroom in a cloud of steam and I couldn't help but laugh at the irony of her entrance. She glared at me and I bit my lip. I watched as she shook out her wet hair and started to apply lotion to her skin. "I can do that for you, if you want?" I asked quietly. My compulsion to be close to her was hovering near extreme need. I hated when she put distance between us, any distance. She moved over to the bed and sat on the edge. I pushed down the straps of her tank and began kneading the lotion into her muscles. She was tight and I moved my hands to massage her neck. I swept back her hair and stopped moving. Her mark had changed, yet again. While still completely entwined, my metal and Patric's stone were unaltered; it was Ana's symbol that had undergone a significant transformation. The tiny star-like jewels that usually adorned her neck were now small, pulsating embers, individual flames that covered the brilliant silver emblem in a wash of red and orange. Stranger still, was that I could actually see the flames dancing and feel the intensity of their collective heat.

"What, what's wrong Nathanial?" She turned her head to look at me. I sighed, how much more was she going to be able to take before she cracked? I didn't really want to know.

345

"It's your mark, it's changed again," I said softly.

"Is it bad?" she asked still looking at me.

"I don't think so, but I'm pretty sure it has something to do with what happened tonight, with what you did." I tried to keep my voice even. She stood up from the bed and I watched as she went into the bathroom.

"Christ, it's always something," she muttered. I motioned for her to come back and sit next to me. She crawled up onto the bed and laid her head against my chest, she was shivering. I moved to put my arm around her, holding her body as close to mine as possible.

"Do you want to talk about it?" I asked her, knowing already what her answer was going to be.

"No," she whispered. "Do you think that Charles will be ok?" She lifted her face to look at me. I met her gaze and nodded.

"Yes, I think he's a bit shaken up and he'll have quite the first degree burn, but yes, he'll be alright." Moments passed as we rested together in silence. I listened to her breathing.

"You know what I want Nathanial?" Again she moved her face to look up at me. I decided not to search her mind and to just let her tell me.

"No Ana, what do you want?" I kissed the top of her head, inhaling the sweetness of her scent.

"I want to live with you. I want us to live together again, and I want to marry you. Will you marry me Nathanial?" I stopped breathing. I couldn't move and I couldn't speak. She was talking again. "I mean, I don't actually have a ring or anything for you, but we could get rings later if you wanted. Although I don't actually know how much time we have before Alec decides to show up, so maybe a wedding isn't the best idea, but if you wanted to, I mean if you wanted to marry me we could do it soon, we could do it on the beach at the commune or something…that's if you wanted to…I don't want to pressure you or—" I cut her off.

"Shut up Ana, just, just…god." I couldn't control myself. I grabbed her face and pressed my lips down hard to her mouth, kissing her as deeply as possible.

"Is that a yes?" She struggled to talk against my sudden attack.

"God yes; I want to marry to you. I love you. I need you. Yes!" I kissed her face, her eyes, and her cheeks, down her neck and over her chest. She was laughing and struggling against my arms, which were binding her tightly to me.

"Nathanial, I—can't—breathe," she gasped. I actually didn't care at the moment and I pressed her closer to me still. I finally loosened my grip on her, only because I wanted to do other things. The events of the evening flew right out of my mind and I reconciled that I would be talking with Caleb tomorrow. Tomorrow we would figure things out, but for right now, Ana was mine and she wanted me above any other; she'd chosen me—forever.

Well, at least I had a *plan* to get married. If it actually happened, that was a different animal altogether. Caleb had agreed to perform the service and we were scheduled to head out on Nathanial's boat and have the ceremony on the beach at the commune this evening. It had only taken us two weeks to get everything together. I had one request, that we not discuss my new "ability" until after the wedding. I didn't want to think about anything that had to do with Demons or Vampires or dark powers—nothing. Besides, I was sure that what had happened that night was just a freak thing, some metaphysical reaction thanks to all of the strange blood I had running through my veins. I didn't really want to contemplate why I was suddenly able to control fire, or why my body seemed to react in such a visceral way when someone was in trouble, all I wanted was to marry Nathanial, to bind myself to him for as long as I had left.

I was franticly driving back to my house to grab my dress; I had left it over at my place because I didn't want Nathanial to see it—it was a bit old fashioned, but I wanted him to be surprised. I left my jeep running and bolted up the stairs to the front door. I burst into the hallway and raced up the stairs to my bedroom, two at a time. I slammed open my closet door and combed through the clothes looking for the long white garment bag. Where the frick was it? I knew I put it in here, what the hell?

"Looking for this?" I heard a voice come from behind me, a voice I knew. Alec. I closed my eyes and slowly turned around.

Nathanial

Where the hell was she? I checked my watch for the hundredth time. Six-thirty. She was a half an hour late. Caleb and I were standing on the docks next to my boat. I took out my phone and called her, also for the hundredth time. Her voicemail picked up. I looked at Caleb; he was staring at me. Something was wrong. He knew it. He could sense it. I shouldn't have agreed to let her go back to her house alone; I felt sick and dizzy.

Ana

Our gazes locked and I wasn't surprised to see that the Alec I had always known, was not the Alec standing in front of me. He was completely unrecognizable except for his eyes; they were still the deep emerald green that I had always trusted, that I had loved. I sighed, feeling slightly numb. "What do we do now Alec?" My voice was surprisingly steady and calm. He was fingering my gown, running the fabric through his hands.

"Kai would have been happy to see this day, don't you think?" he smirked at me. The numbness evaporated and I felt a sudden wave of heat rise in my blood. Something was boiling under the surface of my skin.

"Don't you ever talk about Kai, you son of a bitch!" Again, my voice was holding its calm tone and I found myself stepping

349

forward, closing the distance between us, unafraid. I knew what he'd done; I had figured it out. He laughed and also took a step forward.

"My, my. It looks like the time you've spent with the new and improved Nathanial, has made you lose your sense of self-preservation Ana. But of course, you've tried to kill yourself twice in your life, so maybe you don't actually have a sense of self-preservation at all. What do you think?" He flung my dress to the floor and stepped on it with his boot, moving closer to me. I was trying to navigate the complete shock I was feeling; this was Alec...he was my best friend and my family; I had loved him and cared about him. He gazed at me, his eyes pulsing with deep orange flames. The boiling in my tissues and muscles was getting more rapid and I could feel that my skin had started to swell beneath the surface. My thoughts weren't safe, that I knew. I needed to close my mind. "Good luck with that." Alec laughed, and I felt a sudden sharp pressure squeeze my brain. I gasped and dropped to my knees. "We can make this easy or this can be hard, what do you want to do Ana?" Again my brain contracted, the pain sending a wave of nausea to the pit of my stomach. I heaved forward. He leaned down close to my head and I felt his breath spread across my face. "I really hate doing this to you, I truly, truly do, but you're making things so complicated." I felt him brush my hair back and then he struck the side of my head. That was it. My blood finally boiled over and my skin seemed to erupt in white-hot fire. I jerked my head up, not dizzy, not sick, but strong and steady. I took one step toward him and sent him flying backward crashing into my bed, shattering the frame into a million pieces. I stood up and turned my eyes on him again, locking my gaze to his. I had no idea where any of this was coming from but for some reason, an image of Patric suddenly flashed in my mind, I knew what to do—I had to fight. I waved my hand and turned the splinters of wood surrounding him, into kindling. Fire erupted igniting the curtains and the bedspread. I ran for the door but he was there and he grabbed me around the neck and tossed me into the far wall, I felt the stone crack against my weight. My head was cut, but oddly, I was still holding steady.

Standing in front of me, fire blazing around us, we faced each other and I could see the total shock on Alec's face. It was satisfying. If I were going to die, at least I would make him work for it. I didn't have time to process just how significant it was that Alec had betrayed me or how I was sure that he'd been the one who killed Kai; my survival mechanisms were taking over, not letting me think about anything but my life and the sheer black anger that was now dominating every part of my body and my mind. I felt outside myself, yet completely real, solid in my knowledge of who I was and what I could do. I took advantage of his preoccupation with my unexpected ability and I locked my gaze to his once more, hurdling him backward into the hall and down the stairs.

Nathanial

Flames were coming from the house, blazing out from Ana's bedroom. I yelled for Caleb and he and I blurred inside. I heard a giant crash and saw someone tumbling down the stairs.

351

"It's Alec!" Caleb yelled to me. I saw Ana appear at the top of the stairs, the side of her head bleeding profusely.

"Ana!" I yelled to her, but she flew by me.

"Get out of the way Nathanial!" she said, and I saw her go over to where Alec had fallen. He was struggling to get out from the rubble. "GET UP!" I heard her scream at him. I didn't recognize her voice. I didn't recognize her. "GET UP YOU FUCKING BASTARD, GET UP!" I watched as she kicked him in the face, shattering his nose. Suddenly I felt a whoosh of air and I immediately knew that someone else had arrived. I turned to see Devon calmly walking into the house, his form wreathed in the depths of the fire now fully igniting around us.

"Caleb!" I yelled. Another whoosh of air and I looked up in time to see Ana sending Alec flying through the door to the outside. I ran to the porch but I felt a sudden paralysis of my limbs. I stopped short of the hole where the door once hung. Smoke was filling my lungs and I was having trouble breathing. I needed to get to her, to help her. Devon was squeezing my brain so tightly that I couldn't move a single muscle in my body. I knew that I needed to relax and try to focus. I was stronger than him and I could fight back.

"Let's move this outside shall we? It's certainly not necessary for all us to perish in this mess is it?" I felt Devon shove me outside where I saw not only Ana and Alec beating the crap out of each other, but Patric, he was tied to the ground, a metal stake through each of his palms. He looked at me and in that instant I knew what I needed to do. Where was Caleb? Had he been killed? "She's quite a fighter isn't she?" Devon purred into my ear. "I'm actually aroused just watching her

352

move out there." He took my head and turned it violently to the side. "Let's watch shall we?" I wanted to close my eyes, I didn't want to see; I didn't want to hear.

Alec was standing facing Ana, black blood was pouring from his face and his head. He was taunting her, laughing. A movement from Patric made my gaze shift and I saw his lips moving, his eyes were locked to hers. She turned and I watched as she leveled Alec to the ground and I heard bones crunch. Fire was pouring over our heads and I screamed at Ana as I saw a foundation beam come crashing down right toward her head. She leapt out of the way and I saw Alec grab her from behind. He had her in a strangle hold and he was forcing her to her knees. Something in me snapped and I broke free from Devon's control. I launched myself through the air, tackling Alec to the ground. I heard the clanking of metal and rolled myself over to see Caleb releasing Patric from his bonds, he appeared unharmed. Caleb tossed something to Ana in the air and it landed near her knees, then suddenly, I heard Caleb scream as he exploded into flames. I turned to see Devon on the now crumbling porch, his hands full of dark blue fire. My ears registered Ana grunt and immediately I grabbed her hand and pulled her out from under Alec. She didn't look at me.

"Take care of this!" She spat blood from her lip onto Alec's face, which I now had between my hands. I looked at her. Had she just ordered me to kill? I saw her move toward Devon on the porch. I screamed out for her to stop, but I felt Alec struggling against my grip. I was stronger than he was and with one quick jerk, I snapped his neck, summoned the fire from the burning foundation beam and ignited his body. Patric had blurred to Ana's side and I watched as the two of them stood facing Devon. Blue flames shot out toward my brother and I watched in slow motion as the woman I loved, stepped in front of Patric, absorbing the fire into her body. A guttural scream erupted from my soul, knowing that she was dead, that she had to be dead. I fell to the ground, and I saw that the fire was now *in* her, not *on* her. I watched her suck the flames into her body and fling them outward at Devon. He stumbled backward and Patric moved sending more flames out toward the porch. I blurred to their side, but I was suddenly paralyzed again. My mind was being crushed by a terrible weight and I screamed in agony.

"Go!" I heard Ana shout and suddenly Patric appeared at my side. I heard Ana scream and both Patric and I looked up to see her burning, consumed in blue fire.

"NO!" Patric yelled but before he could get to her, she had once again taken the flames into her body, filtering them through her skin, through her mind and redirecting them, controlling them, aiming them back toward Devon. This time she hit him square in the chest and I watched as his body rose up and crashed down onto the porch, sending the planks shattering. I saw him leap and lunge at her through the air, crashing into her body and sending them both spinning toward the ground. I couldn't believe what I was seeing. This wasn't happening, this wasn't Ana. I collected my mind and managed to catch a break in Devon's concentration. I stood and blurred to her side but I was knocked backward by something, by someone. I looked and saw Ana staring at me. Had it been her? She knocked me back and sent me crashing to the ground, landing me on a soil pile to break my fall. What the fuck? I leapt to my feet and again, I was sent hurdling through the air, this time with unbelievable force.

"Stay where you are Nathanial!" She was holding out her hand to stop me from moving forward. "He wants you to step in, he wants you to have to make a choice. Isn't that right Devon?" she called to him as they circled each other. Patric was immobilized and I saw a semi-circle of blue flames surround his body, creeping ever so slowly toward him. I heard Devon laugh.

"Fit and smart, you're the whole package aren't you? Yes, I do think that it's time that your husband to be, finally make up his mind. He's been playing one to many a role as of late and it's tiring." I moved a fraction of an inch forward.

"I said stay where you are Nathanial, for Christ sakes!" Ana called to me. Her voice was steady and calm, and ice cold. I heard Patric curse as the flames moved closer threatening his skin. They seemed to be in a tug-o-war between two controlling forces; was it Ana or Devon at the helm of the flames? I was wondering why she wasn't just redirecting the flames around Patric, somewhere else, could she not get a hold on them; unless Ana had immobilized Patric on purpose, unless she wanted to face Devon alone. What was going on? A voice penetrated my mind. *The minute she diverts her attention from Devon to me, he's got her, he's got all of us.* It was Patric. *She's already made the decision for you Nathanial. It's over.*

I couldn't figure out why Nathanial was having so much difficulty listening to me. I knew he was used to being the one to give orders, but I thought I was having a bit of a better day, fight-wise. "Why don't you just get on with it Devon?" I called to him stepping forward.

"What, and miss an opportunity to spar with you Ana. No, I think not. I was just telling Nathanial that it's quite a turn on to see you so powerful. It seems that you've acquired a bit of a new talent as well. You never fail to disappoint." He laughed and tried to circle me. I mirrored his movements exactly.

"It's over Devon. Nathanial isn't going to play this ridiculous game. It's really me you want. You've used Patric, Alec is dead and Nathanial will never join you… so you get me as a consultation prize. I made the decision for you, so let's go," I spat at him. I heard Nathanial take a sharp breath in. Devon's eyes narrowed.

"Well, I wish I could believe you Ana but after our last encounter, I'm afraid that I lost quite a bit of trust in you. You can understand that can't you, a loss of trust?" What the hell was he yammering on about? He moved to my right and continued to speak. "Well I'm sure that Nathanial told you of course, seeing that he was about to marry you. You did tell her didn't you Nathanial?" Devon called over to where Nathanial was standing. "I mean it's only natural that he should want a bit of revenge of his own I suppose, after everything you did with his brother, after how intimate you were with him, after you let him take your blood." He was stalling.

"Ana, don't listen to him!" Patric was shouting at me, his voice sounded distant, far away. I flashed my eyes at Devon and sent him stumbling backward several feet. He laughed and sprung back positioning himself within inches of me.

"Well I see I've touched a nerve. Shall we stir the pot some more? Let's see, I'm guessing," he pursed his lips and stared at me, "that Nathanial failed to mentioned all of the women he managed to 'have' whilst in the company of us Vampires."

"Ana, don't listen to him, he's trying to get into your head!" Patric screamed again and it took every ounce of my self-control not to look at him.

"I mean technically, it wasn't actually sex that he was having, but I was under the impression that the blood ritual was much, much better. Am I right Nathanial? It must have been so much more intense, letting those Human women taste you, and you taking from them—god, I bet that was incredible." I heard Nathanial growl and crouch, ready to spring.

"Don't!" I shouted at him, not breaking my gaze with Devon.

"Of course, I don't have to just tell you, I can actually show you what he did. Most of the time he enjoyed his little ritual in our presence. It was quite a turn on for us to watch. I'm sure you noticed just how much Nathanial has changed haven't you? He's stronger, sort of." Devon laughed. "And he's got quite a bit of a darker side that he likes to indulge, more domineering or have you not experienced that part of him yet? Well, maybe on the honeymoon?" He stepped closer.

"I don't actually care about anything that Nathanial did while he was away from me Devon, it doesn't matter." I shot him another flash of my eyes and sent him flying backward, crashing face first, into the barbed wire fence. He smirked and leapt to his feet, wiping the blood from his cheeks.

"We'll see." He hit me in the head with a pressure so deep and a pain so acute that I couldn't call out. I fell forward gasping as his memories filled my mind, pictures of Nathanial kissing women, his mouth moving over their bodies, caressing them between their legs. I couldn't look away, Devon had my mind and he was forcing me to watch. I saw Nathanial lying on a bed, his shirt off and a woman standing naked in front of him. I saw her remove his pants and push his legs open, taking him into her mouth. The image shifted to another woman against a wall, her arms bound by a black, silk scarf and Nathanial moving his mouth down her body as she hung in the air; I saw him press his lips against her stomach releasing a dark trickle of blood that ran down her pale skin. I felt my stomach heave but I couldn't afford to be weak, not now, not ever. I heard myself grunt and I pushed myself off the ground and spun to face Devon. "Had enough already? I have so much more to show you. It gets so much kinkier, are you sure you don't want to see anymore Ana?"

"Ana." I heard Nathanial cry out. He had seen what Devon showed me. "Ana!" He was crouching, ready to spring. I held my hand out sending him spinning around in the air and crashing him back into the trunk of a huge tree. It was probably a bit more aggressive than I needed to be, but whatever.

"Hmm, yes, it seems that I may have created some problems in the relationship…" Devon took a step toward me and I met him inch for inch. "Ana, I don't really want to kill you, especially now when it appears that we have inherited such a similar talent. Wouldn't you like to learn how to use it, how to control it? I could show you. We were friends once, not that long ago and I know that there was a definite attraction that we felt for one another." His voice grew soft as he spoke and he took another step forward. I didn't move. "I mean Nathanial lied to you, even after you were honest with him about your tryst with Patric, and of course Patric betrayed you and then there was Alec; my god what's it going to take for you to start choosing a better group of men to share your time with?" He circled me, coming closer.

"So, what are you offering? I thought that Vampires never negotiated," I asked him, still not moving.

"Well, I told you that I was of course always open to fair negotiations and especially ones from someone so, so seductive and clever. I'm not entirely immune to temptation Ana."

"No Ana!" I heard Nathanial yell. I ignored him and sent his head snapping back against the tree trunk. God, he just wouldn't shut up.

"So?" I asked Devon, who was laughing at my sudden aggression toward Nathanial.

"So, how about this; you come with me and let me show you how donating your blood to a Vampire should really make you feel and the twins get to keep their lives." He waved his hand nonchalantly toward Patric.

"What about me?" I asked, moving a fraction of an inch to the side.

"What about you? Well let's see, you're obviously powerful, strong, smart and you have great potential; perhaps we could discuss changing you into the better species?"

"What?" I said laughing at him. "You would honestly consider turning me into a Vampire, seriously Devon, are you really that hard up for group support?" I moved another inch to the side. He smiled at me.

"Actually, I think you would be a perfect candidate, but of course there are other, more selfish reasons for me wanting to change you." He licked his lips and closed the distance between us in one step.

"What?" I said, my voice hypnotically low. He reached out to wipe a drop of blood from my lip. I watched as he brought the tip of his finger to his mouth and sucked the blood, groaning softly.

"I think that you might be able to withstand all of the things that I want to do to you Ana, things that I want to show you." He ran his tongue across his bottom lip and I felt a sudden pull in my gut, something that made me step closer to him. I couldn't afford to have Devon mess with me physically; sexually he was much better at coercion than I was. The

360

familiar boiling under my skin was starting again; it was stronger and I felt my limbs tense reacting to the sudden surge of energy.

"Ana." I heard Nathanial's voice. It was clear and colored with warning.

"Ok, let's say I agree to your little arrangement," I said, moving so close to him that I could smell his familiar fragrance, the deep spicy musk that had me so attracted to him the first time. "How can I trust that you just won't kill Patric and Nathanial once you've gotten what you want?" He reached his hand up to caress my throat. I could feel my pulse quicken at his touch, but it was not out of fear, that I knew.

"I'll let them go right now, before anything happens between us; they'll be free to go. That's me trusting you Ana, but I'm not partial to second chances so your life and theirs is dependent upon you fulfilling your end of the deal."

"NO! Ana, NO!" Patric yelled. I could feel the tissues under my skin, start to swell and an electric current charged its way through my blood. I stepped toward Devon bringing my body close enough to touch him. I could see Nathanial watching us out of the corner of my eye. He was quiet and still and he looked enraged. I raised my eyes to Devon's and studied his face. His eyes were bright with excitement and anticipation, but his expression was smooth.

"Well?" he said quietly. "Do we have a deal Ana?"

"Just one more thing," I said, this time pressing my hips against him. His arms encircled me pulling me closer to his chest. "I wouldn't mind getting a little revenge of my own," I murmured, breathing softly on his mouth so he could taste my scent. I felt his body tremble.

"You know I don't kiss Ana." He was trying to keep his voice even but I could tell how breathless he was standing so close to me.

"Hmmm, well that's a shame, but you know what Devon, I do kiss," I said and pressed my mouth to his, letting my tongue trace along his lips. He growled and yanked me away, his face was flush and he was panting, his arms still around my waist.

"No Ana, no," Devon said as he pulled me in and locked his hands behind my neck, securing my mouth to his. He kissed me violently and I felt him shiver and tremble, his lips moist and hot. I moved my hands to his waist and ran my fingers across his stomach. He growled again and kissed me deeper. He grabbed my leg and hitched it up around his waist, grinding himself against me. I heard him moan and growl and move his lips to my throat. It was time. In one quick movement I ran the metal stake from Caleb, through his stomach, sending Devon staggering backward. I waved my hand and he flew through the air, crashing down onto his stomach, running the stake clean through his back. He screamed and blood began erupting outward, spraying me in the face and covering Nathanial in a black waterfall. I ran to Patric and pulled him from the flames; Devon's blood was dripping down my face and blurring my vision in a dark haze.

"Ana!" I heard Nathanial scream and I turned to see Devon flying through the air at Patric and me, his blood spraying in all directions. At the same moment, Nathanial leapt from the

362

ground and soared into the air colliding with Devon and bringing them both down in a fury of blood and dust and flame. Patric tossed me back a few yards and blurred to his brother's side. Devon wanted neither of them, he wanted me and within seconds he had shimmered away from Nathanial and was on top of me. I felt my blouse tear as he bit and clawed at my flesh. Blood was gushing from his chest and it was dripping into my mouth, burning my throat. I punched him in the mouth, but he had my hair and he was twisting and yanking. I could feel it tearing at the roots as he snapped my neck back. I thought that I saw Patric wave Nathanial aside and move directly behind Devon. He had my head forced back and I saw him bare his teeth as blood dripped from his mouth onto my throat. His hands ripped the crotch of my jeans and I felt his fingers tear at the remaining fabric. I twisted my hips, trying to heave him off of me, but in his bloodlust, his strength was too much. I saw Nathanial hurdling into the air towards Devon and at the same moment, the swelling in my skin burst and I sent Devon flipping over me, erupting in blue flames. He screamed and I rolled over and tried to stand. The blood was stinging my eyes, blinding me.

"Ana!" I felt someone put their arms around me and pull me to the ground. I punched whoever it was, in the face, and sprung to my feet, ready to fight. "Ana!" I wiped my eyes and tried to bring the chaos into focus. Devon was still screaming and Nathanial was next to me trying to pull me away from the fight. My vision abruptly cleared and in a single breath I could see what was going to happen. Devon shot himself into the air and sent a huge wall of flames right at Nathanial and I, and it was too late—we didn't have enough time to react. Just as I dove, covering Nathanial with my body, I saw Patric leap into the air in front of the wall of fire and I watched as the blue flames consumed him and in their burning of Patric, they grew and stretched. Still covering Nathanial, I watched, focusing. I felt my mind go calm and through Patric's screams and Devon's screams, I shifted the flames outward toward Devon and tossed them right into his falling body. Both Patric and Devon spiraled toward the earth in a shower of swirling blue fire and sparks, they rolled together into a giant explosion and I felt my heart crack wide open, gutting me from the inside. I screamed as I watched Patric's body turn to ash and crumble to the ground and Devon's erupt in blood and fire until he too turned to ash, the particles moved and swirled into the air and disappeared. There was a great gust of wind and I covered Nathanial, protecting his head. I felt the softness of smoke and ash begin to rain down upon us, showering us in a thick blanket of debris. I could smell sandalwood and vanilla on the wind and I heaved and gasped. I couldn't breathe, I couldn't see; I couldn't feel. There was too much silence.

Nathanial was coughing and spitting and I moved off of him to give him air. His face was bloody and his hair was singed, but he looked unhurt. I got to my feet and crawled over to where Patric's ashes had fallen. I looked up and watched the last of my house crash to the ground in a heap of flames and smoke, wood and stone, metal and glass. It was over. I knelt to the ground and ran my fingers through the soft ash, feeling a sudden chill erupt on the back of my neck. I gasped at the acuteness of the cold as it pierced the back of my skull. I doubled over in the grass, almost certain that my head was going to crack open. I screamed out in pain and Nathanial was at my side, kneeling in the debris. He was quiet and he didn't touch me. I screamed again as the pain exploded in my brain

364

and I felt the tears stream down my face. I gagged and choked, sobbing into the dirt and ash. Then it was gone and I felt a surge of warmth envelope my body, soothing me and calming the ache in my chest. Another waft of vanilla and sandalwood filtered passed my nose and I could taste the fragrance on my tongue. I steadied myself and rose from my place on the ground. Nathanial was still kneeling, his head bowed. I heard my wolves howling and they ran up from the ocean leaping into the air. Piyip tackled me to the ground, his nose sniffing the ash and his tongue licking my bloodied and battered face. I patted him softly, whispering in his ear that I was ok; I was trying to calm him down. Kuckuc stood very still and was watching Nathanial from only a few feet away. Her fur was raised and she was crouching in the grass, waiting to spring. "Kuckuc!" I called to her. She looked nervous. Her eyes went to me, then to Nathanial, then back to me. "Kuckuc!" I called again. I saw Nathanial get up slowly from the ground. He turned to face me. I stood as well and stared at him. He looked odd, nervous but also very, very huge. He towered over me with his muscles flexed and his breath coming in short bursts. "Nathanial?" I said and I walked forward. He took a deliberate step back. What was wrong with him? "Nathanial?" I called to him again, taking another step toward him. Again, he stepped back. Kuckuc growled, low and deep. "Hush!" I commanded her. "Nathanial what's the matter? Are you hurt?" I moved again, inching slowly forward and watched as he yet again, stepped away from me. I walked quicker, trying to close the distance. He held up his hand to stop me.

"It was all true Ana," he whispered. I stood still not wanting to upset him; something was clearly wrong.

"What's all true Nathanial?" I asked, trying to keep my tone calm.

"Those things that Devon showed you, the women, me, the blood, all of it is true. I did all of those things," his voice cracked as he spoke. Somewhere in my chest, a fissure ran through my heart. I took a shaky breath and continued to step toward him until I could see his face clearly and I could reach out to touch him.

"So you lied to me?" I asked, still trying to remain calm. I noticed that his body was trembling. His eyes met mine and I could see that they were overflowing with tears. I reached for him, but he held up his hands again to stop me. I moved back and stuffed my hands in my pockets.

"No, I didn't...I didn't mean to... Ana, I...I just didn't remember doing any of those things until...until he showed you his memories. It wasn't me you saw in those images Ana, it wasn't me." His chest heaved and I saw him bend forward to grab his knees.

"Nathanial it's ok, it doesn't matter if it was you or not—" He cut me off.

"IT WASN'T ME ANA!" he yelled violently.

"Ok, ok, it wasn't you." It was my turn to hold up my hands. With everything that had just transpired, I couldn't believe that we were standing out here discussing this. It seemed stupid. His head snapped up and he glared at me. In an instant he had blurred himself right in front of me, his face close to mine. He was breathing hard.

"Do you think the matter of how much I love you, how much I need you, how much I have spent every day since I came back from that horrible night at the University, wanting you, hoping that we would find our way back to each other—do you think that all of that is stupid Ana?" I was guessing that that was a rhetorical question. "Do you?" his voice was low and dark. I guessed wrong.

"No Nathanial, none of that is stupid; I was just thinking that it doesn't really matter to me if you were with other women…" He had closed his eyes and his breathing was getting more and more rapid.

"He drugged me Ana…it had to be…" His voice was manic and urgent "Devon had to have been drugging me for months. He was subtle about it, he made sure the effects were mild, but I knew there was something wrong. There would be large parts of my nights that I couldn't remember. My head hurt all the time and he was constantly trying to get through the chinks in my memories, my thoughts. He was testing me, trying to get into my mind. It was Patric who figured it out, who managed to protect me from the worst of things somehow…" His eyes were still closed. "Those things that you saw, that wasn't me; I would never do that to you, I…" His body heaved and I pulled him toward me, letting his head rest on my shoulder, listening to him sob. I smoothed his hair and wrapped my arms around him and there we stayed for hours, the two of us entwined, bound by everything we were, everything we had been and all that we were going to be together. Nathanial's cries rang clear and heavy in the night and I knew that he wasn't just crying for us, but for his brother, his twin, for Patric who twice now had redeemed himself, who had saved me and his brother in one last testament to who he truly was, and now he was gone.

Chapter Eleven

Nathanial

I tore a check from my checkbook and handed it to Ana's landlord. He'd had insurance for the fire, but Ana had felt so bad about the total destruction, that she was planning on emptying all of her savings to pay for whatever she could. I had more money than I could spend in a dozen lifetimes and I had insisted that she let me take care of things, it was the least I could do. Surprisingly, she had not put up a fight. I shook the guy's hand and watched as he walked down the stairs to his car. I turned back into the house to find Ana, her hands on her hips, staring at one of my book shelves. Boxes were everywhere.

"Honestly Nathanial, just how many books does one person need on the evolution of the human species? I've counted fifty and that's just on this one shelf!" I came up behind her and moved my hands around her waist.

"Well, since I'm marrying a Human—or at least I *think* that's who I'm marrying, I feel it's only appropriate that I completely understand just how you came to be, don't you think?" I kissed her neck, breathing deeply. She jabbed me gently in the stomach.

"Be careful Nathanial. Do you really want to insult someone who has an uncanny ability to wield fire? It makes what you can do seem like child's play." Her voice was seductive as she teased me. She turned, wrapping her arms around my neck.

"Child's play?" I purred, kissing her cheek. "Hmmm, perhaps I should take a few moments and show you just how adult I actually am?" I ran my lips down her throat and I felt her move closer, her body pressing against me.

"I've been here for almost six weeks and I'm still not unpacked; if you keep distracting me, I'm going to have to quarantine you to your study." She laughed and kissed me on the nose, unraveling herself from my grip. I groaned, but left her to dismantling my bookshelves. We were headed to Idaho to get married. She wanted to be away from Indonesia for a while and be in the mountains. I knew how desperately she missed Noni and I was looking forward to meeting this woman who Ana loved so much. Noni had offered us her farm on the Reservation to use for the ceremony and she was also going to perform the wedding. Ana was excited beyond words. Considering just how much had happened the last year, Ana seemed to be doing remarkably well. I tried to keep my guilt from infiltrating our relationship, but I knew that she often sensed my mood, how completely horrible I felt about the things that I had done. She didn't want to talk about what Devon had shown her. She said it didn't matter, but there was something that told me that my time with Patric did matter and the choices that I had made, Devon or no Devon, were not going to be as forgiving towards me as Ana had been. Karma was always a bitch and I certainly wasn't immune.

I had determined that Ana's new ability must be some effect from having Patric's blood. Caleb had left some of his notes and theories behind and I was able to sort through most of them. They offered only a bit of information, but from what I could decipher, Caleb had discovered that my brother was also a fire wielder, that somehow by being both a demon and Vampire, he was able to access certain powers that wouldn't normally be available to him. Caleb's theory about Ana centered around her having some of Patric's blood and my blood in her system. Perhaps the mixing of the two had allowed for Ana to tap into his command of fire as well. I supposed it made sense but still, I was a bit uneasy about Ana being Human and possessing such an ancient power. Bonders and Vampires were not particularly partial to Humans who had acquired powers that they themselves did not usually have. There was something pulling at the deep corners of my mind, something that I couldn't sort out and it was making me anxious.

In a matter of days, we'd gotten Ana fully moved in and we managed to merge all of our belongings or what was left of Ana's belongings, into a cohesive and cozy home. She seemed excited to be here and I couldn't be happier to have her so close to me. She was extremely affectionate as of late, even more than her usual intimate nature and I was enjoying this particular upsurge in her mood, mainly because I didn't feel that I deserved such affections, not after what she'd seen me do. I came down the hallway and found her curled up on the couch reading, the stereo playing softly.

"Hi." She tossed her book on the table and watched me cross into the room. I put my bag down and went to sit next to her on the couch. I sunk back against the cushions and turned my head to look at her. "Rough class?" she asked, moving closer to me, stroking my hair.

"Hmmm, just long," I murmured. "I missed you." Her hands moved to caress my face.

"It's nice to be missed, I missed you too." She bent her face close to mine and softly pressed her lips to my cheek. I laughed quietly. I had been about fifteen minutes late to my evening lecture because she had decided that joining me during my shower was a good idea. She was right. Then, this morning she woke me up in the best way possible, again making me late for a committee meeting and now here we were again. I was beginning to think that I was the one with all of the self-control in our relationship, and that wasn't saying much. I chuckled. "What's so funny?" she whispered in my ear, making me tremble.

"I was just thinking how insatiable your sexual appetite is as of late; I'm three hundred years your senior, I'm not sure if my heart can take it." I grabbed her around the waist and pulled her into my lap. She straddled me and started to unbutton my shirt. I pulled her face to mine and bit her bottom lip. She laughed.

"You don't seem to be having a problem keeping up so far," she said and kissed me deeply. I heard her groan. That did it. The sound of her, the taste of her, I could never hold out, it was pointless and she knew it. I wrapped her legs around me and stood up, fully intending to carry her to the bedroom, but we only got as far as the wall near the fireplace. I had to admit, her level of sexual intensity was unusually heightened, and she was moving her body in ways that were making it very hard for me to control myself. I had torn so many of her shirts in the last month, that I promised to take her shopping this

372

weekend; I felt terrible about the casualties to her wardrobe. Presently, the pattern continued as I ripped her tank in half, splitting it down the middle. I had absolutely no problem holding her up against the wall, but I was thinking that it couldn't be too comfortable for her. I moved to grab her around the hips and she toppled me to the ground, pinning me. I wove my fingers into her hair and pulled her head back, sliding out from under her and switching our positions. She laughed and I felt her undo my belt.

"What do you want?" she asked, breathless. It was my turn to laugh.

"Anything?" I replied, moving her hands above her head, pressing them into the floor.

"Anything," she said as she traced her tongue down my neck. I moaned and brought my face within inches of hers. We were both breathing hard and my mind was racing. I was torn, but in a good way. On the one hand I wanted to feel her mouth on me, to have her in control, but on the other, my need to control her pleasure was much more in my demonic nature, and that had a tendency to win out on most occasions.

"Let me show you what I want," I said, and I used my knee to slide open her legs. She accommodated me and I felt a low rumbling rise deep in my chest. I released her hands and slid my body down on top of hers, feeling the moistness of her skin. Her fragrance was so strong these days that it inevitably brought out the most primal urges that I had, some buried so deep that even I was surprised by their animalistic nature. I had just managed to slide off her underwear and remove my pants, when there was a sharp knock at door. I paused and looked up. Christ, could someone have worse timing?

"Maybe they'll go away," Ana said breathlessly. I smiled at her and resumed my disrobing. Another knock came, this one much louder and longer than the last.

"Jesus," I said, standing and pulling back on my pants. I left Ana half-naked on the floor and headed down the hallway.

"Who is it?" I asked, a slight tone of annoyance in my voice. This better be good I thought.

"UPS," a deep male voice answered. I opened the door and found a man standing with a document mailer in his hand.

"Nathanial Arias?" he asked, checking his handheld computer.

"Yes," I said, eyeing the document warily. I rarely ever got mail. Bonders didn't have bills.

"Sign here." He held out the computer and I hastily scratched my name in the space. He handed me the envelope, nodded and walked back down to his truck. I closed the door and headed back into the living room. To my complete dismay, Ana was fully dressed in another non-ripped tank top and she had her sweats back on. I frowned at her and threw the envelope on the desk.

"What was it?" she asked, curling up back on the couch. I crossed the room and sat down beside her.

"I don't know." I waved my hand dismissively, turning toward her and sliding my hand under her hair so I could stroke the

374

back of her neck. "I'll deal with it tomorrow. Now, I believe that we were in the middle of something…" She smiled at me and stood up, offering me her hand and pulling me down the hallway into our bedroom. I watched as she slowly undressed and came to stand in front of me. She took my hands and ran them gently over her body, closing her eyes.

"Nathanial?" she whispered.

"Hmmm?" I was kneeling in front of her, running my lips over her stomach.

"How long will I live now that I have both your blood and Patric's blood in me?" I froze. She put her hands on my shoulders and I stood up to look at her.

"Ana." I reached to stroke her cheek. "I think that you will live an exceptionally long life, longer than any Human who has not been Bonded and longer still because you have both mine and Patric's blood running through your veins." I saw that she was frowning at me. "What?" I asked

"It's nothing, it's just that the last time you came back and I was sick and Patric was here and you, you sort of completed things between us…" I winced at the memory. "Well, it's just something that Alec said while he was trying to make sure that I survived." She moved to sit on the bed, pulling the blankets around her body.

"What did he say?" I was trying to keep my tone calm, but I didn't like the direction this conversation had taken.

"He said that it was nearly impossible for any human to survive having both types of blood in their system and that there was no way to tell how my body would react to such an onslaught of different chemicals; he said that he didn't know if my life expectancy would be the same as if I had just been Bonded with only you." She leaned back against the pillows and held my hand. I took a deep breath. What she was saying was true. I didn't actually know how long her life would be after everything that happened, but I was counting on what I knew so far and that was that Ana, against all odds, had survived— many times over and beyond that, she now had acquired an extremely powerful ability, again defying what was the norm for those in her species. Caleb had been under the impression that Ana would be the exception to all rules, demon, Human and Vampire, and that would mean that while she had certain abilities that made her a unique combination of all three, it was that same uniqueness that could potentially cause her some problems—just exactly what those might be, we still didn't know. "Nathanial?" I turned to see Ana staring at me, trying to decipher the puzzled look on my face. I moved to lie down beside her, propping myself up on my elbow.

"Ana, I don't want you to worry about how long you will live. While Alec was of course somewhat versed in the medical phenomenon of our different species, he was in no way a definitive expert and it serves no purpose to contemplate what is unknown in life." I caressed her stomach and ran my fingers down the length of her thigh, tracing over her tattoo.

"You're trying to distract me." She sighed and I felt her body move in response to my touch.

"Is it working?" I asked, rolling to place my body on top of hers.

376

"A little. I have one more question for you." She laughed and lifted my chin to her face. I groaned and rolled my eyes.

"What." I was in full physical mode and I had no interest in talking, at least not about life or death issues.

"I could be a bit more like you couldn't I? I mean it's possible for me to…to add on a few more years to my life if I had a little bit more of you in me?" I glared at her and rolled off onto my back, running my hands through my hair.

"Absolutely not. It's not even open for discussion." I stood up and started to button up my shirt.

"You're mad at me?" She sat up, pulling the covers around her chest.

"I'm not mad, I'm just not discussing this with you." I stood by the window and gazed at the moon.

"You're mad and you also suck at communicating. Why won't you just talk to me about this? I'm not saying that we have to do anything about it, I just like to know that I have options." She flung herself back against the pillow.

"You do have options; you have the option to marry me, you have the option to learn how to use your power, you have the option to work or not to work; you have lots of options Ana…" I turned from the window to glare at her.

"Well thanks Nathanial, I had not thought about any of those before. And you know what, you're not the only source that can provide me with what I want…you can go places now you know…" I turned on her, my eyes black with rage.

"Are you suggesting that you prostitute yourself out so that you can tack on a few incidental years to your life? And by the way, have you forgotten the one tiny detail about what it is you are wanting? Have you forgotten that hardly any Human can survive having that much blood in their system? That the potential of you dying is far more likely than you getting what you want!" I was yelling at her, something that I never did. "How dare you even think about threatening me with such delusions Ana." I rounded on her, my rage tensing every muscle in my body.

"You make me sound like I'm being selfish Nathanial, that the only reason I would want to take such a risk is just out of my own need to live some ridiculously long life. I was kind of hoping that perhaps you would *want* me to stick around so we can have a life together, one that's not cut short because I'm human and you're not, but perhaps I was wrong in that assumption?" She yanked the covers off and stood to dress. "Oh, and by the way, don't-you-ever-yell at me again. I'm not one of your cronies who's intimidated by your rage." I watched her grab her backpack from the closet and start stuffing it full of shirts and jeans.

"What the hell are you doing?" I blurred to her side and took the pack out of her hand. She yanked it back, knocking me slightly off balance by the force.

"I don't think that I really want to spend the evening being yelled at Nathanial. I'm almost thirty, not thirteen and I can't remember the last time I let a man raise his voice to me!" She was pulling toiletries out of the bathroom and cramming them into the outer pockets of her pack. I grabbed her elbow as she headed to start down the hallway.

"Ana, I'm sorry." I forced myself to quell the anger and frustration in my voice. "You're right, I should not have yelled at you like that, it was wrong, now will you please stop packing and let's talk about this." I turned her back to face me.

"No! I asked you to talk about it and you refused and then you proceeded to make me feel like I was some selfish imbecile who cared nothing for you and only about my own self-preservation. You don't get to dictate the nature of our relationship Nathanial—you don't control us or me—oh, and if you ever refer to *anything* I do, *anything*, as a mode of prostitution again, we're done!" She pulled away from me, leaving me stunned. I watched her walk down the hallway and out the door, not looking back.

Ana

I had no idea where I was going to stay, I just knew that I didn't want to be anywhere near Nathanial. He was being such an asshole, and I would not be in the same house with someone who felt compelled to yell at me just because I had asked to discuss a topic that made him uncomfortable—he could go fuck himself! After an hour of fuming in my car, I found myself taking the back roads down into Jakarta, a place that I hardly ever went and especially at night. It used to be the capital city, but since the last war between the Vampires and the Bonders, it was now divided into two particularly rough sections, one for the Bonders and one for the Vampires and they hardly ever ventured into each other's territory. Several years ago when I had first arrived, I had made a friend who worked as a bartender at one of the rare Bonder/Vampire pubs. It was an underground club, mostly an underground sex club where Bonders, Vampires and humans met to engage in whatever rituals they wanted. I had been only once and not to participate but to check up on my friend, Rene. They used Rene, especially the Vampires. Now, knowing what I knew about the blood and sex, it all made sense. At the time, I had no idea what she was doing and what they were doing to her; I just knew that her arms and her neck were so often bruised and cut, that I was always worried that she might get some sort of infection.

I found myself driving down through the city, the blinding lights from the clubs and the pulsing music in the streets, filled the space around me. I turned down a narrow and secluded street driving under a small bridge and pulled my jeep into a gravel lot. There were at least three-dozen cars already parked in the space and I had to cram myself between two large SUVs. I sat in the car for a few moments and thought about how pissed Nathanial would be if he knew where I was, then I decided that I didn't care. I grabbed my purse and headed down the steep stairs underneath the bridge. I could smell the club before I even got to the door. The aroma of incense masked the distinct odor of sweat, semen and blood. Immediately I felt my pulse begin to race—this was probably one of the more stupid ideas that I had executed in a while. I thought of how upset Kai would be if he had known what I was doing. My throat clenched and I fought back the tears that were brimming around my eyes. There was a gigantic Demon posted at the door. He was at least seven feet tall, with long white-blonde dreadlocks, pale skin and ice-blue eyes. He eyed me up and down and I swept my hair forward and turned to show him my imprint. I heard him grunt upon seeing the three symbols embedded in my flesh. I turned back to face him, staring him down. His eyes narrowed and he nodded and opened the door.

The smell hit me first, followed by the grinding music that assaulted my ears. Rene told me once that they kept the music loud, just in case things got rough in some of the back rooms. I sighed. This was not a good plan. I scanned the bar and found Rene mixing up cocktails. I made a beeline for one of the only open seats and waited for her to turn my way.

"Holy shit! Ana Tessatore! I can't fucking believe it! I've missed you girl; where have you been?" Rene practically flew across the seats to get to me, where she proceeded to wrap me in a giant bear hug. I loved Rene. She was about twenty years older than me, a bit rough around the edges but besides Kai and maybe Nathanial, she possessed the most beautiful soul of anyone I knew. She was blonde and tan and quick with a smile or an insult depending on what type of attitude you were giving her that particular day. I kissed her on the cheek and pulled back to have a look at my friend. I scanned her quickly and saw that her arms and neck were still covered in slashes and bite marks, some healed, some still looked fresh. Rene was always hoping that either a Bonder or a Vampire would chose her, either to be Bound or to be turned. I held her face in my hands and smiled at her.

"Rene, I've missed you too my sweet friend. How are you?"

"Who cares about me! What are you doing here? I thought I told you that this is no place for a smart girl like yourself...you shouldn't be here," she said lowering her voice and I saw her eyes take a quick scan around the room.

"Rene, it's fine. Don't worry. I just needed to get out of my house for a while and I was thinking about you." She eyed me warily, assessing just how much of my lie she was going to pretend to believe.

"Who'd you fight with this time?" She winked at me and stepped back behind the bar, grabbing a glass and a can of ginger ale.

"No one," I mumbled but I knew she saw right through me.

"Uh-huh. It wouldn't just happen to be an extremely tall, dark and very handsome Demon would it?" She poured the soda into an iced glass and handed it to me on a coaster. Rene knew about Nathanial because I had told her about the wedding. I wanted to fly her out to Idaho so she could be there for me. I kept most of the details about the events in our relationship a secret, but the community was small and I knew that word had spread about the demise of Alec and Devon and I knew that Rene had heard all of this as well—I just didn't know how much she had learned. I shrugged and took a sip from my drink. "Girl, he better be treating you right, after everything that you've done for him, for that crazy brother of his...he better be treating you like a queen!" She put her hand under my chin and gazed intently into my eyes. So she did know more than I thought. I was about to tell her what

382

happened, but someone yelled for her at the other end of the bar. "Don't go nowhere honey, I'll be right back." I laughed as she danced down the bar to wait on her customer. I settled into my seat and sipped on my drink. This wasn't so bad I thought. If you didn't look toward the back of the club where all of the rooms were, it just seemed like any other crowded bar, with the exception of all of the incredibly handsome men around.

"Is this seat taken?" said a very soft voice from my left, something familiar registered in my mind. I turned to look and found Stephen leaning against the bar smiling at me. My heart sunk. Frick!

"Wow! Stephen." I tried to muster some enthusiasm for seeing him, but my heart was thundering so rapidly in my chest, that I was having difficulty speaking. Out of all the Vampires that I had interacted with down in West Papua, Stephen was the most polite and the most considerate towards me. I had no idea just how closely aligned he had been with Devon, but I was guessing that Stephen had most certainly learned of Patric's, Alec's and Devon's demise—this couldn't bode well for me. I watched as he slid up on the seat and swiveled so that he was staring at me. As far as Vampires went, well as far as any species went, Stephen was breathtaking. I hadn't really noticed before because Devon had managed to quarantine me from everyone, but now looking at him, I was in awe. He was probably about forty in human years, tall with chestnut brown hair that was streaked with subtle auburn and copper highlights. He chose to keep the length rather short as far as Vampires went. It hung loose and in thick, layered waves to his chin. His face was rugged and tan with a perfect five o'clock shadow across his strong jaw, but it was his eyes that captivated me the most, they had from the first time we met. They were the brightest blue that I had ever seen, not turquoise like Patric's had been, but the purest, clearest marine blue. So startling was their clarity, that I was convinced that they were emitting some sort of reflection of fractured light. He was missing the flames in the center, the flames that I thought all Vampires had, the flames that I now had, thanks to Patric. I heard Stephen chuckle at my appraisal of his physicality. I bowed my head.

"This doesn't quite seem like your kind of place Ana," he mused flagging down another bartender.

"It's not really." I laughed, trying to remain calm. "I have a good friend that works here." I motioned to Rene who was pouring some liquor into several shot glasses.

"Ahhh, Rene. You two know each other then?" He turned to look at me, holding me in his stare for an uncomfortable amount of time. I nodded and took a sip from my glass; my mouth had suddenly gone dry.

"Yeah, we've been friends for years." I met his gaze. He gave me a crooked smile and looked away.

"And where is Nathanial this fine evening?" I loved Stephen's Irish accent; it was familiar and brought back so many wonderful memories of my time Ireland, a time when I was happy, at least for a bit.

"He's not here," I said quietly.

384

"And I'm betting he doesn't know that *you're* here, am I right?" Stephen laughed. It was a deep and hearty laugh, genuine and kind.

"He doesn't know," I said softly, feeling a twinge of guilt at the mention of Nathanial.

"Hmmm, well I'm guessing that he would not be too happy about you coming here of all places." Again he turned his eyes upon my face.

"I've been to worse," I said stubbornly.

"I'm sure you have Ana, but that's not what I meant." Stephen shifted his body closer to me and I could feel the heat coming off his skin. I could also smell his pheromones, the ones that gave him his distinct scent, the ones that Vampires could manipulate to whatever their particular human prey was attracted to—Stephen's were potent. Of course there was the ever present musky undertone that always got me going, but I could also smell the sea; it was as if I was standing on the sand, with the waves crashing around my feet and the salt spray caressing my face—I felt calm and soothed, but I also felt the dangerous allure of lust, something that I knew that I was not responsible for, at least I hoped it wasn't me. I cleared my throat. Stephen was studying me.

"What did you mean then?" I asked, still meeting his gaze. He laughed darkly and shook his head.

"Hmmm…I'm not sure if I'm the best person to be giving you this information Ana; unlike the rest of my brethren, I actually like you—a lot." A felt a weird tightness in my chest and my throat began to swell a bit. I took a deep breath.

"If you're talking about the women that Nathanial was with, the women that he...that he spent time with when he was with all of you, I know all about it. Devon was kind enough to let me see exactly what happened and Nathanial told me, he told me that Devon had drugged him, that he wasn't himself when he did those things." I was speaking so quickly, that I was breathless. I took a sip of my drink and noticed that Rene was staring at Stephen and me; she looked concerned. I waved at her and smiled. I didn't need anyone else in on this conversation.

" Ana, he *showed* you what happened? Christ, even *I* wouldn't have done that. He must have really wanted you." He shook his head and took another sip of his drink. "I'm really sorry that you had to see those things Ana, but I'm even more sorry to tell you that Nathanial was not drugged." He looked at me and I thought I saw his eyes flash. My heart stopped.

"What do you mean he wasn't drugged?" My voice was no longer holding steady. Stephen sighed and moved a bit closer to me.

"Look, he was having a really difficult time with us, with Patric. Every day he was battling against having to see how much Patric felt for you, how destroyed you were after he attacked you at the University, how intimate your relationship became with his brother, not just physically, but how much you cared about Patric, how much you believed that he would do things differently—that he would help you. On top of all of that, he was dealing with his own memories of you, carrying his own

386

guilt. His mind was full of you and that was dangerous to him. Patric managed to hide most of his desires from all of us, he was much more practiced and skilled at keeping his emotions under control—Nathanial, well, not so much." Stephen looked at me, I couldn't imagine what my expression must have told him, but it was enough for him to take his fingers and tentatively stroke the back of my hand. I was under the impression that it had been Patric that had the trouble shielding his memories of me from the others, not Nathanial.

"What are you saying Stephen?" I felt a slight tingling under my skin and a rush of heat surge through my blood.

"I was with him Ana. He asked me to take him here, to help him to try to forget about you, about what he'd seen through Patric's memory, about his own betrayal of you. He wasn't drugged Ana, depressed certainly, but not drugged. He knew what he was doing and he knew the consequences." My head snapped up and my eyes narrowed.

"What consequences? What are you talking about Stephen?" I jerked my hand away from him. He sighed, his eyes roaming across my face. He looked tormented, tortured and sad.

"Nathanial, in the complete and utter chaos of his mind, took that stupid blood ritual to its farthest point…" Stephen's voice trailed off and he turned away from me. My heart seized and my blood began to boil.

"Stephen, are you telling me that Nathanial turned someone, I mean gave someone so much of his blood that they became more like him than they are human?" My voice sounded distant, foggy and muted. "Are you telling me that he did this for another woman and they survived?" Bile was beginning to sting my throat and I felt my eyes water.

"Two. He completed the ritual with two women," he said softly. I saw that his eyes were looking directly over me and his face froze. I jerked my head around to see Nathanial standing behind me, his chest pressed almost to my back, his gaze locked on Stephen.

I stood up and moved towards Stephen. Immediately, I felt him encircle my waist with his arms, pulling me to the side, away from Nathanial, away from the line of fire. I saw Rene motion out the door and instantly, the giant, white haired Demon from outside was standing in between Nathanial and Stephen.

"We have a problem here?" the bouncer asked. Rene came to stand beside me, her arms around my shoulders.

"No problem at all," Stephen said, not diverting his gaze from Nathanial. The bouncer looked at me.

"Are you alright?" He was giving me the once over, searching for any sign of an unwanted wound or bite mark. I nodded my head, but I couldn't speak. My eyes were on Nathanial. The bouncer gave us all one more, quick look and then sauntered back outside. I tore my gaze away from Nathanial and looked toward Stephen. His eyes appeared as though the ocean had iced over and cracked. His jaw was tight and I could see the pain spreading across his face as our eyes met.

"Ana," he whispered. "I'm so sorry. I'm so very sorry." He turned back toward Nathanial and without a word he shimmered out of the bar. Rene still had her arms around me. I gently pulled free and gave her a hug. I grabbed my purse from the barstool and walked out the front door, knowing that Nathanial would not be far behind. He was already at my jeep waiting. I didn't look at him; I didn't speak to him. I opened the door and started the engine, fully prepared to leave him standing under the bridge. He was in the passenger seat before I could even put the car in gear. I sped into the night with him sitting silent and unmoving next to me. I walked into the house feeling cold and stiff. My head hurt and I just wanted to die. I felt so stupid. There probably wasn't a human alive that trusted a Bonder or Vampire even those to whom they were already Bound. They were weak, manipulative and self-serving and now I had spent over a year trying to forget one, and saving the other. I had fallen victim to the idea of being loved, of loving someone and of hoping, hoping that my life would have some semblance of normalcy, some reason to justify why on earth I was still here on the planet, some tether that would remain strong enough to keep me from falling over the edge. I had thought that tether had been Nathanial and possibly his love for me, and at one time I had hoped that maybe it could have been Patric, at least through friendship if nothing else. I had nothing, no one and not a single reason to continue along this path. I had done all of the noble acts; loving, sacrificing, atonement, forgiveness and hope. They were all there like pawns in some godforsaken chess game that I would never win.

"Ana." Nathanial broke through my internal rhetoric.

"Don't," I said, putting my hand up to silence him. I pressed my hands to my temples and stood close to the fireplace. "It doesn't matter, it is what it is." I was exhausted, spent. I felt him standing behind me; I felt his heat and his power. I felt sick.

"Ana, we need to talk about something, something very important," his voice was dark as he spoke.

"I don't want to talk about anything Nathanial. I just want to get my stuff and get the hell out of here." I turned toward him.

"I'm not talking about what happened at the club; this is much, much more important and I can't let you leave until you know what's going on." My stomach heaved and I went to sit on the couch. Christ, what else could he possibly have done; what else could there be that I would have to endure? He came to sit next to me, allowing for the greatest amount of distance between us. He pulled a large envelope from behind him and handed it to me. I recognized the package from the delivery earlier this evening—it felt like a lifetime ago.

"Nathanial, I really don't feel well, I'm exhausted and I'm not thinking clearly. Can this not wait until tomorrow? I promise I'll come back in the morning and we can talk about whatever you want." I would talk about anything with him, mostly because my decision to leave was already made so it wouldn't matter what he said. He took the envelope back from my hands and proceeded to pull out a single sheet of paper.

"You know that Caleb had left quite a large bit of research he'd done on the inception of your power, on Alec and Patric; he's been trying for months to piece things together. He was fascinated by your ability to survive two Bondings, so to speak, and to have two separate blood exchanges in your system—it just doesn't happen. The night of your party, he was already thinking there must have been some sort of consequence to everything that you had undergone—that something might be lurking just beneath the surface. He instructed me to keep an eye on you, on your temper and emotions, although at the time he wasn't quite sure what we should be looking for." I sighed and put my head in my hands, rubbing my face. He waited for me to resurface. "For weeks since the fire, since Devon, there's been something nagging at me about what it is that you can do, what you have the potential to do…" his voice softened and he turned to gaze into my eyes. I looked away. "Ana, you shouldn't be able to have the power you do—not as a Human anyway. Your ability to wield fire is both something that demons and Vampires have been trying to acquire to various degrees, for thousands of years and only a handful have managed to manipulate the skill enough to make it a useful weapon, Devon of course and Patric to some to degree."

"So?" I asked, still averting my eyes. "So, I can do something that you can't, what's the big deal, it's not as though I use it for anything." Nathanial sighed and stood to walk over to the fire.

"It is a very big deal Ana. Demons and Vampires don't often see eye to eye on much of anything, but the one thing that we can agree upon, is that no Human, no matter how exceptional," he turned to look at me, "no matter how unique, can be allowed to possess such a powerful ability—there are rules among our both species…"

"What kind of rules?" I asked, eying him warily. He ran his fingers over the flames taking them into his palm and watching them intently.

"Rules that allow for the complete evisceration of any Human who possesses such a power; rules that say that no Human can be allowed to live while they maintain the ability to destroy an entire species with a weapon that does not belong to the Human race." He tightened his fist around the flames and I watched as smoke rose from between his fingers. Yep, I was definitely going to be sick. I stood up and left the living room. I headed down the hallway into the bedroom and started throwing my clothes and books into boxes I kept stored in the closet. Nathanial followed me and sat on the edge of the bed.

"So, you're going to kill me?" I asked sarcastically, scooping up my jeans and sweatshirts and stuffing them into a gym bag. He laughed darkly.

"No Ana, I'm not going to kill you, but I'm sure that there are several individuals from both my brethren and Devon's coven who would be all too happy to see you die." His voice was flat and it sent chills down my back. I felt the metal embedded in my skin grow warm.

"Do you think they know?" I asked, still piling clothes into boxes. It was weird having such a conversation with Nathanial, odd that we were yet again discussing my death, but even odder that we were discussing such an event while I was moving out.

"Caleb seemed to think so, he was under the impression that Devon was having you watched." He turned on his side, his eyes following my every movement. "Where are you going?" he asked, his head bowed. I felt my heart drop.

"I don't know yet, maybe Rene's." My voice was shaky and tight.

"Will you call me and let me know where you are?" His head still bowed, he was biting his lip. I sighed.

"I guess, but I'm sure that someone will probably just blow me up on the way out to the car; I really don't think it's going to matter where I am Nathanial." He shook his head back and forth, his hair falling over his face.

"I can protect you Ana, if you stay—I would protect you." His voice sounded thick.

"Yeah, because that's worked out great for me so far, hasn't it Nathanial; you're idea of protection includes lying to me about who you are, about what you've done…no, I think I'll pass on your notion of protection and take my chances." I swung my bag over my shoulders and hoisted the box up to my chest. "I'll be back for the rest of my stuff at some point, if I'm still alive." I turned to the door and looked at him. "You know," I said, dropping the box at my feet, "it's really not the fact that you were with other women. I can understand that, but the fact that you allowed for strangers to be with you in such a way that allowed for them to become more like you, that you in a sense chose to save *them* from their mundane human lives and give *them* a chance to live long and possibly happy lives. That you decided that it was going to be *them* and not me and that you saw more value in them than you do in me and then you lied to me, you lied about what happened to you and took advantage of my trust and my devotion to you—you slapped me in the face Nathanial and I cannot, for the life of me, figure out why you would do such a thing. Do you not love me at all? Was all of this just a charade; I couldn't be that stupid could I?" That last question was more for myself than him. I heaved the box into my arms and turned toward the door.

"Ana, you don't understand. You don't know what was happening to me, I wasn't myself, I couldn't be. You have to know that. I couldn't be the person that you know to have done those things; Devon played with my mind, altered my memories, it wasn't me. You don't know what it was like to leave you that day, to have my brother say that he would kill you if I didn't follow through, to see that he was so outside of himself that he would kill the only woman that I know he loved…please, just let me explain…please let's just talk about this!" His voice became harsh and he stood so quickly from the bed that I wasn't sure if I had actually seen him move. He was in front of me in less than a heartbeat. He took the box from my hands and slid off the bag from my shoulders. "Please Ana—just let me talk to you about all of this." He moved his arms around my waist pulling me close to him. His eyes were black and his jaw was tight. I couldn't swallow and my breathing was coming in short bursts. His fingers moved behind my neck and under my hair and I felt them press into the skin, heating me from the inside. "Please, Ana…you're mine…you belong with me," he murmured, bending his head close. He wrapped my arms up around his neck and pulled me against his chest. "Ana, I love you. I want you, please…" His lips pressed against mine and I could taste honey on my tongue. His fingers dug into my neck and his kiss became

394

rougher and more urgent. He was stepping backward toward the bed, pulling me with him. I tried to breathe, tried to push him away, but his bonds held.

"No Nathanial, no! I can't do this." I tried again to press myself away from his body but he had turned me around so that the backs of my knees were up against the edge of the bed. His tongue plunged deeper into my mouth and the heat from his breath made my chest heave and my body pulse and quiver. I felt my mouth begin to move against his, but from somewhere deep inside I also felt my blood begin to boil and my skin start to swell. "NO! "I said. "Stop! This isn't happening anymore!" I shoved him, hard and he stumbled several feet backward looking stunned. "Just stop!" I held up my hand as he tried to approach me again. "Don't please," I begged him. I just wanted to get out of there. I couldn't do this anymore, not with him, not with anyone. He ran his fingers through his hair and motioned for me to leave. My heart cracked again and I grabbed my box and my bag and left our home for the last time.

****

I trusted Rene and calling her for information was probably the only thing that I could do. I had a plan, desperate as it might be, and I just needed someone to help me navigate through what I wanted. Rene was hesitant but she eventually gave me the directions I asked for and I was now on my way. I hadn't been out to this part of town before. There were old factory buildings that had been converted into large loft spaces; mostly artists and hippies lived out this way. It was a somewhat safe community, but traveling anywhere in Indonesia after dusk was always a bit risky. There were no numbers on the buildings, so I had to go off of the physical description that Rene gave me, not the best thing to do so late at night—every building looked the same. A light in a window caught my eye and I turned my jeep so that my headlights could illuminate the façade of the building. It looked right, old brick with a fire escape winding up four or so stories. The light was coming from the very far window on the forth floor, that had to be it. I parked across the street and walked quickly into the building. There was an old crate-style elevator that looked pretty rickety, and I didn't see any stairs—not the best building to be in if there was a fire, I mused. I pulled the large doors across and stepped inside. It was pitch black except for the tiny glow from the buttons designating the floors. I hit "four" and waited for the elevator shaft to begin its ascent. The contraption shook and jolted from side-to-side and by the time I reached the top floor, my muscles were aching from all of the movement during the ride up. The hallway was also completely dark, but I could see the loft at the end; there was a slight glow coming from the crack under the door. I felt my pulse quicken and my chest contract. This had to work; I wasn't ready to give up just yet. I had to have another choice. I took a deep breath and knocked softly. I heard someone shift inside and move towards the door. A lock clicked and the door slid slowly to the side. I stood back not wanting to seem too eager. I exhaled as my gaze met the clear blue eyes and tanned face staring back at me. "Hi Stephen."

"Ana? What are you doing here?" Stephen looked me up and down; he appeared stunned to see me. "Are you alright?" He peered out into the dark hallway then back at my face. I took another deep breath.

"I was wondering if I could talk to you for a moment. I know it's late, but I just need to…I just would like to talk to you, please." I was stumbling over my words; I must have sounded like a crazy person and I was crazy, going to a Vampire's home, surprising them in the middle of the night. My god, maybe I *had* lost it. Stephen's jaw flexed and I saw a flash in his eyes. The smell of my blood was probably not making him very comfortable. He looked me over once more then stepped aside allowing for me to enter. I heard him slide the heavy door closed and click the lock in place. My heart thumped wildly in my chest; if he could just hold off on killing me until I had a chance to talk to him, I might be ok. I heard him laugh softly and I tried to close my mind. I gazed around. The space was huge. The walls were brick and had high, dark wooden beams reaching up to the vaulted ceiling. Hardwood floors shone beneath my feet; the wood was also dark but with swirls of golden threads woven throughout. There were paintings everywhere, on the walls, set up in canvases and leaning against every available space. An acoustic guitar was lying on the black leather sofa. So, Stephen was a painter as well. I had remembered him telling me that he played the guitar; apparently he was a well-rounded artist. I smiled in spite of my complete terror. Soft music was playing from a huge stereo system built into the wall. It looked like it probably cost more than my jeep. Stephen moved from behind me, he was watching as I assessed his space. "I didn't know you were a painter Stephen. That's amazing. Your work is stunning, really," I said smiling at him. I was surprised at how calm my voice sounded; I was terrified. He cocked his head to the side and shrugged. He walked over to the couch and gently lifted the guitar standing it against the recliner. He motioned for me to sit down next to him. I noticed that the coffee table was covered in sheet music and what looked liked lyrics scribbled on scrap pieces of paper. He noticed me staring.

"I have a lot of free time." He laughed softly. I smiled and noticed that one of my favorite songs was now drifting through the space. It was a quiet piece, just acoustic guitar and a lone male singer. I used to play it over and over after Nathanial left the first time.

"I like this song," I said quietly, letting the music fill me with such an incredible sadness that I was struggling not to cry. I had to push through; it didn't matter anymore, I had to move forward. Stephen was studying me intently, the oceans in his eyes moving swiftly.

"Hmmm... it's one of my favorites too." Stephen stared and our gazes locked. "What's going on Ana?" His voice was soft and earnest. I didn't know how to begin or what I should say. Technically, Stephen should be trying to kill me, at least that's what most Vampires would be doing if a human had been so bold to visit them in their home. For some reason, I wasn't concerned about that, not immediately anyway; for some reason I trusted Stephen, and that was probably a mistake.

"Something has happened," I said, looking down, my hair falling in swirls over my cheeks, shielding my face. I heard him shift and then I felt his hands brush back my hair, smoothing it over my shoulders and down my back. A surge of electricity filled my body and the heat from his touch warmed my skin. The feeling wasn't threatening, but oddly comforting, familiar somehow. I was so screwed.

"What's happened Ana?" He lifted my chin so that our gazes met.

"Well," I tried to take a deep breath, "it appears that I'm a marked woman now." I laughed shaking my head at the absurdity of the whole situation.

"Hmmm...because of your ability to control fire," Stephen replied. He spoke not as if asking if he had the information right, but like he already knew what the problem was, that what I was telling him was not new. I pursed my lips. "It's quite an amazing and powerful gift you have, I'm actually quite jealous." He laughed and ruffled my hair. It was such a tender and playful gesture that I looked at him stunned.

"Humph, I'd rather be able to paint," I said, standing to look at an acrylic painting of a woman sleeping in a bed. I was trying to distract myself from Stephen's heavy emotional tenor. The detail of the painting was amazing. All of the colors blended in such a way that gave the image a texture and fluid quality that you don't normally see using such mediums. The way he had captured the light allowed for the woman's face to be illuminated not from the outside, but it looked as if the glow was coming from inside her body, shining and warming the surrounding canvas. I wanted to touch her, to stroke her hair. "Who is she?" I asked, my voice barely audible.

"A woman I loved once," Stephen replied, an undercurrent of sadness running through his voice. I turned to look at him. I had forgotten that Vampires were made, that they had to be bitten by another Vampire, that all Vampires were human once. I turned back to the painting, looking closer at the sleeping woman. Her hair was dark and curly and it cascaded over her pillow in soft waves. I wondered what color her eyes were.

"Brown," Stephen replied. "She had deep brown eyes." He was watching me studying her.

"May I ask what happened? I mean did you marry her?" I was trying not to be rude, but I was fascinated. I had never really talked to any full Vampires before besides Devon; they usually hated humans and never made any gestures of accessibility to us. It was rare to engage in any sort of civilized conversation. He shifted forward and took the guitar, placing it across his lap. He began strumming quietly.

"I wanted to marry her, but she felt somewhat different." His hands caressed the strings softly. I couldn't imagine any woman not wanting to marry Stephen; he was a dream guy in every sense of the word, handsome, talented, he seemed nice, at least to me. I was sure as a human he would have made a very nice partner or husband. He laughed out loud, of course hearing my internal dialogue. I blushed and pressed my questions further.

"But you told her that you loved her, that you wanted to marry her; she knew how you felt?" I felt sad and upset that someone may have hurt Stephen, it didn't seem right. He laughed again and shook his head, looking up at me. He was playing something familiar; it was the song that we both liked.

"Yes, I told her everyday that I loved her and that I wanted her to be with me forever, but sometimes people make different choices, they take different paths and some mistakes can never be forgiven…" He continued to play but he was looking right at me, his eyes penetrating, searching my face. I listened to the song for a few moments, getting lost in chords he was playing. He was humming quietly.

"What did you do? After I mean, after you realized that you couldn't be together; what did you do?" I knew I was also asking those questions for myself. He sung softy, his eyes never leaving my face.

"I made the worst decision of my life, a decision that was made out of anger, out of despair and out of hurt, a decision that I can never undo." Still strumming, I noticed that the chords were now taking on a darker feel, sadder and more intense.

"You asked to be changed," I said. He glanced up at me, not answering, his fingers moving swiftly over the frets. I moved to sit next to him on the couch, sitting down as still as I could. I put my hand on his shoulder. He stopped playing and turned to face me. "They're going to kill me," I said quietly. "I don't know when, but I'm not allowed to stay alive with the power that I have—a power that I didn't ever want; I wish that Patric had just killed me when I gave him the chance, when I gave him my blood—I wish that he would have just ended things then. He still would have been somewhat strong; he still could have fought to keep his position or whatever it was he wanted. Nathanial would have kept his promise I'm sure. Patric didn't need to use me to get to Nathanial…" I trailed off not wanting to go down that road again and also it just didn't matter anymore. I was here for a reason, I had a plan and I needed help.

"What can I help you with Ana." Stephen turned the full force of his eyes upon me.

"I would like to offer a trade off of sorts," I said, realizing how stupid this must have sounded to him. He smiled at me, showing a full set of beautiful teeth, none of which looked like fangs. He laughed.

"What's the trade off?" he asked still chuckling.

"I was wondering if…well if, if you would agree to turn me and in exchange I would gladly allow for your side…for the Vampires to utilize my power…ability, for your cause." Oh Christ, that had to be the most ridiculous sounding thing I have ever said in my entire life. I was a much more eloquent speaker when I didn't have a knife hanging over my head. I steam rolled on. "I mean if you could change me before I was slaughtered by a Demon or a Vampire, then maybe that would be a fair compromise." I took a breath. "I'm guessing that there are already people waiting to take me out, so why not just do things this way, then everyone gets something; well except the Bonders, I guess they'll be pretty pissed…" I was babbling and I hadn't noticed that Stephen had moved to stand near the window, his back to me.

"You're right Ana," he spoke softly. "One side has already sent someone to kill you and not just for your power but for retaliation for Devon and Alec." I looked at him, wanting him to turn around so that I could see his face. I was already too late?

"Who?" I asked, knowing that it made no difference at all; it wasn't as if I could actually put up a fight. Even with my power, I was still no match for a thousand year old Vampire. I heard Stephen sigh and I went to the window to stand next to him. "Who?" I asked him again. Slowly, he turned his face toward mine, the moon casting a shadow over his eyes, darkening them. My heart sunk and I felt my chest shudder. "Oh. Oh, I see." That was all my brain would allow for me to say. I had willingly walked right into the lion's den and I couldn't have made it any easier for them.

"Does Nathanial know that you're here Ana?" Stephen had turned back to gaze out the window.

"No. I left him, I moved out," I said, quietly defiant. He turned back to stare at me. I met his gaze and held it, not looking away.

"Hmmm," he said, the shadow passing over his eyes once more. "You know when I first realized that you were special Ana?" he asked. I wasn't special, stupid that's for sure, but special, definitely not. He shook his head and grinned at me. "I knew the day that we went to the murder scene of that poor child. I saw the way you held that little girl in your lap, the way you caressed her face. I could feel just how much pain you were in over her suffering, how she affected you, what she made you think of, what she made you want." Stephen turned back to the window, his face turned toward the moon.

"Maria," I said softly, remembering that her eyes had looked like mine, only prettier. Stephen shook his head.

"Yes, Maria. Here you were with a clan of Vampires all trying to not kill you—except Devon, and the Demon that you were Bonded to, who had left you, most likely thinking that you had died, and the only thing that was in your heart, in your soul, was the pain and compassion for that little girl. No fear, no anger, no regret, just the deepest sadness that I had ever felt emitting from a human being—except one." He stopped to look at me.

"You? You wanted to die didn't you, I mean after your relationship ended?" I asked gently.

"I did die Ana. I've made so many horrible, horrible choices, so many wrongs I have committed… until recently, I had thought that every part of who I was as a Human soul and as a man, had also died." Stephen sighed softly. I watched him, my heart suddenly opening a bit, expanding.

"What happened recently?" I asked, confused. He smiled to himself.

"You remind me of her you know, of Laura. Except that you've never betrayed anyone have you?" I thought about Patric and Nathanial. "No, Ana you didn't betray Nathanial. He left you, regardless of whether it was of his own volition or not; he left you and you were no longer obligated to him and you were honest with him upon his return. You never denied your feelings about Patric, you never lied to him…" His head was bowed.

"Did she cheat on you Stephen?" I was sure that I already knew the answer, but I also thought that maybe he hadn't told anyone about what happened. Sometimes in order to heal, you have the say the things that your mind and heart won't let you acknowledge; you have to say them out loud. He swallowed and put his hands on my shoulders, his eyes brilliant and captivating in both their beauty and their sadness.

"Good god Ana! Here I am, telling you that I've been instructed to kill you and you're content to play therapist to me because you think that maybe I need someone to talk to! Unbelievable." He shook me gently. He sighed and moved away from me. "Yes, she slept with my brother and she bore his child. I found them together one evening and there was no denying what I saw." His voice darkened and a slight wash of anger filtered into his tone. I had no idea what possessed me to do what I did next, but I had no control over it, it just felt right. I moved to stand close to him and I wrapped my arm around his waist and laid my head on his shoulder, pulling him to me.

"I'm so sorry Stephen, I'm so sorry that you were hurt," I said gently and I was sorry. Stephen deserved better, he deserved to have the life that he was destined for, to be an artist, a husband, maybe even a father—not a Vampire and certainly not a killer. Odd, but my heart knew this to be true and I couldn't explain why, it just made sense that I should think this way about him. I felt his body shudder at my touch and I quickly pulled away. I didn't want to be too intrusive. He shook his head and put his hand on either side of the windowpane. "Sorry," I said moving to stand behind him.

"What are you sorry for Ana, you didn't do anything wrong."
He sounded upset.

"What happens now?" I wasn't sure if I wanted to know when
he was planning to kill me or if it would be better to not see
what was coming.

"I'm not sure. Your offer should be taken into consideration.
You might be seen as useful." His voice was flat. "I'll need to
discuss this with a few of my brethren before we decide what
to do." He turned back to look at me.

"Well what if a Demon gets to me first and kills me before you
can make up your mind?" It seemed a reasonable enough
question, even though the context sounded unreal to my ears.

"Well that's just one of many reasons why I'm not going to be
able to let you leave I'm afraid." He looked sympathetic. I
hadn't anticipated that happening; I hadn't thought that far
ahead.

"Uh, but you work, don't you? I mean couldn't a Demon or
another Vampire just shimmer into your apartment, take me
out and be gone by the time you got home? And I have a job
too, unless you're planning on making my car payments and
my credit card bills until you decide if you, in fact, will be the
one to…to kill me." It seemed quite strange to be discussing
my financial situation when my impending death had yet to be
determined. He smirked at me.

"I work out of boredom Ana, so me leaving during the day
won't be an issue. As for your bills…" He grinned at me and
walked over to a giant roll top desk. He pulled out a large

406

binder and began to thumb through the various sheets. I noticed that it was full of blank checks, hundreds of them.

"Why don't we make sure that you can comfortably take a sabbatical from your job?" He winked at me and I grimaced. I loved my job and since Caleb died, I wanted more than ever to make sure that his organization continued with his dreams and goals in mind. Plus, I hated the idea of having anyone pay for my debts—that just wasn't going to happen. Stephen crossed his arms over his chest and he stared at me, hard. "You're making my job very difficult Ana." He laughed. "But I suppose we can work something out. How about this, I will take you to and from work and we're going to have to trust each other. I will trust you that you will not try to run away, not that that would be much of a deterrent for me and you need to trust me that I will not let anything happen to you while you are in my care. I promise that I will take your offer seriously and lobby for what you want. I cannot, however, make any guarantees." Christ, this whole scenario sounded redundant. I had to leave my life in the hands of someone who didn't care about me, who had no tie or bond to me, not that it had ever mattered here as of late. I was standing in the middle of a room with a Vampire who was essentially confirming things that I already knew about my own life, that there was nothing, nothing that I could offer to him or anyone, that would make them want to keep me in this world. I knew this; he knew this. I had nothing, and every time I had tried to love, I always ended up losing. I wasn't enough. I could offer my life. I could offer my powers but really that wasn't a true reflection of who I was or am, they were just tangible representations of someone who had already been broken, who had survived for some unknown reason, a childhood that had shattered her and forced her into an adult life that was proving all the things she'd known to already be true; I should have never been born. I was a mistake.

"Ana." Stephen's voice was barely a whisper. He had heard and I'm sure he knew that I was right. "Ana," he said again, his voice cracking. His eyes were brimming. I shook my head and put my hand up. It didn't matter; I was on a collision course now, a collision course with hurt, with pain, with suffering and with death. It didn't matter. I took a deep breath and stared at Stephen.

"Fine. We have a deal, although…I remember Alec telling me that I should never trust a Vampire, much less make a deal with one; you could kill me in my sleep and I'd never see it coming." I eyed him warily as I tried to calm my overwhelming desire to fall apart. Stephen spoke quietly, his eyes watching me, seeing into my mind.

"Alec was right, for the most part and certainly when it came to trusting him, but the difference between me and Alec is pretty crucial Ana." I was still staring at him, not sure if I could trust him. "I actually do care about you, very much and I want you to survive. I think killing you would be the one thing that would destroy whatever humanity that knowing you has managed to resurrect." I looked into his eyes. They were translucent, pure and shimmering like the sea. I sighed and moved to stand directly in front of him. He put out his hand for me to shake. I checked his eyes one more time, and I put my hand in his, feeling the heat of his skin on mine. I pulled him gently to me and pressed my lips softly to his cheek.

"Thank you." I bowed my head and stepped back into the shadows. I was already broken beyond repair, but I was hoping beyond hope that I would awake tomorrow to find my heart a little less shattered and the chasm in my soul not so deep. In my mind, I knew that I had no fight left in me and no one left to fight *for* me; in my mind I knew that I had lost and no matter what the outcome, life as I knew it, as I remembered it, was over.

Stephen

I watched her sleep, studying her breath, smelling her blood; she was intoxicating. I had always thought so. I had no idea how I was going to live with her, how she was going to become part of my existence. How I would be able to resist what she was, who she was. The notion of taking her life was an interesting one. Interesting because I knew just what kind of fighter Ana was and the potential of what she could become, but I also knew from her thoughts, that she was done fighting, done emotionally and done physically. I wasn't usually fond of opponents who had already given up; it wasn't nearly as gratifying to kill someone when they, in a sense, had already decided that they were too worthless to live. Ana sighed in her sleep and I saw images of Nathanial and Patric move through her dreams. I had to admit, Nathanial and Patric's relationship as brothers was an odd one. It seemed to have so many conditions set upon it that neither of them were willing to put away for the sake of family. The way they treated Ana was also odd to me, not in that they loved her, that was a given, but in the way they expressed that love. It seemed selfish to me; they were both cowards in their claim on her heart and neither of them seemed to remember that she had had no choice in her original Bonding, that it was beyond her control and that she'd tried to make some sense of the whole thing. She even allowed for herself to fall in love. I rarely had any problems with either of the Arias brothers, but I also sensed something inherently possessive about the two of them, for different reasons. Nathanial wanted Ana and while I could easily see that he loved her, it was a love that seemed obsessive and he was weak; he'd hurt her terribly, leaving her to die and only after Alec had been sent to him, had he managed to rally and remember how important Ana was to him. Patric was an odd construct as well. He cared for Ana, possibly loved her, yet he wasn't beyond using her, putting her life on the line to accomplish his own desires. I wasn't so convinced that his last show of redemption was not without ulterior motives; Patric was a planner. He was ambitious, greedy, selfish and power hungry; his feelings for Ana caused him great conflict, but not enough to change who he'd chosen to be in his life.

Ana sighed and I moved closer, breathing in her unique scent, it seemed tuned to me and my own cravings and desires, something that Humans weren't able to do and I was surprised at the potency of Ana's, it was filling the room. It was perplexing that she'd chosen to come to me and even odder that I had heard in her mind that she wasn't concerned that I was going to kill her. She was afraid yes, but there also seemed to be an undercurrent of trust that she had in me, and *that*, I couldn't understand one bit. I hovered over her, wanting to touch her face, her lips. I was drawn to her for some reason; I wanted to know her. I was also supposed to kill her. It was a dilemma that I had never been faced with before. I had promised that I would take her offer to the covens, that I would lobby for what she was asking; I'd never been known to keep any promises, no Vampires had except Liam. For some reason I didn't want to betray Ana by killing her, not now while she slept in my bed. It seemed like one more blow to her heart would probably just do my job for me, although I could see that she wasn't really expecting me to fight for her. She was expecting me to betray her and maybe that's why I wouldn't kill her tonight, maybe I wanted to see if I could prove her wrong.

I left the room quietly and went to lie on my couch. I would probably have to convert my study into a second bedroom, especially if it was going to take a while for Liam and the other covens to make a decision. I had never lived with a woman before. Human women, to me, were disposable. I never mistreated them, Liam would decapitate me for even harming or degrading any woman, plus that wasn't my style. I just had no use for them beyond satisfying my own needs and desires. I didn't feed to kill, at least not since joining Liam's coven, it wasn't permitted, but I knew that it still happened—sometimes it was hard to stop. There were always women here and I was beginning to think that that scenario might not be the most respectful while having Ana living with me; for some reason I cared what she thought about me and I didn't want her to think of me as a monster or a womanizer. I was probably somewhere in the middle of the two.

I rose and poured myself a drink and went to stand by the window. Liam would be intrigued by Ana's offer, but he wasn't one to allow for Humans to be Changed; he thought them to be a bit inferior and not deserving of such gifts that immortality offered and he made few exceptions. I had no idea what he would think of Ana's worthiness. She posed an intriguing case and I was fascinated by the possibilities for her not just as a Human but also, maybe as Vampire. I sat on the floor and moved a giant blank canvas into the center of the room. My mind needed to calm; painting or playing music always seemed to center me a bit and help me to process events in my existence. What was happening now seemed to be beyond anything I could have imagined. I smeared paint across the cream surface and waited for it to take its desired shape. It looked like a moon. The tides came next and I could see just what my mind was dictating although I had no reason to be expressing my feelings in such a way; I had no gravitational pull toward anything or anyone. I was no one's moon or tide; I had made sure of that during my Human life, my mistakes not offering me that sort of redemption or to know that kind of bond. I added stars next to the moon and cliffs in the background. The image was blurred, not quite settled in its form. I sighed and sipped my drink.

"Stephen," a soft voice spoke through the darkness and I glanced up to see Ana standing over near the bar, watching me.

"Are you ok?" I had to ask. I wasn't sure; she seemed so shattered that I could feel it in my own bones.

"I can't sleep," she said, running her fingers through her curls. I cocked my head, trying not to let her scent do things to my body; I was out of practice with my self-control. I held out a paintbrush to her.

"Want to paint?" I asked as I noticed she'd shut her mind. That was an interesting talent. She stared at me warily. "Trust me Ana, I'm not inclined to get blood all over my canvases, you're safe." I laughed gently. She moved a bit closer and we watched each other steadily. She sat down across from me on the floor, the canvas paper between us.

"I can't paint," she said, her eyes not leaving my face. I shrugged.

"Everyone can paint," I said handing her the brush. She looked around the room at some the pieces I had on the wall and her eyes narrowed.

"Not like that," she said softly taking the brush. Our fingers touched and I swallowed, feeling the extreme heat from her skin on my own; it was incredible.

"You could if you had centuries to practice." I chuckled trying to quell the overwhelming hunger and desire I was experiencing. I turned up the stereo.

"What do I do?" she asked and I could feel that the question may not have just been about painting, that perhaps she was asking me if she should hold on; if she should still fight, if she shouldn't just let go and fall. I met her gaze and held her eyes deep within my own. I moved to sit next to her and she tensed. I took her hand in mine and I slowly guided the brush onto the canvas.

413

"You trust," I said quietly, watching as our hands moved together, fingers entwined, they seemed to fit. She turned her face to me and I could see her eyes brimming with tears, they fell like liquid stars down her cheeks. Her wall crumbled and I saw her standing on the edge of a cliff, her face turned up towards the moon. I watched as she moved herself closer to the edge and her hand suddenly gripped mine as I saw her mind and her heart making a choice. She looked out at the sea and an image of Nathanial swam past on the waves, he dissolved and Patric emerged, and he too dissolved. I watched as Kai and Alec also appeared. I saw images of who I could only assume were the parents that didn't want her, rise from the water and one after the other, they all disappeared until only a single face remained—mine. I felt myself grip her hand back as I saw Ana jump, and my mind's eye focused as her body moved through the air towards me. She'd fallen and now I would have to decide if I would be the one to catch her.

End of Book One

41600058R20253

Made in the USA
Charleston, SC
03 May 2015